Shattered Veil

BLOODBOUND SERIES
BOOK ONE

NIKA VYRE

Introduction

Selen and Sidra's stories are that of overcoming some of the horrors that life throws at us. This is the beginning of a story of empowerment for both women, but with that being said, there are a few notes to the readers before getting into it.

Triggers:

- Depicted Sexual Violence
- Erosion of Reality
- Mild knife play

Take care while reading. Your mental health matters.

"All that we see or seem is but a dream within a dream"

EDGAR ALLAN POE

To those whose demons are sometimes louder than their own voice...

This one's for you.

His breath lurched as another branch connected with his face, and a warm stream of blood trickled from the wound. Adrenaline pushed him deeper into the dark forest's haunting embrace, the only illumination descending from the moon and the stars. Snow clung to his boots, and as he sprinted, each step felt heavier, as though icy fingers were gripping him to the earth. Wiping any remnants of blood from the gash away with a dirty sleeve, a mild twinge of pain hit him as the muddied cloth scraped the wound—the clothes he had spent weeks ensuring were filthy as this day approached. A smell that could mask his scent. *They* were already too close. If they smelled his blood, he'd be doomed.

He could tell that they were near, if not from the echoed screeches, then from the foul odor that clung to the shadow creatures' essences as they trailed him. He had only experienced a similar smell after walking into an old tavern after a bar fight. Blood, booze, mud, and burning flesh combined to create a scent he'd never forget. A man's brain had been smashed in with a rum bottle, and he'd been half lying in the still-raging fire. So much blood. And now, it was the closest thing he could relate to the smell of the shadow creatures—the smell of death. Their metallic sting inched up his nose and filled his mouth.

Where stars reflected against the freshly fallen snow, sparkles shied away from the shadows that neared. His boots were the only thing that disturbed the fresh blankets of white that veiled the frozen ground. He wrapped his arm tighter around the two bundles he had strapped to him. His heart and soul ached for he had left behind. There was no returning, there would be no forgiveness. He would not allow the past to cloud a future—*his* future didn't matter. He would make this choice in any life. For them.

You cannot outrun me, the dark voice hissed through his mind. It had become all too familiar, like a lullaby that pulled you into a nightmare. Beautiful but terrifying. *Her* voice—the voice that had haunted his dreams and every moment after. A voice that only a being of shadow and ice could have.

He knew he couldn't outrun her. Her mind's reach was further than any lands he could escape to. He'd known this for months as he developed his plan. His goal was never to outrun her.

They belong to me! Her voice scratched the edges of his mind, and he winced as its cold embrace left tremors of terror pulsing through his body.

He looked down at the bundles he carried. Streaks of silver hair escaped from the top of one and black from the other. These two beautiful bundles. *His* girls. The one good thing he'd done in this life, and she wanted to rip them away. One year—that's how long these angels had lived in this world. After everything, this was what he had been driven to. Anger bubbled up through him, warming his body and pushing away any of the tremors left by that *wretched* voice that once held such a different meaning to him.

He slowed just enough to rip his arms out of the muddied jacket he'd cloaked himself with, tossing it on a branch high enough that they wouldn't be able to see it without looking up. He took one moment to glance back at the shadows that followed him, then took off running along an adjacent path to the one on which he had begun. The stench of the shadows slowly faded from his senses as he sprinted through a deeper brush. He knew he had only a moment before they realized that the scent they hunted was housed in his jacket; but a moment could be enough. It *had* to be enough. Steadying his breathing, he pushed on, arms now freshly exposed to the brittle air so sharp branches clawed at his flesh. New canvases for them to shred. He didn't take the time to wince as they dug into him, as the smell of his own blood filled his nostrils.

If he could smell it, so could they.

A roar echoed through the woods, no doubt a response to the understanding she had been momentarily fooled. Now that she knew she'd been following a dead scent, the shadows would follow her sight through the woods based on his tracks. They could only see as far as she could; any distance beyond her sight was based on scent alone.

"Do you take me for a fool?" she howled into the night. Her distant voice rattled the ground and trees that warped around him as he ran.

Just ahead, he thought as he approached the crooked tree that had become a sign of hope. He had walked and run the route so many times that the steps felt like second nature. He passed the tree and pushed through the edge of the wood, into the large clearing.

The moon greeted him as he finally shoved past the last of the brambles that kept him from his destination. As he ran through the open clearing and toward the cliff edge, a wash of relief warmed his bones as he spotted the woman standing at the edge of the steepest part. The cliff was at least a hundred feet down, ending at a raging river. The jagged wall of the cliffside was misleading, as everything below was smooth rock all the way to the water. The lip that the woman stood on overhung the edge by a few feet.

Her hair, which may have once been a sandy shade of blonde, was a faded gray. Large curls took up the majority of space in the hood of the silver-blue cloak she'd wrapped around her shoulders, and though her face showed clear signs of age, her features were just as beautiful as they had once been. Just as he had known them to be. Blue eyes reflected the starlight as she watched him approach, and her familiar gaze calmed his thundering heart.

"I was worried you would not make it," she whispered in a bright, commanding voice.

"As was I," he panted, before handing the bundles over to her. As she held his heart in her hands, he could feel the pull to his girls. To protect them. He wanted to embrace the pair, for it would be the last he saw of them. Tears stung his eyes, and his heart clenched at the thought.

Sensing pain in his lingering gaze, the woman shifted her eyes from the babes and met his.

"They have no life here. She will be the end of them," she said sympathetically.

"If I had known..."

"How could you have?" Her voice sharpened as she continued, "None of us could have known this is how it would turn out."

"When will you take them?" He whispered, looking down at his bloodied hands. He knew the question would do him no good, but he had to ask.

"When she finds you, you will not want to know," the woman stated, looking back at the girls. "I will keep them safe. As we discussed."

"Is it possible to see them again?" he pleaded.

"It is unlikely," she whispered. Her voice was a blade as she spoke again, "Do not search for them in any life."

Her words stung, but he knew it was the truth. He had done all of this for them, and would not risk them being found for his own comfort. He moved to look at their faces, and time stood still as he took in their pale skin and long lashes.

"My night and my stars," he whispered as he kissed their heads. A tear fell onto the cloth that wrapped around them.

"She's coming," the woman said, staring at the brush behind them. He wiped his tears, pushing down his anguish. He knew this was the only way they could have a future.

"Go," he said, turning away from his whole world and facing the oncoming darkness. As he did so, *she* burst through the brush. Her raven hair flowed around her like a hurricane, pale skin untouched by the brush and branches that had caused his injuries. Her eyes matched her hair, and the skin around them blackened as though a rot had spread from her soul through her irises. She gave him a toothy grin that sent shivers down his spine.

She drew each sound out as she cocked her head to the side. "I found you."

"Go!" he screamed at the older woman.

Wrapping herself with her cloak, the older woman looked at him one last time before launching herself off the cliff's edge. A guttural scream tore from the shadow woman, and she lunged forward as the bundles dropped out of sight.

He glanced back as her blue cloak disappeared, then closed his eyes in relief as icy fingers wrapped around his throat.

Chapter One

Selen bolted upright. Sweat caused her hair to stick to her face, and her breathing was heavy as she took in her surroundings. Eyes adjusting to the darkness of the space, her heartbeat began to settle as she realized she was in her bed. *Safe*. She was safe.

Another nightmare.

This was the third this week, another dream where she was chased through dark woods. Each night, whatever hunted her grew closer. She could feel the darkness as it swarmed her feet in these dreams, begging to grab hold of her and sink its claws into her.

She closed her eyes for a long moment, then opened them to ensure that her current state was reality. She repeated this act until her eyes fully adjusted to the low light.

Selen looked over at the figure in the bed across the room. Sidra, her sister, slept soundlessly, silver hair illuminated by the little light that shone through the window from the almost full moon. Selen wiped away her sweat with the arm of her sleeping shirt before realizing it was as soaked in her sweat as her own skin. The small amulet she wore around her neck was crooked and almost behind her—she must have been tossing and turning for it to have become this dislodged. She crept to the armoire at the edge of her room that housed her belongings. Slipping out of the sweat-coated shirt, she found a long tunic and threw it over her body. It was large and shapeless, its color unknown in the dark. She then tiptoed back to her bed and sat on its edge before placing her head in her hands and taking a long breath. She kept her eyes open to avoid ending up back in that *place*.

With the frequency of her nightmares, sleep had become a luxury. She always woke multiple times before the sun came up, if she got any sleep at all. Moonlight trickled through the window, the source of what little light existed in their room. She stalked to the window to look out on the courtyard. The moon illuminated the silver cloak left on the earth by the spring rain. White flowers bloomed from the shrubbery along the path to the front entrance to Celestara.

Their home.

The Academy was enormous. Large stone pillars stood alongside the main doors—doors that stood far too tall for any human to reach their peak. A gaudy entrance. She always imagined it was once the home of a nobleman who had something to prove. A compensation of sorts. Intricate carvings in Gothic design were etched into the stone. Large gargoyle knockers had been placed uncomfortably low on the doors. Wrapping around the building was a large terrace, scattered with mismatched furniture that offered seating to all students who attended the Academy. Though it screamed pretension, the entrance was her favorite place to be this time of year. The spring flowers bloomed from all around, and vines wrapped the pillars and onto the terrace. The world came alive this time of year, masking the darkness that crept into the world throughout the long winters.

While her nights were restless, she found peace in the darkness that encapsulated the land. When the stars were out, she couldn't help but feel a connection to the world and whatever force existed, which was larger than her. When the clouds covered the stars, separating the darkness from the only light it could be exposed to, she felt moments of solitude—as if the clouds were a wedge between the ever-connected stars and darkness. Examining the night through the window, she watched the reflections of the stars as they twinkled on the wet ground. This was the type of night she would love to be outside in, experiencing the connection by existing in its glow. But she was not allowed to leave the school after a certain hour.

A slight twinge of bitterness flickered through her. Selen and Sidra had always had strict rules when it came to curfew —more so than any of the other students. Though, this was likely due to the fact that Deandra, the Headmistress, was their guardian. Deandra had leashed the girls far more than the others since childhood. This led to stealth skills that only one with a strict guardian, telling them that they couldn't do something they had every intention of doing, could possess.

Her thoughts were cut short as she felt a presence beside her at the window. Selen looked to her right, finding Sidra awake and also staring out the window. Her long silver hair shone brighter now that she was closer to the light, the metal from her matching amulet glowing bright. It would be an unnerving sight if she hadn't been wearing it. The amulets had been the only things they'd had when Deandra brought them here as infants, after the war had taken their parents.

Selen blinked away the thought. Thinking about her parents typically led to another bout of living nightmares as the reality of their orphaned state left her feeling hollow.

Selen distracted herself from that line of thinking by examining her sister and trying to determine why she, too, was awake in the middle of the night. Sidra was stunning, with soft features that created an essence of innocence in her appearance. Her eyes were an icy blue that pierced the deepest parts of whoever she stared into. She had pale, flaw-less skin—rarely flushed, even upon exertion.

Selen had always envied her looks. Although they were twins, there seemed to be very few similarities in their appearances. Selen had raven-dark hair and even darker eyes. The only thing separating the color of her pupil from her irises was the gold flecks that spread across them. Her features were a bit sharper than Sidra's. Where her twin had delicate features, Selen's had always been described as 'strong'. While she didn't mind their differences, their constant comparisons by others sometimes took a toll on Selen's mind. Without looking over at Selen, Sidra interlaced their fingers.

"Another nightmare?" Sidra seemed to stare at nothing in particular as she looked out of the window. Her voice was soft and light. Selen had always envisioned it sounding like a feather floating through the air. Wispy and quiet.

"Yes," Selen replied, shifting her gaze back towards the outdoors.

"Me too." Even without looking at her, Selen could feel Sidra's lingering fear.

Selen had always taken on a protective role—Sid had always been the more carefree of the two, ignoring dangers and putting them both into situations that Selen had to find a way out of. They shared a link that had been both a blessing and burden. When she was young, Selen realized she could feel most of her sister's emotions and figured Sid could feel hers in turn. Sidra's emotions were large, and she had never really learned to control them—even though that made up most of their training, as their magic had yet to express itself.

Selen's emotions were far better controlled. She had even learned to put up a wall between her and her sister, so she only shared the emotions that she wanted Sidra to feel, rather than maintaining an endless flow that drained them both. Selen started to build her walls soon after the night-mares had initially begun years ago, almost immediately after their VeilBinding ceremony. Before that, Sidra would wake screaming in a panic due to the feelings that Selen would unintentionally share through the bond. Impenetrable obsidian walls in her mind rarely left space for anything to slip through, but Selen could sometimes feel Sidra tugging against the link, trying to get her to open up, but she knew that it would be more trouble than it was worth.

Without saying anything, Selen sent a small sense of comfort down the link and gripped Sidra's hand. Sid's eyes met hers, and Selen gave her a reassuring grin. Selen pulled her back to her bed and laid beside her, humming and petting Sidra's hair as she drifted back to sleep. Selen's eyes still wandered to the outdoors, and she didn't notice when the darkness of the night was replaced by the backs of her eyelids.

Selen's eyelids curled open as the bright light of the morning sun stung her pupils. She glanced down at Sid, still curled up around her. Slipping gently out of her sister's grasp, Selen padded to the window. The sunrise had melted away any sign of the rain that had coated the ground the night before. The world was now awake, and people moved about the well-groomed path below. The early rising students were scattered throughout the faculty, and others wandered the grounds before the day's structure fell into place. Recently, Selen had found herself in ranks with the early risers, as sleep had become less and less of a normalcy. She dressed as quietly as possible and slipped out of the room to join the morning crew.

Celestara didn't require uniforms, so the styles ranged

heavily among the students. As many of them were over the age of eighteen, parental concern for schooling attire didn't come into play. Selen often found herself in simple clothing like today's ensemble; her dark, long-sleeved tunic matched her hair, and she paired it with equally dark trousers that hugged her to her navel, where they met her tunic in a tuck. Her calf-high leather boots provided plenty of support, but were nothing fancy. She often got odd looks from some of the women at the school, as they were draped in finery and dresses that dragged behind them, but Selen had never been one for fashion. She favored clothes for their more practical uses. Her clothing fit just well enough for her to wield weapons without the concern of cloth limiting her movement. That was all she needed.

Sidra and Selen had grown up at this school, learning to read and write at a young age. Celestara was the primary school in this region for individuals of power. A school of magic and battle training. Those who knew they were developing powers from their VeilBinding ceremonies began their journey with the school at the age of sixteen. Oftentimes, they had little education prior to that unless they came from a family of means. The first two years of schooling were saved for basic education—reading, writing, history, emotional control, and, in a less traditional sense, combat. While all training continued after eighteen, once a person's powers had surfaced, they transferred to another section of Celestara, where they would learn to manage their magic for another two years. Everyone's powers were different, linked to their will and desires, and the essence of whichever Lirium was generous enough to share their magic. People of power often set a celebration for their eighteenth birthdays, when the magic was meant to show itself.

Selen and Sidra's birthday had been quite an ordeal. Selen had very few friends, but Sid had developed quite a following of boys and girls who yearned for her attention, so the event was bigger than expected. As the night had worn on, the anticipation built as midnight approached. But nothing happened when the clock struck midnight. Where most people experienced an awakening, accompanied by a display of whatever magic now flowed through them, Selen and Sidra had felt nothing. The crowd was silent for a few minutes after midnight had come and passed, and after some time, some began to snicker while others had watched the girls, sympathy plain in their eyes. Both were humiliated and spent days in their room, but Sid took it the hardest. For weeks, they tried everything they could to ignite their dormant powers, but after a whole year, Selen came to accept that perhaps nothing would ever come. Their Veil-Binding ceremony had determined that they had magic, but based on their awakening party, Selen could only assume the Seer had made a mistake.

Sid's reputation had taken a hit, but not much had changed for either sister. Most moved on from the mild drama the event had spurred within weeks, and new scandals spread throughout the school. While Selen diverted her energy into combat training, Sidra had converted hers into books and research, trying in vain to understand the magic that consumed this world. Now, having just passed their nineteenth birthdays, they wouldn't have a lot of time left at school to hone any magical ability even if they did acquire powers.

Lost in thought, Selen wandered down to the courtyard and hardly noticed someone was in front of her until she collided with them. She looked up, prepared to apologize, and felt her blood still before quickly finding its way into her cheeks as emerald-green eyes met her gaze.

"My bad," Selen murmured as she looked at the familiar face.

Aleya's green eyes watched Selen with a gentle warmth, and Selen's blood heated further. Aleya had always intimidated Selen. For a long time, she had thought it was envy—but as she got older, she realized those feelings were not born of envy but something deeper. Aleya's long, chestnut hair curled around her face before falling flawlessly onto her beige tunic, while loose curls swept her brow. As Aleya was slightly taller than her, Selen always felt like a troll in the presence of a giant.

"It's a little early to be picking fights, Leni." Aleya winked at her and gave her a gentle nudge with her elbow. *Leni.* A name that only one person in this world was allowed to address her by. It slid off of Aleya's tongue and sent shivers down Selen's spine.

Selen took a deep breath, her embarrassment replaced with a playful annoyance at Aleya's tone. "I suppose you shouldn't stand in people's way then, *Al*," Selen said in the most playful tone she could muster. Aleya grinned and met her eyes again, and Selen's heart stuttered. This much eye contact usually led to a brief moment of entanglement in a broom closet, and flashes of memory sent heat throughout her body.

Selen held her gaze with a challenge, as if to say *not now but later*. Aleya's answering grin bloomed into a full smile, and she chuckled before breaking eye contact. A mild sense of relief crashed over Selen as Aleya returned to her conversation with the two individuals before her, who were wide-eyed and clearly attuned to the encounter they'd just witnessed. The pair exchanged a glance and broke into a laugh. Selen rolled her eyes and kept walking.

Before she left the hallway that led to the courtyard, she felt a burning sensation on her neck that told her she was being watched. Glancing back at Aleya as she rounded the corner, she found a longing stare.

As the first round of classes began, Selen found her mind wandering back to her most recent physical encounter with Aleya. One of many. Selen couldn't help but reminisce about how soft her skin was, or how perfectly their bodies fit together... or how inappropriate it was for her to be having these thoughts while she was in class.

Aleya had been at Celestara almost the entire time the Selen and Sid had. They grew up together as friends, but had only become *more* over the last year. While sexual fluidity was common among her peers, Selen had found that the company of men was far less satisfying than her interactions with women—specifically *this* woman.

She often tried to avoid Aleya if she could. The emotions she felt in those moments had more control over her than she would prefer. Neither had actually ever stated whether there was anything more than physical attraction between them, but her self-control and general discipline went out the window when they shared a space. Aleya had made it clear that she wasn't sure what she wanted and had only recently begun exploring the company of other women. Selen knew she wasn't the only person with whom Aleya was casual, though. While the thought stung, Aleya wouldn't commit to her, and Selen wanted her in any capacity she could.

Selen closed her eyes and re-entered reality as she strained to remain focused on her teacher, who was using the dullest tone she had ever had the displeasure of experiencing. The first class of the day covered the geography of her home country, Vetusterra. The country had ancient roots that went back further than Selen could comprehend. She tried desperately to focus during these lessons, but the teacher's voice coaxed her into a trance of wandering thoughts. Could she blame the teacher entirely for her lack of focus? Probably not. But it was an easy excuse to not know nearly enough about the layout of her country of residence. The one piece of information she had gleaned from today's class that brought a loose bit of humor, was that the land's name 'Vetusterra', quite literally meant 'Old Land'. The comedy being that the ancients who'd discovered and named this land couldn't come up with anything better than *old land*. How original.

Selen's critique of the ancients' creativity was abruptly disturbed when Sid plopped down in the seat next to her, late enough that half of the class had already passed.

"Did I miss anything?" Sid whispered and began to unload her books onto the table.

"Of course you did, the class is almost over." Selen grinned as she looked up at the stuffy teacher who was still giving his nasally lecture, taking notes as best she could from the chicken scratch that littered the board.

"I lost track of time in the... library after breakfast. I found a book on something I *think* you'll find interesting," Sid huffed as she sat back in her seat.

"There is no time in between breakfast and the first class." Selen glanced over at her.

"Well... I suppose you'll just have to share your notes with me." Sid elbowed Selen.

Selen threw her pencil at her sister, sending it skipping across the floor as it bounced off of Sid's face. Both let out small gasps as they tried to keep their laughter quiet.

"Am I interrupting something, *ladies*?" their teacher asked in a condescending tone as he crossed his arms so chalk marred the sleeve of his dull brown robe.

"Not at all, Professor Monton. We apologize," Selen said, sitting up straight. Selen pulled Sidra up by the back of her dress as she leaned over the table, trying to grab the pencil off the floor.

"We were just *really* excited about today's lecture." Sid made the statement with an arrogant air of sarcasm that often got them into trouble as she settled back into her seat. Selen dug her nails into Sidra's leg under the table, and her sister elicited a swift blow to her shin in retaliation.

Professor Monton slowly turned back to the board, keeping a wary eye on the pair as he continued his dreary lecture on only the gods know what at this point. "Glad you could join us, Ms. Dagny," he said with his back turned.

Sidra frowned and looked at her sister. Selen shrugged and grinned at her notes, but as she did, her gaze caught on her sister's bag, still open on the floor by their seats. The spine of a large black book caught her eye: *Noesis and Bulwarks*. Selen frowned as she looked down at the title. An eerie sense of familiarity flooded her, but she had no idea why as she didn't recognize either word.

Selen caught Sid's eye, and Sidra raised her eyebrows at Selen as if to say: *That's what I want to talk to you about.* Selen nodded and went back to doodling on her notes page, but curiosity gnawed at her mind. This was one of the many resources Sidra had brought up. Usually, Selen ignored them and went about her day, but this time seemed different for whatever reason.

Another recent resource Sidra had shown, which actually intrigued her, was on Time Jumpers. Selen had heard of people who could hurdle through time at will—a dangerous and unpredictable ability. Very few people had control of the ability to jump, and even less control over the damage Jumpers could create from ripples in time. From the lessons taught on the power in school and the information that Sidra had shared from her own research, Selen was under the impression that Jumpers no longer existed. The power had been stifled and weeded out after the war eighteen years ago.

Royalty ensured that the power was forbidden after a catastrophic tragedy occurred at the hands of a Jumper from a different time. Due to the nature of the power, Selen imagined there wouldn't really be much that could be done to eliminate it entirely, but there were wards at the gates of this time that prevented Jumpers from passing through... Another interesting topic that had very little practical purpose but took up space in her mind. Selen often had Sidra to thank for these random pieces of knowledge. If the school ever held a session on random and useless information trivia, Selen would definitely win.

Sensing her spiral into the unknown, Sidra's light brushed against the obsidian wall of her sister's mind, and Selen loosed a breath as she stared at the parchment before her. The notes had descended into a jumbled mix of chaos, as she had still been writing as she had slipped into thought. Frowning, she shut her leather-bound notebook and shoved it into her bag as their class began to shuffle out.

Sidra sighed next to her. "Off to the next," she said as she gathered and loaded her supplies, closing her bag over the title that would now sit on Selen's mind.

Chapter Two

Selen breathed deeply as she skidded to a stop at the edge of the fighting ring, her grip loose yet controlled as she held her wooden sword. She watched closely as her opponent circled the opposite edge of the ring. Each step was carefully placed. His arms moved in fluidity with the wooden sword as he glided, leaving no areas exposed as he shifted.

Aeden's skills were impressive for a second year, so much so that he'd joined the upper-level fighters during the second half of the day, which was devoted to either magic or combat. Combat and magic alternated days, but those who did not yet have magic trained in these rings every day. Today was one such day where the magic wielders were off learning to hone their new abilities, leaving the rest of the class to train at a faster pace than usual, as there were less people for the instructor to oversee. Today was a dueling day—Selen's favorite kind of day, where she got the chance to show off all the skills she had been developing over the last three years.

Aeden's movements were fluid and quiet, leaving little room for error, but there was always a flaw. A weakness. Selen had learned to embrace patience and allow her opponents to expose their own weaknesses as they sparred. They often had too much anticipation to keep them on the opposite end of the ring, building and building until they lost control and charged.

This in itself was a weakness Selen could exploit.

They often tried to overpower her with brute force—typically her male opponents—but this opponent was more patient than the others. Regardless, she could sense his rising tension as his anticipation grew, begging her to make the first move. She stared at the boy, weapon at the ready. His eyes flared—he'd expected her to make her move—but she simply grinned at him and cocked her head to the side. Though Aeden had more grace than most, his feral instincts took hold as her grin ignited the anticipation inside of him like a spark against a long-developing bed of fuel.

He lunged, but his unhinged strike missed as she stepped to the side. Without skipping a beat, he swung for her head, missing again as Selen ducked and swept his legs out from under him. The boy's body slammed to the ground, the grunt and gust of air that expelled from his mouth exposed that she had knocked the breath from his lungs. Selen smiled down at him as she lightly rested her boot against his chest and aimed her sword at his throat.

He huffed and shoved off her foot, rising to his elbows as

he grinned at Selen. "You got lucky," Aeden grunted before standing and wiping off the dirt that now covered his clothing.

"Again?" Selen chuckled. "I must be very lucky for that to be my sixth time beating you today, Aeden," she drawled, handing him back his wooden sword.

Aeden grimaced as he reached for the sword, grabbing for his now bruised back. "One of these days, Selen, I'm gonna put you on the ground," Aeden said with misguided confidence as he waddled back to the edge of the ring.

Selen turned her back to him, setting her wooden sword against the edge of the ring wall as she adjusted the sleeves of her tunic.

"I doubt it," Selen grinned, briefly looking down at her arms before her gaze slid up to linger on the empty air before her.

Her attention was wholly focused on the person behind her, so she heard as his foot shifted from the left and stepped to the side as his sword came down right where she was standing. Aeden's eyes were wide and he gave her a bewildered look before she grabbed the back of his neck and threw him at the edge of the ring wall. The wall caught Aeden's hips and sent him out of the ring in a somersault, landing again on his back. Aeden groaned and looked back at Selen.

"You have so much to learn, little boy," Selen laughed as she rested against a wooden pole that held up the roof of the ring.

Aeden smiled and stood as he turned toward her again.

"You would think I'd get sick of this humiliation," he grinned, glancing her up and down, "but when it comes in such a pretty package..." he trailed off.

Selen flicked the space between his eyes as his concentration broke from an area south of her face. He gave her an exaggerated look of betrayal, placed his hand on his chest, and gasped.

"You are drama," Selen chuckled as she grabbed Aeden's forearm and helped him climb back into the ring.

"Perhaps. But if the Afterworld freezes and you start to like men, promise I'll be the first you call on?" he purred as he staggered to regain his balance in the ring.

"You're a toddler." Selen shook her head and shoved her sword into his hands for him to put away.

"I may be younger than you, but I am a man in *many ways*," he winked as he began to walk away with the two swords.

"Ick." Selen shook her head at him, kicking dirt at his back as he walked away.

Aeden had been one of Selen's closest friends since he'd shown up at the academy almost two years ago. His bleach-blonde hair and bright blue eyes were a contrast to his tanned skin. He stood a bit taller than Selen, but had always come up short in their battles. She did have to adjust to the height difference in the last year, though, as he'd been the same height as her when he'd arrived. Selen was tall for a woman, but many of the boys still had several hands of height on her.

Aeden was conventionally attractive, she supposed.

Many of the people at the academy and beyond fawned over him, but he typically showed little interest in them. His earlier crush on Selen had developed into a friendship as they grew together, and his hopes that they might bond romantically were squashed once he discovered that Selen did not share in her peers' sexual fluidity. He knew there was no chance, but it didn't limit his flirting, however misguided. Selen didn't mind; the flirty banter was entertaining as they worked through their training. It had become a normalcy that she didn't particularly care to change. He had become the closest friend she had here, beyond Aleya, who qualified in another category.

The afternoon heat pounded off the roof of the fighting ring she and Aeden occupied. The sound of wood clashing together and the grunts of the other fighters in the neighboring rings swarmed Selen's ears as she listened. About a dozen sparring rings surrounded them, and the afternoon heat did nothing to limit the rise of dust as the other students fought. Selen closed her eyes and listened to her surroundings. A stumble from a fallen competitor, followed by a rich peal of laughter and words that she couldn't identify. A scuffle of movement from two male students, who were pushing each other around after a fight that had ended with wounded pride. A swift crunch as one of the wooden swords broke beneath a foot. Selen pushed her senses beyond the sounds of the rings until she could identify the birds chirping as the spring wind washed through the aspen trees surrounding the property. She grinned as she heard the creek that ran along the edge of their school's land.

Selen pushed her senses every day as a part of her training. It was a skill that many were taught here, but few employed in their training. It could be useful not only for her time at Celestara, but in order to protect herself and her sister, she knew she'd have to be keenly aware of the things that happened around her. Perfecting it now would be the best way to keep them safe if anything were to happen.

A press of a finger on the tip of her nose startled her out of her focus. Selen frowned as she stared at Aeden, his dirt-covered finger still lingering on her nose. She whacked his hand away in frustration at her error, but the scent of wood and dust still coated her nose, eliciting a sneeze she wasn't prepared for.

"Dammit," she exclaimed as she leaned against the edge of the ring.

"You're going too far," Aeden said genuinely as he leaned next to her.

"What do you know, second year?" she said, sharper than she'd intended, then immediately looked at him with an apology in her eyes. Aeden's grin was confirmation that he didn't take it to heart.

"Well... *third year.* I've been training for a lot longer than many here." He raised his hands quickly before continuing. "Not you. I know you're practicing throwing your hearing. It's a neat trick until you get so caught up in what is happening far away that you forget to take note of what is happening in front of your face," he explained. His eyes were wide with sarcasm as he slid his finger along his throat. He dramatically wrapped his hands around his neck and began making gurgling sounds.

Selen stared wordlessly at the scene, waiting for the dramatics to fade before continuing. She wanted to be annoyed at Aeden for mansplaining a skill she'd been honing for years, but she knew he meant nothing by it. It was true. She tended to miss what was happening right in front of her because of how far she was trying to reach.

"You should push for a theater program at Celestara, you'd have a better chance at coming out on top there," Selen told him, now slowly sliding down the side of the ring. He momentarily stalled his dramatic interpretation of a dying man to glare daggers at Selen. The sides of her mouth tugged up into a smile.

Finally, after what seemed like forever, Aeden hit the ground with a huff. He slowly reached a hand towards Selen and let it fall—but not before letting out a croaking sound that drew the attention of their neighboring rings. He closed his eyes and fell limp.

Selen blankly stared down at Aeden's seemingly lifeless body below her. She pressed her lips together, shaking her head as she pushed off the side of the ring towards the exit.

A quick shuffle behind her was her only indication that Aeden's display was complete.

"So, why are you pushing yourself so far? Most people don't give two poops about learning that skill here."

Aeden quickly moved to match Selen's pace. Selen gave him a sidelong glance before sighing and stuffing her hands in her pockets. She may never get used to Aeden's creative language, but she couldn't deny the dread that slithered through her gut when she thought about why this skill was so important to her.

"Life is going to get really complicated after Sid and I leave the academy. In a world full of magic, someone without it..." she sighed and gestured to herself, "is going to need every skill they can muster." She let a small amount of the defeat she felt at her reality slip through her voice.

Aeden looked at her. He must have sensed how uncomfortable Selen was with her vulnerability because he quickly shifted the conversation.

"Well, you could just stay here with me for another year," he shrugged.

"Like I could endure another year with you," she laughed, appreciative of his obvious change of subject.

Aeden strode over to the rack with the wooden swords, grabbing two before moving back towards her. "You uh... you heard from Aleya recently?" Aeden asked playfully, tossing Selen a sword.

Selen caught the sword with ease and glared back at Aeden. She planted her back foot and pointed the tip at him and smiled.

"*That*... is none of your business," she crooned as she lunged at him.

Selen dusted herself off after another two victories against Aeden, putting the swords away for the final time for the day. The sun was still a few hours off setting as Selen and Aeden exited the training ring, and the rings around them were quiet. Everyone else had already headed into the school for dinner, and Selen's stomach ached as she made her way towards the dining hall.

The smell of potatoes and stewed meat filled her senses, causing her mouth to water. She hadn't eaten since breakfast, having gone to the rings early to train after a morning of feeling distracted in her classes. The book that Sidra had skipped their first class to acquire sat firmly in her thoughts. It was probably just another fruitless journey that Sidra was on to find their magic. One that Selen knew she'd have to help Sid recover from, as she always did after a dead end of information. The hope she saw in her sister's eyes was typically followed by a blow of disappointment that left Sid down for days. While her initial instincts told her to blow off the book, something drew her in and kept her from dismissing the thought in the way many had been in the past. Her mind still wandered as she and Aeden sat at the only empty spaces at the long tables that filled the dining hall.

"You're brooding," Aeden stated with a full mouth of bread and stew.

Selen looked up at him, poking at her food. Her appetite had faded as they had waited in line. She knew she was hungry, but her mind was busy enough to distract her from the ache in her belly.

"I'm distracted," Selen said without looking up from her plate.

Aeden glanced up at her without moving his head. "Anything you want to share?"

"Not anything worth talking about," Selen huffed.

"Highly doubtful," Aeden said. Selen glared up at him from her untouched plate. "I'm just saying," he said, putting his hands up. "I might be able to help with whatever it is."

Selen thought about it for a moment as she looked up at her friend. She had never shared much about how she and Sid didn't have powers. She thought that sharing her feelings with others might give them the power to hold it against her. She couldn't imagine that Aeden would do that, but it didn't stop that fear from creeping up whenever it came up in conversation. Selen had shared brief things with Aeden in the past, however, and he had always been supportive. As he approached eighteen, Selen had shared less and less with him, so as not to create any nerves for such a big moment in his life. He was only a few weeks from getting his own powers now.

"Sid found another *lead*," Selen stated, with more bitterness than she intended to let slip.

"Ah," Aeden sat up from his hunched position over his plate and looked at her. "Anything?" he asked, crossing his arms.

He knew how often Sidra found these leads and how quickly they turned into an emotional recovery mission.

"Highly doubtful," Selen solemnly grinned up at Aeden.

Aeden's expression leaned towards something similar to

sympathy, but not quite pity. Either way, Selen hated receiving that look from anyone—and *especially* her friends. Breaking eye contact, Selen looked back at her plate.

"Do you wish it were different?" Aeden leaned forward on his elbow, glancing at Selen with intent.

"Of course I do. Sid was destroyed when we didn't get magic."

Aeden's brow furrowed. "I'm not asking about Sid."

Selen stopped fiddling with the food on her plate and looked at Aeden properly. He had never cared much for Sidra. Not that he disliked her, he just didn't pay her as much attention as others did. What he did know about her, he knew from Selen—and, therefore, how she affected Selen. Aeden was the only one who had helped Selen pick up her own pieces after she took care of her sister. Brief moments of vulnerability that had deepened their relationship, but only as rarely as Selen would allow. It was a protectiveness that Selen hadn't experienced with anyone else that she both despised and appreciated at the same time.

"I have always been fine with my current state. Plus, I have other skills that many others don't." Selen was not in the mood to be pitied.

"Fair enough." Sensing her avoidance, Aeden moved on.

Selen parted ways with Aeden after dinner and was just making her way out to the terrace to watch the sunset when she was halted by the gentle voice of her sister. Sidra was sitting in the headmaster's—Deandra's—office, attempting a poor excuse as to why she'd missed her first class. Selen sighed and turned into the office to come to her sister's defense. *Again.* Pushing the door open, both Sid and Deandra's heads turned towards her.

Chapter Three

Deandra had been the headmaster of Celestara for far longer than Selen could comprehend, and her magic kept her from aging at a normal pace, as was allowed by the laws of the land so long as she continued to educate the future of the country. Deandra's curly, gray hair sat in coils atop her head. Her curls tended to keep her hair at shoulder length, but Selen imagined it would reach to the bottom of her ribs if straightened. She had kind eyes, which had always been a comfort to the girls. She had been their guardian since their parents were lost in the war eighteen years ago. She was kind and caring, but would become stern when the girls tended to act out of order—which they often did—and especially as they'd entered their teenage years. Selen respected the hell out of Deandra for taking them in and dealing with them.

Selen and Deandra had grown closer over the previous years as they bonded over Sidra's fragility, consistently coming up with ways to handle and manage her sister's large emotions. Where no one else could understand, or Selen wasn't willing to show them, Deandra knew her struggle with Sidra—and the love she felt for her. Sid would always be a weakness for them both. Selen hated herself for viewing her sister that way, but after years of protecting and repairing her, Selen had no other way to feel. She loved her sister deeply and endlessly, but it did not limit the weight that Sidra placed on Selen's shoulders. Selen plopped down into the chair beside her sister before Deandra's desk.

"I was just looking for more information on our magic and lost track of time!" Sidra stated defensively.

Deandra spoke with a low but controlled voice. "I understand that, Sidra, but this is the fifth time this month that you have been late or missed Professor Monton's class, and it is getting to the point where your behavior is affecting my position, especially as he is not the only professor who has documented your absences and misbehavior. It is unacceptable, and I will not allow it to continue."

"I am *trying* to solve a problem that neither of you seems to care about!" Sidra snapped, waving her hands at both Deandra and Selen.

"Hey! I came in here to defend you. Don't attack me, Sid." Selen gaped at Sidra.

"Whatever, Selen. You both are so comfortable acting like the fact that we don't have magic is normal. We are literally the only nineteen-year-olds in this school who are powerless!" Sid exclaimed. "Not to mention that we had our

VeilBinding ceremonies, and were meant to get our magic. Does that not at all alarm you?"

Frustration flared through Selen as she watched her sister. The aggressive light of Sidra's emotions pressed against the obsidian wall in Selen's mind, and she had to close her eyes to ensure that the wall stayed upright. Sidra's emotions were more powerful than they had been in weeks.

"Enough, Sidra," Deandra stated calmly. She stood and placed her hands on the wooden desk between them, sending a wave of magic that shut and locked the door to her office.

"No! Not *enough*. We are broken! We were supposed to have power, but *something* happened. We pissed off some god or something." Sidra threw her arms up to the side.

"Sidra, we are doing what we can." Deandra's calm voice blanketed the room.

"And what is that?" Sidra sat forward expectantly. Her face was twisted with rage as she turned her head back and forth, waiting for Deandra's response.

"You have done nothing to help me solve this." Sidra's anger broke with her voice when Deandra said nothing.

Selen stole glances at Deandra and Sidra as she felt a fracture form between them. "Sid. There's only so much any of us can do," Selen said quietly. Sidra's eyes were still on Deandra, but her attention seemed to shift as Selen continued. "I don't know why we didn't get our magic, but it's been over a year..." Selen swallowed air as she brought her eyes back up to her sister, who now stared at her, frustration and pain radiating from her gaze. "Maybe... maybe it's time to move on," Selen said in a near whisper.

Sidra's eyes turned hollow. Her pained expression turned to stone, and her voice was low and cold when she finally spoke. "Our Unveiling was the only thing I had to look forward to—the only thing that made life at this miserable school worth living. And now you want me to *move on?*"

Selen flinched at her words. No matter how many times Sidra had made comments like this, it never ceased to wreck Selen. Knowing how little her sister cared for their life here.

Sid took a deep breath and turned her gaze to the floor. "I'm not some fragile doll who needs to be protected. I am not a mental patient who needs sheltering from reality." Sidra's words were gentle, but shards of glass pushed at their surface. Selen could feel the pressure forming from Sidra's emotions, shoving harder against the walls in her mind. "I don't *care* that you think I should just *move on*. I don't *want* to *move on*. There is no reason for me to *move on*. Not until I've figured out why, after everything that was determined during our VeilBinding ceremony, we sit here, at nineteen, without those magnificent powers the Seer said we would have. I don't understand how you *can* move on."

"We are less than a year away from leaving here—from getting out into the real world. Do you have any idea what's out there?" Selen waved a hand at the window behind Deandra.

"Do you?" Sidra's face formed into a sneer.

"I know that if we don't know how to protect ourselves, we could get killed." An audible flinch came from Deandra behind her desk at Selen's words. "I am training to develop skills that could keep us alive. Your books can't help you if you are being attacked. Your knowledge of the Veil and Time Jumpers won't help you if someone is using magic against you. You *are* weak. *I* am weak. We have nothing to offer this world," Selen spat the words out like venom.

Her entire life—all leading up to this point—had been about protecting Sidra and preparing for what comes after. She was pissed that the magic hadn't bound to Sidra. Maybe the Seer had made a mistake during their VeilBinding. She couldn't even begin to understand which god or Lirium they'd pissed off to hold the magic hostage. It made even less sense for Selen. Was there the possibility that their powers could show up eventually? Sure. But Selen wasn't willing to wait around and get killed trying to solve a problem that was outside of her control.

The girls stared at each other, rage radiating through their bond.

"Girls," Deandra said calmly. "I know that it is... peculiar that your magic didn't arrive during your Unveiling. I am looking into it with others." Deandra struggled to get the words out as she addressed them. Her eyes briefly landed on them before shooting in any other direction, and Selen cocked her head to the side as she considered her guardian. Deandra typically didn't struggle with words like this. Sidra's gaze still seared into Selen, seeming not to have noticed Deandra's momentary struggle.

"I am not going to wait around for fate to decide whether it wants to provide us with our magic." Sidra turned her attention back to Deandra. "The fact you have 'people working on it' means nothing to me."

It was the blow she had meant to land, and Deandra's answering wince was the only indication her words had hit their mark. Selen's blood boiled. This was the woman who took them in. Who had done nothing but love and care for them. Sidra might as well have spat in her face.

"Watch it, Sid. I know you're mad, but come on," Selen growled.

"Selen, you are no better," Sidra stated, crossing her arms over her chest. "Playing warrior isn't going to save you in the real world. You're just as likely to die as I am."

"At least I'm doing something that might help us."

Sidra scoffed and looked towards the ceiling. "Please don't act like you do anything for anyone but yourself."

Sidra shifted her gaze to Selen, fire replacing stone. Selen knew that look; it was the look Sidra wore before she was about to make a poor decision.

Chapter Four

Sidra's eyes still blazed as she leaned over the arm of her chair and towards Selen. She was pounding on Selen's mind now—intentionally, it seemed, as Selen watched her. Each blow against Selen's wall made her vision stutter, and she could feel the migraine that was already forming as Sidra tried to push her way in.

Selen's temper was boiling. She breathed through her nose, using every ounce of self-control she had not to open the gates in her mind and allow her anger and frustration to crash down like a wave upon her sister. Even as Sidra let loose every ounce of anger she could into Selen's mind, the wall held still.

Selen kept her gaze down as she felt the burn of her sister's eyes on the side of her head. Sidra slowly leaned closer, rage still emanating from her like a furnace, but Selen ground her teeth. "All I have done since we were children is take care of your reckless behavior and clean up your messes.

I'm selfish? I have fought to keep your emotions in check and save you from experiencing any of mine." Selen slammed Sidra with eye contact.

"Oh, get off your high horse! We both know the only reason you do any of that is so you can hold it over my head." Sidra angled her head at Selen and shot her a wicked grin that told Selen that Sidra was going to try to cut deep with her next words. Selen shifted her gaze in warning. "At least I'm trying..." Sidra paused, and her grin grew wilder. "Maybe I could just give up and have a go at Aleya. From the sounds of it, she's pretty decent in a broom closet."

And they struck home.

Selen gripped the arms of her chair and her nails began to tear the edge of the cloth. She jumped up in an instant and gripped the arms of Sidra's chair, leaning so close to her face she could feel the heat of Sid's breath. Without a word, Selen opened the gate in her mind, coating Sidra's light in a dark wave of shadows. Sidra's expression transformed from one of aggressive arrogance to something glazed with fear as she fell back in her seat.

But Selen didn't stop, and let the waves of aggression, anger, sorrow, and bitterness wash over her sister as they tore free of the fortress she kept in her mind. Selen watched as her sister experienced each emotion, and reveled in the fear on her face. Shadows clouded her vision as she homed in on that terror.

Let it out, a dark voice whispered in her mind.

All thoughts left Selen's head as she stared Sidra down. Her vision became distant as she felt herself being lifted into the darkness of her mind. The wave of shadow she had let out was not only washing away Sidra's light, but also her own.

More!

She gripped for anything to keep her steady as the darkness wrapped tendrils around her mind and body, but she could still feel the pull. She wanted to stay, but the darkness beckoned, its embrace both cold and warm, terrifying and comforting. Selen wanted nothing more in that moment than to succumb to the shadows and let them take her.

MORE!

She felt her mind's eye closing as the face of a distant stranger looked terrified through the little light that shone through the darkness.

"Enough!" Deandra yelled, and a wave of wind knocked Selen back from Sidra's face.

Selen hit the desk behind her, knocking items from it as she did, and the impact sent a sharp jolt of pain through her hip. As if slamming back into her own body, the shadows in her vision slithered away until she was able to take in her surroundings. Deandra now stood between her and Sidra, an expression that almost looked like fear on her face. Selen covered her mouth in horror as she took in Sidra. Her sister's eyes were glazed with a sense of fear and shock that Selen had never seen before.

Selen snapped the walls in her mind back into place and pushed Deandra aside, lowering to her knees before her sister as all the anger and frustration she felt was replaced by fear and regret.

"Sidra?" Selen whispered as she took Sid's hands. "I'm so sorry. I don't know what happened."

Sid blinked up at Selen, her expression shifting from a glazed fear to absolute rage.

"So that's how you feel about me?" Sid asked calmly, in a much darker voice than she usually used.

"No. No! I... I was angry. And..." Selen stuttered to come up with an explanation for her outburst, pausing after a moment because she had no explanation for what had occurred. For that darkness.

Sidra ripped her hand from Selen's and pushed past her towards the door. She turned to shoot Selen, still on her knees in front of the chair, one last, spiteful look, then slammed the door shut behind her.

Selen's heart splintered as the door rattled. Lifting herself off the ground and slumping into the chair—still warm from Sidra's body—Selen's mind reeled. Sidra had never dug into Selen's personal life to make her feel small. She knew Sidra would never actually do what she had said— but for her to even say something that she knew would cut so deep... That was a line they'd never crossed. Selen pressed her face into her hands and closed her eyes. Why now? Why did she lose control now? What just happened?

Selen reached for the memory, now fading as if it were a distant image. The darkness had encapsulated her vision.

The utter lack of control she'd felt as she stared at the stranger.

No. Not a stranger. *Her sister.*

But in that moment, that is what Sidra had been to

Selen. A stranger. She mentally sorted through the moment and realized that, as that darkness wove through her mind, body, and vision, she hadn't known who was on the other end. It was as if the darkness was the only thing she knew—the voice that had coaxed more darkness from her was a fading memory. Had that been anything more than just her own need for whatever darkness was inside of her? To be consumed by it? Selen felt two cold hands on her knees and looked up to find Deandra looking at her thoughtfully.

"Are you okay?" Deandra whispered.

"What *happened*?" Selen sat back in the chair, keeping her hands on her face.

"I lost control," Deandra kept her voice at a whisper as she looked down at the floor.

She had lost control? Sidra was nothing to be controlled. Selen had tried many times. Deandra had never expressed the desire to control Sidra, only guide her. Selen pulled her hands from her face and looked down at Deandra.

"Sid can't be controlled, and apparently neither can I," Selen huffed as she crossed her arms.

Deandra slowly sat back against the desk, holding Selen's gaze, anguish seeping from her.

"How are you feeling?" Deandra asked as she assessed Selen from head to toe.

Selen didn't know how to answer that. She felt fine, she supposed. Guilty and irritated at the interaction, but fine overall. Something had snapped within her that she had never experienced before, a power that still tugged at her mind. Selen itched at her now-tingling skin.

The darkness. The shadows that momentarily overtook her. Had Deandra noticed them? There really couldn't have been any other explanation for why she had stepped between them. She'd let the sisters fight before, so Deandra must have sensed Selen slipping into wherever she had just gone if she had come to protect Sid.

To protect Sid.

The realization hit Selen as she studied her guardian's face. What had Selen done to have Deandra step in to protect her sister?

"I've never felt that way towards her before. I think I was so mad that my vision got cloudy. Dark." Selen felt that childlike fear and vulnerability wrap around her, seeking comfort in the only consistent person who had been in her and Sid's lives. Could this have been what the Seer and those horrifying voices meant during her VeilBinding Ceremony?

What wanders in the depths is yours to conquer or to claim. What has been broken may be bound, or continue to break. Trust your heart when your mind takes hold, young eclipse.

None of it had made any sense to her then, and even more so now. VeilBinding Seers were notorious for speaking in riddles. Some enjoyed it because it made their Unveiling that much more of a surprise if they couldn't decipher what the Seer had given them, but Selen didn't like thinking back to the moment that still haunted her nightmares.

As if sensing Selen's vulnerability, Deandra leaned forward and clasped one of Selen's hands, before offering a grave smile of reassurance.

"Did I hurt her?" Selen whispered.

"No. Sidra is fine. The cut only as deep as those that have come before it. You both are fine, it seems," Deandra said exhaustedly.

Selen eyed her wearily. "Are *you* okay?" She wrapped her fingers around Deandra's hand.

Deandra gave Selen a look of awareness that quickly flickered into something else. "Though her comment was out of line. Are your... relations with Aleya something that I should be concerned about?"

Color flared in Selen's cheeks as she broke eye contact with Deandra and pulled her hand away. "No. It's—it's nothing." Selen crossed her arms over her chest.

"Do we need to talk about... safety?" Selen looked up as a small bit of color flooded Deandra's cheeks.

A laugh of discomfort slipped from Selen's lips and she uncoiled a bit. "I think the awful presentation we received on the topic in our first year was enough," Selen laughed, and was flooded with relief as a small grin bloomed on Deandra's lips.

"Just please make good choices. Meaning: avoid broom closets for the foreseeable future." Deandra gave her an amused yet warning look.

Selen coughed in disbelief as the words came out of Deandra's mouth. After a quick nod, she stood and headed for the door.

Gods. The anger that she had felt only moments ago was now completely replaced with humiliation, and a small spark of frustration rekindled as she cursed Sidra for putting her in this position, which is the emotion she'd expected after the comment that Sidra had made. Yet, the temper that had actually reared its head was something much, much darker.

Sidra seethed as she stomped up to their room.

What the hell was that?

Her mind raced as she sorted through the memories of what had just happened. It had felt like a tidal wave. Selen had opened the door on that gate she always kept closed, and let her true emotions wash over Sidra. She had felt so entirely helpless and small as she had sat there just watching her sister's face hover above hers. Sidra got to her room and slammed the door, pacing as she wrapped her arms around her body.

Is that really how she felt? A small sob came from Sidra as she continued to relive the moment. She hadn't *recognized* Selen. Her face was the same, but there was so much darkness clouding her eyes that she had never seen from her.

Could that be her magic? It had to be.

She knew that wall in her mind was that of darkness, but she'd assumed Selen kept it there for privacy. Sid had never wanted that wall to be built. She wanted to share things with her sister, see how deep their bond went, but Selen had closed the doors the minute that Sidra's emotions had grown bigger than she could handle. Everything that made them unique and special, Selen wanted to stifle.

Selen wanted to become a *warrior*.

A warrior? Who was she kidding? Neither of them was strong enough to become a warrior. Selen should be trying to help her find how they can get their magic. Sidra knew their powers were there, somewhere—she had always felt them scratching under the surface. She knew Selen had, too. Today was only further confirmation that Selen's powers were begging to be released; those shadows were a sliver of Selen's power, and Sidra knew it. She hadn't really meant to use Aleya against Selen, but she wanted to see how far she could push her before she broke.

Plus, she was angry. Selen and Deandra always acted like she was a doll that needed to be cushioned. She knew that Aleya was a weakness, and she'd wanted to use that. She had wanted to hurt Selen, deeply and unapologetically. And she had—before the darkness had taken over Selen's vision, Sidra had seen the hurt on her face.

They had never attacked each other's personal lives. It was a line they had set to avoid pushing a wedge between them. It had never entirely limited their fighting, but it had kept it from leaving lasting scars. Had she put an irreparable rift in their relationship? Maybe. Maybe that's what they needed to move on to the next phase of their lives. Maybe a change is what they needed to push them over the edge to unveil their powers. Their magic that was still blocked for some fucking reason.

Sidra was shaking as she sat on the bed. Putting her head

in her hands, she closed her eyes and steadied her breathing. She felt both guilty and thrilled by today's discovery, and her mind reeled as she tried to navigate why her tears fell when she also felt joy and hope. She'd never wanted to hurt Selen, but she was thrilled she'd shown an ounce of power.

But how had it slipped through? What was blocking it? Was anger the key? Sidra grabbed one of the notebooks out of her bag and started scribbling furiously.

Anger equals power?

Barrier cracking.

Where does the barrier come from?

Why is it there?

Who put it there?

Her power came when I *attacked her.*

Vulnerability equals... me?

She scribbled for several more minutes—ideas and random thoughts—until her shoulders sagged and she finally looked at the words that were finally free of her mind. The page was chaos incarnate; words of different sizes scattered the page without a defined order, lined the sides of the paper and ran off the edge.

"*I* am Selen's weakness," Sidra whispered into the darkness of their room, and a wave of excitement and anguish hit her as she figured out what she had to do.

Chapter Five

Cracking open the door to their room, Selen peered inside to check if Sidra was asleep in bed and was relieved to find that she was nowhere to be found. After the incident, Selen had visited the fighting rings to beat her anger out on some of the wooden dummies, taking her time returning to their room. However, as the door opened all the way, Selen huffed at what she found. Out of her Armoire, Sidra had strewn Selen's clothing all over the floor and her bed.

Real mature.

Selen gathered her clothes off the ground and began sorting them, but as she did, a small scrap fell from one of the items of clothing. Reaching down, Selen picked up what seemed to be the corner of a piece of parchment. She turned it over in her hands and found that one side had a bunch of scribbles and what seemed to be the ends of words.

—*arrier*

—wer?

—...me

It was Sidra's handwriting, but there wasn't enough left to discern what its meaning could be. After putting her clothing away, Selen sighed and threw herself on her bed. As always, the only light in the room came in from the moon that shone through the window. Turning to look out the window, Selen realized that it may be a full moon based on the size of the goddess staring back at her, and sadness encompassed her. She and her sister usually spent this night outdoors together, sneaking out after their scheduled curfew. Something about a large moon and the darkness made them the perfect pair, like Selen and Sidra. Gods, her feelings towards her sister were so complicated. She loved her more than anything in the world, yet she resented her, too, causing reactions like the one she gave tonight. Well, that had been the first time that had happened.

Selen knew she had some explaining to do, but also expected an apology from Sidra. While it was no secret that Selen and Aleya were seeing each other, Deandra didn't need to know *details*. And for her to imply that she would ever try to hurt Selen by going to Aleya was so out of line.

Sidra's expression of fear and betrayal flashed through Selen's mind as she got herself ready for bed. Had she been so frightening to look at that she instilled that level of fear in her sister? What *had* that looked like? The thought intrigued and frightened her, even as her memories of the event continued to grow more distant—as if her mind wanted to force them out.

Selen sat on her bed and curled her knees to her chest before setting her head on them. She was still staring out the window as a small *knock* echoed through her room, cutting through the stagnant silence. Selen went rigid, expecting Sidra to walk in with a fight, ready to fire, but drew in a breath as Aleya entered the confined space. The room suddenly felt very small.

"I saw Sid going into Leirei's room and figured you didn't want to spend the full moon alone." Aleya's soft voice caressed her skin, sending shivers down her spine as she strolled through the room. She came and sat on the bed, placing a hand on Selen's knee. Her soft skin sent electricity through Selen's body.

"We fought," Selen said quietly, turning her face back towards the window.

"How bad?"

"It was one for the books." Selen gave Aleya a solemn grin before diverting her gaze back to the window.

"What happened?" Aleya asked in a whisper, running her hand down Selen's shin.

Selen sighed and leaned back against her headboard. "I honestly don't even know. I heard Dea and Sid arguing—and naturally I went in to help—but Sid turned on me. Brought you into it. Then *I* turned on *her...*"

Aleya's brow furrowed. "What did she say about me?"

Selen made eye contact with Aleya as her hand slowed. "Nothing really. Just things to rile me up," she paused. "It worked," Selen stated with a small grin.

"I didn't know I had that effect on you." Aleya grinned and positioned herself cross-legged on the bed before Selen.

"*Sure*," Selen laughed and gently shoved one of Aleya's shoulders.

Silence fell, and Aleya reached for Selen's leg again. "I'm sorry. I know how much your fights with her affect you."

Selen's grin fell as she let her knees fall into a crossed position in front of Aleya, who shifted her hand off Selen's leg. "I don't know what happened. I was so angry with her, and I lashed out in a way that I never have before. My walls completely fell, and I buried her with my anger. I have never felt so... *dark*." Selen put her hands over her face. "She hates me," she whispered after a moment of silence.

Aleya grabbed Selen's hand and placed it in hers. "Your sister has a lot of emotions—" Aleya started, but Selen sent a warning message through her stare. It was one thing for Selen to talk negatively about her sister, but another for anyone else—even Aleya. "—but hate for you, is not one of them."

Selen's shoulders released as she realized Aleya's statement held no judgment towards her or Sidra. "You didn't see her face." Selen kept her eyes on Aleya's face as she traced the lines on Selen's hands.

Aleya stilled and turned to lift Selen's chin with her index finger. She cocked her head to one side, sympathy lining her eyes. "She could never hate you," she gently repeated, rubbing her thumb along the bottom of Selen's chin.

Selen sucked in a breath of air at the intimacy of her

touch. She could feel the burning start in her cheeks before slowly moving to her core. After everything, she'd love nothing more than to get lost in Aleya. Feel her skin on hers. But she was too vulnerable. Too exposed.

Selen gently pushed a curl behind Aleya's ear and slid her hand around her neck to cup the back of her head, pulling her in. She pressed their brows together and closed her eyes. She could feel Aleya's breath on hers, slowly quickening as they stayed attached. She wanted the closeness, but wouldn't let her be at her most intimate with her in this state. The tension was thick between them as she opened her eyes, only to be greeted with Aleya's stare, fire burning beneath the surface of her gaze. Her eyes were a deep forest green that always brought Selen to a place of peace, like the green moss that grew on the north side of the mountain trees.

"I can't," Selen whispered, maintaining eye contact.

The fire dimmed, but Aleya's eyes stayed alight, only slightly tinged with disappointment. Aleya tilted up her chin and gently brushed her lips against Selen's, whose heart skipped a beat as the other girl leaned further in. Aleya's soft lips pressed to hers with a tender force that would have made Selen's knee buckle if she weren't sitting down. For a moment, all thoughts left Selen's mind. She could focus only on the lightning which pulsed through their touch, the raging fire between them that begged to be released.

Aleya was the first to pull back, and Selen let out a small gust of air as the blissful distraction was ripped away. Aleya ran her hand through Selen's hair before shifting her body towards the edge of the bed.

"Find me if you need me," Aleya said with a flirty grin, slipping off the bed and out the door.

As she did, Selen felt her fire shift into hollowness. The closeness with Aleya was always temporary. The fire would always be drowned by the reality that Selen never wanted to face. Aleya was always going to be temporary. She'd said as much when they had started their *entanglement*. Selen knew Aleya cared for her, but not in the ways she wanted. She used Selen as an outlet for something she was still trying to understand, but Selen knew what she wanted—or at least, she thought she did. She wanted *her*. She wanted Aleya to stay, even if it meant her not getting the release she knew Aleya had come for.

She wanted more than Aleya's lust, but she wouldn't beg for it. She would let Aleya come to her. But how long would she wait? Should she wait at all? She wrapped her knees up towards her chest once more and looked back towards the moon.

The following day was a blur. After the lack of sleep and her anxiousness to see and talk to Sidra, Selen was convinced that there wasn't a single thing that she had learned in any of her lessons. Sidra hadn't turned up to any of the classes that morning, not that there was much value to their classes, anyway, but worry plagued Selen's mind. Sidra was likely just skipping out of her own anger, but not coming back last night and not saying anything for an entire day was unlike her.

Classes were still in session, but there was little hope of anything being learned while professors distracted them with fun projects. Celestara was buzzing with the approaching Fire Festival that was being set up in the large building, an ancient celebration to honor the spring at its peak as summer quickly approached. Typically, the academy lit two bonfires that would burn into the night. With low supervision from faculty, the event always turned somewhat into a mess. They did always keep a closer eye on the older students, however, as they tended to sneak in mead to share amongst the other students—not to mention the ego-driven magical displays that were typically associated with the consumption of alcohol.

Selen had avoided Aleya since their encounter the night before, obviously dodging her wave in the dining hall at lunch, where she promptly sat next to Aeden before heading out to the training rings. Selen knew there wasn't anything she could say to her that would make either of them feel any better about last night's encounter. Not that anything particularly bad had happened, but she had rejected Aleya's advances, and it was the first time she had done so. Where Aleya may not have felt any awkwardness, Selen knew she wouldn't be able to act normally around her.

"You bringing her to the Fire Festival?" Aeden cut in, throwing a piece of lettuce at Selen, which hit her in the face before plopping onto her tray. The impact startled her, and she slowly turned her head towards Aeden, intentionally contorting her face into an amused frown.

"Do you have to exist in such an unserious state at all times?" Selen asked, throwing the lettuce back at him. Aeden opened his mouth and dipped his head to catch it. Selen's amusement swiftly shifted to disgust.

"That was literally on my face, you absolute goon," she laughed. How some people picked men over women given the choice, she would never know.

"So that's why it was so sweet?" Aeden crooned, winking at her. "Answer the question, you absolute *crone*," he mocked her.

Aeden's brightness tinged Selen's gloom, and she couldn't help but smile. He brought a light to her life that was so effortless; where Sidra's light was her opposite and equal, Aeden's was her lighthouse.

"No. I am not bringing Aleya to the Fire Festival. I'm not bringing anyone," she said, smile fading, and looked down at her tray.

"*Well...*" he said, drawing out the final letter of the word. "I'm not taking anyone, either. So, if you want..." He didn't finish his statement as he waved his fork towards her.

Selen's lip quirked again. "Aeden, would you like to join me at the Fire Festival?" Selen put her elbows on the table and looked up at Aeden beneath her lashes, a play on flirting.

Aeden put his hand on his chest with an exasperated gasp. "Like a date?" Before she had an opportunity to say anything, he went on. "Why, I never thought you'd ask me. Could this be the beginning of a love story?"

Selen cocked her head at him before scoffing and focusing her attention back on her meal. "Absolutely not," she said sternly.

"You are no fun," Aeden huffed, going back to his own food.

After finishing their meals, Aeden and Selen made their way out to the training rings, the former balancing a stolen spoon on his nose as they walked. At least he was entertaining. Selen strived to have his level of carelessness about—well, everything. He always seemed to be having a good time, and even with Sidra and Aleya weighing on her mind, Selen found peace when she was with him.

A door opening from the end of the hallway caught her eye before they left the building. A tall woman with cropped dark hair and tan skin exited Deandra's office, shoulders wide enough that Selen could tell that she was strong, even if it wasn't obvious enough by the muscled arms that peeked out from under her dark brown cloak. Aeden hadn't even noticed Selen had stopped as he exited through the door, but Selen watched the woman turn back towards the door and clasped arms with Deandra.

"It is important tonight more than ever. I can feel the pressure building," Deandra said in a whisper that did nothing to muffle her volume.

Selen furrowed her brow. Who was this woman? What was Deandra talking about? She slid her body behind the wall, trying not to be too obvious.

"It will be done." The woman's voice was low and powerful. She had a slight accent, likely from a land that Selen had been too focused on other things to have learned about in class. They disconnected arms as Deandra closed her door, and the woman slipped the hood over her head. As she turned, Selen got a full view of the woman, and the sight nearly took her breath away.

Her shoulders were broad, muscles rippling down her arms. Her fitted pants did nothing to hide her muscular legs, and she had three white scars, which ran down her face and cut through her tan skin. The woman couldn't be older than her mid-twenties, but the scars that wrapped her arms and face represented a life hard-lived. She wrapped her cloak tighter around her as she walked towards the exit Selen occupied, keeping her eyes low. Nervously turning from side to side, Selen tried to figure out where she might go to pretend she wasn't just listening in on their conversation, before opting to act like she had just walked through the door.

Acting as though she were looking back at friends, even though no one was there, Selen rounded the corner and found herself colliding with the tall woman.

"Oh, I'm so sorry. I was talking to my—" Selen looked back at the door where no one stood and paused. "... Friends." Giving an awkward laugh as she glanced back at the woman, who looked between Selen and her imaginary friends. Giving a slight grin, she locked eyes with Selen.

Selen's breath caught as the woman's amber gaze fell onto hers. Her eyes reminded Selen of the endless sand dunes in the deserts of the east. Gods, she was beautiful. She had a strong jawline and high cheekbones, accompanied by her full lips. Her face was stunningly harsh.

"Be careful, Bird, the imaginary friends are some of the more dangerous," the woman said, her voice low. Her accent caressed each word as it left her lips.

Selen coughed to try and mask the red creeping up her cheeks. She didn't have a chance to say anything before the woman stepped around her, heading towards the exit, pushing open the door to find Aeden on the other side, likely having only figured out a few minutes ago that Selen wasn't walking with him. His eyes widened as he watched the beautiful woman exit the building. Selen shortly followed out the door.

"I was going to be mad at you for leaving me unsupervised on my walk to the rings, but *wow*. She looks like she could ruin my life—and I might... enjoy it?" Aeden gawked after the woman who now strode towards the edge of the property. She moved quickly. With purpose. Selen supposed a woman like that *always* had a purpose.

Aeden shoved her shoulder when she didn't say anything, breaking her out of her trance.

"You're staring more than I am," he laughed, turning around to head back to the practice rings. "Come along, puppy, far less attractive and sweaty fighting awaits."

Selen picked up a pebble and flicked it at the back of his head.

"Call me puppy again and I won't go easy on you today," she laughed, walking beside him.

Aeden let out a deep laugh throwing his head back.

As if she couldn't help it, Selen glanced over her shoulder one more time, watching the woman fade into the cover of the forest.

Chapter Six

Selen stared at herself in the mirror of her open armoire as she got ready for the evening. After sparring with Aeden well into the afternoon, she had needed to bathe before the evening festivities. The ends of her hair was still damp, and left small wet spots on her black tunic, but the rest had dried into their natural waves. If not tied back into a braid, this was how she typically wore it, and tonight was no exception.

She had tried on dozens of outfits, even going into Sidra's armoire for inspiration, but ended up opting for her usual daily attire. Clothing now spread out to cover both her and Sidra's beds, and Selen sighed as she looked around; she knew she'd have to clean this up—but maybe later.

She was just slipping on her boots when her door cracked open, and Sidra slid inside. Her face dropped when she saw Selen was already there.

"Oh. I thought you'd be out already," Sid said uninterestedly as she moved to her side of the room. She paused in front of her bed as she looked at the clothes that littered the space, sending a quick glare in Selen's direction as she worked her way through the garments. Selen internally rolled her eyes at Sidra's annoyance after having cleaned up the mess Sidra had made after her fit yesterday.

"Sid, can we talk?" Selen stood and reached for Sidra's arm.

Sidra quickly wriggled out of Selen's grip.

"I'm here to get some clothes, then I'm going to stay with Xander." Selen grabbed Sidra's arm and spun her.

"*Xander?*" Selen spewed.

"Yes. Xander," Sidra spat, and turned back towards the bed. "I have nothing to say to you right now," Sidra muttered, sorting through the mess on the bed.

"Xander is an ass!" Selen crossed her arms over chest. How could she be seeing Xander? He had made his way through eighty percent of the students at the school, not to mention the fact he was an absolute prick.

Sidra spun back towards Selen. "You're an ass!" Sidra stated and held up a finger.

Selen raised her eyebrows and both girls' anger snagged. A small grin started to brew on Selen's face as she stared at her sister, whose face also began to crack.

Sidra let out a large sigh as she plopped down on the bed.

"Is this done?" Sidra asked, pointing a finger back and forth between them.

"It can be," Selen said, sitting on her bed and resting her elbows against her knees.

"It's exhausting being mad at you. You scared the shit out of me last night," Sidra exclaimed.

"You were being a bitch," Selen said.

Sidra scoffed. "*You* were being a bitch."

Both girls let out a small laugh. The wound between them was still made of newly-healed flesh, and Selen knew she'd have to walk on eggshells to avoid another blowout. They'd had many fights, though this was their worst. It had also been the longest they had gone without seeing each other since forever.

"Tell me you weren't with *Xander* the entire time." Selen hoped that Sid hadn't been stupid enough to give into any of his desires. She had heard some very questionable things about him and didn't want her sister getting tangled up with a creep.

"I want to tell you yes just to piss you off, but no. He caught up with me earlier today and asked if I wanted to go to the Fire Festival with him. I stayed at Leirei's room last night." Sidra propped her head on her hand as she watched Selen, reminding her that Aleya had mentioned Sidra was with Leirei last night.

Selen quickly shook off the memory to avoid reliving what had come after that. Leirei was to Sidra what Aeden was to Selen—without the constant flirting. A tension in Selen's chest eased knowing that Sid hadn't been with *Xander.*

"But you're still going to the Festival with him?" Selen asked, more judgment slipping into her tone than she had intended. Selen put her hands up in surrender before Sid had time to react. "I'm just saying as he has a bit of a reputation."

Sidra sighed. "I suppose the same could be said about me." She glanced sidelong at Selen before sitting up. "I'm just going to flirt a little bit and enjoy his company, then be rid of him," she said dramatically, sweeping her hand through the air.

"Please be careful, Sid, he's not great company," Selen warned.

"Please don't act like I can't handle myself, that's why we ended up in this situation in the first place," Sid stated, standing as she got ready to change into one of the dresses she found lying on her bed.

The comment sparked a small fury in Selen, but she took a deep breath and let it go. Fault often avoided Sidra—*especially* if you asked Sidra.

"I'm going to meet Aeden. I'll see you at the fire." Selen stalked towards the door.

"Finally giving the kid a chance?" Sidra grinned at her.

"Not even a little bit." Selen grinned back and shut the door behind her.

As she entered the hallway, Selen sucked in a deep breath. She knew she had to let go of this anger towards Sid, but that little comment she'd made showed Selen that nothing had changed. She was still the same old Sid. But that was a conversation to have with a counselor later.

Selen hadn't felt Sidra's typical pull in her mind. She reached out a tendril of darkness, searching for her, but the constant light that usually pushed up against her dark walls were far away; a small wall in the space between them. She forced that tendril of darkness to brush against the small wall, and as she did, she felt a flicker and the bright wall hardened. Selen blinked as she came back to reality.

Sidra had put up a wall?

A small bit of anguish ignited in Selen's chest. She had kept one up for years, begging Sidra to put one up so she didn't have to constantly protect herself from the waves of emotion slamming into her mind. But for Sidra to have put one up now, ripping away that constant presence... it left Selen feeling a bit lonelier than she had expected.

Darkness had fallen as Selen made her way towards the bonfires, their glare lighting up the night sky. Aeden had said that he would meet her at the top of the hill, and as she breached it, she spotted him lying on his back, propped onto one elbow, tossing grapes into his mouth.

"Oh, good. I just ran out of grapes," he said, popping up and walking over to her.

"Sidra is going with Xander tonight," Selen grumbled as she stalked towards him.

"You two are talking?" Aeden looked at Selen.

"How did you know we weren't talking?" Selen glanced over as he struggled to keep up with her raging pace.

"This school knows everything." He paused and reached

for Selen's arm to slow her down. "It's not like your fights are quiet. Also... *uh*, Aleya told the twins, and it pretty much spread like wildfire from there."

Selen stopped and turned towards him, hurt flickering in her eyes. "What did she tell everyone?" Her voice cracked as she stopped and plopped down on the side of the hill.

Aeden slid to a stop and sat too.

"She said that you two had another blowout, and that it was 'dramatic as usual'." Aeden played with the tie on his boots.

Selen sat there momentarily, looking down at the large fires below them. Students had already gathered, not so sneakily sharing containers of mead amongst small groups. Selen spotted Aleya with her group of friends, an arm draped around some third year, whose name Selen had never bothered learning. She stared down at them for a moment longer before letting out a sigh. She had the tightness in her chest that she felt so often when it came to Aleya.

"The last day has been shit." Selen propped her forearms up on her knees.

Aeden's gaze followed Selen's to the group below, catching on Aleya and her newest conquest. His shoulders drooped a bit at the sight.

"Aleya's kind of being a dick," Aeden stated, ripping a piece of grass from the hill and tossing it to the side.

"She's just... figuring some things out," Selen justified. She didn't know why she constantly defended her. Aleya had always been very transparent about the state of their relationship, but Selen always assumed she still cared for her.

Maybe not in the ways she wished, but she'd thought it at least would have been enough to not spread their personal conversations around the school.

"You don't have to defend her. She's making a lot of questionable decisions lately—bailing on you being at the top of the list." Aeden gave Selen a grin and stood, offering his hand, which Selen grabbed gladly.

"Aeden," she started, wiping off her backside from the grassy hillside. "I'm tired of moping. Am I annoyed with Sidra? Yes. Am I annoyed with Aleya? Definitely. Am I annoyed with you for not saving me any grapes? Absolutely." With that, she began her trek down the side of the hill.

She had meant it. She was tired of feeling down because of other people. If nothing else, she would enjoy tonight. Avoidance happened to be her favorite form of coping.

Aeden quickly caught up. "If it makes you feel any better, the grapes were not crisp at all. Mushy, even."

Selen couldn't really tell if he was joking. He often said things in such a sarcastic way that she couldn't tell if it was humor or not. So she just moved on.

Sensing her dismissal, Aeden went on. "Anyways, I know a fourth year who has a surplus of mead that we could partake in. He may have brewed it himself, but it has alcohol and based on my nonexistent knowledge of the brewing process, I think that kills any bacteria that could have come from his room."

"That isn't particularly appealing, but I'm not in the mood to *not* have alcohol, so I think it could work." Selen's lips were downturned, but she raised her eyebrows.

"Sweet! Let's see how long it takes before we vomit on our peers!" Aeden skipped, putting up a hand for a high-five.

Selen laughed at his upraised hand and raised hers to meet it. With a quick glance at Aleya, still draped around the third year, they drifted into the depths of the crowd.

Sidra leaned against Xander as his friends attempted to see who could manipulate the fire the most with magic. Being that none of them could actually wield fire, the playing grounds were fairly level.

Xander's arm pressed against the ground behind her back as he chatted with his friends to their right. Selen was definitely right about Xander; he was a grade A prick, but he had a purpose tonight, so Sid played her part. Snuggling a little further into Xander's side, Sid pulled his attention from his friends and down to her. Xander looked down at her with a predatory gleam in his eyes.

He was attractive in every sense of the word. He had dark brown hair that was long enough to display his natural waves. He always let pieces drape over his bright blue eyes, creating an allure of mystery which added to his basic beauty. His eyes were beautiful, but depthless. His tall stature put him a good two hands taller than her. He was the typical attractive man, no more, no less. Sidra often associated his type with dogs—some are capable of caring, but most run on instincts and are just looking for someone to comfort them. Cute as they were, they didn't truly serve a purpose beyond companionship.

Sidra played the best needy sweetheart character she could produce, and looked up at Xander from below her lashes, batting them to emphasize her crystal blue eyes. She knew she had an effect on people. Her looks had always been something she could use as a weapon if necessary. She knew her look hit home when Xander's arms wrapped around her side, pulling her in closer. Pushing the hair on her neck back with his nose, he gave her neck a quick nip before turning back to his friends.

Sidra hated that it still sent a spark through her. Men had many frustrating qualities, but the most frustrating was the desire they could pull from Sidra. She knew that Xander had no intentions of acting like a gentleman, much as she had no intentions of being a lady for him. But, though tonight had a different purpose, it didn't mean she couldn't have some fun.

Sidra glanced up at the crowd that was swiftly gathering. How she had beaten Selen here, she had no idea. She'd assumed that Selen had run into Aleya and found some privacy until she saw the very girl throwing herself at some third year whom Sid didn't know. Anger had sparked in Sidra's gut at the sight. While she was still irritated with Selen, and had used Aleya against her, she was pissed that Aleya would flaunt this little fling knowing that Selen would be here. Aleya had made eye contact with Sidra only once before quickly averting her gaze after that.

Sidra's gaze caught on the two figures perched on the side of the hill overlooking the fires. She would know that head of dark hair—and slightly angry demeanor—anywhere.

Her heart dropped a bit when she noticed that Selen's gaze was fixed on Aleya, but her sympathy quickly transformed into white hot anger. She hated that Aleya just played with Selen's emotions. Selen would obviously be the best thing that would ever happen to Aleya, but she was too stupid to realize it. Flaunting some girl right in front of Selen.

Bitch.

Sidra appreciated Aeden for the friendship he offered to Selen, even if it was rooted in a desire for more. He wanted her in any form that he could get, and that was pure. Sidra knew that if Selen ever gave him the time of day in that way, he would jump at the chance, but would otherwise never push for anything more than her friendship, jokes and all. Their friendship was beautiful, deeper than any friendship Sidra had. Though Leirei was probably the one she was closest to, they just spent a lot of time together, and Sidra often felt as though their relationship was based mostly on the fact that Leirei wanted to get in with the popular crowd. Though, that had never really bothered Sidra; she knew most of her relationships were very surface level. She wanted it that way.

Selen thought Sidra was a gullible, vulnerable fool. While it drove Sidra absolutely insane, she knew that was pretty much all she had presented for years. She had ideas and knowledge that most people in this school would never even come close to acquiring. The walls that Selen had plastered in her mind were an easy way for Sidra to continue playing that part. She had allowed many of her emotions to go unchecked for years and had only just started putting up walls in the last one.

When they hadn't received their powers on their birthday, Sidra had drifted into a state that she had never experienced before, and felt her sister's mental walls growing thicker.

Hiding from Sidra's emotions. Always hiding.

She had finally concluded that Selen hid from her own emotions as much as she hid from Sid's.

But it was because Selen hid so well behind those walls that she overlooked when Sidra had put up her own, far deeper than Selen could actively find without the depth of mental training that Sidra had undertaken. After their fight the other night, Sidra put up a wispy exterior wall that could trick Selen into thinking the rift between them had just begun, but it had really been years since she'd truly lost control as Selen had during their fight.

That hadn't *actually* been intentional. Sidra had been angry and wanted to hurt Selen. While she had been far more intentional with her emotions over the past year, she still had moments that slipped.

Blinking, Sidra realized she had lost track of the two forms on the hill while deep in thought. Tonight was the best time for her to test her theory. With the wounds still fresh from not only their fight but whatever was going down between her and Aleya, Selen was vulnerable. She didn't love that she thought that way about her sister, but this was all to help them both in the long run. Selen would thank her one day.

Sidra turned her focus back towards the fires. Leirei emerged from the crowd and sat beside Sidra in the grass, briefly glancing at Xander before settling her gaze on her friend.

"Should I plan to see you after the festivities tonight?" Leirei asked in her wispy voice.

Sidra grinned, knowing Xander heard the comment as he gave her side a quick squeeze. Sidra gently nudged her elbow into Xander's ribs.

"We'll see," Sidra said with a smile, sending Xander a quick glance, finding him already actively watching her. He narrowed his eyes before turning to his friends.

Leirei rolled her eyes and settled next to Sidra to continue their people watching. Sidra glanced over at Leirei every once in a while. She did care for her. While Leirei and she may not have been as close as Aeden and Selen, she was the closest friend she had, and she didn't really want to lose that. There were moments where Leirei had shown a depth further than the puddle they typically kept between them, one of those having been after the fight Sid had with Selen. Leirei had not even hesitated to comfort her when Sid had stormed into her room. Leirei had shared her bed and her pajamas, as Sid hadn't grabbed anything to sleep in when she left their room, despite slinging Selen's everywhere out of spite. It wasn't her most mature moment, but she'd felt satisfied at the sight of what would soon annoy Selen.

Sidra and Leirei had talked for hours as Sidra worked through her thoughts that night. Most of the time, it was Sidra rambling on and Leirei just listening. She supposed that was a lot of their relationship. Sidra speaking and Leirei listening. She appreciated her for that. It was likely one of the only reasons she had been able to get a handle on her emotions over the last year. Leirei was an outlet for her.

She felt a slight pang of guilt that she hadn't been more of that for Leirei.

Sidra never turned her away when she had wanted to talk —she just ended up doing most of it. She'd assumed that Leirei spent time with her to gain popularity, but she never understood why she listened to her ramblings if that was the case. Likely just because she was willing to work for her popularity? Or maybe she just wanted to be her friend. Sidra knew that she was a bit jaded when it came to friends due to the countless others who had come and gone when they didn't get what they wanted out of her, whether that was status or sex, so, she'd tried to give Leirei the benefit of the doubt, but she still held onto the concept that she was likely here only for herself.

"Thank you for letting me stay with you," Sidra said, realizing that she hadn't yet thanked her for her hospitality.

Leirei frowned at her. "You don't have to thank me. You can stay with me whenever you want." Her frown softened and shifted into a smile.

Sidra smiled in response. She was normally far more comfortable around Leirei, but with Xander so close, Sidra had to stay focused on what she'd come here to do. She knew that Xander pushed boundaries; it was why she had chosen him.

If there were ever a time to test her theory about their magic and what was blocking it, tonight was the night. She couldn't imagine that Deandra would have done what she suspected—but after finding that fucking *giant* book in her office about the understanding of magical barriers and how to suppress magic, there was little doubt that Deandra was behind their lack of power.

Still, she hoped tonight would disprove that. Maybe the Seer hadn't completed her ceremony, and that's why the veil still clung to their magic. No matter what she hoped, all paths led here. To this moment, with Xander of all people, sitting at her side to unknowingly assist in Sidra's somewhat irresponsible plan.

Sidra knew enough self-defense from the lessons Selen had taught her, so she was confident that if things were taken too far with him, she would be able to take care of herself. Selen hated Xander, so if she had any inkling that he was harming Sidra, she would be furious.

And, hopefully, she'd show some of that fury she displayed last night.

Sid knew she was playing a risky game, but she had to know. It had been too long with so few answers that she couldn't *not* try this. With darkness having recently encapsulated the land, she knew it was too early to make her move. But it was coming. Once the mead had taken hold of the majority of the students and the liveliness began to fade, that's when she would act.

Chapter Seven

Selen's vision wobbled as she downed her most recent glass of mead. The sweet honey flavor coated her throat as she handed her cup back to Aeden for a refill.

The live music had started shortly after Selen and Aeden had arrived, and they'd quickly found themselves wrapped up in what had become a makeshift dance-floor. Aeden had been ready immediately, but Selen had needed some liquid courage before joining on the dance floor.

She found that forgetting about the events of the past few days had been easier than she expected. She became lost in the laughter and mead as the world twirled around her with her movements. Occasionally, Aeden would break away to dance with others, as did she, always finding their way back to one another. She had looked over only once to see Aleya watching her, still in contact with the student she didn't know, and did her best to seem as uninterested as possible before going back to whomever she was dancing with in that moment. The music was lively and loud, drowning out the crackles of the large fires. She was yet to see her sister, but then again, she hadn't really looked. Her goal tonight was to forget, so that's exactly what she was doing.

Selen was close enough to the music that she couldn't hear the surrounding chatter; the beat pulsed through her blood and bones, sending her into a state of euphoria. She found Aeden and danced with him again, knowing that he wouldn't get the wrong idea from the interaction. He was also there to have fun. They both laughed as mead sloshed around them, soaking their clothes and boots. If the dirt hadn't soaked up the sweet alcohol, it surely would have been sticky from the amount that missed everyone's mouths. Selen was moving mindlessly as she shifted to the beat, when a hand wrapped around her waist and pulled her close.

Her peaceful state quickly dissipated as she took in Aeden, who was still standing across the crowd, having just gone to get them another refill. Selen swung around.

"What the hell?" Selen spun and shoved the nameless man, whose arms found their way to rest far too intimately around her body.

"Come on, baby, I want to feel those hips move," the man slurred as he moved in closer. His breath smelled disgusting, despite the sweet scent of the mead wafting off of him, and was large—seemingly far older than someone who should've been at this Academy. Stumbling towards her, he outstretched a hand and grabbed her arm.

Before Selen even realized what she was doing, she'd grabbed his wrist and twisted his arm back, eliciting a satisfying yelp from the pig. She took the base of her palm and shoved it up into his nose, a clear crunch sounding from the collision. Blood spurted from the man's nose as he stumbled back, dropping his drink and bringing both hands up to his nose.

"Crazy bitch!" he squealed as he pushed through the crowd and disappeared into the sea of people.

Those nearest to her were giving her weary looks as they continued to rigidly dance to the music. Some sneered, while others gave her a look of disgust. Some didn't even notice the interaction.

"What happened?" Aeden dropped the two cups of mead and rushed over to her, having seen the blood on the ground and her hand.

"Some shit guy just ruined my fun," Selen grunted, "he did *not* leave unscathed." She grinned over to Aeden.

"*Okay,*" Aeden grabbed Selen's wrist and pulled her towards the edge of the crowd. "You have officially reached the level of intoxication that apparently makes you fight random guys. Good to know where that line is."

They got a good distance from the laughter and drew to a stop as the sound of the music was slowly overshadowed by the trickling creek they neared. Selen stumbled a bit as she approached the creek and got down to her knees to wash the blood from her hand.

"So, we're just breaking people's noses in public now?" Aeden asked with his arms outstretched to the sides.

"The creep groped me," Selen said, leaning back, hands now free of the guy's filthy blood.

A moment of silence spread between them—too long to go unnoticed, even in Selen's inebriated state. She glanced back at Aeden, whose eyes were dark as he stared at her.

"He did what?" Aeden growled, turning back towards the fires as if he could see the guy through the crowd.

"Settle down. I handled it." She rolled her eyes, more annoyed by Aeden's need to protect her than she was flattered. Of course, he would—as a man—think that he needed to do something to protect the *fair maiden*.

"You shouldn't have had to," Aeden exclaimed. "Did he hurt you?" Aeden approached her, ready to check for injuries.

Selen raised her hand, halting Aeden before he reached her. "Aeden, I do *not* need your protection, nor do I need your healing skills. I am fine on my own."

She slowly lowered her hand, and the look in Aeden's eyes shifted from fury to hurt. Selen's shoulders curled defensively.

"I'm allowed to care about you, Selen," he said in a low voice. All the light that typically accompanied his words was nowhere to be found.

"I don't need you to *care* about me, Aeden. It's not going to get you what you want, anyway," Selen snapped. The poison in her voice coated her words, even as they slurred. He had no right to be mad at her for defending herself. *What?* Like she should wait around for some guy to protect her from another 'some guy'? Absolutely not.

But Aeden wasn't just *some guy*. Selen knew that, and as soon as those words hit him, the look in his eye shifted, and he stared at the ground.

"Yeah. You've made that pretty clear," his voice a near whisper as he turned to look back at the crowd. "For your information, I've never wanted anything from you other than what we have," he said over his shoulder. "I'll talk to you later, Selen." And, with that, he trudged off.

Whether it was her lowered self-control or her lack of patience from the events of the last two days, she had cut the only person who would never cut her back. She'd known that and still struck him. Selen felt the familiar sense of self-loathing slithering up her spine like the slimy snake she thought herself.

She had never seen that look on his face, and *she* had been the cause of it.

"Why did I say that?" she whispered, and threw a small chunk of rock she found into the creek. She was on a roll. Who else was she going to tear down today?

Selen leaned back and looked up at the stars. They turned at a much faster rate than they normally did, likely due to the alcohol still swirling through her system. She closed her eyes and sighed.

At this rate, you'll be completely alone before summer starts, she thought as her lids got heavier. Whatever damage she had done, she would deal with tomorrow. For now, she was just going to take a quick power nap.

Sidra drew in a breath as Xander pushed her up against a tree. The bark dug into her back, and her breath was cut off as he enveloped her mouth with his. His hands roamed her body with no clear direction, and Sidra looked up at the stars above her.

She let Xander feel all of her as her thoughts drifted. It wasn't particularly because she didn't want things to go further with him tonight, but because she was distracted. She hadn't seen Selen all night, although she knew she was there. She had seen Aeden trudging back towards the fire towards the end of the evening, just before she'd slipped away with Xander. She imagined that Selen was somewhere near him—though, the look on Aeden's face may have suggested otherwise. Sidra supposed that if Selen didn't come find her, she'd at least get something out of the night. Sloppy as it may be.

Xander gripped the back of Sidra's neck, sending heat down her spine until it pooled at her core. She gave him a small grin as he grazed his teeth along her neck. He may be better at this than she thought. Just as she found herself slipping into the moment, Xander put her legs back on the ground and took her hand.

"Come on," he grinned over his shoulder. "I have somewhere I want to show you."

Sidra sighed out of frustration, but followed. She was

actually starting to enjoy this, and he had to go and break her concentration. She stumbled through the woods for longer than she would have preferred, tripping on sticks and getting whacked with branches as they pushed on. Her annoyance almost got the best of her, but they finally broke through to a clearing.

Sidra's breath caught as she took in the view. They were at a cliffside, with running water at least a hundred feet below. The moon and stars lit the night sky, showcasing the cliffside's one jagged edge that reached out further than the others. It was towards that ledge that Xander pulled them, placing Sid in front of him and wrapping his arms around her shoulders to hold her in place as they both took in the view.

This may turn out to be a really *good night,* Sidra thought as she watched the moon hover above them. A grin bloomed on her face as she took it all in.

"This is really beautiful," Sidra whispered, not breaking eye contact with the goddess.

"*You're* really beautiful," he whispered into her ear.

Sidra frowned, momentarily deterred from the beauty of the night by the terrible attempt at flattery. Women were far better at flattery than men were. She often tried to lean further into that part of her sexuality, but she always found herself drawn more towards men. An irritating reality.

Xander slowly turned Sidra around to face him, brushed her hair behind her ear, and took in the details of her face. Naturally, Sidra wanted to run away from the intense stare, and drew her eyes instead to his lips in a silent hint to end the intimate moment and dive into another one.

He took it. Their lips gently brushed once before his were crushing against hers. His tongue roamed the inside of her mouth as he lay them onto the ground, where he lay next to her rather than on top, as his hand began to make its way down her body. He grazed his thumb along her collarbone and gently slid his finger down to meet Sidra's peaked nipple, ripe from more than the cold. She gasped as he twirled one in his fingers, sending pulses down her core. Her back arched against the cold ground as he moved further down her body, leaving her breasts aching. One hand slid down past the spot that she begged him to touch, pulling up her dress to reveal her bare legs, and his fingers slowly made their way up the inside of her thigh, leaving gentle bumps in their wake. Removing his lips from hers, he stared down at her now-exposed lower half.

"I've been waiting to feel you," he whispered, still staring down at her legs.

"Then feel me," Sidra said breathlessly. Her arousal pushed her hips off the ground to try and meet him.

A low growl escaped from deep in his chest as he finally slipped his finger up the center of her. She gasped from the contact that she so needed.

"Gods, Sid, you're so wet," he growled against her skin as he slowly nipped at her neck and collar.

Sidra whimpered as he slid one finger into her, pushing against his hand, begging for more. He obliged by slipping another finger in, palm grazing her bud as he pumped his fingers in and out. His mouth found its home on her breast, licking and biting her nipple, sending electricity into the tension that was building at her core. His fingers continued to move in and out, sliding against the spot that threatened a perfect release.

Her eyes fluttered as her release began to crest. Sensing her impending orgasm, Xander pumped his fingers faster, sending her over the edge that caused Sid to let out a cry as her release engulfed her. The stars above her became multi-colored as she rode out the waves, and Xander continued to pump his fingers until Sidra was limp and breathless beneath him.

He shifted on top of her, spreading her legs further with his own. He moved closer to kiss her neck.

"My turn," he whispered against her skin. Sidra was happy to allow him to get his after the good work he'd just done. "Take off my pants," he said to Sidra, hands on both sides of her head.

She made easy work of the loose string that held his pants in position, exposing him. She looked down at the evidence of what she did to him, momentarily unimpressed by the size. She would've expected more based on how many people fawned over him. *Whatever.*

He grabbed her wrist and brought it above her head, catching the other one within his grip, too, before gently pressing against her entrance. She could feel him pulsing for her, bringing a grin to her face. He then shifted the entirety of his weight into the hand that pressed her wrists down, and her grin faded.

"Ow," she said as a gentle warning that he was causing discomfort.

His eyes flared with animalistic urgency as he drove into her, and Sidra gasped, arching her back as he pushed himself through her folds.

"You like a little pain, don't you?" Xander growled as his hand made its way up to her throat.

"Xander, no," Sidra said as his hand pressed against her windpipe. Panic rose rapidly, replacing the arousal that had previously flooded her system when he didn't stop. Before she could say anything, Xander squeezed her neck, and her vision became blurry.

She tried to breathe, but found her airway entirely restricted, so Sid choked and gasped for air as he continued forcing himself into her. She could feel the bruises forming on her wrists and neck from the force with which he held them, and tears lined her eyes as she struggled underneath him, trying to push him off of her. She tried to free her hands to land any of the self-defense maneuvers she had learned. Tried to push her hips up to press him off of her, which only seemed to ignite Xander's animalistic drive.

This wasn't supposed to happen.

Her ears were ringing, the sounds of the night fading into nothing behind the overwhelming buzz.

It wasn't supposed to go this wrong.

The ache in her wrist exploded into agony as she kept trying to raise them.

Help me.

Her eyes stung, and her tears finally began to slide down the side of her face.

Help me!

Aside from the pain in her body, now engulfing her, Sidra felt the boiling emotions rolling over her. Pain, sorrow, sadness, anger—the waves of feelings that she had kept contained, now cracked against the walls in her mind. She opened the gate. She reached for that obsidian wall that so often ignored her, the wall that housed Selen's mind. She pushed and knocked and opened that channel between them that she had kept so limited.

Help!

"No," she choked. The only words she could get out of her closed airways.

"Shut up bitch, you were asking for this," Xander laughed as he continued.

Her tears now completely blurred her vision as darkness started to press its way in. Her struggles were useless as she tried to kick her legs underneath him, slowly slipping out of consciousness. Just as the darkness was fully taking over, and her attempts to breathe slowed, she felt a weight lifted off of her. Air filled her lungs.

Distant yells sounded as she drifted into the darkness.

Help me, Selen. Please.

Chapter Eight

Selen woke with a start. Her head was pounding from the early onset hangover—but also from something else. Fear immediately gripped her gut and twisted. She glanced around for impending danger, but found nothing amiss. Yet, anger and agony ripped at her.

She spun, looking around once more. Fear rippled through her body until an ache formed around her neck and wrists. She clawed at her skin, trying to remove the invisible danger. Turning yet again to scan the forest, determined to find whatever was causing this. Her heart pounded in her ears, and slight bruises began to form along her wrists before her eyes.

She knew this feeling. She hadn't felt it in years, but she recognized it. A string pulled at her mind, and she took off.

"Sid!" Selen screamed as she sprinted through the forest. The light from the fires had long since faded, and her only light came from the moon and stars which blinked through the cover of the trees. She didn't know where she was going, but she knew she was going in the right direction. She could *feel* the pull as if there were a rope guiding her along. She growled as the aching sensation grew, pulsing across her wrists and neck, and had to take deep breaths to work past the pain.

Was someone choking her? Selen's rage coupled with her fear as she pushed on, through the final section of bushes, and came into a clearing. There, her heart dropped and anger consumed.

Xander's one hand gripped Sidra's hands above her head. The other wrapped around her throat. Sidra's eyes were glazed as she stared behind him, her eyelids slowly closing. Before Selen could even think, she was behind Xander, gripping his hair and ripping him off of her sister. She left him no time to react before diving her fist into his face. Blood spurted as she broke his nose. Two for two for the night.

Xander scrambled to pull up his pants, aimlessly swinging his arms to connect with Selen, who easily dodged his blows. He swung again, barely missing her temple as she ducked and took out his legs with one swipe, but he quickly recovered and moved to tackle her. There was no time to move out of the way as he dropped his shoulder into her chest, sending them both sprawling to the ground. The connection sent the air whooshing out of Selen's lungs, and they rolled, still going blow for blow. Coming to a stop, Xander ended up on top and quickly used the position to push both of his hands into her throat, cutting off her airway.

"Both sisters in one night? What a fucking pleasure," he rasped, breath jagged as he pressed Selen's neck harder. She clawed at his fingers to no avail and reached around her for anything to help. Xander's eyes were those of an animal, crazed and strictly operating on instinct and anger alone.

True terror began to set in, but rage still kept Selen functioning. She couldn't let him hurt Sidra again. She had to win. She slowed her arm movement, feigning unconsciousness, and her hand paused against the jagged side of a rock, big enough to fill her palm. She swung before Xander had time to notice the change in movement.

The rock connected with his temple and immediately knocked him unconscious as he fell to the side. Selen lay there for a moment and stared at the sky before reality settled in, and she caught her breath. Scrambling to her feet, she rushed to Sidra's side and gently lowered her dress so it covered her lower half. She then lifted Sid's head into her lap.

"Sid?" Selen cried as she rocked back and forth. "*Sidra?* Please answer me." Selen gently tapped her cheek in an attempt to rouse her.

The bruises along Sidra's wrist and neck—a more distinct reflection of the bruises on her own wrists and neck—had already formed in the shape of Xander's hands. Selen gently set Sidra's head back on the ground and moved in front of her on her hands and knees.

"Sid. I need you to get up. Please get up, Sid. I can't lose you, Sidra." Selen's voice broke into a sob as she gripped her sister's hand. Pressing her forehead down onto Sidra's hands, she began to rock back and forth as tears streamed down her face. Sobs wracked Selen as she worked back through the scene she'd walked up to. She had felt Sidra's sorrow, anger and fear as Xander hurt her. Selen's anguish crippled her. The damage Xander had done was overwhelming.

How had Sidra gotten here?

Why was she here? Why was she with *him*?

Softly, Sidra's hand tightened around Selen's, who gasped and looked up at her sister. Sidra's eyelids were barely open, but she held Selen's gaze. Reality seemed to grip her as she gasped for air and let out a sob. Selen reached up and gently grabbed her face, wiping away the tears that rolled down her cheeks.

"You're safe," Selen whispered, trying to steady Sidra's eyes on her. "You're safe," she repeated, tears leaving her eyes as she took in her sister's bruises. Sidra's face was deathly pale —a stark contrast to the purple and blue bruises encasing her throat.

"That wasn't supposed to happen," Sidra sobbed, wrapping herself around Selen. "It wasn't supposed to happen like this. I'm so sorry."

"I'm so sorry, Sidra. I got here as soon as I felt you. What he was doing to you..." Selen trailed off as she rested Sidra's head on her chest and stroked her hair. Sidra only let out a sob in response.

"I need to get you back to the school and get you checked out."

Selen's heart ached and writhed at seeing her sister like

this. To have shown up, only to find that scum attacking her. Defiling her. Selen wanted to go over there and bash Xander's skull in until he was nothing but mush. She knew there would be a lot of recovery needed to heal from this, and didn't know how she was going to help Sidra. They'd experienced and overcome harassment before, but... this? Selen's stomach turned, bile rising in her throat, but she swallowed it down and began to help Sidra rise.

Sid's legs wobbled as she tried to hold her own weight, but Selen held tight, gaze entirely focused on her sister as she finally stood. Sid's eyes widened, and Selen felt a presence approaching in front of them, and a sob drifted from Sidra's mouth as her attacker appeared. Xander limped towards them, head leaking blood from where Selen had struck him with the rock.

"What the *fuck*?" Xander yelled, sending rocks and debris sliding around him with his magic. His *magic*. Fuck. He had magic. Selen had forgotten that.

Beside her, Sidra shrank, and Selen pushed her further back.

"Stand down, Xander. You've had enough fun for tonight." She laced her words with caution as he approached.

"*Fun*? You call this *fucking* fun? I did what she"—he waved his uninjured arm toward Sidra—"wanted! And this is what I get for it?" he screamed, power radiating off of him.

Selen knew she had to de-escalate the situation before it got worse, and put both of her hands up in a sign of surrender. The motion made her sick, but she needed to get Sid back to safety and fighting Xander again would only slow them down.

"Xander. Let me take her back to the school." Selen spoke in a low, calming voice, hands still raised.

"Why? So she can tell the whole fucking school I raped her and ruin my life?"

A stillness settled over Selen. He knew. He knew exactly what he had been fucking doing.

Xander's words were laced with hatred and venom, and what seemed to be a hint of desperation, but Selen narrowed her eyes at him, temper raging beneath the surface, threatening to explode. She took a deep breath and spoke again. "She won't say anything. I just need to get her home and tend to her wounds."

A lie. But one that Selen, but a willing one because she knew it would bring them closer to safety.

"Fuck that! There's not a chance that crazy bitch doesn't say anything. She can't keep her mouth shut, so I'll shut it for her." Xander's voice broke at the end of his statement, a show of the desperation which now emanated from him.

A pulsing sensation encased Selen's veins, rage wrapped in darkness pushed at her skin, begging to get out. She was so close to losing control. The absolute audacity this man had after assaulting Sidra. To blame her—to speak to her at all.

Selen's voice dropped low in warning. "I'm warning you, Xander. Take one more step and I will break your *fucking* neck." She let her silent fury rage as she wrapped her arms behind her back and around her sister.

Xander let out a wicked laugh. "With what power?" he

crooned. The desperation in his voice faded into arrogance as he made his decision. Magic swirled around him like a slow tornado, and rocks and sticks lifted from the earth to encircle his waist. He lifted the rock that Selen had used to knock him out, tossing it up in the air. The rock caught and hovered above his hand as his wind magic swirled it around in circles, blood still soaking its surface.

"I don't need magic to kick your ass, Xander." The words slipped out before she had time to think them through. Now was not the time to challenge him.

"Let's see it then," Xander said, raising a hand. His eyes were wide, and his previous rage seemed to shift into a crazed sense of calm as he stared them down. The blue in his eyes swirled with chaos, but the rest of his face was expressionless. Wind began to swirl around them, ripping Sidra from Selen's arms.

Selen whirled as Sidra blew towards the cliff's edge. She reached for her, but found herself unable to move as the wind wrapped its tendrils around her throat, pulling the air from her lungs. Selen clawed at her throat, trying to remove the invisible hands that choked her, and she heard before she felt the collision of something hard hitting her head.

A crack that radiated through her mind. Her vision faltered. He hadn't hit her with the rock hard enough to knock her out, but she was at least concussed. The world spun as she continued to pry against the invisible hands around her neck, as a trickle of blood swept into her eye.

Just as quickly as it had started, the wind died down. Both sisters fell to their knees in unison. Xander let out a wicked laugh and stalked closer to Selen. Before she could catch her breath and stand, a fist collided with the side of her head, right where the rock had struck. Her vision blurred once more, and blood coated the inside of her mouth. When she spit, red consumed the rocks and grass below her. She turned her head as quickly as she could to meet Xander's gaze. His face was close—so close that she could smell his breath. His eyes still expressed that crazed calm. A terrifying look of stillness that seemed more like a wild animal examining its prey, rather than a human. He grabbed her face and squeezed her cheeks, pointing her face towards Sidra.

"This time, there won't be anyone to save her, you useless bitch," Xander whispered, pushing her face into the ground. He gripped the back of her head by her hair and lifted her, nearly unconscious. She had no strength to fight him off as he dragged her. Xander was a sick fuck, but she hadn't realized how entirely screwed up he was until this moment. He rarely slept with the same person twice. Was this why? Was he raping them then threatening them to keep them quiet?

Selen scrambled to try and dislodge his hand from her head, but couldn't calm her heart enough to think coherently, let alone function following the two blows to her temple. Sidra let out a rough scream as Xander dragged Selen to the edge of the cliff. Selen watched as Sidra reached for her, but she knew there was nothing Sid could do to help.

Selen made eye contact with her sister, as if to say *I'm sorry I couldn't protect you.* Tears fell from Sidra as she shook her head in reply. Selen had to say goodbye in some capacity.

If this was to be her end, then she at least wanted Sidra to know how she truly felt, but there wasn't time.

"Such a tragedy," Xander stated, condescension and humor coating his words. "The lovely Dagny sisters fought at the cliff's edge, the crazy one pushed the other off the side, then jumped herself. A very sad murder-suicide no one saw coming."

Leave it to an arrogant 20-year-old man to voice his entire plan to his victims before ending them.

Selen struggled under his hands, very aware that any sudden movement might induce her tumbling to her death. Xander kept hold of Selen's hair as she faced the waters below. The swift current pushed and pulled at the waters below. If she didn't die on impact, the water would surely pull her under.

"Let her go!" Sidra croaked.

"What was that?" Xander asked, holding a hand up to his ear as if he didn't hear her. "Your voice sounds a little rough there, angel," He said with a maniacal laugh.

Her voice was raspy, but unwavering. "Let. Her. Go." Sidra rose, stumbling slightly as she planted her feet.

Selen could only see her out of the corner of her eye as she faced her impending death. Sidra stood so steady after what she'd been through. She faced her attacker with the will of an army, and Selen felt a burst of pride. If she were going down, she would at least go down with the knowledge that her sister was a fighter. Selen closed her eyes for a moment, releasing the walls in her mind. She wanted Sidra to feel how proud she was of her. She wanted her to know that she was okay and that Sidra was going to be okay. Sid wrapped her light around Selen's darkness, and Selen knew Sid felt her in her mind.

Comfort enwrapped Selen.

"Let her go?" Xander asked.

"Xander," Sidra warned.

"I can let her go," he said with an air of arrogance.

"Xander!" Sidra cried out this time.

Selen felt the fingers on her hair loosen and the earth slip out from under her. Her stomach clenched as time slowed. She reached desperately for anything around her to steady her, but he had held her too far from the edge for her to have any chance of escaping the fall. Her fate was sealed.

"Sidra, *run!*" Selen was able to get out before she felt the wind rip her words away as she fell towards the river.

The last thing that Selen heard was a blood-curdling scream—from her or her sister, she didn't know. She knew she was falling fast towards the water, but time felt as though it continued to slow.

She shifted in the air until her back faced the water, and her hair wrapped around her face as the wind gusted by. Her limbs swirled around her, trying desperately to slow the pull of her descent. All of the anger and pain transformed into calming acceptance. She had nothing to hold on to. There was no reason for the darkness that raged against her skin to be held back. Selen had no one to answer to but the gods, she supposed.

All her childhood memories flashed before her. Sidra yelling at her for breaking all her dolls with a wooden sword.

Deandra chasing them after they'd jumped into the creek without permission, getting water all over the school's floors. All the fights they'd had faded into nothing—brief images of petty spats. Selen saw Aleya and Aeden's faces. Aleya's face as she watched her dance with someone else. The disappointment in her eyes at their latest interaction. Aeden's face before he'd walked away from her. The pain in his face. Pain that she had caused. So many unsaid words that would never be said. Finally, Sidra's face showed up as it was moments ago, broken and enraged, tears streaming down her face.

She couldn't leave it like this.

It awoke something in Selen. Cracked something deep within her. The swarming darkness beneath her skin exploded. Shadows swirled around her. It felt like she'd been hit with a shock wave, and the sound was just as loud. The darkness that had pulled her throughout her entire life rose to the surface, pulsing from her as she drifted towards the water's surface.

She closed her eyes and let whatever power this was leap from her—a release she had never known she needed. It was beautiful and dark and uncontrollable. She let the darkness take hold of her, wrapping itself like a cocoon around her—a terrifying and warm embrace that brought her comfort. Selen opened her eyes and through the darkness she saw a light bloom on the cliff just before she hit the water. Then, a different darkness took hold of her.

Chapter Nine

The feeling of Sidra's hand sliding into her own broke through the haze in Selen's mind. She blinked a few times to push away the blur in her eyes and bring the surrounding light into focus. The trees overhung the path, and white strings of light magic weaved through their branches to dangle from them. They illuminated the stone that Sidra and Selen walked on, equally beautiful and ominous as they approached the sparkling pond at the end of the passage. Her anticipation for this moment was too much for Selen's mind to remain clear, and Sidra's hand shook in her own, as she, too, experienced waves of excitement and panic as their vision of the Being floating in the pool became more defined.

The Being stared unseeing, or all-seeing, at the ceiling of trees that drooped towards it. A Seer. Its long, dark hair splayed around it and gently floated in the pool, clinging to the exposed skin above the water. It was draped in a sheer black cloth that covered very little of its pale flesh, and a smoky quartz sat embedded in its forehead. Selen knew it was the grounding stone, used to bring the Seer back to their body when they entered the unknown. She assumed that this Seer must have once been a woman by the shape of its body—but Seers transcended human-based identification and societal labels and names when they transitioned into their powers.

It was both a blessing and a curse from the gods and the Lirium to be gifted a Seer's powers. Most families saw it as the highest honor—even though their child would soon take on this form. It wasn't always a shock. Most children begin to show flickers of what magic they will be bound with at a young age. Without the Seers, there would be no one to bind the Lirium magic to each person, and they would all be without magic entirely. They were a living conduit of power and sight, a necessary step in the evolution of those who had magic. Magic is just one living piece of the universe, known in the world as the Lirium. They cannot exist in this world without a host, and while they may choose to give some or all of their essence to a host, they rarely offer all of themselves to one person. By giving up all of themselves, a Lirium gives up its corporeal state and becomes a powerful parasite that can only be passed along through bloodlines. Seers spoke to the Lirium and bound their essence to its host, which was why Selen and Sidra were here.

Today was Selen and Sidra's twelfth birthday. The standard time for the VeilBinding ceremony to take place. Selen had been preparing for months, but the sight of the floating body before her still sent shivers up her spine. This was a task only she and Sidra could go through, so Deandra waited for them outside the entrance of the MistralWood. Selen so badly wanted to look back at the entrance of the forest, to lean on Deandra's comforting gaze, which always gave her confidence, but the ceremony began as soon as they entered and could not be altered.

Selen squeezed Sidra's hand as they stood at the edge of the pool, looking down at the Seer who had yet to acknowledge them. Slowly, the Seer began to inhumanely rise from the pool, and Selen's stomach turned. They rose without bending their legs, as though they were being lifted, until they were standing in front of the girls. The Seer stared down at them with pale eyes that Selen had only ever seen on those who had no sight.

She took a deep breath and did not avert her gaze from the Seer's curious eyes, feeling Sidra do the same. Selen knew that Sidra had to be pushing out her chin and squaring her shoulders at the Seer—that was often Sidra's power move when things were frightening, but she didn't want them to know that they'd frightened her.

"Sidra and Selen Dagny." The Seer's voice was a slithering sound of multiple voices combined to create one.

Male and female, and everything in between and beyond spoke through the Seer as it looked both girls up and down, its head cocked to the side. "An interesting pair." It floated closer to them in the water. "One said to be wreathed in starlight"—it glanced at Sidra, taking her in once more before snapping its head at Selen—"the other said to be as dark as night herself."

"Where might one begin and the other end?" The Seer continued, seeming not to be asking the girls but something beyond. It grabbed the ends of the girls' hair in its bony hands, which ended in long, cracked nails. It took all of Selen's willpower not to cringe away from the touch as it rubbed their hair between its fingers before snapping its head up to Sidra.

"You." It dropped Sidra's hair and pointed at her, hand flowing in the air like the water it stood in. The Seer hooked its long nail beneath Sidra's chin and lifted her face. "You shall go first." The Seer spat the last syllable out like venom.

Moving its nail down Sidra's neck and shoulder, the Seer continued until it reached her arm, where she gently pulled away and splayed out its hand for Sidra to take. Hesitantly, Sidra lifted her small hand and placed it in the Seer's, who grinned and began leading Sidra into the water.

Selen's breath caught at the sheer predatory nature of the Being. She briefly reached for Sidra as the creature pulled her into the pond.

"Do not fear, child," the Seer told Selen, not breaking eye contact with Sidra.

They stopped in the center of the pool. The Seer towered over Sidra, and Selen realized that the Being was floating above the bottom of the pond. Sidra's pale blue dress floated around her waist, water-soaked, while the Seer was barely submerged up to its shins. It gently settled into the water in front of Sidra, still a good three hands taller than her.

"May the gods bless you with wisdom. May the Lirium grant you an essence of their power," the Seer stated, forcing out the words in ceremonial normalcy. The Seer took Sidra's hands and its head shot back, looking up at the sky between the trees, and Sidra jumped slightly at the movement. Its eyes rolled back in its head, and it began chanting in a language Selen didn't recognize. The air thickened around them as droplets of water began to circle the Seer and Sidra. Selen's pulse quickened at the sight; she had known this was coming, but it didn't settle her unease.

A lifetime later, light seemed to trickle between the branches above them. It slithered through the air, reaching with tiny fingers for the pair. It swirled into a mist that wrapped around them, intermingling with the water droplets, and Sidra's face alit with wonder as she glanced around.

Soon, the slithering stopped and the light faded, until it was only the mist and water which swirled around them. The Seer's chanting quietened until they finally snapped their head back towards Sidra. Time seemed to still as the water around them fell away, leaving only the mist which sat still in the air.

"You have been granted the essence of the Lirium of starlight," the Seer said in its slithering voice. "Do not take advantage of this gift, for what is bound can be unbound."

As the Seer's last words left its mouth, the mist shot towards Sidra. The Seer released Sidra's hands and slid away from her.

Sidra's eyes were no longer her own, but those of starlight. Selen gasped as Sidra began to glow. Sidra gazed at the trees above her with unfamiliar eyes, arms spread out as she continued to shine. Her body rose from the water until her feet floated slightly above the pond.

Deandra had somewhat prepared them for the dramatics of the event, but Selen had no idea that it would be like this. Sidra still shone as she slowly dropped back into the water, but as soon as her feet touched the floor of the pond, it stopped. Her eyes dimmed back to their natural state, and she blinked as she glanced at her surroundings, as though she was seeing something she hadn't before. Selen loosened a breath that she hadn't noticed she'd been holding in.

"It is done." The Seer's multitude of voices reignited Selen's anxieties. She was next. After watching Sidra's experience, the realization brought more fear than excitement. Still, Sidra's eyes met hers—filled with pure joy and power— and Selen smiled back, despite the unease seeping through her.

Sidra made her way out of the pool and stood beside Selen, shaking slightly—from either her newfound power or something else, it wasn't clear.

Selen's breath caught as the Seer approached and stopped before her, slowly turning its head from side to side as it took her in.

"Be gone, starlight, your time here is complete." The

sharpness in its tone penetrated Sidra's joy, and she stumbled back slightly.

"But... she was here for mine," Sidra tried to push back.

The Seer snapped its head to her, signifying that Sidra's time here was, in fact, complete. Sidra flinched and began to move back as Selen's heart raced, fear leeching its way through her veins. Sidra was a comfort she'd expected to have here for this, and knowing she wouldn't be there brought tears to the corner of her eyes. Sidra made eye contact with Selen, pity and frustration in her gaze, before quickly turning and running back to the entrance—likely to try and get Deandra to interfere.

Selen's focus was pulled back to the Seer as it grabbed her hands, and Selen gasped as her breath began to match her heartbeat.

The Seer's head snapped back. It stared at the ceiling of trees above them, head twitching and its lips moved in a silent chant. Selen's breath continued to quicken as the Seer seemed to drift into whatever space existed between realms. Its voice was nothing more than a mere whisper as it spoke.

"An ally of the night." Its head twitched and bent unnaturally to one side. "What wanders in the depths is yours to conquer. To claim." Its head moved to the other side. "What has been broken may be bound, or continue to break." A horrifying cackle left its throat; several voices seemed to come and go. Selen could hear the whispers as they surrounded her, but couldn't decipher what they were saying, only that they grew in volume. Selen looked around her, hoping to identify the origin of the disembodied voices.

She wanted to scream, but her lungs closed. She could see nothing around her but the trees, but she could feel them everywhere. What *were* they? She could feel the growing intensity of the voices—until, without warning, they all stopped and spoke as one.

"Trust your heart when your mind takes hold, young eclipse."

Selen froze. She was far too terrified to even begin to understand what any of that meant, and just as quickly as it had begun, the Seer looked back to her with an angled head, almost as though nothing had happened.

"You are different from the other," it said, taking a step closer. "You do not have the essence of magic surrounding you." It studied her further and moved closer to sniff her neck. Tears leaked from Selen's eyes as she tried to force her face as far away from the creature as possible. It inhaled again, then let out a sharp cackle, and a small whimper slipped from Selen's lips as her caution turned to fear.

"You are... BloodBound!" it hissed. "How interesting that your sister is EssenceBound, while you, who share her blood, house the powers of something ancient."

It stood in silence for a moment. If it was waiting for a response, Selen was at a loss. To imply that an ancient Lirium had bound itself to one of Selen's ancestors, and was now bound to her through blood, wasn't something she was fully prepared to comprehend.

"We got rid of your kind a long time ago, girl. How are you here?" Its words turned from curiosity to a cold bitterness that made Selen's skin crawl.

The Seer stepped further out of the pond, gripping Selen's jaw as it pushed her further down the path. Selen clawed at the Being's hand and wrist, and its cold skin sent icy shocks through her where their skin connected.

"You're... you're not supposed to hurt us." Selen tried to reason with the Seer as she struggled against its grip.

"You are not supposed to be alive!" the Seer hissed.

Selen yelped as the Seer tightened its grip.

"Your existence threatens the balance." It began dragging Selen towards the exit, mumbling as Selen kicked and screamed.

Selen's jaw ached where the Seer's fingers had dug into her flesh. "I didn't do anything!" she sobbed, tears streaming down her cheeks.

Selen could hear muffled yells from the edge of the forest before the distinct sound of footsteps rushing towards her became clear. Hope flooded her senses as Deandra's voice called out for her as they approached.

The Seer rasped a harsh laugh and threw Selen on the ground. "You brought me a BloodBound?" the Seer growled at Deandra.

"I didn't know," Deandra breathlessly voiced.

"Either you are a fool or a liar." The Seer pointed its boney finger at Deandra, who had her hands raised in effort to calm the Being.

Selen continued to lie on the ground between the Seer and her guardian, looking back and forth between the two. She didn't understand what was happening, she only knew she wanted to get away from the Seer.

"Selen, I need you to get up and wait with your sister," Deandra said calmly to Selen without breaking eye contact with the Seer.

Selen didn't hesitate to jump to her feet and sprint as far away from the Seer as she could. She never wanted to see that Being again. As she was running, however, she heard the conversation start back up between the two.

"This doesn't have to be a battle, Seer. What do you want?" Deandra's voice was harsher and more aggressive as she spoke this time.

"There is quite a price for a BloodBound. There's also quite a price for one who hid her." The Seer spoke calmly.

"I will pay more for your silence." Deandra's desperate rasp were the last words Selen heard before she broke through the edge of the forest, colliding with Sidra. Sidra squeaked but gripped Selen as they lay on the ground.

"I was so scared!" Sidra leaned into Selen's chest.

Selen looked at her sister with frustration. The image of Sidra running away from her ran through Selen's mind. She knew she had been scared, she could feel it. She didn't want to make her sister feel worse than she already did, but she was scared, too.

Selen sighed and wrapped her arms around Sidra and stroked her hair. "It's okay." Selen whispered as Sidra sobbed into her chest. "We're okay."

After some time, the girls sat up and curled their knees to their chests as Deandra burst through the edge of the forest, startling them enough to make them jump.

"Get up, girls. We're leaving." Her voice was urgent as she reached for both of their hands.

Selen quickly stood as she looked back towards the entrance of the forest, the Seer's magic opening the edge enough to see its full silhouette watching her as they moved quickly away from its fortress.

Chapter Ten

Fire scorched Selen's lungs as she gasped for air. Darkness surrounded her as she tried so desperately to fill her lungs. Her chest ached, and she could feel that her body was full of something that didn't allow any air to enter; there was nothing but the pain that seared through her.

Pressure hit her body, cracking through her chest. Another blow came, and she felt movement from the force inside her that blocked her air. Another swift wave of pain, and Selen's eyes flew open, just as she turned to the side and vomited. Water forced out of her, and she gasped as air finally filled her lungs, but the relief was coupled with searing pain in her throat. Her coughs and gags continued as she gulped as much precious air as she could manage. Once she finally caught her breath, her heart slowed, and she realized she could hear someone else breathing behind her.

Fast enough to make the world spin, Selen jumped to

her feet and whirled to face whoever was behind her. Darkness clouded her vision, and her body ached in protest at the quick movement. Enough so that she immediately fell to her knees. But, she recognized the face of the woman who knelt in front of her. Water dripped from her short, dark hair as her desert eyes watched Selen. Her tanned skin glistened from the water that beaded upon it. The three scars on her face reflected the moonlight, and she panted as if she had just swum through the harsh waters to retrieve Selen—which was likely exactly what had happened based on the current state of them both.

"How am I alive?" Selen let out in a rasp.

The woman sat silent for a moment, thinking through her answer to the question, or just catching her breath. "I don't know." Her accent was heavy as she spoke.

The lack of detail in this answer annoyed Selen. She didn't understand why this woman was even in the area to find her. While Selen appreciated the fact that she wasn't floating lifelessly down the river, her internal defense sparked at her presence.

"Who are you?" Selen asked, still forcing air into her brutalized lungs.

"I am the person who just saved your life," she said in a low, calm voice.

"I saw you at the academy," Selen stated.

"You did," the woman replied, watching Selen cautiously.

"*Who are you?*" Selen emphasized.

"My name is Deryn," the woman said in a smooth voice as she stood, extending a hand to help Selen up.

Selen wobbled as she stood, smacking away the woman's hand. Her mind still reeled from having just thrown up what seemed like her body weight in water. She backtracked through the events that had gotten her here. The darkness. The collision with the water. The warm embrace of a different darkness. The explosion of power. The fall. Xander. Sidra.

Sidra.

Selen's heart started pounding even louder in her ears.

"Sidra. Where's Sidra? My sister. Where is she?" Panic consumed her. What had Xander done with her? She gripped her stomach as the memories came flooding back and held in a sob with her other, pressing it against her mouth. Either holding back a sob or another round of vomit.

"I don't know where your sister is," Deryn said, no ounce of panic or urgency in her voice.

Selen could feel the world closing in around her, and her breath quickened to a pace she couldn't control. She breathed so much, but no air found its way to her lungs.

"Look at me, girl." Deryn's distant voice cut through the darkness she felt closing in on her.

Selen looked up at the woman, her vision blurred from tears and the swirling darkness around her. She couldn't tell if it was just in her head or if Deryn was actually wrapped in darkness.

"You need to slow your breathing." Deryn's voice lowered to a darker tone. Less calm and more demanding.

Something in the woman's eyes told Selen she didn't want to know what she was going to tell her. Selen took a step back, loosening Deryn's grip on her.

"We need to get you back to Celestara."

"Not without her," Selen said breathlessly, pushing Deryn's hands away entirely as she shoved past her.

Deryn stood back for a moment, eyes darkening as she stood tall. "That's not an option."

Selen looked up at her. The pulsing in her head and veins was becoming unbearable.

Not an option? she thought.

What does that mean?

Selen's mind raced as she looked aimlessly at the world around them. Was Sidra hurt? Was she... dead? The thought made Selen gag. The earth around her moved too fast for her brain to process. All the training she had gone through fell to the back of her mind, rendering it useless. She was strictly operating on emotion.

Selen took off into the woods. Not looking back to see if Deryn followed. She had to find Sidra.

"Shit," the woman's distant voice said as Selen sprinted away. The pulsing converted to an enraged ringing in her mind. She reached deep into her mind to find Sidra's light, but found only swirls of darkness.

Waves crashed behind her skull until the pressure became too much—the tie that had held Selen and Sidra together was lost somewhere in the darkness.

Where was she?

Selen's heart ached at the absence that was her sister's presence.

She couldn't be gone.

The ache spread into her bones.

She had to be fine.

The ache turned into a searing pain that pushed through her veins.

She had to be alive.

Selen screamed as the pain ripped through her body, and darkness exploded around her. The surrounding trees toppled over, the grass tore from the ground, and swirls of shadow were left in their wake.

Selen slumped to her knees in the crater that now inhabited where she had stood. The pain had eased after the explosion, but the pounding in her head made her sway. She suddenly felt more exhausted than she had ever felt before, and there was no bodily control as she fell to the side. Her last thought faded as she slid into unconsciousness.

Sidra.

Sidra felt as though the world around her was empty. When she opened her eyes, her feeling was confirmed. She sat in darkness —though, sat wasn't the right word. She was floating. The only thing she could see was her own body, illuminated by the light coming off her skin. She could feel it combating the darkness. She felt powerful, even in her current state of probable danger.

She grinned and turned her hands in front of her face, taking in the power which emanated from her. She tried and failed to push her magic out through the darkness.

It worked. She had gotten her powers.

Had she died in the process?

Is that where she was now?

Had she *actually* died in the process of trying to ignite their powers?

Sidra thought back through the evening leading up to... her death?

Fucking Xander.

That stupid fucking asshole had... raped her. *Yeah.* That's what he did. Anger boiled up inside her, and her light responded by brightening and pushing through the dark.

She had been in control... at least she thought she had been. Until she wasn't, she supposed.

She guessed it was a good thing, then. That she'd died. That she didn't have to feel the pain, or relive that moment. She could still feel the ache against her throat and wrists and... other places.

She couldn't even get rid of that in death?

That was bullshit.

Maybe she could haunt Xander and ruin his life that way, since she wouldn't get revenge in life.

Selen was going to be pissed. At least she had her powers. Maybe she'd survived the fall after Xander threw her off the cliff. Sidra hoped so. She hadn't done anything to ignite their powers, so it must have been Selen.

Of course she'd needed to be thrown off a cliff to ignite their powers. She wouldn't be surprised if Selen's uptightness is what had caused the block in the first place. They say not to talk ill about the dead, but can the dead talk ill about the living? Or the dead talk ill about the other dead? That felt more appropriate.

She guessed it didn't really matter now.

All she remembered was the wave of darkness that had flowed over the edge of the cliff a few moments after Selen had been thrown off of it. That image ached. She hated Xander for what he had done to both of them. Selen had been right about him.

Of course she had.

How annoying.

Anyway, the wave of darkness had flowed over the edge of the cliff towards them. Sidra hadn't really moved after witnessing her sister's murder, per se. After Selen was gone, Sidra had felt something boiling inside of her, just below her skin, clawing to get out. She'd recognized it as her magic; her powers had tried to claw their way out before when they were much deeper. This time, they had been much closer to the surface.

So, *the wave of darkness flowed over the edge of the cliff,* and as soon as it had hit her, it felt like a flood gate opening. She didn't remember much after that. There was darkness, a flash of light, and an epic release.

Much more of a release than the orgasm that stupid fucking pig gave her.

Then there was more darkness.

Now here she was.

Dead?

She still wasn't entirely sure.

"Sidra." A woman's voice cut through the darkness.

"What the fuck?" Sidra tried to spin around. "Are you a god?"

The disembodied voice let out a sharp laugh.

"I am no god, child," she said, amusement still dripping in her tone.

"Okay?" Annoyance flooded Sidra's system. "So, who are you then?" She continued to try and spin in the darkness.

"That will come in time," the voice said.

Sidra's brow furrowed. "Can I not even get peace in death?" She threw her arms out to the side in frustration.

"You are not dead," the voice answered blandly.

Sidra was aware that the bit of disappointment she felt at this was not a good sign for life. Now she would have to deal with everything that had happened. The rape. Selen's potential death. Selen's wrath if she was alive. Having to gut Xander.

At least she'd get to use her magic. She'd spent enough time researching in the last year that she deserved to get to use her magic.

"Okay. Well, where am I then?" Sidra wasn't trying to play nice. She thought she was dead a few minutes ago, so she didn't really feel like she had anything to lose.

"I'm here to answer all of the questions you've been asking your entire life."

Well that's vague as fuck.

Although, if this Being was capable of tossing Sidra into another dimension, or wherever she was, then maybe she did know things. It could be useful getting information from someone now that she actually had magic.

"Can you help me master my magic?" Sidra asked. She might as well get something out of this weird fucking situation.

"Of course I can," the voice said.

"Well, okay. Can you take me out of this darkness thing then, so I can meet you?"

"Are you prepared to take on the past?" the voice asked.

Sidra wasn't exactly sure what that meant, but she supposed she was. She didn't know much about her past. Maybe this person knew something.

"Sure. I guess."

"I need you sure, child."

"Yes. I'd like to *take on my past.*"

"Your manners are lacking. We shall remedy that."

Sidra was about to say something in retort, but the darkness snapped away, and she landed hard on the ground. The pain of the evenings events rushed back to her, and she was left to groan and roll onto her side. Any smartass comment she'd had ready to fire was no longer loaded. Her neck, wrists —and entire body—ached. Tear tracks pulled at her cheeks. All the emotions she hadn't needed to face in the darkness rushed back to her at once, and she let out a quick sob.

Closing her eyes, she tried to calm her breathing, but when she opened them again, her breath caught in her throat.

Kneeling beside her was a woman. Her hair was dark and stringy, and her eyes were somehow darker than her black hair, though bloodshot and slightly sunken in. She looked sick, but had a face that might have once been beautiful. A crone was likely the best description Sidra could come up with for this woman, and there was something familiar about her, but she couldn't place it. It was an unsettling face that looked down at her.

"Hello, Sidra." The woman gave a toothy grin.

Chapter Eleven

Selen inhaled deeply, lungs filling with the scent of leather and wood. She knew this scent very well. Her eyes snapped open. She was in Deandra's office, on the floor, trying to calm the rising headache.

"She could have *killed* you, Deryn," a woman's voice whispered. A voice that Selen didn't recognize.

"But she didn't," Deryn's smooth voice retorted without shifting to a whisper.

"This just got a lot more complicated," a man's voice chimed, equally as calm as Deryn's but coated in frustration.

"This changes nothing," Deryn said in a much more commanding voice. "We are here to do a job. We will do the job."

All grew quiet, tension coating the room as the sound of silence grew louder.

Deryn was the first to break it, her voice falling to a low

whisper. "We cannot do our job when we've lost one of them. We have to get her back."

Selen sat up straight and glared at the group who huddled around Deandra's desk. Even through the protest of her achy body, Selen moved quickly.

"Where is Sidra?" Selen asked urgently. Getting her back meant that she was alive. But was she taken? Had Xander kidnapped her?

The group snapped their heads over to her in surprise. The woman who had spoken initially was short, with long blonde hair that draped down the side of her shoulder in a thick braid. Her dark blue eyes regarded Selen wearily, and she wore a scowl that matched her biting voice. Selen glanced over to the man, whose hard face darkened further when he took in the sight of her. He had deep brown hair, accompanied by gray eyes that glared down at Selen. He stood about the same height as Deryn, both towering over their companion. Selen's eyes slid to Deryn, who watched her with a tilted head.

"Eavesdropping again, Bird?" Deryn asked, no real humor in her voice.

Selen's mind was clear, even with her aching body and impending headache. All the panic she had felt last night faded to a calm control. If Sidra had been taken, she had to stay calm to get to her. To save her.

Selen stood, crossing her arms across her chest as she squared her body up to the group. "Who are you people?" she asked in a low voice.

The man's eyebrows rose as his expression lightened.

The small woman scoffed, crossing her arms as she leaned against the desk.

"Hell of a way to talk to the people who saved your ass," the woman spoke, voice sharp and direct.

"As I recall, there was only one person who got me out of the water. So *who* are you two?" Selen pushed, commanding her voice to stay steady.

The man let out a low chuckle as he glanced over to Deryn. "At least she's feisty." His sidelong glance at Deryn was met with Deryn's own.

"I asked you a question." Selen's patience was wearing thin.

"Don't poke the bear, Varric." Deryn shifted her attention to Selen, eyes shifting from mild humor to a calm intensity. "Your sister has been taken."

Her breath caught, but Selen did her best to remain expressionless as fear flooded through her.

Taken. Selen had suspected that was what had happened, but having it confirmed was like a dagger in her heart. "Was it Xander?" She lowered her head, her gaze fixed on the desert eyes that stared into hers.

"That weasel is in a coma in the infirmary. He was barely alive when we found him," the small woman scoffed.Selen's brow furrowed. If Xander hadn't taken her, then who had? As if sensing her confusion, Deryn spoke.

"We don't know who took her." Deryn's expression softened. "Varric and Nys tracked you both to the cliff's edge, and were coming up to it when they saw a burst of light. The pulse forced them to duck behind trees to avoid the blow. I assume we can thank your sister for that," Deryn continued. "Xander was in a heap on the ground when they could finally leave the trees."

"Where was Sidra?" Selen cut in.

The man, Varric, continued the story. "When we left the cover of the trees, all we saw was light intertwined with darkness, then nothing."

"That's it? There was no other person?" Selen prodded.

The man hesitated, looking over at Deryn and the other woman, Nys. His expression exposed the defeat in his eyes.

Fear and hopelessness slid through Selen, and she released her power stance. She slid into one of the chairs in front of Deandra's desk, the cloth still ripped from when Selen had dug her nails into it. That felt like years ago, even though it had only been days. Selen pressed her middle and index fingers against either side of her temples, gently moving them in small circles, massaging the area to ease the headache.

A loud bang tore through the room as the door flew open as Deandra ran in.

"Selen!" Deandra's voice was panicked, and a small sob escaped when she found her sat in the chair. She ran over and grabbed the sides of her face, turning her head back and forth as though examining for injuries.

"I'm okay," Selen said through smushed cheeks.

Deandra let out a loud sigh and dropped her hand. Her composure turned from that of a concerned guardian to the fierce Headmaster she was to everyone else.

"What *happened*?" Deandra turned to the three individuals huddled around her desk.

Each of their cool exteriors shifted when met with the commanding presence of the woman who had run this academy for decades without incident. Even Deryn's eyes widened as they took in the force before them; they looked like students who had been caught in a lie.

Deryn cleared her throat, settling her gaze back into its calm expression. "Things took an... unexpected turn," she said in her velvet voice.

"An unexpected turn?" Deandra spat the words out like venom. "Sidra is missing. Selen almost drowned. What exactly went *right*?"

None spoke, but Deryn never broke eye contact with Deandra. "You didn't tell us how powerful their magic was," Deryn growled at Deandra. "We were all almost killed when they blasted through the veil."

Selen froze. Their magic. Is that what had come from her—what she had felt as she was falling towards the water? She did feel lighter than she had in years. Had Sidra finally broken their powers free? Selen's mind raced. The short conversation she had just witnessed brought up so many questions.

Still, a small shred of hope rose within her. If Sidra had her magic, she might be able to put up a fight against whoever had taken her.

"Hold up." Selen stood, putting her hands up in front of her. "One—" she held up a finger. "*Veil?* Two—" she held up another finger. "Deandra, why do you know these people? And three—" she lifted a third finger and paused. "We have *magic*?"

Deryn raised an eyebrow at Deandra, who glared back at her. Selen glanced between them expectantly, frustration raging when no one spoke.

"Someone say something before I lose it," Selen commanded.

"This is not my story to tell," Deryn said, sitting in the chair behind Deandra's desk.

"Selen..." Deandra hesitated, "I will tell you everything. Just please give me some time to sort through things with these three. I will come to your room soon."

Selen scoffed in disbelief. After everything that had just happened, she expected Selen to just wait patiently in her room? Absolutely not.

"Dea, too much shit has gone down in the last few hours for that to be an acceptable answer." Selen was pissed.

Her sister was missing— having been *abused*. She wasn't even sure if they were aware of that, but she would make sure that Xander would deal with the consequences of his actions if he ever woke up. And if he didn't, she couldn't say that she would feel any kind of sadness. She hoped it was the blow from Sidra's power that had knocked him into a coma. She deserved at least that much.

"Now is not the time," Deandra said. "I will tell you everything very soon."

Selen was stunned into silence. She glanced between the three strangers in the room and back to Deandra.

"Is that a fucking joke?" Selen asked.

"Watch your mouth," Deandra warned.

Selen laughed in disbelief. Was this for real?

"Deandra, you have clearly lied to us about *something*, likely everything," she said, gesturing to herself and the three strangers. "So, rather than withholding more information and pissing me off, how about you actually tell the fucking truth. What is going on?"

Selen didn't hide the fury in her voice, and Deandra stared at her, concern and guilt warring. It didn't seem like she was going to even *try* to give an explanation. Selen glanced around in disbelief.

Deryn watched her with what she could only describe as stony sympathy. She had been right. This wasn't her story to tell; it should have been told by the woman who had taken care of Selen and Sidra since they were babies. The woman they had looked to for everything for so long. A small string snapped in her as she met the gaze of her guardian. She didn't feel the warmth that she always had when she watched her. Selen felt the trust between them break as the reality of Deandra's lies being what had potentially led them to this point settled in.

"Fuck you, Deandra," Selen growled before storming out of the room. She didn't have time to fight her. She had to find her sister.

Chapter Twelve

Selen slammed open the door to her room, heart lurching when she saw their clothes still thrown across their beds and floor. The space, once so full, now felt empty and broken, like ghosts of the life that she had known only hours before.

Her blood boiled from her interaction with Deandra and the mystery trio. Why did Dea know them? What was going on? Her trust in Deandra was steadily fading as she sorted through her emotions. She had to go find Sidra—there was no other option. She sat in her bed and closed her eyes, trying to work through what she knew.

They had said that Xander was in a coma, meaning he couldn't have anything to do with this. The trio could have taken her and lied about it later—but if they knew Deandra, maybe worked for her, what would their motive be to take her?

Money. *From whom?*

Deandra? *No way.*

She didn't particularly trust Deandra right now, but she knew she'd never put either one of them in harm's way.

Intentionally.

Though, perhaps she could have brought danger into their lives without knowing it... but Dea thought everything through. Likely even had a good reason not to tell Selen everything in her office.

You're giving her too much trust, an inner voice spoke.

Selen's eyes shot open. She'd always had an inner monologue, but this voice was different. Older. More of a living thing than her own thoughts.

She silenced her thoughts for a moment, waiting for the voice to come back. After a moment, she sighed when the voice said nothing else. It must have been her imagination.

You know me, girl.

Selen jumped from the bed. She spun, searching the room for the source of the voice. Her heart beat quickened.

You've always known me.

"Who are you?" Selen said out loud as she continued to spin.

I am you. I am many things.

The voice coated her mind, as if coming from every direction.

"Are you... are you my magic?" Selen whispered. Her heart pounded, but that didn't quieten the voice at all. She was still looking around the room as if she would be able to see the entity speaking to her. *Through* her.

Your *magic. Ha!* The voice grated through her mind as its dark laughter faded. *I am owned by no one.*

"What do you want?" Selen's voice grew smaller and smaller.

I want to help you. It's raspy voice pulsed through her head. It felt like it was flying around her mind.

"Help me do what?"

I want to help you, the voice rasped, fading slightly on the last words.

Selen waited for a moment. Fear still plagued her at the mental intrusion, but if this... *thing* knew where her sister was, she might be willing to work with it.

"How?" she whispered.

Let me show you.

As the last words faded, Selen felt the world slip away. She fell into darkness, and her body tumbled through nothing as it continued to grow.

Selen felt as she connected with some surface, yet no pain ran through her. As quickly as she had been ripped from the world, she slammed back into another.

Selen's head spun as she tried to take in her surroundings, and panic spread when she realized she couldn't move anything—not even her eyes, at least not intentionally. She felt like she was looking through a short tunnel. Sound dissipated into her senses as she realized... she was... talking?

Where am I? She spoke through her mind, as her mouth would not open.

Answers. The distant sound of the shadow voiced in reply.

Selen wanted to ask more questions, but she quieted when she heard what it was her body was saying.

"You are not in danger." A voice that was not her own came from her body. Her gaze turned and looked at a figure she knew very well.

Selen jumped and tried to reach for her sister, who was curled on the ground in front of her. She tried and failed to get her body to move towards her. To comfort her. Sidra's face was tear-stained and contorted in pain. Her body waved a hand, and darkness encompassed Sidra. Selen screamed silently and continued to thrash against whatever restraints kept her from moving or making a sound.

Immense relief flooded Selen as Sidra rose through the wave of shadows with a bewildered look on her face. The bruises around her wrists and neck were almost completely gone. Sidra stood and placed a hand on her abdomen.

"There's no pain." Sidra spoke softly as she looked at Selen with mild fear and curiosity.

Was this an image of the future? Selen continued to try and speak—to force this body to listen to her at all.

"This is a mere tendril of what our magic can do, girl." The voice that wasn't hers came from her again.

Sidra looked up at her again after having fully assessed her body for injuries.

"How can I repay you for your kindness?" Sidra spoke carefully. Deandra had instilled manners in the girls from a young age, and Selen recognized that this was how Sidra acted around strangers.

This isn't my body.

The realization gripped Selen. She was seeing through someone else's eyes. At a distance, it seemed, but through someone else's *body*.

Whoever it was had saved Sidra. She was thankful for that, but cautious as to how this stranger had found her—and why she had her now. At the realization, Selen stopped attempting to control the body. Almost in reply, the stranger let out a relieved sigh.

"I have many things in store for repayment, girl." A sinister feeling twisted within Selen at their insidious tone. From the look on Sidra's face, she felt the same way.

"I don't want trouble." Sidra raised her hands. "Please don't hurt me. I've been through enough."

The desperation in Sidra's voice cracked something in Selen. Her stomach lurched. She wanted so badly to reach for her, but again, she could not move in this state.

"No harm will come to you," the stranger spoke, sounding almost bored.

Sidra's arms dropped, and her manners slipped as she spoke.

"Then what do you *want*?" There was far more fervor in her voice than Selen had expected. However, she imagined that anyone who had just gone through what Sidra had might have the determination to keep themselves from danger, but she could also tell that Sidra's patience was wearing thin. Selen just hoped she wouldn't do anything stupid that would get her into serious trouble. Selen had to trust that this stranger would keep their word—at least until Selen could find her.

She felt as her fear and relief were replaced with sheer determination. *Sidra was alive.* That was all she had needed to push forward. Now she just had to find her. She looked through the eyes of the stranger, searching for anything that might provide an indication of where they were.

There was greenery all around, and they were in what looked like a lightly wooded area.

The entire country was lightly wooded, so that didn't help.

Scattering the area were rocks—otherwise it was covered in dirt and grass.

Just like everywhere else.

The stranger glanced up briefly, their eyes catching on a mountain range that stood beyond a vast forest below them. Selen's breath caught.

She knew that mountain range. She knew that forest.

The MistralWood, they called it. In other words, an enchanted forest. One that Selen had visited only once before–during her VeilBinding ceremony.

Chapter Thirteen

elen burst through the doors to Deandra's office and found her guardian sitting with her head in her hands, though she quickly looked up at the intrusion. The trio who had been here before had separated, leaving only Deryn of the three. Selen's frustration continued to burn through her as she turned, shut the door, and silently moved to the chair in front of Deandra's desk. The chair that, just a day ago, Sidra had sat in.

"Sidra is alive," Selen said, crossing her arms in front of her and leaning back into the chair.

"You saw her?" Deandra's gaze was fierce as she watched Selen.

"Yes." Selen paused. "I had a vision... I think." She looked up at Deandra, searching for the right words to explain how she had seen through the eyes of another Being. However, she had no idea how to begin that conversation, so she didn't. "It was through our bond," Selen lied.

"Where is she?" Deandra stood, placing her hands on the desk. Deryn stayed quiet, and leaned against the window frame. Ever so calm. Selen hated how, even in the midst of the current situation, Deryn seemed relatively unfazed.

Selen knew that Deandra had been lying to her and Sidra, but she didn't know the extent. She so badly wanted to tell her what she had seen. Tell her about the voice that was now apparently going to be a part of her daily thought process... but she couldn't trust her.

"I don't know exactly," Selen said cautiously, leaning forward. She refused to meet Deandra's gaze and heard a small shuffle from beside her desk, where Deryn now stood watching Selen with an angled head.

Selen narrowed her gaze at her, as if to ask, *What?*

Deryn's assessing expression didn't change as she continued to stare her down. Finally, Selen looked back at Deandra, who was watching her closely.

"If you have seen her, you might be able to lead us to her," Deandra said with a sigh as she gripped the bridge of her nose with her thumb and index finger.

"I'm leaving to find her," Selen said firmly.

Deandra stopped and looked at her. "I know."

"Before I leave, I need you to tell me what you know. What you've done," Selen stated.

"I know I do," Deandra sighed. Any semblance of the powerful headmaster's mask she commonly wore was not present.

"I don't even know where to begin, Selen." Deandra put her head back in her hands.

Selen watched as Dea continued to rub her forehead. There was so much about this woman that she didn't know. She had been so confident that she could trust her—yet here she was, having lied to her and Sidra their entire lives.

"The story started a long time ago." Deandra looked at Selen then quickly over to Deryn, as if examining whether or not she truly wanted to get into this.

Sensing her hesitation, Selen pushed. "I need to know, Deandra."

Deandra sighed again and continued. "When you girls first came to me, it was out of protection. You had barely been on this earth for one year before it became apparent that your lives would always be in danger. I knew I had to keep you girls safe, no matter the cost, so when you began showing the symptoms of magic, I knew something had to be done." Deandra paused and looked at Selen deeply. "I had no idea you were BloodBound."

"*Hmph*." Deryn grunted, causing both Deandra and Selen's gaze to land on her. Selen examined Deryn's face with curiosity and a bit of annoyance. The look she had wasn't one of surprise, but more so of disgust. It made Selen's stomach turn in a way that she hadn't expected. She didn't care what this pretentious stranger thought of her, yet... something still tugged at the idea that Deryn thought less of her because of something she couldn't control.

Deandra dragged her gaze back to Selen.

"I had expected the magic to be what it was, but I didn't know you were BloodBound. You showed a large influx of magic from a young age, which should have been an indicator, but I had hoped that you were just more connected to the Lirium than your sister. After your meeting with the Seer, I knew I had to step in."

Selen knew from her experience with the Seer that she was BloodBound, but she hadn't entirely acknowledged what that would mean for her. Especially when they didn't get their powers at eighteen. She had hoped that the Seer had made an error, however unlikely that was.

"Why does my being... BloodBound have anything to do with this situation?" Selen asked.

"Those who are BloodBound have full access to their powers from the minute they are born." Deandra's words slammed into Selen like a wall.

"I've—I've always had my magic?" Selen remembered that she had felt connected to magic as a child, but had always equated it to her imagination once the connection ended as she grew.

"Yes, Selen. I hadn't even considered the reality until I saw your sister running out of the MistralWood during your VeilBinding ceremony. At that moment, I knew I had to do something to protect you."

Selen looked at Deandra with confusion. "Are the powers of a BloodBound so dangerous? Once someone turns eighteen, wouldn't they have the same levels of powers, whether BloodBound or EssenceBound?"

"A BloodBound doesn't just have the *essence* of a Lirium. They have the entirety of their magic. Plus, the concern doesn't just concern when they turn eighteen, but every year before that, too. Can you imagine a child with the full magic of a Lirium? There would be too many chances for danger. Too much power for one person. Which is why they were... eradicated a very long time ago."

"So how am I here?"

"That's a very good question that I don't know how to answer right now."

"Okay... So, I'm a BloodBound who only exists because of some mystery that no one has any answers about. What does that have to do with Sidra? And why are we *here*?" Selen gestured to herself and their surroundings.

"The origins of your magic are unknown. Since the Lirium gave itself entirely to someone in your bloodline, it's been forgotten and passed down only through your blood. Without knowing the origin of your magic, we cannot know the extent of it. In order to protect you I had to... block it." Deandra looked down at her hands, guilt coating her last words.

"You blocked it." Selen sat back, trying to process what Deandra was saying.

"I veiled your powers manually. When you go through the VeilBinding ceremony, the Seer typically lifts the veil between the person and their Lirium so the Lirium can bind their essence to the person. I placed a veil over your powers, and because of your connection, your sister was veiled as well. It didn't entirely sever the binding between your sister and her Lirium's essence, but it did keep them separated. It wasn't as effective as I had hoped. Though I'd never needed to place a veil between a person and their BloodBound Lirium, I knew it was becoming fragile. It would only take one traumatic event for you to be able to shatter that veil. I knew that if your magic broke through the veil, Sidra's would follow."

Images of the previous night flooded Selen's mind. She saw Sidra being attacked by Xander, felt her blood boil, and experienced the pain of seeing Sidra lying on the ground, bruised and broken all over again. When she looked back to Deandra, a dark haze seemed to settle over the room.

Deandra glanced around the room and at the darkness that now crept into the space.

"You and Sidra have a connection through your magic, even though it is bound separately. The veil was the only thing I could do to keep you both safe. It was a temporary solution to a long-term problem I was trying to solve. I just thought I had more time." Deandra spoke cautiously.

Of course it had ended up being Selen's fault that Sidra hadn't gotten her powers. She'd never hear the end of that once they found her. The reality of the situation pressed itself to the forefront of Selen's mind. Sidra was missing. Taken by a mystery person, on whom she still had no information.

"Would there be any reason that someone would want to take Sidra?" Selen had to get them back onto the topic that mattered. There would be time later to discuss the strangeness of her magic and its origins.

Deandra sighed and looked away from Selen, who sat forward in response.

"Deandra. *Would there be any reason that someone would want to take Sidra?*" Selen felt that flare of frustration again bloom within her, and as she spoke, the room grew darker. Deryn moved to a standing position by the window.

Glancing around again, Deandra's face showed a sense of nervousness that Selen wasn't used to seeing on her.

"There are many who fear the powers that could come from you both. There are—" She glanced at Deryn. "Societies that track those who pose a danger to the current world." Selen didn't miss the look she gave Deryn at the mention of societies.

"And you are a part of one of these societies?" Selen didn't hide the accusation in her voice as she looked at Deryn.

Deryn's hard expression didn't change as she addressed Selen. "My people are not the ones who took your sister."

"You knew that these people viewed us as a threat, yet you still worked with them?" Selen gestured to Deryn but directed her frustration at Deandra.

"Your magic was pushing too hard against the veil. I didn't have anyone else to turn to in order to protect you both."

"Protect us?" Selen scoffed.

"Yes. Protect you. You have no idea what you are capable of."

"*You* have no idea what I'm capable of. How could you put a bandage on a fatal wound and pretend that it wouldn't bleed through?" Selen could feel that itch under her skin beginning to form as the room grew ever darker. "What could they have done other than harm us if your *veil* didn't work out the way you wanted it to? Is that what you wanted?"

"Of course not, Selen." Deandra stood from her seat behind the desk.

"You could have trained me to control it. You could have limited the threat by just teaching me how to handle magic," Selen fumed.

"She needs to calm down." Deryn spoke to Deandra.

"Do *not* tell me what I need to feel." Selen glared at Deryn.

"Selen, I just needed reinforcements. I had no idea that your powers would shatter the veil so soon." Deandra put her hands up in caution.

"How could you know..." Selen drifted off. "How could you know that Sidra would be *raped* and I would almost die trying to fight off one of *your* students."

Deandra's face dropped. "What?"

Selen dropped her arms and pressed against the desk. "Did your *reinforcements* not tell you? I found Sidra being attacked by Xander, half dead, and I had to fight him off to *try* and save our lives. Oh! And he threw me off a cliff."

Deandra's gaze turned molten as she looked to Deryn.

"*What?*" Light began to leak from Deandra, combatting the shadows that were overtaking the room.

"We did not know that was occurring. We only found them after the incident." Deryn's cool facade altered slightly as she glanced between Deandra and Selen. Her gaze lingered slightly on Selen, and she could have sworn there was remorse in her eyes.

"Deandra, your decisions led us here." Selen could feel how sharp her words were coming out. "If you had told us what was going on, we could have prevented this from ever happening." She waved her hand, and an explosion of shadows erupted from it, knocking several things from the bookshelves on the opposite wall.

The devastation on Deandra's face is what made Selen's fury falter. She had intended for her words to hurt—had wanted them to. It was true, right? If Deandra had told them even a fraction about what was happening, they might have prevented this course of events. Selen couldn't focus on the pain that look brought. She had to turn this into something productive.

So, she knew that their powers had been veiled by Deandra because she was BloodBound, essentially illegal in this world. She knew that the veil shattered when she was thrown from the cliff. She knew that Deryn and her two friends were a part of some secret society that was meant to protect the world from her and others who posed a danger to the world. She knew that Sidra had been taken by a mystery person whom neither Deryn nor Deandra knew.

The boiling beneath her skin simmered as a cool calm settled over her, and she focused on the one thing she knew she must do.

She had to find Sidra.

Chapter Fourteen

Selen didn't have much time. If the stranger had taken Sidra to the MistralWood, she had to move soon or risk losing track of them in the dense forest. That meant she had little time to get supplies and go.

Their powers had already broken through the veil she had created, but neither of the girls had any formal training with their magic. Selen knew that was a liability, but she had a lot of emotional control—or, at least she thought she had until recent events. If her magic had spoken to her, maybe they could guide her to learn control. While the idea of the disembodied voice speaking through her head again made her nauseous, if there was a way to utilize it to help with this situation, then she would take it.

She made it back to her room around midday, mind racing with the information that Dea had shared. There were still so many missing pieces to the story, but she didn't have time to stroll down memory lane. Once she had Sidra back, she would hear the rest of it. Ask the rest of the questions. She threw some clothes into a pack and slung it over her shoulder, planning to head to the kitchen area for some food. She was just reaching for the handle when the door flew open, and Aeden rushed in, pausing when he found her. His eyes were wide with fear and concern as he slowly approached and threw his arms around her.

"I'm so sorry." Aeden's voice broke towards the end, and Selen, stunned, wrapped her arms around him before resting her head against his shoulder.

For a moment, her mind flashed to the image of him walking away from her—to the anger and sadness on his face as her words cut into him, and to how she had thought she'd never see him again as she fell from that cliff.

"I didn't mean anything I said. I'm so sorry, Aeden," Selen said, face still shoved against his shoulder.

Gently, Aeden guided her back so he could see her face, a hand on either shoulder. "I don't even care about that. We were both drunk." His face darkened, and silver lined his eyes. "I heard so many versions of what had happened last night that I didn't know if you were alive or not. I ran to the infirmary to see if you were there, but it was just a few people from the rings and Xander—who looked like he'd been thrown into a fire. I didn't know where you were. I didn't know if you were as hurt as he was..." A tear loosened from his eye, and he looked towards the ground.

"Oh, Aeden," Selen whispered, wiping the tear away with her thumb.

"I left you there," Aeden said quietly, still not meeting her eyes. "You were drunk, and I left you in the woods."

"Aeden, none of this is your fault," Selen whispered, her hand still on his face.

"I could have helped." He finally brought his eyes up to hers. Sorrow and guilt swirled in his gaze, and it broke something in Selen. She had never seen him with such pain in his eyes. She wanted nothing more than to ease that pain.

"I got my magic, so there's that." She gave him a slight grin.

Aeden's expression shifted into one of surprise. "How?"

Her grin faded as swiftly as it had come as she thought back to the events that had caused her magic to break through their cage. "It's a long story." Her eyes glazed over as she looked past Aeden.

A moment passed again before either spoke.

"Sidra is gone?" Aeden whispered softly.

Selen nodded. "I'm going to find her."

Aeden straightened up at that. He wiped his face with his sleeve. "I'm coming with you," he said confidently.

"I need you here, Aeden." Selen had anticipated that he would try to join her as soon as she saw him, but she had made her decision about it before he had said a word.

"I need you here to keep an eye on that *trash*, Xander, while he heals, before the Guard comes for him. I need you to protect the people here." She looked back at him. "Aleya. Deandra... I can't be here to protect any of them."

Aeden looked at her sharply, but understanding and

acceptance glazed his eyes. "I still don't understand what is going on."

"I know. I wish I had time to tell you, but I have to go." Selen separated from Aeden and began to head for the door.

"Please make it home, Selen." His voice was a near whisper as he turned his head slightly towards her over his shoulder. His eyes didn't meet hers, but she could feel the pleading that emanated from him as she looked back for a brief moment.

"If you're here, I will." Her heart ached; she knew what she was leaving behind. What she might never see again. Of all of the things that would break her if she didn't make it back, Aeden was near the top of the list. She wanted more than anything to sit and tell him everything, but there wasn't time. She was just glad she had actually gotten to see him.

She took in every detail of his face before shutting the door behind her, leaving him standing in her room.

Rain was falling hard by the time Selen had finally gathered her supplies and was ready to make her way out of the school. Her entire life had been in these walls. Rarely had they made trips beyond a few miles of this area.

She turned back to the towering building, the fear of the unknown creeping, soaking through her skin with the rain. Water droplets rolled down the stones of the school, seemingly alive with the activity of the students. She watched through the windows as students moved about the lower levels. Some paid attention to the instructor at the front of the room while others were drawing, staring off into the distance, or messing with their friends. Simple acts that, deep down, Selen knew she may never experience again. Light was slightly visible from the upper levels where their rooms were —likely from some students skipping their classes to rest after the night of festivities. This world she had created and become so accustomed to—none of it meant anything if she didn't have Sidra with her.

Only a day ago, her biggest concern had been that Aleya might be interested in someone else. Now the world seemed to shift. Things were happening, and they were bigger than any of them. The origin of her powers was still unknown, the voice silent after the vision. How any of it pieced together was still a mystery, but she hoped it would fall into place once she found her sister. Perhaps it was a childish hope, but she had to hold onto something.

She looked over to the flowers growing on the green bushes that lined the courtyard. The water pelted them, causing them to buckle and bend, but each time they resumed their place, rising higher after the water washed away. She had to believe that this was her rain. Events would bend and break her, but she would only rise up stronger. There wasn't another option.

Selen turned her face to the sky so the rain brushed her cheeks and closed her eyes. She let the droplets wash over her, focusing solely on the mission ahead. Every instinct she had told her to go back into the school. To comfort. She had no idea what dangers awaited her on this path, but if Sidra was on the other end, she would not be afraid. Taking a deep breath in, she lowered her face back towards the muddy earth and took one last look at the world she was leaving behind. She managed one step before she was abruptly halted as three figures stepped into her path.

"Where are we going, Bird?" Deryn spoke with a grin as she took in Selen's appearance.

Selen scoffed. "*I* am going to find my sister." She pushed past Deryn and her two friends. "I don't know what you three are doing."

The small woman, Nys, Selen remembered, made a huffing sound before all three turned and followed Selen as she pushed on.

"I thought you might be interested to see what my companions found near to where your sister was taken," Deryn said, sounding amused.

Selen stopped. Why hadn't she thought to go back to the spot Sidra was taken? Frustration washed over her as she turned back to face the group, heat creeping up her cheeks.

"Didn't you wonder where they were earlier?" Deryn asked.

"Not even a little bit," Selen bit out. "What did you find?"

"Rude." The man, Varric, spoke as he reached his hand out with a small amulet that Selen immediately knew. Instinctively, she reached for its twin, tied around her neck.

She grabbed for it just as Varric moved his hand backwards, out of reach. He grinned at her.

"We are coming with you." Deryn's voice was stern.

"No. You are not." Selen tried to reach for the amulet again, just for Varric to put his hand behind his back.

"We are coming either way, Bird. So I think it best if you worked with us willingly."

"Are you seriously *threatening* me right now?" Selen's anger was beginning to manifest into that itch that warbled across the surface of her skin.

The other two took a step back as Deryn raised her hands.

"There is no threat from us. We mean only to finish the work we were brought here to do." Deryn spoke softly, caution coating her words.

The itch began to fade as Selen watched the other woman. There was a sincerity in Deryn's gaze that Selen wanted to trust, but she didn't appreciate the idea that she and Sidra were just a job to her and her friends. Not that she wanted Deryn to think of her as more, but the idea that Selen was the only one on this mission who had any emotional stake in it left her uneasy.

There was no doubt that Deryn made Selen nervous, but she didn't entirely know why. It wasn't the kind of nervousness that she felt around Aleya, but it fell within a similar field. She was annoyed that this person—who had supposedly been hired to protect Selen and her sister—had not only failed at her job but now wanted to join her in saving who she had already failed to protect.

Her instinct was to tell Deryn she couldn't come; so she did.

That didn't work.

And, although Selen should have continued to push for her *not to* come, part of her was intrigued by Deryn's presence. She wanted to see what she had in store. Her scars indicated experience in the outside world, something that Selen lacked. So, maybe the idea of having her along for this would be more beneficial than Selen had initially thought. Plus, the other two must have experience as well. Selen was confident, but she knew that she might be in over her head going into this alone.

She huffed out a sigh before conceding, "You're coming. But I will be involved in every decision, and you will keep nothing from me." Selen pointed her finger at Deryn, then the other two, in an effort to come off as intimidating. From the grins that spread across Deryn and Varric's faces, it didn't seem she was successful. At least she knew they feared where her powers were concerned—or when they were about to explode from frustration. She should really get that under control, if nothing more than to keep this group in line.

"Come on, school girl. We got places to be," Varric taunted as he passed, tossing her the amulet.

Selen caught the amulet and turned it over in her hands, taking a deep breath as she envisioned it dangling around Sidra's neck; it was the only place she had ever seen it. Holding it in her hands now made Sidra's absence feel concrete, and a weight lowered onto Selen's shoulders.

She looked up at the three in front of her, supposing

that this was the best sort of team she was going to create to save her sister. She wanted so badly to run back inside, grab Aeden, and bring him along—but she needed him at Celestara, away from danger. She needed his light to guide her back.

Selen tied Sidra's amulet around her neck and moved towards the group. With that, she glanced back at the building behind her, and said her final goodbyes to the life she knew.

Chapter Fifteen

Selen was aware that she knew very little about the depth of her situation. She had no idea where the three people in front of her were from, or how they had wound up on this path together. But she knew that she needed to learn more in order to trust them enough to forgo the MistralWood. While it was a place of beauty, there was an eerie essence to it that made Selen uneasy.

She had heard stories; those who entered sometimes didn't come back. Where some believed they'd found a haven in the wood, others claimed that they'd found their demise. Selen was skeptical enough not to have solidified an opinion on what became of those who never returned... although, she'd leaned more on the latter option based on her brief experience with the Seer in the MistralWood. The image of the Seer's milky eyes and hollow features flooded her mind, sending shivers down her spine.

The group had been travelling for a little over a day, and

at night, Selen was riddled with nightmares of the events that had led to the present moment.

She saw Sidra staring blankly at the sky, lying on the ground.

She felt the wind as it had whipped around her when she'd fallen, and woke only when she hit the icy water.

Every time she closed her eyes, the nightmares plagued her. So, sleep had been limited. Her nightmares prior to these events had made sleep challenging enough, but now? It would be almost impossible. The weight of exhaustion was beginning to settle on her, but there wasn't really the option to slow down or stop. Time was not on their side.

"Eat, girl." Nys's harsh voice pulled Selen out of her spiraling thoughts.

She realized that the steaming meat in front of her had turned cold due to her wandering mind. She poked at it. The texture resembled jerky... or leather. Selen held back a gag as she continued to prod at the carcass, and looked up to find Nys staring at her from across the fire between them.

"Is it not up to your standards, milady?" Nys asked mockingly.

"It's... I've not had anything like this before." Selen tried to keep her voice level as the entire body of the small animal they'd killed for their meal was splayed across the stick she held. She imagined it was some kind of rodent based on its size and... stature.

Selen looked away from the crispy rodent and met Deryn's gaze, who was seemingly amused by Selen's disgust.

"You wear your emotions on your face, Bird." She grinned as she took a bite from her stick meat.

Selen attempted to wipe the disgusted look off of her face, with little success, it seemed, based on the reactions from the others. Varric snorted as he started in on his second stick rodent.

Deryn continued to grin as she took her attention away from Selen and looked to Nys. "What path are we taking tomorrow?" she asked.

Selen snapped her head up from her 'meal' and looked at Deryn. Selen knew the way, so why was she asking Nys?

"We are going to cut through the WestWood," Nys said without looking up.

"Why would we cut through the WestWood? There's a road that leads directly to MistralWood." Maybe she hadn't chosen the right crew.

All three stopped to look at her, and Selen felt heat creep into her cheeks from their undivided attention. Not to mention that it seemed as though she had made an error in judgment, from the looks on their face.

"If I were a magical kidnapper, I'd likely have every road leading to the place that I was keeping my kidnappee watched and potentially riddled with traps," Varric stated, head tilted to the side.

Selen's cheeks heated further as she realized her mistake. She hadn't even thought of that. Why hadn't she thought of that? It felt like all of her common sense was useless in this situation. She had no idea how to track a kidnapper or what to expect.

"What... *Um...* What experience do you guys have with kidnappings?" Selen asked. She hated asking for help, but she was clearly underqualified to be leading or making decisions on this journey. She wanted an idea of who she was working with.

The three exchanged looks before Deryn spoke for them.

"We have dealt with few kidnappings. But we have tracked those who do not want to be found. As a kidnapper falls within that category, I think our expertise may be... useful."

Selen looked between all of them. Their expressions, previously coated with amusement, now fell solemn, as though each reminisced a particularly morbid memory. She knew better than to pry at the memories of someone she didn't know, so she didn't ask. She would, however, tuck this moment away to readdress another time.

"What can you tell me about people who do this?" Selen wanted to know as much as she could. She didn't want to seem weak, but knew she had a lot to learn. If she had any chance of finding her sister, she needed to learn how kidnappers thought. If she knew how they operated, she could learn how to beat them.

"There are a lot of different things to consider when you're tracking those who have a *habit* of taking others against their will," Varric said. "These people often function with motives tied to things like power dynamics, exploitation, or ideological agendas rather than mere opportunism. This abductor's actions suggest a calculated approach, implying familiarity with both tracking magical individuals and evading detection. Based on the fact that they left something behind, this may have been more spontaneous than their skills imply. With how quickly your sister was tracked after your magic shattered the veil, there's a chance that your specific powers were being monitored by this person."

Selen tried to keep her mouth from dropping open as Varric spoke. His words came out so effortlessly as he meticulously described the kidnapper. Silence fell over the group as he returned to his meal without hesitation.

"How could you possibly know that?" Selen asked.

Varric gestured to Deryn without looking up from his food.

With a groan, Deryn replied, "Varric is a Mindweft." Being that Selen had no idea what a Mindweft was, she continued her look of bewilderment towards Varric. Seeing this, Deryn continued, "A Mindweft perceives the threads of thoughts, emotions, and intentions that make up a person's mental and emotional... Being. A person is a tapestry of interwoven strands. Each strand represents a different aspect of a person's mind. Varric is able to look at those strands individually, so he can see what makes up a person's... tapestry." She glanced at Varric, who briefly gave her a look of appreciation before turning back to his meal.

"What Lirium provides that magic?"

"I have a small essence from Elathir, of Threads and Truth," Varric replied. "Not enough to manipulate or read minds, but enough to be able to understand them."

"I didn't even know that was a thing," Selen said. She

had only seen powers that manifested into outright forces of nature—never anything to do with the mind.

"That is because you go to Celestara," Varric laughed bitterly.

"What does that have to do with anything?" Selen asked.

"Celestara is made for destructive magic." He said it as if it were common knowledge.

"What do you mean?"

"There is no one at Celestara who is trained to use their magic for anything other than as a weapon. Magic can be the hammer, rather than the nail."

Selen looked at him. "Can a hammer not also be a weapon?"

Varric pulled his attention from his meal to Selen and sighed. "If we're sticking with the metaphor, the hammer drives the nail. A nail has one purpose; without a driving force, the nail will never meet that purpose. A hammer on its own, however, has multiple uses."

Selen crossed her arms. "Sounds to me like the hammer is more dangerous than the nail."

"Used incorrectly, it can be." He raised a brow in challenge.

"A nail isn't destructive. It's literally used to build things."

"I think you're taking the metaphor a little too literally."

"It's *your* metaphor. It's not my fault it sucks."

Varric narrowed his eyes at Selen, glanced at Deryn and Nys, and went back to his food without a response.

She hadn't thought of magic as anything other than an

extension of the user. Like a sword. To be used in battle and nothing more. The idea that magic could be used for something other than force seemed unessential, but based on Varric's description of the abductor... if it turned out to be true, it may change Selen's opinion.

"How have I not heard that other schools teach this type of magic?"

Varric looked up at Selen without moving his head, eyes veiled slightly by his brow.

"Because Celestara doesn't acknowledge magic that cannot be used to destroy lives." He spoke low, the lightheartedness in his voice was completely gone now, and he sounded almost threatening. Selen started to close in on herself.

"Whoever you're mad at, it's not me." Selen knew she wouldn't earn any points with the group for snapping at Varric, but she could feel the accusation in his tone and wouldn't accept being blamed for someone else's mistakes. The impulsiveness of her reaction must be a symptom of having to make up for Sidra not being around. Can't be too much at peace. Especially now.

The air shifted. Not from any magic, but from something else. The energy around them had grown heavier than it had been before, and based on Varric's ongoing look, Selen assumed there was a story behind those words that she was a little too frightened to address.

"There are many things that I believe you will come to learn the longer you are away from your school," Deryn said. Her words cut through the rising tension.

Varric sneered and walked away. Selen's temper boiled at the action.

Once Varric was out of earshot, Deryn spoke, "Varric has been through much in his life. He has first-hand experience of the pain destructive magic can cause. Specifically, from those who have studied at Celestara."

"How could I possibly have known that before asking?"

"You couldn't," Deryn sighed. "But you could try and convince him that not everyone from your school is as bad as he thinks." She stood and began moving back towards the tents they had erected prior to their meal.

Before entering, she turned back towards Selen. "And you're not off to a great start."

Chapter Sixteen

Selen watched as Deryn closed the flap on her tent. Her head hurt with all of the new information she had gained in the last forty-eight hours.

Why had Deandra not told her about the other schools? She mentally added that to the list of things that Deandra had lied about and would need to explain.

She thought about what Varric had said about the kidnapper. It was impressive that he could just figure out someone's entire personality based on their actions. She really needed to pick his brain about that when he wasn't mad at her. Which, based on what she'd gathered, was a very small window of time each day when he was fed and not too tired. Selen's only advantage within this group was that she knew she could fight. She had to show that she had value beyond her connection with Sidra and her erratic magic, which seemed to be attached to emotions she had no control over.

You have me, the voice in her mind spoke softly. The intrusion was enough to make her jump. A cool sensation crept up her spine as she tried to keep calm. She glanced up at Nys, who still sat across from her at the fire, now watching her.

Go away. Selen spoke the words in her mind. She didn't have time to deal with this group thinking she was insane on top of being useless.

"I'm going to bed," Selen said, setting her untouched cooked rodent on the fire's edge. "Aren't you going to rest, too?" She asked Nys before opening the flap to her shelter.

"I'm on first watch tonight. Can't let the ghouls get to the princess." She sat back on her hands and tilted her head, wearing a condescending grin.

Selen refrained from saying anything snarky, instead opting to roll her eyes as she closed the flap to her tent.

You didn't think that I was gone, did you? Selen flinched at the voice emanating through her mind.

I don't know what you want from me, she replied.

I want only to teach you. The voice grew slightly louder, moving from a distant whisper to something seemingly closer to her.

"Teach me what?" Selen whispered out loud.

How to use your magic.

"So are you just here, like, all the time now?" Selen moved to her sleeping spot and sat. She figured if she can't get rid of the voice, she might as well learn more about it.

I live in your mind, always, but I do not live in your

thoughts. I am here only when you allow me to be. When you seek answers. When you call for me.

"I didn't call for you."

You wanted to know how to control your magic. You wanted to be useful to the group.

"That's not what I said. Or asked for."

Perhaps not, but it's what you desire. Which is why I am here.

"I don't have time to be worrying about managing a voice in my head that shows up at inopportune times."

I am so much more than a voice. You can be rid of me whenever you want.

"Then why didn't you go away when I told you to?"

Because you didn't want me to.

Selen felt drenched in frustration. Squeezing her eyes shut, the image of a shadowy figure entered her gaze from behind closed eyelids. Swirls of black and gray encompassed a human-shaped Being, that ominously floated in the nothingness. Selen gasped and opened her eyes, pushing backwards in her seated position. Her heartbeat pounded in her ears as frustration turned to fear.

I exist in your mind. Meaning, you can see me in your mind.

Selen wished the voice away. Her fear caused her breath to quicken and her heartbeat to get louder. She wanted nothing more than to be alone in her mind. No matter the reassurance the voice provided, she feared it. When it was present, it took up space she didn't realize she had and pushed aside parts of her just to exist there.

"Go away. Go away. Go away," she whispered and wrapped her arms around her legs. She didn't want to close her eyes in case she saw its form again.

A sense of relief and isolation coated her, and she let out a heavy breath at the realized the shadow voice was gone. It felt like her mind had been compressed, and she was finally able to release it. Tears slid down her cheeks before she even noticed she was crying, and she forced herself to sob silently, so as not to cause alarm for the others.

A deep sense of loneliness slithered its way into her mind. She didn't miss the voice, but the reality that she was living alone with this made her ache. She had no one to talk to and no one to help her understand. A weight of exhaustion hit Selen like a wall, and before she knew it, she was forced into a deep sleep.

The earth was frozen beneath Selen's feet, but she couldn't feel the cold as she moved barefoot through the night. The trees around her were coated in a soft dusting of snow. She smiled as the moon made the snow around her twinkle, and wore a long white dress that she had never seen before. Its long train draped behind her, floating across the snow, leaving swirls in its wake. It clung loosely to her legs, shuffling with every step. Selen looked down at her bare feet in curiosity. There wasn't

any pain, even though she knew they should have been burning from the cold.

Her hair draped across her shoulder, and she could feel its length running down to her waist. She knew that her hair was not that long, but it made sense here for some reason. Wherever here was.

Selen continued to walk through the woods, gently brushing branches with her hands as she passed. She felt at peace. She felt powerful. She smiled and spun in the snow, creating flurries around her. When she stopped, her breath caught at the sight in front of her.

Aleya stood before her, emerald eyes shining brightly against the snow, accentuated further by the green velvet dress she wore. Her beauty took Selen's breath away.

"What are you doing here?" Selen smiled. Her voice sounded distant and muffled.

"I missed you," Aleya said as she approached, and Selen's breath caught as her stomach flipped. Aleya placed her hand gently on the side of Selen's face, stroking her thumb along her cheek.

Selen's eyes drifted closed as she leaned into the touch. A fire formed in her core as she opened her eyes again to catch Aleya's blazing look as it began to form—much like the many she had seen from her before, but with more affection. More desire.

"I can give you what you want," Aleya spoke softly as she brought her face closer to Selen's.

"And what do I want?" Selen asked as her breath began to mingle with Aleya's.

"Me." Aleya crashed her lips into Selen's, and Selen's whole body lit on fire. She brought her hands up to entangle in Aleya's hair, and could feel her soft curls looping around her fingers.

Aleya's hands drifted down to Selen's waist as they became lost in each other. Their hands roamed each other's bodies in every way that Selen needed. Each movement was a question followed by an answer. Selen wanted nothing more than to lose herself in their closeness.

Aleya briefly broke their entanglement and ran her hands up to caress Selen's face.

"I need you. I need you more than I've ever needed anything." She spoke with a gentle grin.

"You have no idea how long I've wanted to hear you say that." Selen smiled and moved in for another kiss, but was abruptly stopped by Aleya's hands, still bracing the sides of her head.

"What are you doing?" Aleya's smile had faded, eyes shifting to something Selen hadn't seen from her.

Fear.

"What do you mean?" Selen's own smile faded as Aleya's eyes became panicked.

Selen reached for Aleya's wrist to provide comfort, but when she looked down at where she was grasping Aleya's wrist, a darkness began to form where her fingers made contact. Her own hand began to turn black, and she ripped her grip from Aleya's as the other girl stumbled back and started screaming. The blackness ate away at her skin, leaving a hollowed, mummified limb in its wake. She beat and scratched at the darkness swallowing her limb, her screams echoed around them as she continued to glance back and forth between her arm and Selen with horror in her eyes.

"I don't know what's happening." Selen reached for Aleya, and shadows shot from her, hitting Aleya in her shoulder.

"What did I do to you?" Aleya screamed at Selen, continuing to hold her shoulder. Horror struck Selen as she realized that the darkness was spreading again from the spot she'd accidentally struck with her magic.

"Aleya…" Tears ran down Selen's face as she helplessly watched as the darkness continued to eat away at Aleya. Whenever she tried to reach for her, more darkness would form and threaten to worsen the damage she had already done.

Aleya dropped to her knees. Everything from her neck down was covered in the rot of her darkness. Her eyes were pleading and broken as she looked up at Selen.

"You did this to me," she whispered.

Selen felt something crack inside of her. Aleya's face was soon swallowed by the darkness as well, leaving nothing but a husk of a human, rotted and hollow.

Selen fell to her knees and began screaming. She had done this. She had destroyed this beautiful human. Darkness swirled around her, knocking the snow off the branches and encompassing the entirety of her surroundings. She shook as she looked down at the husk that was once Aleya, and rage filled her.

She had done this.

With one final scream, Selen looked to the sky and shattered the world.

Selen woke to Deryn shaking her shoulders.

"Wake up!" Deryn screamed as Selen's eyes finally focused on her surroundings. Her confusion deepened further as she looked around, finding her tent had been ripped to shreds, ribbons streaked in black. She scrambled away from Deryn and hit a rock behind her, smashing her head against the hard surface. Once more, her vision blurred, but she squinted and forced herself to take stock of her surroundings. Her tent wasn't the only one that had been shredded. Both Deryn and Nys' tents matched the remnants of her own, and their fire was now nothing more than ash spread throughout their site.

Selen gasped as she realized what must have happened. *She* had done this. Her skin still tingled, threatening to unleash what lay beneath. Her breaths quickened as panic settled into her bones. Dragging her knees to her chest, she placed her hands over her ears.

"Stop. Please stop," she whimpered, rocking back and forth.

Breathe. That voice in her mind spoke softly and, this time, Selen didn't flinch. In fact, she welcomed the invasion.

Breathe. It repeated. This time, Selen focused and took a deep, shaky breath. The tingling lessened.

Breathe. She did.

Again. She did.

As her breathing steadied, she noticed Deryn kneeling before her, a hard look of frustration laced with something else coating her face. Concern? Selen couldn't tell. Her mind still reeled from the impact of the rock and the nightmare.

With a glance at Deryn, she found she was being carefully watched in silence. Selen's stomach dropped. Deryn was covered in what looked like ash—but her hands were black. The darkness of shadows.

Selen surged forward and grabbed Deryn's hands, the motion causing Deryn to flinch. She quickly turned her scarred hands within her own. There was no rot, only darkness. No husks beginning to form.

"I'm so sorry," Selen said frantically. "Are you okay? Does this hurt?" She ached at the idea that she had caused Deryn pain—that she had caused anyone pain.

Looking past Deryn, she found Varric tending to Nys's wounds—wounds that *she* had undoubtedly caused. A strangled sob burst from Selen's throat at the sight. She didn't want to hurt anyone. She couldn't be the monster that did what she had seen in her nightmare... but maybe she was.

"Bird." Deryn grabbed her chin with the hand that Selen wasn't holding in a death grip, forcing their faces level. "Look at me, Bird."

Selen breathed hard but tried to focus on Deryn, despite

how her vision began to darken around the edges. Removing her hand from Selen's hold, Deryn placed a palm on either side of Selen's face.

"Breathe, Bird. You have to breathe." She somehow spoke both firmly and gently. Looking deeply into her eyes, Selen saw those eastern deserts that were housed within—the winds that carried the sand on destructive journeys, brutalizing everything in its path. She saw the calm dunes that sat untouched on a hot day and the oasis offering refuge to those lost in its endless grip.

Deryn blinked, breaking Selen's contact with their depths. However, when Selen managed to refocus on Deryn's face, she found it lined with confusion. The look was quickly replaced with one of relief. Selen blinked a few times and sat back against the rock.

Both women were silent for a moment, until Selen spoke. "I hurt you," she said quietly.

Deryn looked up and offered a small grin. "It will take much more than that to hurt me, Bird."

A small sense of relief crashed over Selen. She knew that she could be destructive with her unknown magic, so it brought her some semblance of peace to know that she couldn't hurt Deryn as badly as she could the others. That must have been why she was always the one to find her when Selen was having a magical episode.

Something about this moment with Deryn felt far more intimate than Selen was comfortable with. Pulling her gaze from the other woman's, she looked back towards the wreckage of their camp.

"Nys." Selen scrambled to her feet and ran over to where Varric and Nys sat. The morning light was beginning to show over the horizon, exposing the true damage Selen had done to their camp.

"Night two, and you've already destroyed our shelter," Nys hissed as Varric tended to a cut on her cheek. It ran almost all the way from her nose to ear. It didn't seem deep, but the other scrapes and bruises on her face told Selen that she had taken the brunt of the damage.

"I'm so sorry, Nys. I didn't mean to hurt you." Selen felt heat creep into her cheeks.

"What could have possibly awoken that level of power while you were sleeping?" Varric asked without looking at her.

"She was dreaming of a lover," Deryn said, approaching where they sat.

Selen felt her cheeks heat as frustration swept over her once again. Any apology she had felt stirring melted away with the heat of her embarrassment.

"You don't know what you're talking about," Selen snapped.

"Is Aleya not your lover?" Deryn asked, tilting her head to the side as she looked at Selen. At this point, both Varric and Nys were looking at her.

"She... I—it's complicated," Selen stumbled. "And none of your business."

"Well, it seems to be our business if your wet dreams are going to destroy our camp every night," Nys grumbled.

Utter humiliation.

"Man, I wish I had a lover that was good enough in bed to make me shred tents in my sleep," Varric said light-heartedly and stood. Nys punched him in the stomach, eliciting a grunt that was soon followed by a snicker as he backed away from her.

"How are you all being so casual about what just happened?" Selen was entirely embarrassed by the fact that they now all knew about the dream that had preceded the horror show, but she couldn't wrap her head around the fact that they were acting like nothing had happened.

"If we went into panic mode every time your magic posed a danger to our situation, our stress levels would be too high to function," Nys bit out.

Selen's breath caught, and Deryn scowled at Nys, elbowing her in the ribs. Was she that unpredictable that they had already created coping skills to deal with the stress she caused?

"What Nys means is that we have seen some of what you can be capable of when your emotions are heightened, so we've developed systems to... compensate for when those situations arise," Deryn spoke calmly.

"So, you're worried I'm going to explode and kill you all?"

"There is a concern for that," Varric said as he sorted through Nys's shredded shelter.

"So, why not just lock me up then?" Selen threw her arms out to the side. "If I'm such a danger. Lock me in an iron box and pull me on a cart," Selen snarled.

"Well," Varric wiped his hands on his pants and looked

back at Selen, amusement brightening his eyes, "we don't have a horse to pull the box." He shrugged before turning back to his task.

Selen let out a sound of exasperation, and Nys snickered before moving to help Varric salvage what they could from the wreckage.

Deryn stayed and eyed Selen. "You have to understand that we have to take precautions against an unknown power. Your strength is a mystery even to you, and you are as much a threat to yourself as you are to your surroundings."

A *threat*. That was what she was, wasn't it? Selen took a deep breath and sat.

"I don't want to be a threat." The statement came out more pathetic-sounding than Selen had intended, but she didn't care.

"I don't really think anyone does unless they have malicious intentions, but the lack of control you have over your powers *is* a threat," Deryn stated.

She looked over at Deryn, who watched her closely, eyes roaming over her face, as if searching for something. "It is." Selen scrubbed at her face. "I don't know how to control it. I don't know where to even begin."

"Varric may be able to help," Deryn said, looking towards the two. "Mindwefts are skilled teachers as they can glean the best techniques to guide each individual."

Selen considered as she looked up at the two. She had a teacher in her mind as well. *Literally* in her mind. It knocked at that obsidian wall, requesting to be let in and add to the conversation, but she quickly denied it and strengthened the wall. She had to try with Varric before she let this voice lead her. As much as she wanted to believe that it was there to help, she couldn't help but feel some level of hesitancy in allowing it in fully.

"Okay, I'll work with Varric," Selen nodded.

Deryn turned her attention back to Selen. "Well, since you are in a considering mood, let me teach you how to fight," she grinned.

Selen scoffed and grinned back. "Now, that's something I *can* do."

Chapter Seventeen

"So, we are waiting for *what,* exactly?" Selen asked, throwing rocks against one of the many trees that surrounded them in the woods that she couldn't name. It was before the WestWood and far before the MistralWood, but beyond the woods that surrounded Celestara, which, now that she thought about it, she didn't know the name of either. She really should have paid more attention in Mr. Monton's class.

"There is a royal caravan scheduled to pass through this area over the next day or two and we cannot risk being seen on the road," Nys said sharply. Her tone matched the anxiety emanating from her, if her bouncing leg was any indication.

"We're expected to just *hang out* until it passes?" Selen sat up from her lounging position. Royalty had always been intimidating, but to avoid them entirely, slowing their journey by an entire day at least, felt like too much.

"Trust me." Nys looked back at Selen. "You do not want to be caught in the path of a royal caravan."

"Why is that?" Selen's interest had been piqued.

Nys sighed and rolled her eyes, shifting her gaze from the road to Selen. "Have you ever had a royal encounter?" she asked, condescension coating her words.

"That I have not. Anytime they came to the school, Deandra would have Sidra and I disappear." Selen paused at the end of her statement, realizing now how peculiar it was that Deandra had limited their exposure to those who ruled. She had never given it much thought.

Celestara had only had a handful of visits from the Royals in Selen's lifetime, but she had never actually met them. Perhaps Deandra had been hiding the twins—specifically Selen—from them. Perhaps they would have known about Selen's... condition, if they had met her.

"They have a tendency to limit survivors during their encounters," Nys spoke quietly.

"Every time they visit Celestara, a few kids go missing from the group afterwards." Selen stood. "Is that where they could be going? Are they sacrificing students?"

They all turned to her with exasperated looks on their faces. Not *sacrificing,* then. Perhaps she had let the idea of corrupt government cloud her vision of reality. But, who was she kidding? The only encounters she'd had with royalty or any other governing body was in the books that she read —and *they* all ended up being corrupt. So, while the idea seemed realistic to her, perhaps these were not the royals of her novels.

"Are they *not* corrupt?" Selen asked hesitantly.

As though rehearsed, the three laughed in unison. "Of course they're corrupt. Not sacrificing-school-children corrupt, but corrupt nonetheless," Varric laughed.

Selen felt that annoyingly familiar heat bloom in her cheeks. This consistent lack of knowledge drove her insane. She felt like an ignorant school girl out in the world for the first time. Which, she supposed, was accurate.

"You have so much to learn, Bird," Deryn laughed and walked over to Nys. "You should work on controlling your magic while we have time." She glanced over to Varric, who gave her a curt nod.

"Let's go, school girl. We got *a lot* to work on," Varric said as she stood. Selen glared over her shoulder at Deryn, who gave her a sympathetic wince before looking away. The sheer playfulness of the interaction had Selen's stomach doing somersaults, which were quickly stifled when she turned to look at Varric, who wore a shit-eating grin.

"You ready?" he asked.

"I was," Selen side-eyed him warily. "But now that you've given me that look, I'm not so sure," she said, only slightly joking.

Hours passed before Selen finally let out a sigh of defeat. "This is absolutely no use," she said, throwing up her arms.

"It is not my fault that you are wound so tightly," Varric stated, sitting back. "I can crack people within minutes, but you have this... wall. This big, dark wall that blocks me from seeing your tapestry fully."

"It's obsidian," Selen said mindlessly.

"So you know about it? It's intentional?" he asked, sitting forward.

"Well, yeah. When you share a mental bond with another person, there have to be boundaries."

"You learned this from being connected with your sister?"

"That's an understatement." Selen typically didn't share much about herself, let alone about her relationship with her sister, but something about this moment made her feel the need to open up. She quickly looked up at Varric. "Is this a part of your magic? Getting people to talk about themselves?"

"I suppose so. Or it could just be my charm." Varric grinned, sitting back.

"Nope. Definitely not that." Selen scowled across at him. He was charming, and his wit reminded her of Aeden. Her heart ached at the thought of him.

Varric frowned but sat forward. "Anyway, you have a complicated relationship with your sister. Your guardian veiled your powers for the better part of your life. And now you are struggling to control these newish powers because of emotional instability, which wasn't as much of an issue prior to your magic." His face hardened, focusing on the ground in front of him before looking up at Selen with a puzzled look. "There are strings that are missing. The walls in your mind are solid, so I can't access all of the information I need to be able to help you. What aren't you telling me?"

Selen sat back against the tree behind her. How in all the worlds was he able to do this? His magic made no sense to her. So, he had the power to understand a person's mind. But *how*? How was he able to weave the 'tapestry'? As he called it.

"If you need this much information from me, how were you able to figure out so much about the person who took Sidra?"

"Ignoring the fact that you are changing the subject, some people are simpler than others. Their tapestries are strung looser. Those who have simple desires are the easiest to understand. I don't know everything about the captor. I just know enough to be able to profile them. I'd be able to tell you much more about them if we'd met; that's when I really get to use my magic. I suppose that it gives me advanced knowledge of the human mind."

The idea that someone who'd kidnap another could be labelled as simple was off-putting to Selen. There seemed to be nothing simple about their situation.

"There are scholars who study the human mind and share that information." How was his magic special if people without magic could do the same thing?

"And you think they don't have magic?" Varric raised an eyebrow.

Fair. She had only assumed that the scholars had no

magic because they weren't out battling or using their magic as a force.

"So, what can you tell about my *tapestry* so far?" Selen moved to change the subject, trying to come off more playful.

Varric sighed. "You come off as careful, observant, and someone likely shaped by a deeply ingrained fear of harming others, which might be tied to past trauma or a strained relationship with a dominant sibling. Adopted as an infant, you have a lot of unanswered questions about your origins. That can lead to a desire to prove your worth. Even though you seem empathetic and resourceful, your self-doubt and aversion to conflict keep you from fully committing to actions or decisions—people pleasing, if you will. This internal struggle between caution and a yearning to make an impact, and can lead to unpredictable behavior if your fears are triggered. Being that you now house a known yet unchecked source of magic within you, your fears are, in fact, triggered. Which is why you had an episode yesterday. You harmed someone in your dream."

Selen paused, staring at Varric. "I don't like that," she said after a moment.

Varric let out a laugh that Selen hadn't been expecting. His eyes shone with actual humor, opposed to one of the cautioned grins she had seen from him thus far.

"It's not for you to like." He shrugged his shoulders and sat back. "Now, can we get back to what you're keeping from me?"

"You seemed to have done fine without any extra information." Selen felt the words on her tongue. But how was she going to explain that she had a shadow voice in her head that popped in and out on command and wanted to teach her how to use her magic? She'd sound insane—and since she was already a liability, she knew this could potentially push them over the edge with her.

"So, there is more." Varric tilted his head. Selen wanted to pinch herself. She felt like she was on a mild truth serum being around this guy. But there were ways to state the truth without giving away its depths.

Don't tell him about me; he won't understand, the shadow voice spoke in her mind. Selen looked up at Varric, like she was trying to see if he'd heard it too. She knew her eyes must have shifted because of Varric's own shift in expression.

I won't, Selen replied. *Now go.*

The voice's presence dissipated, and Selen released a breath that she didn't realize she was holding in.

"What was that?" Varric studied her.

"I have moments where I feel like a part of me wants to give in to the shadows." Selen looked down at the ground. "It's almost like my magic is a whole separate Being that I'm trying to live with." She was skirting this line very closely. She would have to word this next part very particularly so as not to raise suspicion. "I know it's just because it's new, but I'm afraid that if I give in to it, I won't be able to come back. Or that I'll hurt people I care about."

Something small lifted from her shoulders with the

confession. While she hadn't told him of the voice, she had shared something far deeper than she had with anyone else.

"Selen—" Varric said her name, and it felt foreign. "You will hurt people you care about by *not* learning to manage your magic. Which means you have to actually let them in. They are sitting outside of that obsidian wall, begging to be let in."

Selen stared at him for a moment. Somehow she felt intruded upon. He had never actually been in her mind, yet somehow, he'd dissected her inner self based on the very little information he had. She *really* didn't like this. He was right. Gods, did she know he was right, but something in her fought back. Something told her to not go there.

"I don't have time for this. We have to find my sister." Selen moved as if to stand, but Varric grabbed her arm and pulled her back down.

"*What?*" Selen pulled her arm out of Varric's grip.

"I wasn't really giving you a choice." His expression was serious, and his accompanying tone made Selen's blood run a little cooler. Any humor that had existed before was completely gone. "You have a very powerful magic that is simmering under the surface, and without proper control, you could kill countless people. Now, I want to *help* you, but I can't do that if you fight me due to your own stubbornness. We will find your sister. But it will not be of any use if you kill all of us following another nightmare about your girlfriend."

His words were a knife, being slowly pushed into Selen's gut. She couldn't think of another time anyone had been that direct and harsh with her. Taking in a deep breath, she sat back. She felt as though she had just been scolded, and part of her wanted to snap back, but something in his gaze made her remain silent.

"Fine," Selen said sharply, trying to push away any unease she felt. "But I want to know what your problem is with destructive magic."

Varric glared at the challenge, but his expression lightened and he finally answered. "Fine, but only after you've proven that you are actually trying."

Chapter Eighteen

Selen and Varric worked for hours to try and push through the wall that she had in her mind, to no avail. Exhaustion weighed on her before the first sight of dusk skittered around them.

"You had said you've done this before," he said. His frustration was obvious, and matched Selen's.

"I have, but I was really pissed and it was before the 'veil' broke or whatever," Selen huffed.

"What triggered it?"

"My sister being a menace." Selen slumped back against a tree. "But being that she has been kidnapped, and we are currently doing nothing to find her, I don't imagine she can help." She gave Varric a pointed look.

"As I have said probably thirty times, we cannot go anywhere until the caravan passes."

"Yeah, I know. It doesn't annoy me any less."

"Currently, you are annoying me."

"Currently, *you* are annoying me," Selen mocked.

Selen crossed her arms and huffed, eliciting a dramatic eye roll from Varric.

They had been trying to access the moments where her magic had recently shown itself. Each moment seemed to have been triggered by trauma or fear, whereas the moment with her sister in Deandra's office had been the only stand-alone experience.

She remembered darkness closing in around her, and almost losing herself to it. She remembered being pulled into her own mind and watching her sister through new eyes, until it was almost as though she didn't know her. There had been no explosions of magic, but that had been prior to shattering the veil. The pressure of her power against the veil had been all consuming, but she had control. Her anger had driven her. Sure, she had been angry when she was fighting Xander and was being thrown off a cliff—of course. But her fear of losing her sister was greater than her anger.

Now, she feared never getting to see Aeden again. She feared for the life that she would lose if she failed. In that moment, she realized she had nothing to lose, so she let loose. She had no reason not to let out every bit of emotion, pain, heartbreak, happiness, fear, and anger that lay within her—and *that* is what broke the veil.

The other time, in the forest, while they had been sleeping, that had been strictly out of fear—it was uncontrollable and had gripped her, ripping apart her composure.

The only thing they had figured out during this little explorative extravaganza was that the level of control she had over her magic was based on which emotion she expressed prior to its arrival. Anger seemed to be the most controlled. Fear, the least. Which essentially meant they had not figured out a way to control her magic. She couldn't just get angry every time she needed to use them. It had to be more than that because even in those moments, her magic would be volatile. An explosion waiting to happen.

"We should try to find out where your powers are housed within you, so you can learn how to access them without feeling overly emotional." Varric paced in front of Selen, sparking an idea.

She hadn't tried to identify where the shadows lay inside her. Honestly, she had been a little afraid to. But if she could find and call upon them at will, she might have a chance at controlling them. Varric's words gave her an idea, but the reality was that there was a huge piece of her magic that Varric didn't know about. The piece that truly made her fear accessing her magical basin. She worried that by finding out where it resided within her, an endless pathway between them would form.

"We could try that." Selen tried to sound convincing. Every other time they'd tried accessing her magic today, Varric had been connected to her physically through their hands. "I want to try without you."

Varric stopped pacing and looked at her. "Why?" His eyes were as curious as they were cautious.

"I just think I might do better if I'm not connected to someone I'm not entirely comfortable with." If she was going to do this, she needed to do it without worrying that he might pick up on the other Being in her mind.

"Fine. But I'm not going anywhere," Varric said, planting himself in front of Selen.

Selen cracked her neck from side to side as she settled into her seat, mentally preparing for the door she was about to open. Selen gave Varric one last look before closing her eyes, and the world around her faded. She began to lose focus of the senses that she had just settled into. The ground no longer pressed against her. The tree bark no longer dug into her back. She stood in darkness. Facing the large obsidian wall of her mind, Selen looked around. All she could see from side to side was the wall—everything above and behind was darkness. Selen felt herself shaking, if only in her mind-body.

Alright, you got what you wanted. Please help me.

Selen spoke through her mind, pulling open the wall that she closed when keeping the voice at bay. Her heart raced as the shadowy figure came into sight beyond the wall. It swirled and writhed, never settling. Almost as unpredictable as the magic that it brought.

So, the Mindweft convinced you to come to your senses.

Selen scowled and spoke cautiously, *He didn't suggest this. I did.*

The only response the shadow figure gave was to float before her.

I need to be able to control my magic if I'm going to find my sister.

Something seemed to ignite in the figure—a spark of

interest. Selen wasn't sure how she picked up on that, but being that they existed in the same body, it made sense, she supposed.

You know I can help you control the magic that flows through you. I've told you as much.

What do I do?

A heavy silence settled as Selen waited for the voice to give her instructions. The nerves she had pushed to the side in order to reach out to the shadows slowly bubbled to the surface. She was still deep within the thralls of her own mind, but that shadow figure just writhed and twisted in front of her. There was so much of her that feared this creature that lived within her, but there was another part that wanted to learn about it. Wanted to learn *from* it, and allow it to work alongside her. Almost as though the voice was rising from being muffled, it spoke again.

You need to open yourself to the magic—to me. I cannot live as a separate entity in your mind. Your fear will limit you. Limit us.

The words hung between them. Had it been speaking the entire time, but Selen hadn't noticed? Or had she pushed its words out from fear of what it would say, because she didn't really want the answer. She wanted it to say it couldn't help her, and she could move on and keep being the girl she was before. The minute she accepted this... thing— this part of herself that she could get lost in it.

Will I still be able to be alone when I push you out? Selen's inner voice was a whisper as she regarded the shadow.

Yes. Just as you just did before, you can close yourself off to me. But it will be only temporary. Once you've let me in, we will be more deeply woven together.

I don't want to live with someone else in my mind.

Then I cannot teach you. I cannot help you find your sister.

Selen let out a heavy sigh and closed her eyes. Behind her eyelids, it was just as dark as her surroundings when she opened them. The only reprieve from the absolute darkness was the shadow figure. She needed to find her sister, but in order to find Sid, she needed to master her magic. In order to master her magic, she needed to remove the separation between herself and this entity. She *needed* their tapestries to be woven together. It was a means to an end. No matter what happened to her, she had to do this. For Sidra. For Deandra. For Aeden.

It didn't matter what happened to her.

It had never mattered what happened to her.

She was always a means to an end.

Selen reached out a hand towards the shadow figure, as if to shake its hand in a deal.

I will open myself to you. I cannot help my sister without you. But... please allow me freedom. Allow me moments of peace.

Although there was nothing but swirls, she sensed a smile on the figure's face.

I will help you, Selen Dagny. You have my word that we will be woven, and you have my word that you will have peace.

The shadows reached out, and Selen sucked in a breath. Her heart rate heightened as the shadows slithered up her arm, coming closer and closer until she was in their embrace.

They were *within* her; she couldn't tell where she ended and the shadow began.

She supposed that was the point, wasn't it? There *was* no difference. Where she ended, the shadow ended. Where she began, the shadow began.

Selen felt a surge of power throughout her mind-body. Looking down at her arms, she found swirls of shadows twined around her forearm, leaving dark lines in her skin. Tattoos of her connection. Her submission. The bits of power she felt before were nothing compared to the depths of this. Before, where she had first felt a pond to pull her magic from, there now lay an ocean—an endless sea of power that both terrified and excited her.

Selen shoved the fear and disappointment deep in her mind, locking it behind the door that led to the inevitable. Once the shadows stilled, and all that was left were the dark marks on her skin, she felt that tingling begin to form under her skin.

The tingling that so often led to disaster.

You may command the magic to your will.

The voice came from within and all around her. A whisper in her ear. A shout from a distance.

That's it? Selen put her arms out and shadows shot from them, fading into the darkness of her mind. *How do I control them?*

They are not to be controlled. Can you contain a wildfire once it's burning forests? Can you control the raging pull of the sea? You respect it and allow it to take its course. The voices all around her sounded frustrated, as if the idea of controlling them, or her magic, was absurd.

So, I just have to let the magic take control of me? Let it rage? I have no say in this? Selen felt rage and panic wash over her. She had made a huge mistake by letting the magic in, by giving in to it. Her heart rate spiked further as she desperately tried to look around the darkness surrounding her for a way out.

A calm settled over her, and it was as though someone else were calling the shots on her emotions. But she didn't resist. It calmed the panic, but she still felt in control. She took a few deep breaths.

Listen, child. We are woven. Our tapestries intertwined. I have no more control over you than you have over me. We are one. You are not victim to the wildfire. You are not drowning in the ocean. You are *the fire. You are the ocean.*

A mirror shot towards Selen through the darkness. She flinched at its approach, putting her hands up to protect herself from the inevitable impact, but when she looked up, the mirror had halted before her, illuminated slightly by light that seemed to line the frame itself. Selen took a step towards it, intrigued by it being the only thing other than herself and the shadows that seemed to exist in this part of her mind. The words that the voices had told her rang in her ears.

We are one.

She didn't know whether it was repeating them or whether she was. She closed in on the mirror, her stomach plummeting when the reflection she saw was nothing but shadows. The dark, unpredictable swirls of shadows encompassed her body. She couldn't even see her face. Fear held her in place until she was unable to look away.

Slowly, the shadows gave way. First, she saw her nose. Then, her lips, and then the rest of her face emerged from the shadows as if rising from a pool. She lifted her hand up in the mirror, and the shadows parted, leaving her now shadow-marked hands in their wake. The fear began to subside as she watched the shadows shrink away, exposing the rest of her.

No. Not shrinking.

They were *absorbed* into her.

She looked away from the mirror, down at her body, and watched as the rest of the shadows soaked into her skin. Finally, she looked back up and into the mirror. A darkness rumbled in her eyes, the only unfamiliar thing staring back at her.

She could feel it. She could feel the magic now, not as an itch under her skin, but as a piece of her. It felt as natural as a sword in her hand or the clothes on her body. She watched the shadows swirling in her eyes until they faded into the darkness of her eyes, and a small grin tugged at her lip. She didn't know why. Perhaps it was because she finally felt the turmoil that had raged within her settling.

Perhaps because, even if it was just for a moment, she felt peace.

We are one.

Chapter Nineteen

When Selen opened her eyes, the sight she was greeted with made her jump. She had entirely forgotten that she had been sitting in front of Varric, who now wore an expression of absolute confusion, sprinkled with a small bit of horror. Selen could still feel the calm that she had within her mind now she was in her physical body.

"What?" she asked after a moment. Varric's look of bewilderment hadn't changed since she came back to reality.

"Wha—You... What just happened?" His words were rushed, like he was struggling to find them.

She had yet to see him speechless, so whatever he had seen while Selen spoke with the voice in her mind must have really been something.

"I opened myself to my magic, just like you said I should." Selen knew she was holding back but she hoped that he wouldn't pick up on it. She had no idea what he had seen.

"Who were you talking to?" Varric's face shifted further into caution than bewilderment.

"I was talking? What was I saying?" A small twinge of panic skittered up her spine, but she tried her best to not show any emotion.

Did I talk out loud? Selen asked the Shadow.

I don't know. I was in there, with you, it replied nonchalantly.

Selen huffed and let her shoulders drop in annoyance. How very *not* helpful.

Noticing that Varric hadn't replied, Selen readjusted to face him. She had intended to come up with some kind of excuse, like she was in a deep, meditative trance and was speaking with a spirit guide or some shit. He didn't know her religion. But, before she got the chance to make up an excuse, Varric spoke quietly.

"I don't know what happened in your mind just now, but you... you're different. Your tapestry has changed. Not a little bit, either. A lot. It's like you're a different version of the person who was sitting in front of me a few moments ago." His voice, while still low, was now rushed. Frantic. "I watched it happen. There were shadows and tattoos that are no longer there. You were talking to someone like they were right in front of you. Selen, I have never seen anything like that. I don't think anything like that has ever even been recorded in history. Then again, I haven't read all of the books." Varric's words were becoming jumbled. He was no longer looking at her but staring at the ground as he continued to ramble.

Selen reached for Varric's arm to pull him from whatever this was, but as soon as she touched him, his eyes shot to hers.

"What are you?" he asked viciously.

Selen didn't know how to answer that. She hadn't really wanted to ask that of herself.

"I don't know," she conceded.

There was no hiding this from him, she determined. He had seen the shift in her. He had seen her tapestry change. She wanted to tell him everything. Moreso, she wanted to tell *someone*, but didn't have anyone she could trust.

"I can't be locked away. I can't be a test subject. I need to find my sister." She lowered her voice, holding his gaze.

As if sensing the implication behind her words, Varric shifted closer. "Selen, I need to know what happened in there. I won't say anything to the others."

Selen sighed and closed her eyes. Once she opened them, she willed the shadows to be visible in them. She knew it had worked when Varric sat back, caution and curiosity coating his expression.

"I am BloodBound to a Lirium, or whatever they become when they give themselves to a bloodline," she started.

"I knew that. That is not news," he said.

Selen glared at him but continued. "I have always felt... *something* within me that I didn't understand. That I feared. It wasn't until I shattered the veil Deandra had put in place that I started hearing..." She paused, and her eyes flicked up at him sheepishly. "A voice."

"You've been hearing a voice? Since that night at the cliff?"

"I have. And I'm about ninety-nine per cent sure that it's my magic. My ex-Lirium. The one that I'm BloodBound to. It's been trying to convince me I should let it teach me how to wield my magic. Which, obviously, I was cautious of. But, after these last few incidents, I knew I needed to control it. And if I have a voice inside my head—that is actually a shadow figure in my mind—why wouldn't I utilize it to help me master these powers and help us find Sidra?

"When I did my meditation thing just there, I was essentially letting it in. I was embracing the binding. In turn, our tapestries were woven together, which is what you saw. Essentially, I am now interconnected with this Lirium... thing. And I have more control of my magic, I think. That about sums it up."

As Selen finished, she knew how absolutely insane she sounded, and based on the look on Varric's face, he thought so too. She watched him sort through the information, and each new emotion he encountered showed on his face.

This was it, she thought. He could go running back to the others and tell them how insane she is and that they need to lock her up in their secret society dungeons—which she now realized she hadn't asked much about. But at this point, what did she have to lose? A lot, really, but she felt a large flood of relief after word-vomiting over Varric's sanity.

After a few tense moments, Varric finally spoke. His

voice became more serious with each word until he was more like the man she'd come to know over these last few days. "This voice," he began. "What types of things has it been telling you?"

Memories of all of the conversations she'd had with the magic—her shadow figure friend—over the last few days flooded Selen's mind. Specifically, the conversation that led her to having a vision of her sister, through another person's eyes, came to mind. Gods, even she was beginning to think she might be better off locked up.

"It's been brief conversations mostly. Nothing concerning. There was a brief moment where I..." She planned to say these next words as quickly as possible to get them out there. "I saw Sidra alive and near the MistralWood through the eyes of a stranger, with no control over what was happening."

Selen clicked her teeth together while waiting for Varric's reply.

"This... is absurd."

Here we go. He's going to grab the chains.

We could break them, the voice whispered.

"Not now," Selen said out loud. Flinching when she heard her own voice.

"What? Is it talking to you right now?" Varric sat forward.

"Yeah. Are you not freaked out by all this?" Selen side-stepped her internal conversation.

"Of course I'm freaked out. But there hasn't been a BloodBound in centuries, and all research that had been completed on them was barbaric, most lost with time. This could be a normal BloodBound experience. I don't know. It's a little outside of my knowledge base."

"Honestly, same." Selen had been looking toward where the other two were when the question she had yet to learn the answer to popped into her mind. "If there hasn't been a BloodBound in centuries, how can I exist?" She had asked Deandra this question, but received no answer. Deandra had no idea how she existed. "Is it possible that the magic could lay dormant in a person's bloodline until it somehow... comes back?"

"Like I said, Selen, there is very little information on the BloodBound. Although, from the small amount I understand, a Lirium who has given themselves over to a bloodline risks their existence, because unless someone within that same bloodline is bound to their magic, they cease to be. Clearly, however, that information may be incorrect because you do, in fact, exist." Varric threw up his arms in frustration and sat back, placing his forearms on his knees.

Another unanswered question.

Selen wanted to keep pushing Varric for information that could help her understand her situation, but the reality was, Varric may now be her only true ally. He had all of the information and still sat here, no ropes or chains prepared to take her away to be locked up for insanity. There was comfort in that.

"You said that if I worked on this, you would tell me why you hate destructive magic—specifically those who were trained to use it from Celestara." Selen was desperate to get the conversation away from her if she wasn't going to get answers.

Varric's energy shifted, almost as though he was remembering that he was speaking to a potential threat. He carefully observed Selen, expression unreadable. He clearly wasn't done asking about her new *tapestry*, but he sighed and began speaking.

"I grew up in a village that sat outside of the Mistral-Wood. It was a peaceful place. Those who left to study their magic often came back—except for those who left to study at Celestara. I didn't think much about the differences between those with destructive magic and those with other kinds, it had never affected my family or me. Once I was bound to the essence of the Lirium who gave me magic, I went to study at Luminaris—a small academy north of the MistralWood. I was taught incredible things about magic and learned how to wield my powers to help people through challenging times. I learned how to pick apart the tapestries of the mind and identify the one thread that sets an entire person off balance. Soon, we realized that magic can also be used to understand people who don't want to be understood, which was a useful tool for those in positions that maintain balance.

"I spent years honing my craft and finally left and went back to my small village. Throughout my years studying, I had been recruited to many societies, and that did not stop when I returned home. But I wanted to help the people of my village. I wanted to use my magic to bring them peace. And I did—for about a year.

"Peace is a funny thing. It feels so permanent when you have it, yet so unattainable and chaotic when it goes away—which it often does." Varric paused, face falling solemn as Selen felt the energy of the story shifting.

Dread radiated off of him as he continued, "A group of Celestaran students, upperclassmen, came to our village in search of knowledge. They wanted the powers of the MistralWood. Being that we were the closest village to it, they assumed we would have studied it—and perhaps that had been a reality at one point, but my people only wanted to live peacefully and in harmony with the magic of the Wood. Not to conquer or control it.

"They plagued our homes for months. Once they realized we had no information, they remained only to toy with us. They knew we were no match for them, and came and went as they pleased, using their magic to destroy anything and everything. As we had no destructive magic wielders in our village, they had complete control... I could do nothing to stop it. My magic was nothing compared to theirs, and I hadn't learned to wield it for anything other than peace. Eventually, they had driven out most of the townspeople and our village was cold and empty. But we stayed. We had hope that our home could be saved." Silver lined Varric's eyes as he stared at the ground, lost to his memories.

"One day, they came as usual, but something was different. They were more vicious than usual. Where there was typically a cruel humor to their actions, they came with hatred and disgust. They had grown tired of their toys and wanted to be rid of them." He threw the stick he had been picking apart against a nearby tree, and stared at where it connected with the trunk, breaths deep.

"What did they do, Varric?" Selen kept her voice low as she spoke. She needed to hear the rest of the story. She hated that this had happened to him and his people. If she had known...

He slowly looked at her from below hooded eyes. "They got rid of their toys."

The coldness in his voice sent shivers down Selen's spine.

"They ravaged what was left of the village. They raped what was left of the women. They burned every structure that stood. Then, as if we were nothing but old dolls that had rotted from the rain, they ripped my people to shreds."

Selen couldn't help the audible gasp that came from her. These people *killed* his family and friends. She had expected something horrible, but she hadn't known how horrifying it would truly be.

Varric's face was as hard as stone as he watched Selen. "I only survived because they thought that I had burned in one of the structures they'd destroyed. I escaped, though. I watched them rip my mother, my father, and two siblings apart after having been forced to watch them defile my mother and sister... and I could do nothing. I had to decide if I was going to march in there and die with the rest of my family, or live and try and bring them justice. So, I finally joined one of the societies that had been seeking me out. I needed to restore balance. *That* was not balance. *This* is not balance." His words were almost a whisper as he looked down at the forest floor.

They sat in silence for a moment. Selen had no idea what to say or how to comfort someone who had gone through something so horrific.

"I'm so sorry." She couldn't look at him. She couldn't imagine the pain he must be feeling. "How long has it been?"

"Two years, Selen." His words were another blow. She had studied with these people. She had been younger, but she likely knew them—had likely fought against them. She drew in sharply, realizing how fresh this wound was to him. Knowing that every time he looked at her, it must be like looking at the people who did this.

"So, you can imagine why I'm not entirely trusting of someone who so carelessly functions with destructive magic." His words were venom.

"Varric, I didn't know. Why didn't Deandra do anything to stop them?" Had Deandra known that this was happening? Did she know that her students were leaving the school and destroying people's homes?

Varric let out a bitter laugh. "Why stop something so few care about?"

The words settled over Selen. Deandra may have known and chosen to do nothing to stop these people. She felt as though she was going to be sick, and searched the ground with her eyes as if it would offer a response—give her the words to comfort Varric. But she came away empty.

"I'm not like them," Selen whispered, still keeping her eyes from his, though she felt the weight of his gaze.

She finally found the courage to look at him, and as if waiting for this, he replied, "I hope not."

Chapter Twenty

The sun had almost completely faded over the horizon when Selen and Varric made their way back to where Nys and Deryn had set up camp. Varric walked a few steps ahead of Selen, and the tension from their previous conversation still lingered between them. Deryn glanced over and immediately took a double-take when she saw their faces, then stood and took a few steps towards them.

"What happened?"

Varric offered a small glance back at Selen before leaning against a tree close to the fire.

"We made progress." His voice was low.

Selen could tell that the story had brought up memories that still haunted him, and wished she could go back and never ask about it at all. She wished she could go further and prevent whoever had destroyed his life. She wished *Deandra* had stopped them. Uncertainty roiled in her gut. Everything she thought she had known about Deandra, about her school, was shifting the further away she got. If she had so blindly believed everything she had been told—or had been led to believe—what else was she missing? What else did she not know?

Deryn eyed him, then shot a questioning look at Selen, who shook her head slightly in response before making her way to the shelter they had created for her.

She sat there for a while, staring at the bark and branches they'd used to build her shelter. After having destroyed the tents the night before, she supposed she was thankful they'd given her anything at all.

Varric's story played on repeat in her mind, followed by images of her childhood. She had been so trusting. So naive. Was she still so trusting? Did the people surrounding her pose more of a threat than she had initially thought? She had immediately believed this group to be experienced enough to help her find Sidra. Not that she'd entirely had a choice on them coming along, but she had found comfort in their experience, where she had none.

She'd pieced together that Varric was likely around twenty-three or twenty-four years old. Deryn and Nys seemed similar in age, but it was hard to tell as Selen knew that someone's looks didn't typically expose their age. A heavier life seemed to age people faster, and of course, people could negotiate with the Royals to slow the aging process through a very specific type of magic Selen didn't understand. That's what Deandra had done. Her aging had been slowed because she ran Celestara to the Royal's expectations.

Selen honestly had no idea how old Deandra was. She had shown clear signs of aging since Selen was a girl, with graying hair and wrinkles around her eyes when she smiled. Could Deandra be in the pockets of the corrupt Royals? After everything that had occurred over the past few days, she could believe it, as much as it pained her to even think about.

A slight rap on the side of her shelter startled Selen from her thoughts, and looking up, she found Deryn leaning against its entrance. The moonlight illuminated the scars on her face, making them look almost white, and she had on the dark cloak that she so often wore, draped behind her shoulder so it exposed her muscular arm. Selen's cheeks heated when she realized she had just been staring at her, and a slight grin was loose on Deryn's lips as she waited for Selen to finish her examination. Selen coughed to break the silence and shifted where she sat.

"What's up?" Selen's voice was an octave higher than usual, and she scolded herself internally with a cringe.

Deryn let out a low chuckle that skittered across Selen's skin. Her voice was sultry without even trying. Selen despised the effect that she had on her. She had been sulking. Couldn't Deryn let her sulk?

"How did it go with Varric?" Deryn asked, without moving from her position.

The heat immediately left her cheeks as she thought back

to her day with Varric. "It went... fine," Selen said, her face shifting to a scowl. "I accessed my magic in ways that I hadn't known I could do, so that was progress."

Selen didn't want to get into the day's details. It had been exhausting in so many ways, and explaining meant she would have to divulge her little friend in her head.

"That's promising." Deryn crouched in front of Selen, causing her breath to still. "Tomorrow, you will learn battle practices when we rest from travelling." Selen wanted to object to having to be trained at every moment they weren't gallivanting through the woods, but she didn't hate the idea of training one-on-one with Deryn.

Deryn hesitated, looking at Selen deeply. "He told you, didn't he?"

"Yes." Selen knew what she was asking about. A look of sadness befell Deryn's face in a look Selen hadn't seen before.

"You understand his hesitancy when it comes to destructive magic wielders, then." Deryn sat now, seemingly intent on staying for a while. "It even took him time to come around to Nys."

"I wish I had known... I could've—I probably *knew* those people. I should've done something." Selen's stomach turned as she thought about what she would've done had she known what students in her school had done.

"What could you have done as a sixteen or seventeen year old? You were no more than a child." Deryn's words stung. It hadn't been *that* long ago.

"I'm not a child anymore." Selen wasn't entirely sure

what she was trying to accomplish, but it was important to her that Deryn didn't view her as a child.

"But you still have so much to learn, Bird." There wasn't any ounce of humor in Deryn's voice. "Varric's magic gives him a deeper insight into others, which everyone else must work harder to learn. If we all had his magic, the world might be a better place."

Selen sat with that for a moment. It was likely true, but he knew too much. People with that much knowledge could be dangerous.

"What is Nys's magic?" Selen sat forward. Her interest piqued when she realized she hadn't asked what Deryn's powers were either. "What is *your* magic?"

Deryn chuckled at Selen's enthusiasm, the seriousness of her previous comments fading into the light of her eyes. "For a shadow wielder, you seem to shine when you are interested in something." The statement took Selen back. It had almost come across as a compliment. Before Selen had a chance to say something ridiculous, Deryn continued. "Nys is gifted with the essence of Thalrion."

Selen gaped at Deryn. Thalrion, of earth, was one of the four elemental Lirium. The others being Pyrenis, of Fire, Aquyra, of water, and Zephyros, of Air. Many Lirium were interconnected, but the elemental Lirium had the most connection in their magic, which meant that those with their essence were connected as well. Often, those with elemental magic kept close, forming cliques of sorts. It wasn't common for them to wander alone, even after their school years. Where Pyrenis and Aquyra had a habit of binding their essence to many, Zephyros and Thalrion essence was rare. Water balanced fire, so for every essence from Pyrenis, there had to be an equal of Aquyra. The same went for the other two. They were always depicted as two sets of twins within the same sibling group. While Lirium didn't operate that way, it was a way for educators to connect the knowledge with something children might understand.

Unfortunately, Xander was one of the few bound with the essence of Zephyros, which is what had given him the magic he'd used to defeat Selen on the cliffside. He was the only one at the school with that magic, which is another thing that had made him so popular. There had been none at Celestara who had the essence of Thalrion. Selen hadn't even heard of anyone with that magic. Although if Xander existed, then somewhere the balance must too.

Attempting to regain her composure, Selen cleared her throat. "I've not met anyone with Thalrion's essence."

"Many haven't. Which is what makes her useful to our cause, among other reasons." Deryn spoke of her with affection. Not the type of affection that Selen might have expected after having *met* Nys, who seemed small and angry. That was about all Selen had gotten from her.

"So, Varric is a Mindweft. Nys has elemental magic. What is your magic?"

"Mine is far less exciting than the other two." Deryn looked at Selen, and when their eyes met, Selen felt that spark of excitement that she so often did when Deryn was near.

"I doubt that." Selen grinned and leaned forward. A confident move that was genuinely nothing more than intrigue, and a desire to learn more about the other woman. A fire lit behind Deryn's eyes, catching Selen off guard.

She sat back. She couldn't read that reaction.

She wanted it to be something more than it likely was, but knew it was probably annoyance or something of that nature. So, she stayed put.

Deryn didn't take her eyes off of Selen as she spoke. "I have the essence of Kaleid; a lesser Lirium which many do not know. And, I'm assuming from the look on your face, that you do not either."

Selen had tried to make it seem as though she knew exactly what Kaleid's magic was, but she had no idea—and evidently hadn't done a good job at hiding.

"Like I've said, Bird, you wear your emotions on your face." Deryn chuckled and continued. "My magic gives me the ability to decipher magical patterns. I can see weaknesses in one's magic, providing an opportunity to strike for those with destructive powers or weapons. Often, my kind are used in the front lines of wars."

"What does that look like?" The strings of Selen's interest had been pulled. She wanted to know all about this. It may have had something to do with the fact that the person it was coming from was equally as intriguing to Selen, but she wanted Deryn to tell her everything.

Deryn seemed almost taken aback by the question, but grinned at Selen after a moment. "A peculiar Bird you are. No one had ever asked me that before."

Selen's stomach flipped a bit at the use of the nickname Deryn had given her when they'd first met. She had no idea why. She would ask eventually.

"Have you seen a Kaleidoscope?" Deryn turned to face Selen.

"I have not," Selen said matter-of-factly.

Deryn laughed. "Well, they are devices created by people with magic from Kaleid, where it got its name, and is used as a training device. When you look into it, the light reaction creates colors and patterns that are beautiful and symmetrical. Those with the essence of Kaleid view magic in that way. Magic, as it passes through the world, creates similar patterns that change and shift with every movement. When a magic wielder has little control and intention over their magic, there are... holes in the patterns. When we see those holes, we see their weaknesses."

"That... is really cool." Selen sat back and looked up at the stars which peeked through the holes in the branches. The fact that she had known nothing about this type of magic was so frustrating. Selen turned her eyes back to Deryn. "What does my magic look like?"

Deryn's brow furrowed for a moment, as if remembering a deep-seated memory. "Yours is large. Chaotic, mostly. There is very little pattern to it, and I cannot find holes in your patterns because there isn't much of one. It's rather frustrating."

"I apologize for causing you frustration." Selen's tone was playful, but she was actually sorry for having caused frustration. So much inner turmoil coiled within her, that brief moments where her focus could be on something else, like this, were welcome.

"You have no idea," Deryn said as she stood, ready to make her way out. "You are an unknown, Bird. Many fear the unknown."

Deryn made her way out of the shelter but looked back again as unease ruffled Selen. Selen's tone turned serious. "Do you fear me?"

"I do not fear the unknown; I fear only what can be known." With that, she left.

Selen's mind was a swirling mess. She was confused by Deryn's statement, yet intrigued by this new knowledge of magic. She was terrified of her new magical partner in crime, and then there was the exhausting and frustrating situation of her sister's kidnapping.

"Hey, shadow-voice?" Selen whispered as she leaned back, staring again at the stars through the gaps in the branches above.

Yes? The voice sounded amused.

"What's your name?" If Selen was going to live with this thing, it was time to accept it truly. Meaning, she had to get to know it.

There was a long silence. Long enough that Selen had to double-check that she hadn't blocked it out again.

I do not remember the name I had in my other form. A sense of loss that worked its way into Selen's emotions. It was not her own, yet it very much existed inside of her.

"What about Velros?" Selen asked. The name had popped into her mind. It was similar to a name that she had heard in one of Sidra's books, 'Velrath,' that loosely meant veiled power. It seemed fitting for the situation.

Velros. She could feel the shadows working the word through itself. Testing it out. *Velros will do.*

"Alright, Velros. Can you tell me how I saw my sister through you?" Selen wanted to get down to business. She didn't really have the time to play questions and answers with Velros if it didn't lead to her end goals.

No. The voice was stern. Unmoving.

Selen huffed. "I bound myself to you. I gave in to you so you could help me, and now you refuse?" The stirring she felt within indicated that Velros was as frustrated with her as she was with them.

That is not information I can share with you.

"Because you won't?"

Because I cannot.

Selen realized that the frustration was not aimed at her, but at whatever was keeping Velros from confiding Selen.

"Why can't you tell me?"

There are things beyond your understanding, girl.

"That's becoming apparent," Selen grumbled quietly. "Can I see her again?"

It takes a lot of magic to do that. It will be many days before I can project into another's mind.

Following that, Selen felt a bit deflated. After a day of working through her magic, learning about the horrible things that Varric had experienced, learning about Deryn's magic and the emotional ups and downs that came with that experience, she was eternally exhausted.

Fine. I will not access the magic for a few days, so we can try to reach her again. Selen spoke internally and waited, but there was no response.

The presence that lingered when Velros spoke to her was slowly fading, as if they, too, were exhausted.

Chapter Twenty-One

The wind rustled her hair as she stood and looked over the cliffside. She could feel the swell of magic that had just exploded over the edge. It was what had called her here. She watched as the light one's magic shot from her, blowing back the wind wielder.

That the essence of Zephyros granted to such a wretch of a human was truly a tragedy. Fortunately, the light one's explosion of power seemingly took him down—and hopefully, it killed him. She stared down at the unconscious body of the light one. Sidra. Oh, how the sight of her was so pure. Her eyes, before she fell unconscious, were a bright shade of blue, like the icy blue caps of the northern mountains. She knew those eyes. She despised those eyes. But she had finally found them. They had finally exposed their magic so she could find them.

The dark one was not lost. She was lost to her for now, but not in this life. After her journey, she did not have the power to retrieve her from the waters below. So, the dark one would have to come to her. This was not ideal, having one but not both. But if she kept the light one, the dark one was bound to come. Their connection was too strong. She could feel their bond, frayed as it was. It was still the most powerful she had encountered. She could feel their anger towards each other. Their resentment. Their kinship. It was an undeniable tether rooted in love.

What a weakness it was. *Love*. It would surely be the key to unlocking their abilities. How much easier this would have been if they hadn't been separated.

A shuffle from the wood behind drew her attention, and she glared in that direction, sure that someone was approaching. Likely drawn by the power emanating from this area. It had been a location of great power for a very long time. But now? Now the twins had left their mark, it would become truly sacred.

Her fingers twitched at the idea of death—of draining the life of those who walked out of the wood in the matter of heartbeats—tugged at her desire. Her head twitched to the side, and she pushed away her primal urge. Her magic was nowhere near recharged enough to take on other magic users, no matter how weak they were. She gritted her teeth and reached down for the light one. She had just enough energy to transport them.

Where the light goes, the dark follows.

Chapter Twenty-Two

Selen stood on the edge of the cliffside and looked down at her falling body until it was entirely engulfed in the raging water below.

She was here, staring down at... *herself*.

As soon as her body hit the water, time seemed to stop. The particles in the air stilled along with the waters below. This happened the night after the full moon, yet the moon was nowhere in sight, and the stars had been snuffed out by the clouds that hung overhead.

She swiftly turned behind her, expecting to see Sidra's and Xander's bodies on the ground, but there was nothing. Not even the scorch mark she had seen moments ago. When it was her... but not. She was standing exactly where she was mere moments ago, but this mind and body were her own. She looked at her hands, covered in the dark swirls of shadows that had covered her when she let Velros in.

Velros.

"Velros?" Selen shouted in the darkness. The eerie energy that existed around her was unbearable. She needed to understand what was happening. "Velros, are you here?" Her voice seemed muffled yet simultaneously echoed as she yelled.

A shadowy figure emerged from the wood behind her. The shadows fell away, leaving a mirrored image of Selen that made her stomach turn.

"Is this what you look like now?" Selen said cautiously, slowly circling the space between them.

"Would you prefer the shadows?" Velros's voice always startled Selen. Here, their voice sounded like a thousand layered voices were being forced from one Being. It was unnerving, and Selen wasn't entirely sure whether she would prefer the shadows. It was like looking into a mirror, but their eyes were different—made entirely of the swirling shadows that Velros typically manifested as.

"I suppose not," Selen said, unsure of her answer. "Where are we?" she asked, looking around at the familiar space around them that felt so foreign.

"We are in your memories," Velros said, tilting their head at Selen.

"What about before?"

"We were in the other's memories," Velros said, as if it wasn't an impossible thing to understand.

"How were we in someone else's memories?" Selen pushed.

"The same way you saw through someone else's eyes. You asked for answers that I could not give. But it takes far less magic to access memories than it does to access some-one's conscious mind."

Selen supposed that made sense, even though she still didn't understand how they could access someone else's mind in any capacity at all.

"How can we see into someone else's mind or memories?" The question had burned Selen's mind since that first experience.

"Connected magic speaks to one another." Velros glanced behind Selen, to the cliffside, and looked at the spot Selen had been thrown from. "How do you imagine *she* tracked you?"

"Who is *she*?" And how was Selen connected to her?

"She is the one you seek."

"That is unhelpful." Selen crossed her arms.

"There are some answers I cannot give you, girl." Velros's stance mirrored her own. "Now would you like to learn your magic or not?"

Selen dropped her arms from their defensive position and took a step toward Velros. "That's why we're here?" She couldn't help the swell of excitement that bubbled up inside. Since their moment with Varric in the woods earlier today, she'd been anxious to see what their magic looked like without someone else present.

"What can you teach me?" Selen's tone did not mask her anticipation. However, masking seemed unimportant given that they were inside her mind.

"Much." Velros let out a curt laugh. "Sit, girl." They gestured to the ground before them.

Selen did as told and sat in front of Velros who, up close, made her even more nervous. She was identical to Selen, clothes and all. Selen watched those shadowy eyes as Velros took up a mirrored position.

"Do you see the ocean of your magic?"

Selen closed her eyes and tried to access her mind's vision, before quickly realizing she was already in it. Opening them again, she found that they had been transferred into the dark space where the edge of the cliff once was, only now it was an endless ocean of black water which calmly lapped against the cliff's edge.

"Woah." Selen didn't know what else to say. She had just thought about the magic she had felt when they had woven their tapestries and... here it was.

"This is the well of your power." Velros waved an arm at the endless horizon.

"The *well*? There's no end," Selen said exasperatedly.

"I assure you that it is not endless."

Selen turned back towards them, gaze locked on the shadowy swirls that matched the ocean that sat around them.

"How can I access it without losing control?" Selen asked. They were not far from the MistralWood, and she had to master some semblance of her powers before then. There was no other choice.

"The magic is not to be controlled. As we have discussed," Velros began, "it manifests as an ocean because it is as unpredictable as one. You are not to control the ocean; you work *with* it. You borrow its power with the respect that it could consume you at any moment. Unlike the oceans, the magic will show you the same respect you offer it."

"Are *you* not the magic?" Selen scrunched her brow. Everything she had learned about Lirium led her to believe that Lirium was magic and magic was Lirium.

"I am a sentient manifestation of the magic," Velros said. "I suppose I am the magic, but after today, you are as much the magic as I."

"So, I have to respect it and not control it. But it *is* me? And also you?" Selen's head hurt... inside her mind. Which made her head hurt more.

"Precisely."

Selen could detect a hint of an almost-grin on Velros's face—which was slightly horrifying, as it didn't even remotely meet their eyes.

"You wield a piece of what exists inside you. Your human mind is not meant to understand the depths of magic, especially that which is bound in blood."

"Okay." Selen hesitated, trying to navigate how to ask the right questions to get the answers she needed. "How can I access the magic in a controlled way so it doesn't get out of control in the real world?"

"Firstly, this is as real as the waking world, I assure you." Velros's voice held an air of annoyance. "Secondly, just as you have limited my access to your thoughts, you can access the magic when you call upon it. You've successfully blocked me out and opened your mind to me. Therefore, you've successfully blocked your magic and opened your mind to it as well."

"That was a *test*?" Selen hissed. She had no idea that when they had first been talking, Velros had been teaching her to open her walls not only to them, but to the magic as well.

"As I said, the magic is me. The magic is you. When you block that part of me—that part of *yourself*—you block your magic. The same goes for when you want to access it."

"I don't like games, Velros," Selen growled.

"There are no games in magic wielding," they said sternly. "Your mind was overwhelmed. I gave you only what information you could handle."

Selen was torn between her annoyance and the fact that she knew Velros was right. "I suppose that's fair." Maybe it was the fact that they shared a mind and a body, but she felt the reality of what Velros said. There was no lying here; this was her *mind*. The emotions she felt were relayed to Velros, and there was no denying that.

"Take only as much as you need from your well. Draining your magic would be draining your life." The actuality of Velros's statement hit Selen like the water she had just watched herself fall into. It was an explanation of how to access her magic, which is what she wanted, but the reality that doing so could potentially cause her death wasn't something she was entirely prepared to comprehend.

"Do the EssenceBound have the same concern with overusing their magic?" Selen was curious and wondered if Deryn knew the same thing. If not, she wanted to warn them, as it seemed no one else could have conversations with their magic.

"No. This is uniquely a BloodBound warning." The statement was almost as a growl.

"Why..." Selen started, trying to word this without offending them in some way. "Why am I BloodBound? Why did you give yourself to my bloodline?" The question was another that she had been wanting to ask, but had been cautious about it.

"My reasons for binding to your bloodline are my own," Velros snapped. "And left to the memories of your ancestor."

"Okay." Selen held up her hands. It was a sore spot. Clearly.

"You want to access your magic without blowing up?" Velros stood from their sitting position and began walking away.

"Of course I do!" Selen shot up, ready to chase after them for answers.

"Fill a cup from your ocean. Begin there. The more you need, the more you take." Velros looked over their shoulder, and dark shadowy eyes met Selen's. "Do not drain us, girl."

The shadows began to spread from their eyes until they encompassed their face, moving down their body until they were the swirl of shadows that Selen first saw them as. The unpredictable floating mass shot out shadows and pulled them into themself all at once. She decided that she did prefer Velros in their mirrored form, as this form was too unsettling to stay focused on.

The shadows turned away from her and moved into the woods, leaving Selen standing on the cliffside. She turned again to look over the edge, and watched as the ocean dissipated into the raging river below that she knew too well. She searched for her body in the rapids, and suddenly felt an invisible hand press against her back, sending her sprawling into the open air.

Her breath caught, and panic set in as she relived the fall. She turned herself in the air, just as she had before and looked up at the cliff's edge. Her mind stalled when she saw herself standing at the edge, and the snarl of a grin on her own face was the last thing she saw before she hit the water.

Chapter Twenty-Three

After the Royal Caravan had finally passed, the group was able to continue their journey. They moved quickly through the WestWood with Nys at the front, scuttling over fallen trees and branches that Selen would trip over moments later. Both Deryn and Varric also moved with ease, and Selen wasn't used to being the slowest—or clumsiest—in a group; she often led groups and laughed at their stumbles. Her restless sleep last night wasn't helping her general functionality, but she couldn't tell anyone why she had slept poorly. The experience was humbling to say the least.

Finally, after what seemed like an eternity, the group stopped moving when they hit a large opening between the trees.

"We'll stop here to rest and eat," Nys said, still looking around. "Varric, help me build a perimeter."

Selen was breathless as she stopped behind Deryn, who

looked back at her with a grin. Selen attempted a smile and gave Deryn a thumbs-up, but the other woman just laughed and moved to the far side of the perimeter that Nys and Varric were already setting up. Her laugh sounded smooth and confident, just like everything else about her, it seemed.

"Rest for a moment, Bird. Then we'll train." Deryn set her bag down and started pulling out food.

"Do—" *breath.* "We—" *breath.* "Have—" *breath.* "To train—" *breath.* "Today?" Selen collapsed on the ground nearby Deryn, who was prepping the food for the group.

Deryn grinned and shook her head. "I thought you were the top of your class for fighting. How are you so out of shape?"

Selen gave Deryn her best glare, but gave up, realizing it took too much effort. "I might be dying," Selen said, staring up at the swirling trees above her.

"You didn't eat last night or this morning. You didn't give your body fuel to take on this journey." Deryn didn't acknowledge Selen as she worked away, cutting their meat and bread.

"Nevertheless, I think I'm dying." Selen could hear a smooth chuckle come out of Deryn, and knew she was shaking her head without looking at her.

Selen finally caught her breath and propped herself on her elbow to look at Deryn. Her short hair hung over her eye as she focused on her work. The scars on the other side of her face reflected the sunlight, shining silver. She was the silhouette of perfection. Selen was comfortable thinking that; she had felt it was so since she'd first met her. Who knew that cutting meat could be an attractive activity? Selen knew only knew it was now Deryn was doing it.

I don't need to be here for this.

Velros's voice startled Selen. Enough so that she flinched, pulling Deryn's attention to her.

"I leaned on a stick," Selen said with an awkward laugh, trying to justify her small outburst. Deryn eyed her, but returned to her task.

Could you not do that while I'm in front of people who don't know you exist? Selen didn't try to hide the annoyance in her voice.

You summoned me. You were panicking.

Selen looked up at the sky. She *had* been panicking because she couldn't breathe and summoned the presence of her magic mental companion. She really needed to get in better shape.

Bye. The presence dissipated, and she took a deep breath.

Selen, again, sat up on her elbow and watched Deryn.

"What is this society that you all are a part of?" Selen asked, slightly distracted as Varric, threw a stick at Nys, who retaliated by kicking up a far too-large rock from the ground with her magic before sending it flying at Varric. He dodged it easily and laughed, and Nys huffed and turned away from him, redness creeping up the sides of her face. Seeing someone with earth magic was a peculiar sight. She wanted to ask Nys about it, but she frightened her, however small she may be.

"It is called Nexis." Deryn's voice pulled Selen's focus

back. "It's a group dedicated to maintaining balance in the world."

Selen sat up, expecting more of an elaboration, but Deryn silently went on doing what she was doing.

"And?" Selen pushed.

"And what?" Deryn smiled knowingly, continuing to work.

"And is there more to it? Is it just you three?"

"We are not the only ones who are a part of Nexis. There are many. We are just the few in this area."

"Is that why you ended up at Celestara?"

"So many questions, Bird. And before we've eaten?" Deryn shoved food into Selen's hand, who, this time, didn't hesitate before digging in. The hunger from not having eaten for the last day had settled in about halfway through their morning journey.

Varric and Nys joined them, sitting and eating silently.

After the ache in Selen's stomach had passed, she sat up straighter and faced the group.

"How did you all join this 'Nexis' group?"

They all exchanged glances but said nothing, and Selen's frustration ignited at being ignored.

"*Hello*?" she asked, with far more sass than she had the energy to defend.

"You've heard my story." Varric spoke. "Each person's story is unique, and *they* decide when to tell them."

"They could've just said that." Selen sat back with a huff. She didn't doubt that she looked like a pouting child, but she had been put in her place far more times during this journey than she would have liked. It seemed to be wearing at her pride, along with her maturity.

The sun warmed Selen's face as she lay on the ground and stared up at the sky. The trees swayed with the wind, all in perfect harmony with one another. Now that she had eaten and didn't feel like her lungs were going to crawl out of her and kick her ass for putting them through that, she truly got to take in the beauty of the WestWood. Many of the woods looked the same—the same trees and the same foliage. The WestWood didn't differ from the woods around Celestara, but there was something more magical about it that Selen couldn't put a finger on. Something peaceful.

She closed her eyes and allowed the sun's warmth to seep into her skin. She hadn't realized it until now, but there was a calmness to her spirit that she hadn't felt before.

What was it that made everything so peaceful?

Images of Sidra's body, laying as it was atop the cliff, popped into her mind. She could see her from the corner of her eye as she was thrown from the top. With the explosion of their magic, something else had snapped, too.

Selen realized *that* what was missing. Sidra.

The string that was always so taught between them now lay loosened and barely visible inside Selen. She felt her brow furrow as she reached for it. Pulling lightly, she reached for that bond that had kept them so close all of these years. The string tugged slightly back, as if Sidra was pulling it on the other end.

Relief rolled over Selen. While the lack of their connection had brought Selen peace, it wouldn't matter if Sidra was in danger. The peace and calm was slowly becoming determination, but Selen felt guilt trying to work its way in as well.

After days, this was the first time that Selen had even tried to pull on that bond. She chalked it up to being overwhelmed, but there was a part of her that wondered if it was because she relished the peace that Sidra's absence offered. This only made her feel guiltier.

A shadow blocked the sunlight, pulling Selen from her thoughts. She opened her eyes to find Deryn standing over her with a grin. She didn't mind opening her eyes to that face.

"Can I help you?" Selen asked with a sly grin.

"Not likely. But I can help *you*," Deryn said, reaching her arm out to help Selen up. "It's time to train, Bird."

While the idea of training made Selen want to throw herself to the ground and partake in a particularly childish tantrum, the idea of training with Deryn was intriguing. It annoyed Selen how much space Deryn took up in her mind. There wasn't really any reason for Selen's crush on her, other than her looks... And the fact Deryn had a sense of confidence that Selen envied and admired.... And that she was really graceful... And those *eyes*.

Okay. She may be a bit infatuated with her and these last few days hadn't helped. She had been drawn to her from the moment they'd first met outside of Deandra's office. Everything was so simple then. Her biggest concern was Aleya and her wandering eyes... and hands.

The thought of Aleya made Selen's stomach turn. Why

did she feel guilty? Aleya sure as shit wasn't waiting around for her. Even when Selen was there, Aleya didn't bother to keep to herself. Aleya wasn't loyal to Selen, so a crush was fine. Even if something were to happen with Deryn, which it likely wouldn't, Selen shouldn't feel any guilt. Nope. She wouldn't feel any guilt.

Images of Aleya flashed through Selen's mind as she followed Deryn to the wood's other side. She remembered her lying in her bed. She remembered her loosely draped over the bench in the broom closet they frequented, eyelids drooping with lust. She was a masterpiece. One that Selen would love to have all to herself... but that would never happen. She had to let go. And what better way to do that than to get with someone else? But could she really use Deryn as a pawn, a rebound, for the sad excuse for a relationship she had with Aleya? Would it even *be* a rebound?

Selen nearly ran straight into Deryn's back, having not realized that she'd stopped. Deryn turned, seemingly startled by how close Selen was.

"Typically, our fighting stances start a bit further away." Deryn grabbed Selen's shoulders and gently pushed her back. Selen felt heat creep up her neck and into her cheeks.

"I-I know," Selen stuttered. "I wasn't paying attention."

"Not a great start to battle training." Deryn took a step back and prepped her stance. She slowly moved one foot back to stabilize herself, and Selen pushed all thoughts of Aleya—and of her crush—away, and tried to focus solely on her training. She was the best fighter in the school, so she was sure she could hold her own against someone experienced. While she didn't know Deryn's experience, the fierceness of her stance and the cold calm that fell over her face was an indication. This was not the woman she had a crush on. This was an opponent.

Selen found her own stance that mirrored Deryn's and focused on everything she knew. The main thing that had made Selen the fighter she'd become was her patience. She could wait until her opponent showed weaknesses and then take advantage of those. Surely Deryn had a weakness. Selen just had to wait and find out what it was.

"No magic." Deryn's voice was low and serious, no hint of the grin she had given her previously.

"I don't need it."

"Arrogance will get you nowhere here, Bird." Deryn began circling her, and Selen followed, step for step. "Show me what that school has taught you."

Selen felt the tension building, as it always did, and the anticipation made her grin. This thrill was why she loved hand-to-hand combat. She kept her body relaxed and watched Deryn's movement. There was little to no error in how she strode. In all of Selen's previous fights, she had typically seen some sort of imbalance in how her opponents moved—even in the first few moments. Deryn had none. She wasn't concerned, though. She had faced a few who hadn't shown weaknesses at this stage.

Deryn took one step closer, and Selen noted it without moving forward herself. Deryn's eyes blazed, and for a moment, Selen shifted her focus to her eyes, then to her mouth. Her full lips, begging to be—

Noticing the distraction, Deryn lunged. One arm quickly shot for Selen's face, but she easily moved to the side, deflecting Deryn's blow from making contact with her right forearm. She then dropped her left arm and sent a fist into Deryn's side.

Right. Not the time for admiration.

"Good." Deryn shifted back, seemingly unfazed by the blow.

Selen didn't let a fraction of her surprise show. That blow typically knocked the wind out of Aeden. Then again, he was sloppy.

Deryn moved fast, striking again. This time, Selen didn't have time to send her own attack and simply shifted her footwork backwards. She moved in defense, but met Deryn blow for blow, footwork mirroring the more experienced fighter in every motion. Her moves were fast—faster than Selen was used to—and she noticed that her own defensive movements were barely fending off Deryn's attacks.

Deryn spun and kicked, and Selen found her opportunity. She grabbed Deryn's foot and twisted, forcing her to face Selen. Deryn's eyes flared as she glanced down at her foot, and Selen grinned. However, her glory was short-lived as Deryn shifted her weight and drove her foot forward, slipping out of Selen's grip and connecting with her chin. Selen stumbled back and grabbed her chin and glared at Deryn.

Selen shook her head and resituated her battle stance. She had to get a blow in. She hadn't expected Deryn to actually kick her. This was training. But she guessed they weren't holding back. She wasn't at Celestara anymore.

"Do not expect your opponent to hold back. This isn't school." Deryn's words were short. She clearly was not impressed, which hurt Selen's ego more than she cared to admit.

Selen moved first, going in with a left hook and expecting Deryn to block it, before spinning until her back was facing Deryn. There, she sent her elbow flying for her head. Deryn moved just in time to block that movement, too, but Selen used the momentum of Deryn's block to drive her body forward until they were facing again. Heat flushed her cheeks. She felt her magic crawling underneath the surface of her skin. She wanted to let it out. Her frustration begged her to, but this wasn't a true enemy. This was training. Even if her normal tactics weren't working.

Selen jumped back and began circling Deryn again, who stood and mirrored Selen's actions. The sheer nonchalance of her movements drove Selen insane. Deryn acted like Selen wasn't even a threat.

"I can see that you observe your opponent before attacking," she said. "Which is fine until you face an enemy whom you cannot allow to make the first blow. It could be your last poor decision."

Selen growled and began to slowly inch towards Deryn, fist flying towards her face. It was sure to be a knockout blow, but Deryn grabbed Selen's arm with both hands and sent her knee flying into Selen's chest. Selen coughed and tried to play off the impact like it hadn't knocked the wind out of her, and Deryn took the opportunity and lunged for Selen. Selen tried to prepare for a frontal attack, but was taken by surprise when Deryn turned her arm and rounded Selen's shoulders with her arm still firm on her neck, twisting again until her legs were wrapped around Selen's neck.

She hadn't seen this move before. That was about the only thought she could get out before she was thrown to the ground with the weight of Deryn's body and momentum.

Selen lay on the ground, panting, staring at the trees swaying above and the stars that now blurred her vision.

What was that? Selen had never seen someone use their body like that to take an enemy down. She'd never even read about it.

Deryn gently placed a boot on Selen's chest, indicating her loss, and Selen turned her attention to Deryn's face. She was panting slightly, but other than that, there was no indication that they had been fighting.

"I've never seen that move," Selen grimaced, pushing Deryn's boot off of her and leaning up on her elbows. Her pride was hurt, but she was more impressed with Deryn than she was ashamed of her own lack of success.

"Your movements are smooth. You were controlled before I got my first hit on you, and I can tell you've worked on that, but the minute your opponent can best you, you lose your composure." She went on, driving the knife further into Selen's pride, "You know the basics and are good at them, but you have much to learn."

Deryn offered her arm to help Selen up, and she took it reluctantly. Deryn slid back into a defensive position.

"Again!" she called, and jumped towards Selen.

Chapter Twenty-Four

After what seemed like an hour of Selen getting her ass handed to her, Deryn finally announced that the training was over. To say her pride was hurt would be a colossal understatement. She was the top of her class; how could Deryn have taken her out so easily? Doubt rose in Selen's mind—doubt for all she had been taught at Celestara. Their history. Their magic. Their fighting. All seemed to be missing so much. She resented how little she seemed to know about even the things she'd thought she excelled at.

They were one day from the MistralWood by the time they stopped for the evening, and Selen's mind raced as she wondered what to expect. Her education was clearly lacking, but the little she knew of the MistralWood was the mystery surrounding it. It played games on the mind, and could even make a person think they were hallucinating. It was a form of protection for the Wood; it wasn't meant to be explored by those who weren't worthy of it, so it tested people. Considering how unstable she'd been over the last week, she worried she wouldn't make it out alive. She had to believe that she would. There wasn't any other option. If she didn't, Sidra might not survive. Selen wouldn't allow that to become reality.

Selen stood by the edge of the fire Nys had built, chewing on her nails while the other three chatted quietly on the opposite side. Selen wanted to know what they were talking about, but she was too engrossed in her own mind to try and eavesdrop. The moon was half its full size and the new moon was approaching—the light She did emit was clinging to the leaves of the trees surrounding them. The woods had gotten thicker throughout their afternoon travels, signifying the end of the Westwood and the beginning of the plains that sat between them and MistralWood. It was typically where all of the border towns sat.

It's where Varric's town had sat.

Selen shoved her hands in her pockets and stared into the flames. With every flicker and crackle of wood, Selen felt the anticipation building until her anxiety crackled alongside the wood.

She couldn't fail.

Selen's mental state had to be her priority. Her instability posed a real threat to their success once they entered the MistralWood. It played games with a sane person's mind. She couldn't imagine what it could do to someone who was struggling between what was and wasn't reality.

She knew she could focus on what she'd learned from

Deryn during their brief fighting session, just as they'd have another lesson tomorrow—but two training sessions before heading into enemy territory didn't give Selen much confidence in her abilities. She hadn't even gotten a chance to practice her magic today, but wanted to practice what Velros had told her about accessing it.

Selen barely noticed when Deryn came to stand with her. Her presence took up more space than Selen was entirely prepared for.

"You're anxious," Deryn said, looking down at the place in the fire that Selen had been staring holes into.

"That obvious?" Selen tried to sound casual.

"I've told you, you wear your emotions on your face. It's relatively easy to see." Deryn's voice eased a small amount of Selen's anxiety. For some reason, the smooth composure Deryn held was enough to pull her from the hold of her mind. Deryn often seemed to have that effect on her.

"I'm just nervous," Selen confessed. "I've been to the MistralWood once, and it wasn't a pleasant experience. And this is the longest Sidra and I have been apart. I know she's okay– I mean, she has to be okay... but she's... distant. I'm not used to that." Selen was a little surprised by how much she was admitting, but she had been asking so much about the group and had yet to share much of herself... although they didn't really ask.

"The MistralWood is a force that brings uncertainty to us all," Deryn started. "As far as your sister goes, have you felt anything else from her?" Deryn's tone was so genuine that it hurt Selen's heart to lie or bend the truth.

"I felt a pull from her earlier, which has to mean she's okay. I'd know if she was hurt," she said with certainty, nodding her head as if in an attempt to convince herself.

"I am sorry if I hurt you during training." Deryn looked down and spoke with a sincerity that Selen hadn't expected. "I understand there's a lot Celestara hasn't taught you."

Selen glanced at Deryn, taking in her expression. She looked serious. Selen wasn't expecting sympathy from this group, let alone her. She hated it as much as she appreciated it.

"I learn quickly. I won't make the same mistakes again." Selen's tone was colder than intended. She was determined to learn, but she wasn't angry at Deryn. She was angry at Celestara for failing to teach her. She was angry at Deandra for allowing the school to teach ignorance rather than knowledge.

"Noted," Deryn said quickly before turning to move towards Varric and Nys.

Selen looked up and quickly grabbed Deryn's elbow. Heat flared at their connection, and Deryn looked back at her, surprise flaring before being rapidly replaced by calm. Deryn glanced down to where Selen gripped her elbow, then back up to her, lifting a brow.

"I didn't know I knew so little." Selen released Deryn's arm, heat rising up her neck. She didn't want to let her go. She wanted to keep Deryn's calm and controlled presence nearby. "I didn't realize Celestara prepared us for so little." Selen didn't try to hide the disappointment in her voice.

Deryn shifted, facing Selen this time. "You cannot know what you do not know."

Selen looked at her. She was right, but Selen hated that it made her vulnerable. Deryn's eyes shone with understanding; it wasn't the critique she'd expected.

"I've always just taken what they told me and done it. I didn't question it. I didn't question the knowledge they shared with me." Selen felt the shame sink into her bones.

"A people without the hunger for knowledge are just voids in the world waiting to be filled with corruption and misinformation. How might a person know if their knowledge is just that, or that which they are led to believe?"

Deryn studied Selen, and a moment of silence passed between them.

"By asking questions, Bird," Deryn answered herself and angled her head at Selen. Who grinned.

"That was... profound." Selen let out a solemn chuckle.

The humor in Deryn's gaze shifted. "There is nothing profound about leaders guiding people into blindness, keeping sight to themselves." A note of sadness wrapped in bitterness accompanied her words, and Deryn turned to the fire again. Her arm brushed Selen's, and she felt a small spark ignite where their skin touched. Deryn glanced down at where their skin touched, no space between them, and shot a look at Selen before stepping away. Selen felt the absence of her touch far more deeply than she wanted to. It was unlikely that Deryn shared Selen's feelings. This connection between them, much like everything else lately, was in her head.

Selen cleared her throat. "Have you been to the Mistral-Wood?" Selen wanted to change the subject, but didn't want Deryn to leave.

"I have." Deryn's brow furrowed, as if recalling a memory.

"Do you have any advice?" Selen grinned sideways at Deryn. Deryn had already seen Selen without her pride, so what was another moment?

"The wood plays games with your mind. You will question things that you once knew without a doubt. The Guardian will determine our path, which is the most unnerving. They are... not known to be fair."

Selen turned to Deryn, confusion overtaking her. "Who is the Guardian?"

Confusion that rivalled Selen's own marred Deryn's face. "The Guardian of the MistralWood," she said matter-of-factly. Selen shook her head in response, hoping that it was enough to show Deryn that she had no idea what Deryn was talking about. "The *Seer*," Deryn pushed.

The color drained from Selen's face, and based on Deryn's expression, she saw it, too. *The Seer*? The horrifying Being that had been ready to kill Selen at her and Sidra's Veil-Binding Ceremony. The creature that knows the state of Selen's powers. The creature that threatened to turn Selen in for simply existing.

"What is it, Bird?" Deryn gripped Selen's shoulder.

"I can't go to the Seer." Selen felt herself slipping back into her twelve-year-old self's mentality as fear crept into her mind. Shadows blackened her vision, and she wrapped her arms around herself before sinking to the ground.

Deryn followed her.

"What's happening?" Nys's voice sounded distant as the world started to close in around Selen.

She closed her eyes. She had to control her breathing. She had to get control of her emotions. Why was she so unregulated since her magic had shown up? She could only see the images of the Seer's milky eyes glaring into her. She could feel its cold, bony fingers clamping around her face. She could hear its unearthly voice hissing at her.

"Varric!" Deryn's voice sounded almost panicked, and Varric instantly became another presence beside Selen. He placed his hands on her shoulder.

"Selen. Where are you? Where did you go?" His voice was calm.

The question confused Selen, but she found herself trying to find some grounding.

Where was she?

Where was she?

Her vision was blinking in and out. Shadows came and went. She saw Varric and Deryn for a moment, and then, with a blink, she saw the MistralWood. Another, and she was on the cliffside in her mind. She slammed her eyes shut to ground herself.

Where was she?

She was twelve years old, stuck in the MistralWood with the Seer—the Guardian. She was horrified. She was alone.

She'd always been alone, but now she was *really* alone. She was standing in the pool where the Seer lay. No—she was *drowning* in the pool where the Seer lay. Thrashing. Struggling to breathe. Crying out for someone, anyone, to save her. She saw Sidra run from her. She saw Deandra standing at the edge of the entrance, abandoning her. She saw a figure she couldn't make out turning from her as she drifted ever-deeper into the water. The Seer's bony fingers wrapped around her throat and shoved her head underwater. She had to get out. She had to fight. No one was coming to save her. She had to do this herself. She felt the itching under her skin. She felt Velros's presence.

A cup, girl. Only a cup. Velros's voice was soft, almost comforting.

Selen did exactly that. She scooped from the ocean that was her magic and let that flow through her. Magic shot from her, knocking the Seer back. She was free. She had saved herself. She would always save herself.

Her eyes shot open. The only sound she could hear was the fast thrumming of her heart. She looked around, and her stomach immediately dropped. Deryn, Varric, and Nys were all on the ground. Their fire was loose embers around them. Nys and Deryn looked at Selen in horror as Varric scrambled to Nys.

Had *Selen* done this?

Selen moved toward Deryn.

"Are you okay? What happened?" Selen asked frantically, reaching for Deryn, who flinched away. Selen retracted her hand, cold realization washing over her.

She *had* done this.

"*You* happened." Nys shot to her feet and pushed Varric's inspecting hand away from her. "You let your emotions control your magic. *Again*!" She was nearly yelling by the time she reached Selen.

Selen shrunk back, curling her knees into her chest. What was going on? Why was she suddenly so unpredictable?

Nys approached her like she was on a mission. To hit her? To kill her? Either would be understandable to Selen. She couldn't be trusted.

Deryn stood and pushed her body between Nys and Selen. "You do not harm her." Deryn's tone was stern. Nys seethed and looked between the pair, clearly trying to decide whether or not she wanted to end their problem right then and there.

"She is going to kill us before we even get to the Mistral-Wood to save her precious other half!" Nys pointed at Selen, who glared at how she'd spoken of Sidra, but Nys's eyes might as well have been daggers from how they dug into Selen.

"She is not to be harmed." Deryn's voice dropped, and she pointedly glared at Nys. After a moment of their stand-off, Nys shot Selen a warning look before huffing and spinning back towards Varric.

"I'm so sorry," Selen whispered.

Deryn crouched in front of Selen. Any of the previous sympathy or gentleness she had shown was gone, leaving behind an emotionless mask.

"What happened in there?" Deryn tapped on her

temple, and Selen flinched away, the movement anything but affectionate.

"I don't know... I-I was here. Then I was... *there*. Back with the Seer." Selen closed her eyes.

"You've seen the Seer before?" Deryn questioned. "There are two Seers closer to Celestara. Why were you brought here to the Guardian of the MistralWood?" She'd likely put together *why* Selen had seen the Seer—it was an experience all magic wielders shared. Probably not in the same way Selen had, however.

"Deandra brought us here. I don't know why." Selen felt the fire of a headache forming at the base of her skull.

"What happened at your Ceremony, Selen?" Deryn's use of her name instead of the nickname she'd given stuck out. Selen lifted her eyes to meet Deryn's.

"It sensed that I was BloodBound," Selen said coldly, trying not to slip back into her memories.

"And it didn't turn you in?" Deryn's brow scrunched.

"Clearly not," Selen cut.

"Why wouldn't it turn you in?" Deryn seemed to be asking herself more than asking Selen.

"Why haven't *you* turned me in?" The question shot from Selen before she realized how much she needed to know. There was this giant secret that she'd been forced to hold in, and the only people in the world who knew were her, Sidra, Deandra, these three, and the Seer. Which, evidently, was quite a few people. BloodBound magic wielders had been *eliminated*—whatever that meant— centuries ago, when they decided they were too much of a liability to be kept alive. Selen's existence was illegal. So, why had these three not turned her in? Why were they protecting her and Sidra?

"You are not the biggest threat to the balance." Deryn's words sank into Selen.

"Right now," Selen finished quietly, stating the words that hung silently at the end of Deryn's sentence.

Deryn's expression softened. "You are not the threat," she said quietly. "You are helping to create balance... but you are dangerous without control."

"Did I hurt any of you?" Selen searched Deryn for injuries, looking past her to the others. Nothing seemed broken. No shadows swirled around them—no shredded cloth.

"You just shoved us back. While this fire may not recover, we will."

Selen sighed and interlaced her fingers behind her head. They were one day away from the MistralWood and she couldn't control her emotions at the mere mention of an unpleasant memory. After being bounced between her own mind, the mind of the kidnapper, her reality, and apparently her own distorted version of her memories, she wasn't entirely sure where her head was at any given time. The lines were blurring, and reality was becoming another unknown.

"What's happening to me?" Selen whispered without looking up.

"The veil blocked more than just your magic." Varric stood and came towards her despite how Nys clearly tried to hold him back.

"What do you mean?" Selen looked up. Varric's face was covered in soot from the fire, but he seemed otherwise unharmed.

"You are feeling a range of emotions that you didn't have access to before."

What the fuck? As if enough wasn't changing already, she now had new emotions to deal with, too?

"She's a hazard," Nys quipped from behind Varric, who sent her a glare from over his shoulder.

"She's been set up for failure since she was a kid," he bit at her. Nys visibly flinched at his words. It was clear that he didn't often stand up to her like this.

"Enough." Deryn stood. She looked between Selen and Varric, then over to Nys. Her word was final, it seemed, as both Varric and Nys turned and headed to their designated sleeping arrangements.

Deryn looked back at Selen, who still sat on the forest floor. Deryn crouched in front of her, and Selen's heart skipped a beat. Deryn reached up to Selen's face and brushed her thumb over a bit of soot that seemed to have gotten on her in the chaos, eyes staring at the spot where their skin met. Selen couldn't take her eyes off of Deryn. She seemed troubled, more so than just by the events that had just taken place.

"The world will not be easier on you," Deryn said after a moment.

Selen felt small, dwarfed by Deryn's presence. Everything had a place at Celestara. Almost everything had made sense. She wanted to go back to that simplicity—her heart ached for it. Was Sidra feeling the same way? If Selen's emotions were amplified after the veil shattered, surely Sidra's were too. With how volatile they had been before the shatter, Sidra was likely to be worse off than Selen... unless this was what Sidra had felt like the entire time, and Selen was just now catching up. Perhaps Selen's emotions would now be as volatile as Sidra's had been all these years.

"You're spiraling, Bird." Deryn's voice forced Selen out of what surely *was* a spiral.

"I can't trust myself with my own emotions. How am I going to save her? I'm a monster." Selen felt the sting of tears at the corner of her eyes as she watched Deryn.

"You know what control felt like before your magic. Find it again—and fast." Her words were harsh, but her tone was soft. Deryn placed her hand on Selen's knee. It was a simple act of comfort that shouldn't have meant anything to Selen, but it did. She so rarely sought or allowed comfort from others, but for some reason, she wanted it with Deryn. She wanted to lean into her for support.

But she didn't know her.

She didn't trust her.

Selen shifted her knee away from Deryn's touch before she could think better of it. Deryn looked down at where her hand had just been essentially pushed away from Selen's leg, and Selen could have sworn she saw some emotion cross Deryn's face before settling into the nonchalant expression that she typically wore. Deryn pressed on her knees and stood.

"Try and rest tonight. We have a lot of travel and training tomorrow." Deryn turned and walked towards her shelter.

Selen watched as she walked away, steps faltering slightly as if she wanted to turn back. Selen wanted her to. She also *didn't*. Things were already so complicated. Did she really want to complicate it further with what she felt for Deryn? Although, if it wasn't anything but physical, maybe it wouldn't be that detrimental to their goal.

Deryn looked back over her shoulder, and relief flooded Selen.

"You don't have to be the monster, Bird." Deryn's words weren't that of comfort, but that of a warning, and the relief Selen had felt pulled taught. Unease washed over her. It wasn't a comfort that she was not the monster she had claimed to be moments ago, but confirmation that she could become exactly what she feared.

And not only did Deryn not deny it, she agreed.

A twinge of pain in Selen's chest made her flinch as she watched Deryn lie down, facing away from her.

Chapter Twenty-Five

"Am I the monster?" Selen whispered to herself as she leaned against the tree her shelter was built around. She looked up at the canopy of leaves above her, still illuminated by the moonlight that shone through the veil of branches.

Velros? Selen whispered in her mind.

Yes? Velros's voice spoke throughout her thoughts. Their presence moved over Selen like a blanket.

Am I a monster? Selen wasn't sure what she expected to hear from the voice that existed within her, but she needed to talk to *someone.*

Who is to say what a monster is and is not?

Selen scrunched her brow. *Does this power make me a threat to the balance?*

The balance for whom?

Selen wasn't entirely sure how to answer that. Whose balance was she fighting to keep? Magic and Lirium had a natural balance, so her minuscule existence couldn't throw those powers out of equilibrium, or there would surely be a counter-balance that outweighed her.

For the kingdom, I suppose.

Who is to say that you do not exist as the balance to another?

Are you accustomed to answering all questions with other questions?

Are you accustomed to believing everything others say to you about your place in the world?

Evidently, yes. Selen curled her mouth to the side. She was actually having an argument with a voice in her head, but Velros did have a point. Selen had believed everything she'd been told about herself, and how she should feel about her magic. Ever since she'd found out she was BloodBound, she feared what it would mean for her. She was relieved when their magic didn't manifest at eighteen, but always felt as though she had to make up for what she was. Perhaps if she was so much more, she wouldn't become a danger—like she'd heard those whose magic was bound in blood had been. Granted, she had avoided the conversation almost entirely. Deandra has tried to educate her, but her knowledge had been forced and vague.

They said BloodBound were monsters. A danger to the world around them. Selen spoke softly in her mind. *I always assumed that I could control it. I always assumed that because I didn't have any fits after our VeilBinding, it was because of control.*

Are you any more danger to the world than others who are granted magic through essence?

Again with the questions. Selen rolled her eyes.

I do not exist to answer your questions.

But, like, you could. Selen wasn't sure taunting the magic within her would really do any good, but it was kind of fun. Based on the silence in her mind, she imagined she had irritated Velros enough that they were perhaps not going to answer.

Do not let the rest of the world tell you who you must be. It is only for you to decide.

Selen's grin fell as she slowly shut the wall in her mind. Velros's presence dissipated as she continued to lie on the ground. Selen couldn't help but feel a small bit of validation. It *was* only for her to decide. Why should anyone else get to tell her who she was supposed to be, or how her magic was so dangerous? Everyone's magic was dangerous if misused. She knew that if she was afraid during a fight, she would surely lose. Fear created doubt, which was what she had been feeling for days; fear for what this new magic meant for her, whether she was to become like those who came before her... Not that she actually knew who had come before her.

Her mind raced as she stared, unseeing, at the ceiling of the shelter. She didn't realize she had fallen asleep until the sun peeked through the trees around her, waking her from a rather unrestful sleep.

Selen jumped back, panting, as Deryn rounded her. She had memorized every movement Deryn had made the day before, and didn't allow any of those same tactics to best her today. They had shifted into using blades today, rather than just going blow for blow with their fists. Selen had felt slightly uneasy at the idea of drawing blood, but the image of her blood on Deryn's blade created a unique tightening in her core that she didn't have the mental capacity to dissect right now.

Deryn's own breath seemed to be heavier than it had been yesterday. Selen had woke with a new sense of confidence. She wasn't entirely sure why a small weight had seemingly been lifted, but she wasn't going to complain. They were a half a day from the MistralWood, meaning tomorrow morning they would meet with the Guardian. *The Seer.* Not only did Selen need her confidence, but she needed control. She could not allow the sight of that Being to elicit the same response that the memory of them had. She got to choose what broke her, and the Seer was not it.

Selen had two daggers, one strapped to her thigh and one in her hand. She pushed forward, taking Deryn's advice from yesterday. She couldn't wait for her enemy to strike; she had to lead in advances. Deryn's grin had been an indication that she approved of Selen's renewed vigor, and there was a spark in her eye that Selen hadn't seen since their first meeting.

Selen moved fast, aiming a strike at Deryn's shoulder. She knew that Deryn would anticipate the movement and likely grab Selen's wrist in an attempt to twist her arm backwards, loosening her grip and exposing her most vulnerable areas—which she did. This time, however, as soon as Deryn went to twist Selen's wrist, Selen looked at her. Deryn's eyes blazed, and a cocky grin coated her lips. Selen remained for a moment, allowing Deryn to believe that she had caught her off guard.

It was Selen's responding grin that had Deryn faltering. Selen spun, twisting her arm until her palm faced the ground. She dropped the dagger from her arm, held in Deryn's grip, and into her other, waiting hand. The movement was fast—and just enough of a surprise—that Deryn's hand slipped from her wrist. Selen shoved her forearm into Deryn's neck and pressed the dagger into the leather that protected her heart.

Deryn couldn't mask her surprise, and she looked down at the closeness of their bodies, lifting her eyes to meet Selen's. Pride swelled in Selen's chest. She had actually bested Deryn. Gods, had she needed to feel that familiar sense of accomplishment.

"I was wondering when you'd show up." Deryn grinned and shoved Selen back. Selen gasped but didn't lose her focus as Deryn stood with her arms crossed in front of her.

"What do you mean?" Selen kept her stance, but relaxed slightly.

"You think we only just knew of you before the Fire Festival?" Deryn cocked her head to the side. Selen narrowed her gaze at Deryn. Honestly, she hadn't entirely thought too much about it. Her thoughts had been otherwise preoccupied. "The woman I've seen would not have been bested by the basic maneuvers yesterday."

Selen stood fully then. "Two things." Selen held up one finger. "One. Have you just been watching me at school? Cause if so, *creepy*." She raised another finger. "Two. That last move you pulled on me yesterday was far from a 'basic maneuver'."

Deryn's gaze slid over her slowly, and Selen felt heat rising in her cheeks, her questions falling to the wayside. Selen didn't need answers if she kept looking at her like *that*. That wasn't the look of a curious fighter, sizing up their opponent. There was a hunger in her gaze that Selen knew well, and she didn't cower at the intensity of it but pushed into it. A challenge. She wanted to see if Deryn was as confident in this area as she was in others. Deryn's gaze snapped back to Selen's, no less intense than it had been when she was devouring Selen with her eyes.

Selen flipped her blade so that it pressed parallel with her forearm, then bent into a fighting stance, lifting two fingers that gestured for Deryn to come at her. She tilted her head in a grin as Deryn threw her head back and laughed—actually *laughed*. The sound was the most beautiful Selen had heard, and it's silky tendrils wrapped around her senses. There was so much warmth in her laughter. She didn't know how, but she knew she needed to hear that sound again.

Selen's momentary distraction had apparently been very obvious, though, as before Selen knew what was happening, Deryn was lunging for her.

Selen went on the defense, blocking each of Deryn's calculated attacks. Deryn struck Selen's wrist, sending her dagger flying to the ground. Selen watched as it landed blade-first in the ground, snapping her gaze back to Deryn, who stood before her with a ravenous smirk that made Selen's blood boil. Selen moved, fists flying with control. They spun and moved in perfect unison.

Deryn's arm flew at her with a strike that would surely draw blood, but Selen grabbed her wrist before the blow could land. She slammed Deryn's wrist against a tree once, then again—until Deryn let out a frustrated grunt and dropped the blade. Selen grinned as she met Deryn's gaze.

Selen's flare of pride at disarming Deryn was quickly replaced with mild concern as Deryn's gaze locked on hers. Her head tilted. Suddenly, Selen lost her footing and Deryn spun her until her back was pressed against Deryn's warm body. Selen's breath caught as she felt Deryn's body form perfectly behind her. Deryn's arms wrapped around Selen's shoulders, and her blade pressed into her pulse, close enough that if she moved, she'd bleed. Selen glanced down with her eyes only and saw that Deryn's blade at her thigh had been unsheathed. She had no idea when she had done that, but she was impressed.

"You cannot win in a battle if you leave any weaknesses open, Bird." Deryn's breath caressed Selen's ear as she spoke. For a moment, the adrenaline that spiked from the heat of battle shifted into something else. Selen was consumed by the scent of her. Leather and vanilla. She savored the warmth of having her so close—the sensation of her hair brushing gently against her neck.

Her body held firmly against her back. Any and all life preservation faded from priority as Deryn's breathing continued, caressing her skin. Selen didn't care about the slice of the knife as she turned her head to face Deryn. The warmth of her blood flowed from her neck and pooled at her collarbone. She had felt Deryn shift the knife slightly as she turned; not enough to *not* draw blood, but just enough that it wouldn't kill her.

Their eyes locked, and Selen's pulse quickened. Deryn didn't break eye contact, nor did she remove the blade. Selen knew that Deryn's cool demeanor wasn't easily swayed, but she took pride when she felt, more than saw, Deryn's breath accelerating as they remained still.

"Are there some battles worth losing?" Selen's gaze slowly dropped to Deryn's lips. She thought about what they might taste like. Would they taste the way she smelled? She'd love to find out.

Selen could see Deryn's self-control shifting and knew she wanted to give in to her lust as much as she did. A battle took place in her eyes.

Something shifted in Deryn's gaze, and the right side of her mouth quirked. Selen gasped as Deryn spun her until they one another faced once more. This time, the blade was just under her chin.

"Not if you want to live." The hunger in Deryn's eyes hadn't entirely faded, but it was masked with hardness.

Deryn dropped the knife and took a step closer, her thumb coming up to the small slice in Selen's neck. She wiped firmly enough at the wound that Selen hissed at the sting. Deryn looked down at the blood coating her finger.

"You should clean that so it doesn't get infected," she said, not looking away from her blood-coated thumb.

There was something so sensual about the way Deryn moved, but having some of Selen's blood on her sparked a hunger for more in Selen.

Deryn shifted her eyes back to Selen, and something in those desert eyes told Selen that Deryn was as hungry as she was.

"We're a half a day out from the forest," Deryn said, beginning to turn from Selen, as if it hadn't been the entire topic of the morning. She stopped before beginning to walk, glancing slightly back over her shoulder. "Get some rest before you get into things you aren't prepared for."

And with that, Deryn walked back to their camp. Selen let out a deep breath that she didn't realize she had been holding in, skin still flushed from more than the exertion from the fight. The pride she had felt earlier had been completely replaced by a burning sensation that she felt far below the surface, that faded with every step Deryn took from her.

She wanted to keep reminding herself that Deryn had essentially called her a monster the night before, but her actions weren't those of someone who thought Selen monstrous. Plus, why wouldn't she act on what she felt? She could very well die tomorrow.

Was this dissociation? She had learned about it in one of her classes on emotional control. She supposed she and Sidra had both become good at it. If she got truly upset by every big or little thing in her life, or thought too much about the fact that she was an orphan... Or about how Sidra didn't seem to care about her emotions. Or that Aleya readily fucked other girls while Selen had waited for her. Or that her sister had been kidnapped by a mysterious Being, whose mind she could peer into. *Or* that she was sexually attracted to a woman who pretty much stated that she thought Selen was a monster. *Or,* how she had a fancy little shadow friend who spoke to her in her mind! Well, she'd just shut down—and that wasn't helpful to anyone.

So, dissociation it was.

Selen grimaced as she relaxed, feeling every bruise that was forming after their sparring session. She grabbed her knife from the ground and sheathed it at her ribs. She'd never be okay with being a victim, and tomorrow was not going to be an exception.

She thought back to the entire experience she'd just had with Deryn. Had she said that she had been watching Selen while she trained at school? How long had that been going on? It didn't make her feel the unease she thought she should feel. Although, maybe after she'd had some time to cool down, she might think differently. She bit the inside of her cheek and thought back to her training. She thought back to Aeden. Where would Deryn have watched them from? Typically, Selen tried to stay aware of the things happening around her.

What was Aeden doing? What were they *all* doing? Had Xander died in the infirmary? She hoped so. Was Aleya sleeping with other people? Definitely. Was Aeden still his goofy, carefree self? Gods, she hoped so. She hoped the world hadn't sunk its claws into him yet. Hopefully, he wasn't thinking about her all the time, and was just going about his day. She pictured him in the fighting rings and tossing grapes into his mouth. The world had gotten darker with his absence. She supposed that was why he was her light —her beacon home.

Just the thought of his floppy grin brought a smile to Selen's face. Many people had assumed they were always more than what they were, and yes, she loved him. She loved him deeply, but in a very different way than people expected. She'd never felt obligated to care for him. She'd never felt guilty for choosing herself, as he encouraged. He loved her for who she was, and that had been enough for him. Even when she knew he would gladly allow her to love him in other ways, he had never expected her to—that wasn't really in the cards for her, anyway, as her 'preferences,' as he called them, lie elsewhere.

She sometimes envied those who were attracted to all genders, and wished she could be more fluid in her sexuality, but men had never granted her a fraction of what she felt with women—trust, she'd tried. She had tried several times, with several men, and there wasn't a drop. Women were beautiful creatures—far more so than men, anyway—but an attraction to only one gender did limit a person's availability for monogamy, especially at this age. Nineteen was not the time to find a soulmate. Her twentieth year approached in the coming months, and she wanted to say she had been in love—but that would be a gross lie. What she felt for Aleya was not love.

The blunt admittance to this mildly surprised Selen. The thing that had existed between them was a fire—a blue flame that burned bright and hot without kindling to keep it alight. Would that be what would become of her and Deryn? Was there anything to even catch fire? There had definitely been sparks.

While that definitely shouldn't be a priority, Selen couldn't help but latch on to that attraction. In all the mud, it was her clarity. It was something simple in a world of complication. While, sure, it was far from simplicity in reality, but by comparison to all Selen faced, it was one of the easier things to comprehend.

And, the idea that her feelings for someone were the least complicated emotions she was experiencing for once, was... interesting to say the least.

Chapter Twenty-Six

The sun clung to the swaying grass as they pushed through its blades. It glistened as it moved, leaving a warm, golden glow on their surroundings and bodies. The WestWood had come to an end a little over an hour ago, and they could just begin to make out the edge of the MistralWood, a bustling town between them and it. The faint hum that came from the wood was nothing in comparison to the energy that emanated from the townspeople. The town was alive, and a strong scent of food wafted from the surrounding buildings, at what Selen imagined was their town center.

Selen hadn't realized how hungry she'd been until then. People laughed and mingled openly in the square, and while people mingled at Celestara and its neighboring villages, there was something so... inviting about *this* village. Children chased one another around a statue in the center of the square.

A man had his arm draped affectionately over a woman's shoulder, who seemed equally as interested in physical connection as he was, based on the look she gave him. Another two women held hands and sat on the edge of a stone wall. One said something that made the other laugh, and the answering look from the first woman made Selen's stomach flip. There was so much admiration and care in her gaze. So much love. Would Selen ever sit on a stone wall and look at someone she loved with admiration like they were? She wasn't sure, and her heart hardened slightly at the thought. Would her existence ever be simple enough that she could love openly?

Selen was so infatuated with watching the townspeople that she hadn't realized that Deryn had fallen back to walk beside her. Selen glanced at her before averting her gaze back to the ground. She couldn't help but envision her and Deryn sitting on that stone wall, staring into each other's eyes. The thought brought a smile to her face, but the sweet taste of joy was sufficiently soured by the reality they faced. There was no world where Selen and Deryn, or Selen and Aleya, or Selen and anyone, could sit on the edge of a stone wall and experience the same level of carefree affection that was required to feel the joy she saw in those two. When she looked for that life, all she saw was shadows.

Her existence was a far more complicated story than that of a love story. She knew that finding her sister was not the end of a journey, but the beginning of one. Selen shouldn't exist; several people have expressed that sentiment. Forces, far larger than she understood, had taken notice of her existence—and not in a favorable way.

Besides, it hadn't gone unnoticed by Selen that if Deryn and the others knew of her, so too did their 'society'—that she knew next to nothing about. If the Seer knew of her, so too did the forces that created balance, that she *also* didn't know much about. She had hoped to avoid all of that when her magic hadn't manifested, but reality was slowly trickling in as she became more grounded in her magic.

"Your mind wanders," Deryn spoke softly, and Selen looked up, almost having forgotten that she was there.

"It does," Selen replied, keeping her gaze locked on the people of the town in front of them.

"I imagine you have not spent much time in places like this." Deryn didn't phrase it like a question, but it seemed to be one.

"I have not," Selen said, kicking a rock along their path.

"I have been here a few times, myself, and the people are always kind. Welcoming to outsiders." Selen stopped walking and looked over at her. Deryn stopped a few paces in front of her and turned back.

"I'm not particularly interested in engaging with the townspeople." Selen furrowed her brow. They were to meet with the Seer in the morning, and Selen didn't need any distractions in her mental preparation for that moment.

"You are not interested in *living*?" Deryn tilted her head at Selen.

"Of course I'm interested in *living*." Selen shook her head. Slight annoyance flitting through her at the casual nature that Deryn held. "I just don't have time to *socialize* when I have to prepare for whatever we face tomorrow."

Deryn chuckled. "Tomorrow will come whether you live today or not."

Selen side-eyed her. Deryn seemed... playful, compared to the stoic, nonchalant character she had been the entire morning. She wondered if the moment they shared at the end of their training yesterday hadn't been entirely one-sided after all.

Selen had thought about it on and off throughout the day; she had recognized the look in Deryn's eye. She had worn the same. Her desire had been written all over her, but Deryn's attitude the entire day, up until now, had made Selen question whether or not she had made it all up out of hope, or desperation for human connection.

Could it truly hurt to enjoy the evening? Sidra wasn't really going anywhere... she hoped. But they wouldn't enter the woods until tomorrow... Deryn was right, tomorrow would come whether Selen wallowed or enjoyed the evening. She glanced at the couple sitting on the stone wall and looked back at Deryn.

"What did you have in mind?" Selen pushed out with a sigh. She was mildly overwhelmed with the idea of the next day and beyond, but Deryn was *intriguing*, per usual.

They met the others at the edge of the stone wall and opened the small wooden gate that led into the town. Selen took a deep breath as her gaze skittered across the plethora of people. Their conversations mingled into a wave of noise that consumed her senses, considering they had had nothing but themselves and the sounds of the forest for days. She glanced at the one- and two-story stone buildings that made up the town. It was quaint but busy; she could easily blend in here. No one knew she was BloodBound. No one knew that she had little control over her magic. No one knew that her sister had been kidnapped. There was something so curious about slipping into a state of unknown, to be another face in the crowd. She craved it, she supposed. She could be whoever she wanted to be here. There were no expectations from the people around her.

Deryn held out a guiding hand to Selen. Nys and Varric had already become lost in the crowd in front of them. The look on Deryn's face said that she, too, felt the excitement of anonymity. Selen looked down at her hand, monitoring every inch that passed as she did so. One more responsibility slipped away. One more expectation faded. One more potential outcome for the future fizzled. Selen's hand connected with Deryn's, and the rest of the world fell away. Selen made eye contact with her, and a moment passed where they just looked at each other. There was no conflict, no pain, no questions. If Selen was going to live today, then she was going to *live*. A corner of her mouth lifted, and in response Deryn's did the same.

An unspoken agreement passed between them; today they would live.

Deryn guided Selen through the people until they reached an opening in the crowd.

"Why is it so busy here?" Selen leaned in so Deryn could hear her over the crowd, and caught herself as the smell of leather and vanilla wrapped around her senses. She stayed near Deryn's neck, partly to hear her response, partly to stay close.

Deryn's head turned so that she, too, was close to Selen's neck. Selen felt her breath on her skin, and a burning ignited in her core.

"This town is always alive," she whispered in Selen's ear.

Selen tucked her chin and looked at Deryn. The sounds of the surrounding crowd fell away as their breath intermingled, and Selen couldn't help but look at Deryn's inviting lips, now in her direct line of sight. Her heartbeat quickened. There was nothing else in the world but the draw to lean in and taste...

"Are you hungry?" Deryn asked, pulling away from her and interrupting Selen's thoughts. Their surroundings rushed back, and Selen's eyes briefly widened as she looked toward the ground.

Get a grip, Dagny, she thought to herself.

She *really* had to get herself together when it came to this woman. Leveling her gaze back out, she looked at Deryn. There was a sparkle in her desert eyes, and Selen couldn't help the flutter in her stomach. This wasn't the overly serious leader of the trio. This wasn't the stoic member of a secret society that could potentially view her as a threat. This was a woman. Right now, they were nothing more than Selen and Deryn.

"I am." Selen smiled, and Deryn's smile dropped as she stared at her. Selen felt her smile slip as well. She angled her head at Deryn in question.

"I've not seen your smile," Deryn said, still staring at Selen's mouth.

"You've seen my smile," Selen said with an embarrassed giggle. A *giggle*? She wasn't sure why she had giggled. She *never* giggled. But of course, she giggled now. Her cheeks heated as Deryn's look persisted.

"Not like that, Bird." Deryn grinned as she met Selen's gaze. "Let's get some food," she said as she pulled Selen toward one of the many buildings in the square.

They burst through the doors of what seemed like a tavern, where music played in the corner. The wooden tables and dim lighting created a calm ambience that Selen appreciated, compared to the chaos outside. The energy was just as vibrant here, but the gentle sounds of the crowd calmed her mind.

"The food here is the best in town," Deryn said without looking back, and led Selen to a small booth in the back of the room. Deryn plopped down in the seat across from her and pulled one leg close to her chest, resting her head on her knee as she looked around the tavern. She seemed so at ease here, for whatever reason, and Selen had yet to see the side of her that was just a girl. Deryn's gaze slid to Selen's, and she grinned.

"Hi," she said with a smile.

Selen chuckled. "Hi." Selen watched her for another moment. "You seem so at ease here. I don't think I ever expected to see you so... happy?"

Deryn chuckled and put her leg back on the ground. "I don't often get an evening to relax. There are many responsibilities that I have to attend to. Right now is an exception."

"I suppose that's fair. But it's just... unexpected," Selen stated.

"You were a bit unexpected yourself, Bird." Deryn set her elbows on that table and leaned forward.

"What do you mean?" Selen was genuinely curious.

"You are one of two beings who exist uniquely in the world. You cater to your sister and those you care about with no regard for yourself. You watch the people you care about actively choose other people." Deryn gave a pointed look that had Selen looking down at the table. She had known Deryn had been watching her for a while—likely at Deandra's request—but she hadn't known how closely she'd been paying attention. "You actively worked to better yourself when something that was supposed to pass to you was taken before even in your possession." Deryn's gaze moved to the table, and her brow furrowed slightly. "I knew you were strong, that much was of no doubt. But I hadn't known to what extent. You have not lived enough to have dealt with the darkness life has provided you."

Selen was moderately taken aback. No one had ever credited her for that. They were just things that she... did. She protected Sidra. She dealt with Aleya's... whatever. And she adjusted to the punches life threw. That was the life she had lived since she was a child; it felt unnatural to be acknowledged for it now.

"That's just life, I suppose," Selen said, looking down. She didn't really want praise, and she didn't understand how those things made her 'unexpected'. "What had you expected me to be like?"

"Honest?" Deryn raised her eyebrows.

"Honest."

"I thought you'd be far more broken. I thought you'd be a shell molded to those around you," Deryn said warily.

"I see." Selen felt heat creep into her cheeks. Had that been how others perceived her? The thought drove a knife into her gut and twisted.

"But," Deryn reached for Selen's hand, and the connection broke Selen's spiral. "It did not take me long to see the truest side of you. The strength you have."

Selen looked up, Deryn's sincerity was clear in her eyes. While she appreciated what Deryn had said, she wanted to change the subject more than anything. "Why do you call me Bird?"

Deryn sat back with a grin and tilted her head, breaking the contact of their hands. She examined Selen with an intensity that made her feel slightly unsettled, but also ignited something in her that spiraled ever lower. That was a confusing phenomenon that she could address later.

"A bird, at first glance, seems fragile and breakable. A bird in a flock has the strength of others, but alone, they are often in danger. Unless, of course, they are a bird of prey. Complex creatures who look gentler than they truly are, but are dark—more powerful than they are given credit." Deryn's gaze heated. "And they are beautiful."

Selen's gaze widened as she quickly glanced away. A foe twice her size in the arena? No problem. A blatant compliment from a woman she had a crush on? She wanted to curl into a ball.

"Oh," was all Selen could gather from that.

"Oh?" Deryn laughed. "In truth, I had said it the first time I talked to you in that hallway without thinking, and it stuck."

Selen's gaze snapped to Deryn's. "So, you just made all that up?" She let out an exasperated laugh.

"Oh no, I've thought long and hard about why that has become your identifier in my mind."

Selen pursed her lips. That would mean that Deryn had thought about her. Often?

"*Hm,*" Selen said as she pushed back against the seat back.

"You want food, you come order it from the bar." A nasally voice cut through the tension as a barmaid approached with an armful of empty glasses, cutting through the tension that seemed to have developed between them.

"So we shall," Deryn stated, gaze unflinching from Selen's.

"So we shall," Selen repeated quietly.

Chapter Twenty-Seven

Deryn went to place their order, and Selen stared at the space where Deryn had been sitting. She was mildly confused at how the evening had progressed. Deryn had called her beautiful, which was unexpected. She had also said she thought Selen was strong. Both compliments were unanticipated, but she particularly hadn't expected them from Deryn.

When Deryn sat back down, their conversation turned far more casual than Selen ever thought she could have with anyone, let alone Deryn. She found out her favorite color was orange. She found out that Deryn had actually wanted to be a professor at her school in the East before she was recruited to the Nexis. Their food had come and gone, but they were still deeply enthralled in their conversation.

"So, tell me, Bird. Why did you never question the fact that your magic didn't manifest?" Deryn asked the question in a casual way, but Selen knew it was anything but.

Selen studied Deryn for a moment. There didn't seem to be any level of judgement. "That's a complex question."

"Well, we have time." Deryn angled her head, and Selen grinned.

"I suppose we do." She paused, pulling at a loose piece of wood on the table. "We had the party, as everyone does at Celestara. Sidra planned and made it into a whole event. She was always the more *socially* oriented sister. She... *uh*—when midnight hit, and our powers didn't show, Sidra's disappointment, frustration, anger—and a whole range of emotions—were about the only thing I had space to feel. It wasn't until several days later that I realized my own emotions weren't that of disappointment or anger, but of relief." She glanced up at Deryn, who watched her intently. "I had found out that I was BloodBound when we went to the Seer for our VeilBinding, and sat with that knowledge for six years, waiting for the day Sidra's powers manifested and I didn't have to hide mine. I hadn't realized that Deandra had placed a veil over our magic, putting a temporary hold on Sidra's manifestation. I thought that I had control, which was why there weren't any episodes after the VeilBinding."

The truth spilled out of Selen. She hadn't realized how much she had actually wanted to talk about all of this until her words continued to flow.

"I think I was just in denial. It didn't make any sense that our magic wouldn't come to the surface. Looking back now, I could feel it. Pressing against my skin. The tension was building and building. The veil lasted seven and a half years, but it shuddered that night. The night of our eighteenth birthday. I think having Sidra's and my powers pressing against it really just made it a ticking time bomb. And, *man*, was it a bomb." Selen let out a bitter laugh. "Sidra turned to studies to understand what could be holding our magic back, and I turned to fighting. I was relieved our magic hadn't manifested, but that awakened a whole new set of concerns. If we had no magic, then how the hell were we going to survive in a world of magic users? She was desperate to find a solution. So desperate, in fact, that she started hanging around dangerous people to see if it would ignite something. I suppose it worked." Selen's voice quieted. She didn't look up when Deryn's hand gently wrapped around hers, but she appreciated the touch. It grounded her just enough to work through the rest of her story.

"When I found Sidra... that night... with *him*—" Her stomach soured as the memory resurfaced. She audibly swallowed and continued.

"I felt the veil splintering, but it wasn't until I thought I was plummeting to my death that I truly let go. That was when the veil shattered. That was what got Sidra taken."

Selen's shame took on a physical shape as she curled her hands into fists. Deryn's grip around her hand tightened.

"You are not the reason your sister was taken." Deryn's voice was gentle.

Selen looked up at her, vision was blurred with tears that she hadn't realized were forming. Deryn reached up and wiped a tear from her cheek. It took every ounce of willpower in Selen to not turn from the intimate touch, and she felt a small weight lifting from her shoulders after making it through the entire story. No one had asked her how she felt after their eighteenth, aside from Aeden.

"I made it sad." Selen forced a laugh through her tears.

"You didn't make it sad, Bird. You answered my question." Deryn's brow furrowed, but was quickly replaced with a seemingly forced grin.

They sat in silence for a few moments. Selen was scouring the depths of her mind to find something, anything, they could talk about that could take her mind off that night.

"I'm sorry you had to experience that." Deryn spoke without looking at Selen. "I'm sorry you had to go through all of that alone."

"Which part?" Selen asked.

"All of it." Deryn was scowling as she looked up to Selen. Her eyes were filled with concern and... admiration? "You've faced more alone than most could handle with the support of others. It makes me sad for you."

Selen pushed back. Shame slammed into her like a wall. *Sad* for her? Her cheeks flushed, and she pulled her hands from Deryn's, crossing them around her midsection.

"I don't need your *pity*," Selen spat. Was that why she had done all of this? Pity for her situation? Frustration surged Selen, and her walls, which had slowly been lowering, slammed back into place. Coldness crept over her as she watched Deryn's stunned face.

"I don't pity you." She shook her head.

"Don't you?" Selen's voice was coated with resentment

that surprised even her. "Doesn't everyone? If they're not pitying me, they fear me because I'm unstable."

"Selen." Deryn wasn't trying to hide the hurt in her expression. It probably wasn't hurt. It was probably *pity*.

"Don't." Selen put a hand up and moved quickly from the booth, making her way to the exit. She briefly heard Deryn say her name again before darkness began swarming her vision.

She pushed out into the street, which was still bustling from the day. The overstimulation slammed into her like a tidal wave, and her breath caught as she tried and failed to gain control. Darkness clouded her vision as she pushed through the crowd. There were sounds of clear displeasure as she shoved some out of the way.

As much as I would love to see what you can do with your magic, now is not the time. Velros's voice was a welcome companion to the chaos within her mind.

Deryn thought she was weak. She pitied her. There were so many emotions taking over. Anger. Sadness. Anguish. She had felt a real connection with Deryn today. Had none of that been real? Had anything she'd felt been real?

A strangled sob left Selen.

Gods, girl. Get it together, Velros snapped.

I can't breathe. Selen tried to force breath through her lungs, but it felt like sandpaper in her throat. Her teeth tingled. *What's happening?*

Selen fell against the stone wall that surrounded the town. She wasn't sure when she had passed through the entirety of the crowd, but she welcomed the slight hum that came from the town without it being overwhelming. The darkness lessened in her vision as she rested against the wall, sucking deep breaths in through her nose before releasing them through her mouth.

You let your emotions control you. Velros's voice was softer now.

Selen sunk and placed her feet flat on the ground, letting her arms rest on her knees. Her head hung between her shoulders as she continued to breathe. With each breath in, she felt the control slowly coming back to her.

Clearly, Selen said after a moment. *Why don't you ever step in before I get to this point?*

Is it my responsibility to control your emotions? There was sass in Velros's voice.

With her emotions more under control, Selen felt a deep ache settle into her. While her reaction may have been a lot, the reason they had started... hurt. Deryn pitied her.

Do you think any of it was real? Selen asked. She was aware that she sounded desperate, but she didn't really care. She also knew that Velros already knew that those emotions existed in her.

I am Magic, girl. I do not have the slightest comprehension of human feelings, Velros said curtly.

Yeah. That was what Selen had expected, but she'd had to ask.

I will say, after centuries of existing within your bloodline, I've gained some understanding of the nature of human emotions. Based on my knowledge... you overreacted.

Selen's head shot up, a scowl washing over her expression.

I did not, Selen replied. Rude.

Surely, you did. You were ready to blow that town to pieces because the one you desire said she was sad for you.

You were listening? Selen was sure she looked absolutely insane as she did not try to hide her frustration as she argued with the voice in her head.

You have not secured your walls enough to not have some things slip through, especially when your emotions become larger than the wall.

I never asked for anyone to feel sorry for me.

I am aware. You also don't get to decide how other people feel.

Selen frowned. In what world had Velros become the voice of reason? In the moment, that had felt like the most logical reaction to the situation. Looking back, Selen thought through what was actually said and how she reacted. She supposed anyone else might also see that.

At what point did I become as unstable as my sister?

I imagine it was when you got thrown off a cliff.

Selen sat silently for a moment. The darkness had completely left her vision, and she watched a figure move through the grass in front of her. The sun had completely dropped behind the horizon, so the only light was the darkening blue it left behind. Selen stiffened until she realized who approached.

Deryn was panting as she stood before Selen.

"How the hell did you get out here so fast?" Deryn asked

breathlessly, putting her hands on her knees and dropped her head.

Selen frowned. She had walked—well, panic-shuffled—out here as anyone would.

Deryn plopped in front of her, startling Selen.

"Selen." Deryn's eyes bore into Selen, and her frown deepened. That was maybe the fourth time she'd heard Deryn refer to her as anything other than her nickname for her. She wasn't entirely sure she liked it. "I do not pity you. I only said I was sad for you because you've dealt with a lot. I only see strength in you." Her words were bordering on desperate.

After a moment, Selen spoke. "I know."

"You do?" Deryn sat back, clearly exasperated.

"I do." Selen looked down. She wasn't entirely sure how to put into words what she needed to say.

"Then... what... This?" Deryn's lack of words was slightly amusing.

"One thing I didn't mention when I told you my story was that before... what I now know to be the veil's work, Sidra and I's emotions were entirely interwoven. I always thought she was the reason everything felt so... volatile. Now? I think it was probably both of us. I've always felt like there were two people in my head battling for control. I always assumed one was Sidra, but she's gone, and there is still a battle."

"What do they fight about?" The question surprised Selen. She hadn't ever had anyone entertain the idea that she had another Being in her mind, which now took on an entirely separate reality, but Deryn didn't need to know that.

"One is chaos and volatile emotions, while the other is a voice of reason, of sorts. She tries to talk the other down when she gets too messy. Most of the time, she can shut things down internally, but sometimes the other one comes through. I don't like her much, but she's seemed to be in control this last week. The logical one is quiet." Selen hadn't admitted this to anyone before. Velros was a whole other conversation, but that wasn't what she was talking about right now. So the current count of Beings in her mind was... three. Not including herself.

"Where do you fit into that?" Deryn's voice was soft. She didn't try to reach for Selen, but the tension between them told her that she wanted to.

"I think I'm just a bystander who is directly impacted by their decisions." Selen let out a small laugh. This wasn't funny really, but she needed to ease the tension.

"Maybe you could ask them to let you in on what they're thinking?" Deryn chuckled. "Then you can relay that information to me?"

The weight on Selen's chest lifted slightly. "You don't think I'm nuts?"

"Well, I didn't say that." Deryn grabbed Selen's hand, breaking the lingering tension between them. "But at least if you're going to have bouts of insanity, I can be better prepared." She grinned, and it sparkled in her eyes.

Selen laughed and squeezed her hand around Deryn's.

Selen's grin faltered as she traced the lines of Deryn's

hand. "When did *this* happen?" Selen asked without looking up at Deryn.

"What? The scars?" Deryn asked, looking at the spot Selen's fingers traced.

"No," Selen chuckled. "This comfort. This... whatever. Between you and me."

"I'm not entirely sure, Bird. I've not thought about its origin as you're likely about to."

"Oh, I've been thinking about it for a while."

"I'm sure you have." Deryn scooted closer to Selen until their knees touched. "I have been curious about something, though."

"Okay." At this point Selen truly didn't have much to hide from Deryn.

Deryn hesitated and played with the leg of her pants. A nervous tick that she had never seen from someone so in control. "This... *Aleya*." Selen froze at the name. "Who is she to you?" Deryn's gaze met Selen's in caution.

"Aleya..." Selen rested her head back against the stone wall. "Aleya is someone who took up a lot of space in my mind, but I take up little in hers."

Deryn furrowed her brow and looked back to the ground. "Do you care for her?"

"I wanted something from her that she couldn't give me. I did care for her, but I've accepted that my place in her life would never be what I wanted, and I wasn't willing to wait around for her to change her mind."

"Interesting."

Chapter Twenty-Eight

Selen looked at Deryn. She wasn't sure what she was expecting to see, but the intensity of Deryn's stare ignited something within her. As Deryn's gaze shifted from Selen's eyes, Selen couldn't help but gently bite her lower lip, slowly releasing it through her teeth. Something flashed in Deryn's gaze, and she moved.

Deryn's mouth collided with Selen's and the world fell away and was replaced with swirling colors and sparks as Selen let Deryn in. They moved in tandem. Deryn's hands slid from either side of Selen's face and into her hair, pulling them closer. Selen grabbed Deryn's knees, pulling her on top, until Deryn was seated on her lap, legs straddling her. Their kiss deepened, and Selen felt a fire burning inside, slowly moving down her spine until it reached her core. She wrapped her arms around Deryn's hips as Deryn's hands continued to roam through her hair. Selen didn't have time to second-guess what they were doing. She didn't want to. A small groan slipped from Deryn's lips, and it made Selen's blood boil.

Selen's hands roamed Deryn's back as their mouths moved together, finding their home with one on Deryn's hip and the other at the nape of her neck. Selen pulled Deryn's head back just enough to move to her neck, and grazed her teeth along her jaw and down to her throat. Selen planted kisses wherever she went, gently nipping at Deryn's pulse and turning her breathing into pants that made Selen's core weep for her. She traced every line and scar on Deryn's exposed neck with her tongue.

Deryn's hand gripped the back of Selen's head by her braid and pulled her back, severing the connection of Selen's lips from her skin. Selen's grin was feral as she looked up at Deryn, who had Selen's head pulled back enough that Selen had to look down her nose at her.

Deryn leaned close to Selen's ear, and her heavy breathing became the only sound Selen ever wanted to hear again. "Shall we live, Bird?" she whispered, grazing her teeth against Selen's ear.

A different kind of darkness consumed Selen, one that she wasn't afraid to give into. She let out a low growl and pushed off the wall, startling Deryn enough that her eyes widened. Selen cushioned Deryn's back with her arm as she settled herself on top, and Deryn's legs were wrapped around Selen. Nothing felt more natural than having their bodies intertwined.

Selen ran the back of her index finger along the scars on Deryn's cheek. She admired the power this woman had; it showed in every movement. Every scar. She truly did want to live. She wanted to forget the rest of the world and exist solely for this moment. She wanted to worship her. *Taste* her. Her lips *did* taste like she smelled—leather and vanilla. She had every intention of tasting the other parts of her to see if they, too, tasted of that all-consuming scent that plagued her.

Selen lifted her gaze to Deryn's, and the hunger in them drove Selen insane. They stilled for a moment, staring into one another's eyes, as if looking for an answer to a question that neither knew how to put into words.

Selen gripped the side of Deryn's face and brought their lips together again, and Selen could've sworn that actual sparks ignited at their connection. Deryn smiled against her lips, and Selen's entire stomach flipped.

"I suppose that's a yes," she said breathlessly.

Selen pressed her forehead to Deryn's and nodded. She didn't open her eyes. She needed to feel everything—keeping her eyes closed meant she could focus more on other sensations.

Selen briefly opened her eyes and was met by Deryn's mischievous grin. Selen angled her head in a question, which was quickly answered when Deryn shifted her weight and pushed one side of her hips up into Selen, sending them to the side. Selen landed on her back with a grunt as Deryn now straddled her once more.

Selen laughed and looked up at Deryn, whose eyes were ablaze as she leaned over Selen. Her loose, dark hair fell in front of her eyes as she kissed Selen deeply. This felt far more controlled and intentional. Their kisses grew languid, explorative, a quiet declaration of their curiosity and desire for each other. It was a different kind of intensity that made Selen squirm.

Selen pushed to try and get Deryn on her back again, but was quickly halted by the cold press of metal against her neck. Selen grinned and raised her hands away from Deryn's body. Deryn was still close to Selen, but the hand that had been roaming Selen's body now held the dagger from her thigh.

"Try to move me, Bird, and you will bleed for me," Deryn whispered in her ear, breath fanning across Selen's skin, leaving bumps in its wake. Dear *gods*, that was hot. Why? She was unsure. But she wasn't about to question it.

Selen kept her arms raised as Deryn leaned back, tracing the blade down from Selen's neck, between her breasts, and even lower. Selen's breath caught as she watched Deryn, who was entirely enthralled by watching the blade move down Selen's body.

"You two about finished?" Both heads snapped up to find Varric waiting with his arms crossed. "You are aware that there are children in this town that could have wandered upon this entirely indecent scene?"

It was as though a bucket of freezing water had been dumped on the heat that had consumed Selen. Deryn laughed and stood, and while Selen glared at her for laughing, she took the arm offered to her. They dusted off the dirt and grass that had made its way onto their clothes from their... entanglement.

"Nys and I found an inn that has rooms available. Two to be exact. We were a bit concerned because both only have one bed"—he glanced between the pair of them, amusement glittering his eyes—"but I see that won't really be an issue."

The inn seemed to be on the quiet side of town, as the people still swarmed the area they had originally entered the town. Deryn didn't seem at all ashamed of how they were discovered, and Varric didn't seem to be holding it against them, so, as mortifying as it had been for Selen, she was going to let it go and pretend she didn't want to throw herself face-first into the nearest wall.

The building was a bit rundown, but the energy in the inn was calm and relaxing. A small pub acted as the main entrance to the building, and a stairwell in the far left corner led to their rooms upstairs. There were only a few patrons here—a group of clearly intoxicated townspeople at the bar, and a couple in one of the booths along the wall. Nys had been waiting for everyone while leaning against the bar, scowling at the drunken townspeople.

"What have those poor men done to earn that look?" Varric asked, leaning into Nys.

"They stink." Nys's lip curled back over her lip.

Selen couldn't help but laugh. Nys was a terrifying and small human who had no problem standing up to people two to three times her size. She also had a deeply rooted disdain for humans that Selen couldn't help but find comical.

Nys looked Selen up and down with the same disgust she'd regarded the men with. "*You* stink," she said to Selen.

"*Annnnnd* with that, we are off to bed." Varric wrapped his arm around Nys's shoulders and guided her to the stairs. "This one gets a bit feisty when she's had a few."

Nys threw an elbow into Varric's stomach, and he let out a strained laugh, glancing back at them with a grin.

"Only when she's had a few?" Selen laughed.

Deryn smiled and took up a seat at the bar. "Drink?" she asked, looking back at Selen.

"After that cold plunge? I need something to warm my system back up," Selen said, sitting on the stool next to Deryn.

"Well, we could just skip the drink and go straight to the bedroom, which I imagine will warm you right up." She grinned, and Selen choked on... air? Coughing, Selen tried to regain her composure as heat crept into her cheeks.

Deryn chuckled and waved down the barkeep. He was an older man with a scraggly beard and slicked-back hair. The lines around his eyes indicated a life full of smiles and laughter. His clothes were worn, but not disheveled. A smile crept across his face as he approached, confirming that the lines on his face were from just that.

"I haven't seen *you* here in ages," he said, placing both hands on the bar. Selen looked over at Deryn, and the smile that she wore was equally as warm as his.

"I don't find myself here much anymore, Devril." His smile deepened at the mention of his name.

"Callyn will want to see you," he said, turning away, as if to grab someone. He swiftly turned back and raised a hand. "Drinks?"

"Two, please," Deryn said affectionately.

Devril nodded and turned back to the bar, where he seemed to turn in place about three times before he finally decided what he was going to do.

"Devril and his partner Callyn have offered us housing many times when we've come through here." Deryn leaned toward Selen, speaking quietly. "The townspeople aren't as... accepting of them as the rest of the world might be."

Selen's head snapped to Deryn. Not accepting of them? What could possibly lead these two to not be accepted? Because they were two men together? That wasn't out of the ordinary. In fact, it was extremely ordinary.

Deryn continued. "It's not often that a magic wielder ends up with one who has none, especially this close to the MistralWood."

Oh. Outrage averted. Kind of. While the concept of same sex relationships was normal, the idea that people treated them differently because of one's lack of magic, was an entirely separate outrage.

"Why would anyone ostracize them for being a mixed couple?"

"The MistralWood calls to those who wield the magic of the Lirium. Those who do not are viewed as taking up space in places of magic." Deryn looked over to where Devril had poured one of our drinks and gotten distracted by something that kept him from pouring the other. That distraction came in the form of another older man in a white apron with dark hair, streaked with grey. He, too, bore the lines of someone who had lived a joyful life. Devril and Callyn embraced, and Callyn pulled back and brushed his thumb over Devril's cheek. Love radiated from them. Selen couldn't help but smile.

How could something so pure be looked down upon?

"Which has magic and which does not?" Selen asked, still watching the couple.

"Does it matter?" Deryn watched them too.

"I suppose not."

As if remembering that other people existed, Devril jumped and pulled Callyn's arm toward Deryn. Callyn chuckled and followed more than willingly, eyes lighting up when he saw Deryn.

"Well hell, Deryn, I thought you might never come back to grace us with your presence." Callyn's deep voice held nothing but affection.

"I haven't needed to come this way in some time," Deryn grasped his forearm and matched Callyn's warm smile. "I wasn't sure if you two were still running this place."

"I can't let this old gal go any more than I could keep Dev's focus on one thing at a time," Callyn laughed, and they all turned to see a tap overflowing into an already full glass, where Devril had turned to chat with the group at the bar. Callyn chuckled and moved to close the line before patting Devril on the shoulder. Devril—or Dev, as Callyn had called him—turned and grabbed the glass as if he hadn't wasted an entire pint's worth of ale from overflow. Callyn made his way back over to Selen and Deryn.

"So, what's new, Dery? Other than your new friend." Callyn leaned over the bar and stuck out his hand. "Sorry for the delayed introduction, Dery here has never been much for manners."

Selen smiled at the man and took his hand. The nickname for Deryn was a hilarious tidbit that she would have to circle back to later. "My name is Selen."

Callyn gave her an inquisitive look before returning to the bright smile he naturally wore.

"Hello, Selen. How do you know each other?" He leaned back against the bar along the wall and crossed his arms over his chest.

"We're... friends?" Selen said, almost flinching as she spoke.

Callyn let out a booming laugh that made everyone in the room turn their heads towards them. He didn't seem to care much about their shift in attention. "Deryn's had lots of 'friends,'" he said with air quotations. "But none she's brought to meet us."

Selen felt her cheeks heat. Deryn glanced sideways at Selen and then back to Callyn. "This is not a formal introduction, Cal. Yours was the only place in town that had rooms," she laughed.

Callyn dramatically put a hand on his chest. "We weren't your first choice?"

"I didn't get a choice at all. The small, angry blonde one

makes those decisions—but I would have come to say hello anyway." Deryn wasn't smiling anymore, but her eyes still held warmth for the man.

"You better of, or Dev would've taken it personally."

"Just Dev?" Deryn grinned.

"Yep! Just Dev. You know, he's the more emotional of us. Gets his feelings hurt when family doesn't visit."

Deryn laughed and looked down at the bar. Selen side-eyed Deryn. *Was* this her family? Why hadn't they stopped here immediately, and why hadn't that even been brought up? Was she really meeting Deryn's family after having just done what they did? She'd never met anyone's family—well, none of the people she'd been with. She hadn't even met her own family. Not that there were any to meet... But, she hadn't really been with anyone in a capacity where she would meet families. Was this that? *No.* They showed up here by chance. It wasn't Deryn's choice. She had said as much. This meant nothing special.

"It was wonderful meeting you, Selen, but I need to get back to the kitchen." Callyn's deep voice pulled Selen from her thoughts. "Enjoy your drinks!"

"Yeah, you too." Selen waved. "I mean, not 'enjoy your drink,' because you're not drinking right now. Not that it would be an issue if you were. But if you do have a drink, you should enjoy that... probably—" Someone needed to stop her.

"Have a good night, Cal." Deryn interrupted, putting her hand over Selen's still waving hand and gently pushing it down to the bar top.

Horrifying. That had been *horrifying*.

Deryn slowly turned her upper body toward Selen with wide eyes. "Interesting time to forget how to interact with humans."

"Did I just meet your family?" Selen stared at Deryn equally as wide-eyed.

Deryn's gaze softened and immediately formed into a smile. Her head went back and she laughed. Loudly. This, again, pulled the attention of the people in the pub. "Oh, *gods*. I didn't even catch that." She was having a hard time getting the words out between bouts of laughter. Selen felt a burn in her cheeks that settled and likely wouldn't be going anywhere anytime soon. "Is that why you forgot how to speak?"

"Well, yeah. We made out once. I'm not ready to meet your family." Selen let out a small yet awkward laugh. Deryn reached for her stomach, tears leaking from the corners of her eyes.

Selen stared at the bar, trying to figure out how to navigate this particularly excruciating moment. In hopes that she wouldn't further dig her own grave, she stayed quiet.

Deryn finally caught her breath and leaned against the bar. "They aren't my family by blood." She breathed in. "They were my first shelter and job when I came over from across the sea. They took me in and cared for me." She still had a smile on her face when she plopped her head down on her folded arms in front of her. "Your panic is adorable."

"Glad you find my humiliation endearing." Selen looked

down at her hands. "How did you end up here? This isn't the first town nearest to the sea."

"I came here for the same reason many do. Purpose." She sat back up and fully turned to Selen. "I sought the MistralWood."

"What did you think you'd find here?"

"I wasn't sure. Anything was better than where I came from—and it called to me."

Selen glanced over at Deryn, who still watched her without humor, curious about the horrible life she'd left that could make the unknown of the MistralWood appealing.

"So, you weren't brought here for Nexis?" Selen asked. She had assumed that she, like Varric, had been recruited in school.

"No. I was not brought here by Nexis. I came of my own free will."

Selen furrowed her brow. Of her own free will. That's an interesting way to describe a society that supposedly gives its members the option to join. She tucked that into the back of her mind, not wanting to press so hard that Deryn shut down.

"Why did you leave your home in the East?"

"Didn't have any reason to stay."

Selen could feel Deryn's walls slowly closing, so she stopped asking. While they had broken through one barrier today, many still stood between them.

Chapter Twenty-Nine

The room was quaint, with just enough space for a bed and a window as the sloped ceiling cut through half of the room. There was a small bathing chamber adjacent to the entrance—nothing special, but it had plenty of space to suit their needs. Aside from the bed, that is, which was just big enough for Selen and Deryn to lie shoulder to shoulder, *maybe*. Selen eyed the bed as Deryn sat and removed her boots.

"Do you often share quarters with Nys and Varric?" Selen asked as she looked around the rest of the space. She couldn't imagine three people comfortably staying here.

"Typically, I have my own quarters. Nys and Varric tend to share space," she said, and slid off her other boot, ripping the socks off both feet. She leaned back on her hands and wiggled her toes on the floor.

"Clearly," Selen stated, looking down at her now exposed feet.

"Do my feet bother you, Bird?" The humor in her voice was apparent.

"I just don't often see people's toes." Most of Selen's interactions included shoes. There was something weirdly vulnerable about having exposed feet. It made the reality of them sharing a bed settle in a bit more than Selen had previously processed.

"Well, alright," Deryn said and stood, heading towards the bathing chamber.

And now Selen was thinking of her bathing.

Sleep may not come easily tonight.

Once the door closed, Selen flopped onto the bed. She ran her hands over her face and stared at the ceiling. She was sharing a bed with Deryn. The woman she had just had a *moment* with in a field. After having a breakdown that her inner self had needed to talk her down from. Where she then proceeded to meet people that *same woman* considered family, proceeding then to make an absolute fool of herself in front of said family.

Selen put her hands back on her face and groaned. Gods. When did she get so embarrassing?

Selen sat up and began removing her boots. She didn't have much for sleeping clothes, as she hadn't entirely expected to be sleeping in a bed on this trip, nor did she expect to share that bed with anyone. She untucked her shirt and let it flow down. She had some undershorts and a long tunic that would have to work for tonight.

She'd just begun undoing her braid as the bathing chamber door clicked, indicating that it was opening.

Deryn stepped out in just her pants and a wrap around her breasts. A towel was partly draped around her shoulder and partly in her hand as she dried her dark hair. There were still water droplets on her shoulders, and her pants were partly unbuttoned. Her skin was a deep tan that Selen rarely saw in this part of the world. The silver marks on her body weren't the only indication of her lifestyle—she was incredibly fit as well. Muscles lined her abdomen, and the definition in her arms was apparent as she reached the towel to her hair once more. Deryn noticed Selen's gaze and grinned.

Selen felt her face warm as she tried to remain focused on her task, looking away from Deryn. Once Selen finally got all of her hair out of the braid, she began running her fingers along her scalp. There was nothing quite like the feeling of giving her hair freedom after it had been trapped in a braid for days, even if it had been loosened by their previous encounter. She closed her eyes for a brief moment and opened them to a stare from Deryn that would likely get them in trouble. She had stopped drying her hair, but still held the towel against her head. Selen dropped her hands and looked back.

"What?" Selen was warm from head to toe now. In part due to her ongoing embarrassment, in part due to some other emotions that typically controlled a location much lower than her face.

"You're fucking stunning, Bird." She dropped the towel onto her shoulder and leaned against the doorframe to the bathing chamber.

"I stink, according to Nys." *Okay*. That was a way to respond to a compliment.

Deryn tilted her head, amusement glittering in her eyes. "There is a way to remedy that." She grinned, gesturing to the bathing chamber. "For Nys's sake, of course."

"For Nys." Selen stood and began making her way toward the bathing chamber. "Okay. Yep," she said as she slipped by Deryn, who still took up part of the doorway. It was seemingly intentional, and Selen was in enough of an awkward headspace that she squeezed by, pushing herself as far as she could to the opposite side of the door frame. She felt Deryn's gaze on her as she quickly slid the door shut, and took a deep breath before leaning her head against the wood.

There was a decent-sized tub on one side of the room, with a designated spot to relieve oneself on the other. There was fresh water in the tub, and Selen tilted her head as she looked at it. Deryn had clearly bathed. Had she replaced the water for her before coming out? That was kind.

Selen slipped out of her clothes and gently lowered herself into the water. Every sore muscle and bruise that had developed over the last few days both stung and eased in the steam. She took a deep breath when she finally settled; she hadn't realized how much she needed this. She knew she had likely smelled, as Nys had claimed—especially as there hadn't been many opportunities to bathe in the woods, and her body immediately relaxed.

Exhaustion coursed through her as she leaned her head against the back of the tub, and Selen knew she wouldn't last long if she stayed in there too long, so she made quick work of washing herself and her hair. Sufficiently un-smelly, she leaned her head back again, soaking in the last moments she would get to enjoy this, the lavender soap wafting her senses.

She hoped she hadn't made too much of a fool of herself in front of Callyn. While it may not particularly matter now, perhaps it would later. She also hoped that she hadn't embarrassed Deryn too much today. Did she regret what happened between them? Would something like that happen again? Selen hoped so. Selen had been so confident in that moment, and recalling the following was like watching as someone else controlled her body and made her do and say stupid things in horror. It had not been her ideal aftercare to the moment they'd shared.

She wasn't aware she had fallen asleep until a gentle shake of her arm rattled her awake. Selen snapped up, looking around in every direction. She was in water. The pool in the Seer's lair? No. It smelled like lavender. The water was warm. Had she slept here all night? Selen grabbed the edge of the tub and sat fully up. She looked to the side and did a double-take, realizing that Deryn was crouched beside the tub.

Deryn was beside the tub. That she sat in. Nude.

Completely nude.

Selen looked down at her exposed breasts and back at Deryn, who wore a surprised yet amused look on her face.

Selen groaned, quickly dropping into the water so it rose up to her neck.

"The water is clear," Deryn said, angling her head.

"Gods!" Selen shot up and grabbed her towel, covering

herself as much as she could. Heat rose back up in her cheeks.

"How long have I been in here?" Selen asked as she tried and mostly failed to cover her entire body with the small towel.

"About thirty minutes. Had to make sure you hadn't drowned," Deryn said nonchalantly.

"I didn't drown," Selen said defensively.

"Clearly." Deryn looked Selen up and down.

"Okay. I'm getting dressed," Selen said, attempting to get out of the tub, but her foot caught on the edge and she tumbled forward, falling directly onto Deryn, who laughed as she caught her. She had lifted her hands to catch herself, leaving the towel free will as to how it covered her body— which evidently left her entire backside exposed to the elements.

"You're a bit of a mess, Bird." Deryn grinned, looking over Selen's shoulder to where her ass was sufficiently exposed. "I'm not entirely upset about it, I'll admit."

Selen muttered incoherently to herself as she rolled off Deryn and did her best to keep the towel around her as she stood. She quickly made her way back into the main room and put her tunic over her head, not at all worried about her soaking hair that left wet spots on it almost immediately. The tunic covered enough that she didn't immediately put on the sleeping shorts and moved to dry her hair a bit before it ruined her only extra shirt.

Deryn moved silently behind her and sat on the bed. Selen was almost annoyed by how relaxed she seemed when

Selen had been a ball of embarrassment for the last several hours.

"What flusters you, Bird?" Her voice was soft, languid.

Selen paused, trying to think of what to say. Clearly, words had not been her friend today, so she decided on the truth. "*You*," she said. "You fluster me."

"I'm honored." Deryn chuckled.

Selen took a deep breath and looked out of the window and into the night. The energy buzzed from the Mistral-Wood. Did it make them act differently? Perhaps. But she didn't want to make a fool of herself, however *adorable* it made her to Deryn. Earlier in the day, she had decided that she would live in the moment with Deryn. She was sharing a bed with her tonight, and she knew exactly where she wanted it to lead.

She closed her eyes again, breathing in through her nose and out through her mouth. She was nervous, but this was something she knew how to do. Something she *wanted* to do. With everything else in chaos, she could control this. She could *have* this.

Selen turned towards Deryn. The shift in her demeanor must have been noticeable, because Deryn's gaze shifted from amused to curious and then immediately to under-standing as she sat on the edge of the bed.

Selen moved until she kneeled in front of Deryn. Neither broke eye contact. "We have unfinished business," Selen said. Her voice was hoarse.

"That we do." Deryn reached up and stroked her thumb along Selen's cheek, and heat immediately pooled in her core. Everything else fell away as she stared up at Deryn's desert eyes. There was a story in them that she intended to learn, one moment at a time.

The weight of everything they'd soon endure hung between them, but Selen put her hands on Deryn's knees and leaned up into her. Deryn's breath caught as Selen stopped just before their lips connected.

"I don't know what waits for us tomorrow," Selen said, closing her eyes as she relished in the feeling of Deryn's breath against her skin. "At this moment, I don't really care." Selen slowly moved her hands from Deryn's knee, running them up the side of her body until they cupped behind Deryn's neck. Deryn's breath quickened in those brief moments. "I do know that I want this. That I want you." Selen opened her eyes and found that Deryn was as lost in their connection as she was. Her eyes were closed, and her features softened.

"Do *you* want this? Do you want me?" Selen whispered after a beat. She didn't need Deryn to tell her that they had a future. She didn't need her to confirm whether they'd ever even speak after this. She just needed to know that she wanted this as much as Selen did at that moment.

Deryn's eyelids flicked open, blazing with unsheathed desire. "More than you know, Bird."

Selen surged forward, lips capturing Deryn's with a force that spoke of desperation, of hunger, of all the words she couldn't say—the feelings she couldn't share. The brief moment they'd shared, that had left them both needing more, finally came undone. Selen gasped against her mouth but didn't hesitate, hands tangling in Deryn's short hair. Unlike their moment earlier, this one seemed far more intentional. Far more intense. There was no humor to be found as they explored one another.

The kiss deepened, becoming a tangle of breaths and moans. Selen's hands slid to Deryn's waist, pulling her closer as if afraid she might vanish. Deryn pressed against her, warmth chasing away the sorrow that lingered in Selen, quieting her inner demons.

When they parted, gasping for air, Selen cupped Deryn's face in her hands. "Look at me," she said. Her hands were trembling, but her voice was firm.

Deryn obeyed, her chest heaving as eyes shimmered with a fire that burned deep below the surface. Selen wasn't sure why, but she needed to memorize the lines of Deryn's face. She needed to allow this moment to wash over her entirely. Deryn leaned forward, this time slower, softer, as if she too was memorizing every curve of Selen's lips.

Deryn cupped the back of Selen's neck and quickly swapped their positions. She hoisted Selen up onto the bed, removing her top. Deryn kneeled before Selen and stopped only to fully examine every inch of Selen's now naked body. Her hands trailed down every curve, watching every spot that her fingers touched. The act was intense. Selen said nothing as she watched Deryn admire her. As they sank back onto the bed, Selen's fingers trailed over the ridges of Deryn's scars, tracing the history of her pain, her perseverance. And when Deryn's hands continued to roam her body, it wasn't with the urgency of before; it was like she was touching something sacred.

When their bodies pressed together, the world outside ceased to exist. There was only the warmth of their skin, the rhythm of their breaths, and soft gasps that filled the room. Deryn buried her face in Selen's neck, her lips tracing a path of quiet devotion, while Selen arched against her, fingers gripping her shoulders as if she could anchor herself to this moment.

Selen's breath caught as Deryn's mouth moved down her body. The anticipation of where it might lead left Selen aching. Her body needed this. It *craved* this. Every sweep of her tongue felt like an awakening Selen wasn't aware she'd been missing.

She watched as Deryn made her way down her body, stopping only to worship her peaked breasts. Her nipples pleaded for the friction of Deryn's touch. Once supplied, Selen felt her mind blur. A slow moan escaped Selen's mouth as Deryn's closed around her. Selen arched into her, and the desire for Deryn's mouth to close around another part of her erupted into a flame she alone couldn't extinguish. The ache in her core was almost too much to bear.

She needed Deryn there. Deryn kept her mouth on Selen's nipples as she slid a hand from Selen's stomach down to her aching clit. Deryn swirled her finger once before letting out a low moan that Selen felt in her core.

"You're so fucking wet for me, Bird." Deryn's voice sent shivers down Selen's spine. Her only response was a groan, which she hoped conveyed to Deryn that she needed to feel her. She needed everything she could give her.

Selen gasped when Deryn gently pressed one finger inside of her. The pressure ignited her soul. She felt every thrust of Deryn's finger and begged for more. Selen rocked her hips into Deryn's hand, needing more pressure, more friction.

"Tell me what you need, Bird." Deryn's words were breathless, and her teeth grazed her very sensitive nipple before moving lower.

"I need you. All of you." Selen whispered. She wasn't exactly sure what that meant, but she hoped that Deryn knew. Selen could feel Deryn's grin against her skin as she worked lower and lower down her stomach.

Deryn stilled over where Selen needed her touch. It throbbed for Deryn as her breath caressed every crevice of Selen. Every breath teased her. She clenched around nothing as Deryn removed her finger, leaving Selen bare and wanting.

"Deryn," Selen whimpered. Deryn stilled.

Her voice was low. "Say that again."

"Deryn," Selen obeyed, and Deryn's answering two fingers sliding inside her, causing Selen's breath to catch and her eyes to roll back. Deryn toyed with Selen's clit with her thumb, bringing Selen closer and closer to the brink of exploding.

Selen opened her eyes and found Deryn's desert eyes watching her with a feral hunger that brought the edge nearer. As she continued to move her fingers in and out at a pace that made Selen's toes curl, Deryn kissed her stomach, thighs, and every inch of skin she could reach from her position. Selen had never felt so... worshipped.

Finally, Deryn moved her mouth over Selen's swollen clit and gave one swipe of her tongue. Selen cried out at the sensation, and Deryn chuckled against her sensitive flesh. She closed her mouth fully around Selen and moved her tongue in ways that Selen didn't even know were possible.

Deryn spoke barely above a whisper, "You taste so fucking good." Selen felt every vibration of her voice against her flesh in excruciating detail. "Look at me, Bird."

Deryn's demand left no room for argument—not that Selen would, anyway. She looked down, and Deryn's face was half-hidden as she feasted on Selen. The image was wholly erotic and almost too much to handle.

Deryn wrapped her arm around Selen's leg and pressed down on her lower stomach, continuing to move her tongue in stunning and intentional patterns that pushed and pulled at Selen's sanity.

Deryn quickened the pace of both her tongue and her fingers, and the pressure that had been building in Selen's spine finally crested, sending her crashing into an entirely mind-blowing climax. Her body shuddered and jerked as she screamed Deryn's name. There was no other thought in the world other than pure bliss and the taste of Deryn's name on her lips.

Selen came down, panting and twitching from the overwhelming sensations that had rocked through her, and whimpered when Deryn slowly removed her fingers. Selen leaned up on her elbows and watched Deryn. Deryn tilted her head in Selen's direction, though remained kneeling before her. Then, she slowly brought those fingers that had just been inside Selen to her mouth and licked them clean.

"So fucking sweet."

Selen watched in shock and fascination as Deryn finished tasting what was left of her on her fingers.

Fucking *gods*, that was hot.

Deryn crawled on top of her. At some point, she had removed her pants and was now bare from the waist down. The wrap around her breasts was the only covered part of her. Selen's mouth watered with the desire to taste her as Deryn pushed one of Selen's legs back with her knee until it was held straight in the air. She then grabbed it and trailed her tongue down the length of her leg, leaving bumps in her wake. Deryn grabbed the back of Selen's knee and pushed her back slightly, until her core was entirely exposed. Selen didn't object to anything. Deryn could quite literally do anything in this moment, and Selen would likely go along with it.

Deryn watched Selen closely as she brought her other leg over the top of Selen's other side. Selen got to see almost all of her at this angle, and she begged for more.

"Please, Deryn," Selen begged for her. The anticipation of whatever was about to happen was unbearable.

Deryn grinned and nipped at Selen's calf, slowly lowering herself. Selen gasped at what she was about to do.

This was something she had not done with Aleya.

As soon as Deryn's swollen and wet flesh connected with Selen's, Selen felt all of her senses ignite. The low whimper that came from Deryn indicated that she, too, felt the intensity of that connection. They sat like that for a moment before Deryn moved. She ground herself against Selen, and the sensation of their most sensitive areas rubbing together drove Selen quickly back to that edge.

Selen gripped Deryn's hip, silently pleading for more, and Deryn dropped Selen's leg, leaning forward until she could grip the back of Selen's head. She gently pulled her hair, just enough that she could control Selen's movements, but not cause her pain. She brought their mouths together as they moved. Pulling back slightly, Deryn pressed her forehead against Selen's. Their breaths mingled as both Deryn and Selen came closer and closer to unraveling.

Selen broke first, the friction becoming too much. She bucked against Deryn's steadily grinding body, which seemed to push Deryn over the edge. Her pace quickened, then quickly turned to a stutter until her accompanying moans and gasps mirrored Selen's.

They stayed pressed together for a moment before Deryn gently disentangled herself from Selen. Both seemed to shudder at the removal of the connection.

Deryn leaned over and brushed a strand of raven hair from Selen's face and smiled—a small, rare thing that lit up her features: a true smile. Selen had seen very few of those, and her heart warmed.

Deryn plopped down on the bed next to Selen. Both lay silent, still breathless from their release, until Selen felt Deryn shift on the bed beside. She looked over to find Deryn propped up on her elbow, watching Selen.

"So, that's something I'm definitely doing again," she said with a mischievous grin.

Selen stared at her for a moment. "Right now?" she asked. Selen didn't have the energy for another round, although the idea of it made her exhausted clit throb.

Deryn rolled onto her back and laughed. "No. Not right now. But again."

A small amount of relief overwhelmed Selen, accompanied by a hint of disappointment. "I suppose we could make that happen," Selen said, still breathless. "We just have to survive the MistralWood."

"Even more incentive." Deryn chuckled.

"...Than living?" Selen laughed.

"Yes." Deryn nodded adamantly.

Chapter Thirty

elen? A familiar voice roused Selen.

Selen, are you here? She knew that voice better than she knew her own. Selen shot up. But she wasn't in the bed at the Inn; she was on the cliff. Darkness swirled around her as she took in her surroundings. This was her mind. This was the place where she had last met with Velros.

Selen! The voice was louder now, and Selen spun around to find an all too familiar face. Icy eyes met hers as silver hair swirled around her.

Sidra? Selen couldn't believe what she was seeing. Was this a dream?

Yeah, you fucking goob. Who else would it be?

Selen frowned. Yep. Definitely Sidra.

Is this a dream? Selen asked as she took in her sister who stood within arm's reach.

No. It's not a dream. I'm in your head, she said, twirling her pale skirts in the wisps around her. *This is kind of weird, isn't it?*

Are you okay? Are you hurt? Selen reached for—and actually touched—her. She grabbed her forearms and held them, examining every inch for injuries. Relief flooded through Selen in waves as she took her in. There were no marks. There weren't even bruises along her wrists and neck anymore.

Sidra scoffed and shook off Selen's touch. *Of course, I'm okay. No kidnapper could truly hurt me,* Sidra said with far more confidence than anyone who'd been kidnapped should have.

Selen watched Sidra with wide eyes. The last time she'd seen her... the bruises...

Sidra's eyes softened. *I'm okay. I fucking hate Xander and will happily fillet him when we get home, but I'm okay.*

Sid, he—. Selen breathed, trying to find the right words. *He hurt you. I found you. I thought I'd lost you.*

Sidra sighed and grabbed for Selen's hands. *And I watched you get thrown off a cliff. It was a* really *fucked up day.*

How are you so okay after what happened? Selen didn't understand many things about this moment. How was Sidra in her mind? How was she handling everything so well?

I've found a renewed sense of self-empowerment, Sidra stated.

While kidnapped? Selen raised an eyebrow.

Actually, yeah. She hasn't hurt me. She's kind of just left me alone, and I've learned a lot about my powers. Sidra grinned and brought her eyes to meet Selen's. *We have magic!* She nearly squealed.

Selen swallowed, but felt her heart lighten. Sidra was... Sidra. Not a broken shell. Not in any obvious pain.

Who took you, Sid? Selen didn't know how long they'd have, and she needed answers.

Sidra was silent for a moment. *I don't know her name,* Sidra stated with an airy voice, gripping the sides of her skirts as she used them to swirl the shadows that twirled around her feet. *She has shadow magic, though. Kind of like yours used to be.*

What? Selen snapped her head up to Sidra's face, who was oblivious to the shock on Selen's.

Your shadow magic. Hers is like yours, Sidra stated again.

How do you know anything about my magic? You were gone by the time it showed itself. Selen examined her more closely.

Sidra stopped twirling and tilted her head at Selen. Something felt... *off* about her. *You had it long before you shattered the veil.*

Selen glared at her. She wouldn't know that—she wouldn't know about the veil. *How do you know any of this?*

Sidra pursed her lips and began twirling again. *She knows much.*

Who is she? Selen pushed.

I don't know her name, Sidra said again, grinning as she spun. *It's peaceful here. I might stay for a while.*

Sidra's voice had grown distant, and she seemed in a daze. Selen watched, unease settling in her stomach.

Sidra stopped spinning. She faced away from Selen, towards the woods. *You're not alone in here,* she stated. The lightness of her voice was gone. Tension coated the air. Sidra slowly looked over her shoulder.

Selen's stomach dropped as her sister's face shifted and contorted. It moved between the bruised and swollen eyes of when Selen had found her on the cliffside—her normal face, a horrifying grin, and an unnaturally downturned frown. She slowly turned toward Selen, and started moving toward her.

Selen stumbled back. She didn't know what to do. Sidra's flesh started to droop and seemingly melt from her bones as she stumbled, then crawled, toward Selen. Low moans of agony escaped her, and Selen screamed as the Being that had been her sister reached for her with bony, wrecked fingers. For a brief moment Sidra's face was entirely her own.

Temple.

That was the only word she spoke before the Being's form contorted. Long teeth seemed to form in the melting flesh. Selen stumbled and fell onto her back, and she scrambled until she felt the edge of the cliff. Her breaths were ragged, sharp shards of glass that tried to work their way into her lungs. She had nowhere else to go.

Horror wrapped its hands around Selen's throat, and she suddenly couldn't breathe at all. Shadows shot from the woods and collided with the Being atop her that had once been her sister. They wrapped around the entity, and it began to screech. Unholy wails rang through Selen's ear as the shadows pulled it over the edge of the cliff.

Wake, girl! Velros's voice pierced the horror.

Wake up. She had to wake up.

"Fucking, gods. Selen, wake up!" Deryn's voice was near a cry as Selen woke to her shaking her shoulders.

Her face ached, and her throat was dry as though she had been screaming. She sat quickly and glanced around her, breaths still ragged as she took in her surroundings. Relief enveloped her as she fully processed where she was; she was in the Inn. In bed. With Deryn.

With Deryn.

She looked over at Deryn and quickly reached for her face. Oh, gods, had she hurt her?

"Are you okay?" Selen gripped the sides of Deryn's face and turned her from side to side, examining her for injuries. "Did I hurt you?"

Deryn took a deep breath and closed her eyes. "I'm fine." After a few more breaths, she opened her eyes. "Are *you* okay?" Deryn gently pushed one of Selen's hands away from her face and placed hers on Selen's cheek. Her thumb gently pressed, stroking her wet cheek. Had she been crying?

"You were screaming. You were crying." Deryn's voice was quiet. "I... I didn't know how to help you." Her voice broke at the end.

Selen's heart splintered with her words. She hated that

she had caused Deryn any emotion that would make her feel that way.

"I'm sorry," she whispered. "I didn't mean to scare you." Selen closed her eyes and pressed their foreheads together. "Did—did the shadows..." She didn't know how to finish that question.

"No. There were no shadows," Deryn said calmly. "Just your panic. Which, honestly, was almost worse." She gave a forced chuckle.

Selen breathed through her own forced laugh. "Almost?"

Deryn pulled back and held Selen's face in her hands. "What happened?"

Selen thought back to her dream... or, not dream. Whatever she had experienced had been a nightmare, whether it had been real or not.

At first, it had felt so real. She had felt Sidra. The bond between them had been so taught, but had slowly begun to slip with every twirl Sidra performed.

"It was Sidra," Selen sighed. "She was there, in my mind, then she was... something else. I thought it was just a dream at first, but then I felt her. Then she *became* something else." Selen closed her eyes as the image of that... thing flashed into her mind. "I think she was in my head. Maybe through the bond? But then it was like something was slowly possessing her, and it took over her body. Then she was—" Selen's voice broke as a sob worked through her. "I lost her, Deryn. It's my fault. All of this is my fault."

Deryn pulled her head against her chest, and Selen

couldn't help but let her tears fall. She had been so confident that Sidra had been okay—the beginning of their encounter had been further confirmation that she was, but after, seeing the different contortions of her face... Selen wondered if the image she'd seen in her mind was simply a manifestation of her hopes and not the reality Sidra faced.

The weight of what had happened finally crashed down on her. The sorrow and anguish of losing her sister—what had happened to both of them before Sidra was taken, and everything thereafter.

The tears came in sobs that left Selen feeling depleted. Deryn just held her. No words were exchanged. She sobbed in Deryn's arms, and Deryn expressed nothing but comfort. The gates to all of the areas Selen had locked away in her mind slammed open, and the sheer mass of it all crippled her.

"I can't do this. I can't save her," Selen whispered as the tears began to subside.

Deryn gently pushed Selen's head back until she was looking into her eyes. There was sympathy there, and under-standing, along with a determination that Selen didn't know how to place. Deryn was silent for a moment, seemingly working through what to say.

"You have to," Deryn said quietly, still holding her face.

"I don't know how." It was a plea. Selen realized that she wanted Deryn to tell her that she didn't have to do this, that everything would work out and that she wouldn't have to fight to find Sidra. She wanted her to lie, and tell her every-thing was going to be okay.

Deryn frowned slightly. "You do, Bird." She stroked a hand down her hair. "And I won't let you fail."

There was confidence there, in those words. They weren't what Selen wanted to hear, but they helped ease that ache in her chest slightly.

"These things cannot break you. The world is dark and full of cruelty and horrors. This will not be your last encounter with what it can bring. I cannot keep you from experiencing such things." She paused, eyes searching Selen's face—for what, she wasn't sure. "But you have control over how you react to them. Sidra was taken. She is potentially being tortured." Selen flinched, but Deryn continued, "And there is nothing you can do about what has already been done. But you *can* control what you do from here." Deryn sat back, the face of the fearless leader of the trio settling into her features. "You can sit and hope that the world goes easy on you. Or you can fight for the things you care about. I will not coddle you, as the world will not coddle you."

Her voice had gone cold, and she spoke as though she were telling herself these things as much as she was telling them to Selen. It didn't make those words sting any less. The warmth that had grown between them the entire day—even moments before—dulled slightly; a wall rebuilt between them.

Had Selen made a mistake opening her emotions to Deryn? Had she made a mistake by opening up other parts of herself as well? Selen shrank back a bit, closing herself off.

Deryn's eyes softened slightly as she reached for Selen's

cheek. Selen flinched slightly, but didn't pull back as Deryn brushed away a tear.

She hadn't wanted pity, but desired protection. Comfort. It hadn't been a fair ask, even without it being actually said. She didn't want Deryn to think less of her, but she had hoped that she would be able to express a bit of vulnerability with her. Perhaps it had been too soon. Perhaps they hadn't reached that space yet. Selen pulled back those heavy emotions which begged to be nurtured and locked them in a box deep in the back of her mind, for this would be another task she faced alone.

Chapter Thirty-One

Selen stood outside the entrance to the lair that so frequently robbed her of sleep. The trio was behind her, but Selen had almost entirely forgotten about them as the energy of the MistralWood pushed and pulled at her. It called her in and warned her to stay away in the same instant. Her instincts, or her inner child, told her to run—to stay far, far away from the Being who certainly sat in that haunting pool within the cover of the trees.

Somehow, this space was isolated from the rest of the Wood. The entrance was an arch of tangled tree roots, draped with branches that bowed and swayed in the wind. Selen knew that as they drew closer, those branches would lift and expose the long corridor that led to the haunting waters at its end.

The trees wrapped and warped the space, as if they, too, avoided contact with the Being that existed there. Seers were few and far between, but they were just people who had been chosen by the Lirium and the gods to be a conduit of their magic. They existed between worlds. Once chosen, they were no longer human, she supposed. This one in particular must have been older to have acquired their own title outside of 'Seer'.

The Guardian of the MistralWood.

She hadn't known that was their role when she had last been here; however, she *had* been more focused on her and Sidra's VeilBinding Ceremony, when Deandra had somehow convinced the Seer to not turn her in for being BloodBound. What had she offered her? Seers didn't particularly live by the laws of humans, but they benefited from the mortal leader's favor. They had no moral obligation to turn Selen in, but potentially had more of an obligation to end her life if she truly threatened the balance of the universe with her existence—which was the true force they served. Would today be the day the Seer would change their mind? Would today be when this Being brought balance back to the world by ending her?

She hadn't wanted to come here first. She had wanted to barge into the wood without approval of its Guardian, but the dangers associated with that were too high. None of the others knew Selen's VeilBinding story. She imagined they may have pieced together a version of what had happened that day based on her reaction to coming here. Although, she wasn't sure if they knew that her life was in danger by seeing this creature again, but she had to risk it.

For Sidra.

Guilt ripped at her soul, especially after last night.

Pathetic. Pathetic was what she had felt when Deryn had called her out. The world would not coddle her, Deryn had been right. Coddling wasn't what Selen had wanted, anyway. She would likely resent Deryn if she had. Her words had hurt, though, and proved to Selen that Deryn may never be more to her than the stoic leader of their group when it truly mattered.

None of that really mattered now, though. Not as she moved towards the entrance of her potential death. No one spoke. There were no words of encouragement or caution as Selen headed for the branches that began to slowly lift away. Selen's breath caught as the memories of the last time she had been here ghosted through her mind. She stopped, briefly closing her eyes and pushing those memories out.

She felt the magic stir below her skin; *it* sensed the danger as much as she did. It was weirdly validating and entirely unsettling that Velros, too, was worried about what awaited them. The familiar itch beneath her flesh provided comfort to her as she pushed through.

The air was still as they entered nature's corridor. The specks of dust one would typically find floating in a forest sat still in the air before them. How unfortunate it was that these specks seemed to have wandered in just as the space was created. How long had they been stuck floating in this prison of time?

Magical light weaved through the branches and trees that created the corridor, and the path was worn beneath their feet as the light led them exactly where they needed to go. It would be beautiful if it weren't for the unease that anyone could feel the moment they set foot here, even without knowing what lay at the end.

Selen felt a warm presence come closer to her. They smelled of leather and vanilla. Deryn gently brushed her knuckles against Selen's as they moved forward. Selen wanted to grab her hand; she craved the security it might provide, but Deryn's words rang through her head.

I will not coddle you, as the world will not coddle you.

Perhaps she had intended to inspire Selen. Perhaps she had wanted to force the hard reality of their situation onto her, to strengthen her.

But Selen's issue had never been a lack of strength. She hadn't wanted to do this. She hadn't wanted to fight to free Sidra—who would? Who would want to put themselves in danger, no matter the situation? Selen hadn't *wanted* any of this. She would have fought for Sidra whether Deryn had comforted her last night or not. She had the strength to fight through her fear. She had the strength to fight through the unwanted. What she had needed in that moment was for Deryn to show her that she wasn't alone.

That hadn't happened.

Deryn had said that she wouldn't let Selen fail, but it felt like less a statement of support and more of a declaration of loyalty to the mission. Maybe some would see that as the same thing, but there was a huge piece missing that Selen couldn't help but hold onto.

The world wouldn't coddle her. Nor would Deryn. She hadn't expected either to—so, she pulled her hand gently towards her and away from Deryn's warmth.

The corridor of warped and wrapping trees widened and raised as they approached the pool. Just as before, the Seer floated on the surface of the water, its oily black hair drifting around, with only its face and part of its body exposed to the air.

"The BloodBound returns." The Seer's voice—or voices, rather—slid over Selen. Its milky eyes still stared at the ceiling of branches above, as if it could see into the universes beyond. Selen's spine tingled as the Seer floated up from the water. It stopped and stared down at Selen, white toes barely above the surface of the pool. "I have been waiting for you, Selen Dagny."

Selen's blood chilled as she met the gaze of the ancient and horrifying Being.

"We come to seek your blessing to access the Mistral-Wood." Deryn spoke from behind Selen, and while her voice was strong, there was a level of uncertainty in her tone.

"I know why *you* come," The Seer said, not looking away from Selen. "I care not for the voices of those who follow." The Seer tilted their head in that serpentine way that made Selen's skin crawl. "I care only for the voice of they who has been silenced, yet still threatens our very existence."

Selen narrowed her eyes. It could just say that it wanted to talk to her.

"We've come to find my sister," Selen said sternly, refusing to break eye contact with the Being.

"Ah, yes," it whispered. It pulled its gaze from Selen's and hovered on the opposite side of the pool, back facing them. "The one of starlight. Your opposite, yet not your equal." It slowly turned until it was facing them again. The Seer finally looked over Selen's shoulders to where the trio was. Cocking its head, it looked back at Selen. "She lies in these woods with one who, like you, does not belong here."

Selen stepped forward. "Who is she? Why has she taken Sidra?"

The Seer lifted a bony hand towards its face, a mockery of contemplation.

It *knew*. It knew more than any other being in all the realms. It was cruel to withhold information as it was likely deciding to do now.

"The one you seek haunts your mind." Old news. *Next.* "Yet you share much with it. With *her*."

The Seer's brow furrowed as it looked down at Selen. Clearly, the expression was not a regular one for the Seer, as its skin stretched and cracked with the movement.

"It speaks to you."

Selen stilled. She wasn't prepared to explain Velros's existence to anyone right now—let alone this larger-than-life entity.

Selen felt Deryn's gaze burning into the back of her head, but she refused to look back—refused to take her eyes off the Seer for even an instant.

"*Who is she?*" Selen attempted to hold its focus.

The Seer rasped a bitter laugh. "You've known her. In another lifetime. Yet another Being who exists outside of the constraints of balance." The Seer clicked its teeth. "She sought you out. She seeks your power, BloodBound."

"Enough of your riddles." Selen's blood was boiling. She

wanted to know enough about whoever *she* was that Selen could defeat her and get Sidra back.

Truly, though, they had come to obtain the Guardian's blessing to enter the MistralWood; the rest was simply extra information which may benefit them.

The Seer looked back to Selen, taking her in, eyes roaming in curiosity. The look was so intense that Selen took a small step away, finding a hand at her back. It stabilized her.

"It will not end." The Seer's voice was soft with a gentleness that was at odds with its nature. "It will not stop with her."

"If you won't tell me anything about who took Sidra, will you at least grant us your blessing to enter the Mistral-Wood?" Selen was tired of playing games. Tired of hearing the Seer's voices.

"Tell me, BloodBound." The Seer's tone was back to its piercing voice of many. "When you allowed that parasite into your blood to become woven with your soul, what was the cost?"

Selen felt Deryn's hand still. Feet shuffled behind her, no doubt Varric shifting around uncomfortably at the information he had not shared with his companions. Selen felt a small pull inside of her—where Velros had recoiled at the initial meeting of the Seer, it now writhed under her flesh again.

"What did you do?" Deryn whispered.

"Don't." Varric's whisper was even quieter as he gently pulled Deryn back, and the loss of Deryn's contact was almost a relief; Selen hadn't enjoyed feeling her every reaction through that connection. While it was no news to the trio that she was BloodBound, the only one who knew that her magic was accompanied by a mental companion was Varric– at least until now.

Selen sighed, knowing she'd have to face the consequences of keeping that bit of information to herself—but she couldn't focus on that right now. She had to focus on getting into the wood and finding Sidra. *That* was the only thing that mattered.

"If I answer your questions, will you grant us access to the MistralWood under your blessing?" Selen steadied her breath and racing heart.

The Seer made a show of thinking it over. "If you answer my questions, you will be granted access to the MistralWood with my blessing."

Selen studied the Being for a moment. Fear still ran through her veins, but it didn't paralyze her as she had expected. She often lived in fear, she realized, as she stared into the milky eyes of the creature before her. A phantom memory of its cold, bony fingers as they'd wrapped around her jaw threatened to push her deeper into that fear, and she wondered if that was partly the Seer's magic, testing to see how much it could draw from Selen. This was a power play. One that Selen had every intention of winning.

"Ask your questions, Seer."

An amused expression played on its features. "When did you first hear the voice of your magic?"

Selen blocked out the presence of the three behind her

and focused solely on the Seer. "Soon after the veil over my and my sister's magic shattered, but I imagine it may have been there long before."

"And what has she shown you?"

She? Interesting. "I've seen into the mind of who took Sidra. I had no control, but I was there. I've also had dreams that were memories."

"Do you fear it?" The Seer tilted its head.

"I did at first, but now... now they're just a part of me." Selen clenched her jaw. She was trying to display nonchalance, and schooled her features into a mask of boredom as the Seer continued.

"What has it taught you?"

"To hone my magic."

No more. Velros's voice startled Selen enough that she flinched. She quickly schooled her features again, but the small movement hadn't gone unnoticed.

The Seer tilted its head, and its eyes widened.

"It speaks." There was an emotion that seemed almost like excitement on the Seer's face. "Come out and play, ancient one." Its voice was taunting.

Selen felt a pressure in her chest that made her gasp. It felt like someone was knocking on her ribcage from the inside out. Selen placed a hand on her chest, trying to ease the pressure.

"Ask your next question," Selen pushed. She wanted to get this over with.

"I am done speaking with you." It seemed to be staring through Selen, as if it could see into the depths of her mind.

"So, we have your blessing?" Selen attempted to stand straight as that pressure continued to grow.

"No, girl. I'm done talking to *you.*"

Selen didn't have time to question what it meant before the Seer's hand shot to her chest and shoved Selen back, right at the spot that had been building pressure. Except— Selen's body didn't move. The world around her darkened at the edges, and she felt as though she was falling. Her limbs flailed as her vision became distant, and she watched in slow motion as the Seer's face contorted into a grin.

She didn't feel anything around her, only the darkness of her mind as she slammed into a hard surface behind her. There was no pain on impact, but fear trickled throughout and all around her. One arm shot up without her guidance, and was shackled to the obsidian wall she couldn't move from. She looked to her left as the other was locked into the same position. She was shoved into a corner of her mind, trapped to the unmoving obsidian wall that encompassed her mental Being.

She felt as though she were looking through a tunnel— and at the end of it was the Seer's haunting face. This was just as it had been when she was seeing through the eyes of Sidra's captor, but she was... she was in her own body.

Panic swarmed Selen as she tugged and pulled on the shackles. She screamed Deryn's name. Varric's. Even Nys's. She looked to her right and found Velros standing there, staring at the end of the tunnel that was their shared vision. The swirls of shadows that encompassed their body were seemingly pulled towards that tunnel's end. A level of remorse seemed to come from Velros that Selen couldn't understand.

Get me out, Selen said to Velros. *Unchain me!*

Velros only watched as the shadows were pulled more and more through the tunnel. Selen bellowed as Velros shot through the tunnels and shadows wrapped around the light, blanketing Selen in absolute darkness.

Chapter Thirty-Two

Deryn

Deryn watched in horror as Selen's body was wrapped in a swarm of shadows. She had reached for her when the Seer had moved to shove her back, but it seemed as though the Seer's hand just stopped on Selen's chest.

Deryn couldn't tell if Selen had put up a wall of darkness or how she had stopped the Seer from pushing her.

Her head was reeling. Selen's magic *spoke* to her? She hadn't said anything—and that stung more than anything, truly. Varric clearly knew, which pissed her off. The simmering rage rolling off of Nys was the only sign she'd figured out that Varric knew, too. He'd get his ass kicked for that.

After everything so far—after last night... For them to still have this huge wall between them felt like a weird kind of rejection that Deryn hadn't anticipated. She hadn't been entirely open with Selen, she had kept her secrets. But this? This was too big. It impacted too much for Selen to have not said something.

Deryn wanted to pull Selen out of here just so she could yell at her. Hug her. Punch her. Kiss her. The range of emotions she felt was almost as useless as she felt watching the Seer, which still had a hand on Selen's chest.

There was a brief moment where time seemed to stop. No one breathed. The Seer didn't move. Then, all hell broke loose.

Shadows shot from Selen more aggressively than they ever had before, and the trio barely had time to flinch as that darkness shot towards them. Deryn tried to shield herself, but the sting of impact never came. She looked up as the Seer was pushed back from where it had previously been, its eyes wide with shock. The ground around them looked as if it had been scorched—everywhere except where they stood. Some part of Selen's magic had kept them from harm.

Deryn looked to Nys and Varric, and their matching expressions of awe and confusion mirrored her own as they looked around them. Varric looked in terror toward where the Seer was, frozen by whatever he saw. Deryn shot her gaze to Selen, and what she saw made her heart drop.

Selen was wreathed in shadows, floating above the ground. Her raven hair flowed around her like she was in water. Her arms were outstretched, and her face pointed toward the sky. Everything about the space seemed to shift in her presence. Something... was so different. It wasn't her. Her energy seemed... old. Where the patterns of her magic were normally chaotic and unreadable, they now sat in a perfect pattern of unbreakable, smokey glass.

Selen's arms slowly dropped to her sides, and her head leveled as she examined the Seer, who shrank at her gaze. Actually *shrank*.

"Selen," Deryn whispered. She wasn't sure what Selen was going to do, but Deryn wanted her to know she was here. With her.

Selen's head snapped to where Deryn stood, and Deryn's throat constricted. Those *eyes*. They were not the eyes of the woman she had spent last night with; they were ancient, *cruel*—a depthless void of shadows.

Deryn stumbled back into Varric. It wasn't very often that she was shaken, but this...

The eyes narrowed—almost in recognition—before snapping back to the Seer.

"You speak like one who knows the secrets of the world, yet you cower like a child." The voice that left Selen was not of this world. It wasn't like the many voices of the Seer, but the depth of it—the absolute control that hissed from Selen's mouth—made Deryn queasy. Something had control of her.

The Seer straightened in an attempt to compose itself, but it still emitted an essence of fear.

"Speak your piece, Seer." That voice sent spiders of

unease down Deryn's spine; she could do nothing but watch.

The Seer gaped at Selen as if it were looking at the gods themselves.

"I mean no disrespect, ancient one." The Seer tilted its eyes down, but not before Deryn caught the twinge of familiarity that sparked in its eyes. What a peculiar sight, to witness a Being as cold and demanding as this Seer essentially bowing to whatever it saw in Selen.

"I am no fool," Selen spat at the Seer, who flinched at her words. "Did you not taunt me for this very thing?"

"I-I did not know. I did not know the extent of control you could have on your vessel." Its hands clasped—seemingly to stop them from trembling.

Vessel? As if Selen was no more than a suit to be worn or armor to don.

"You would not, as you know nothing of my kind," Selen hissed at the Seer with the clear authority of one who outranks another.

The Seer tried to steady itself. "I only wish to learn."

This felt like an interaction that Deryn and the others shouldn't be privy to.

"You refer to my kind as a parasite, yet you once served with me as your master. What of your weak loyalties? What of your cowardice in the presence of true power?"

The Seer dropped its gaze.

Selen continued when the Seer didn't speak, "You asked her what the cost was." She paused, assessing the Being like a predator assesses prey. "The cost of being granted absolute power was *nothing*."

The Seer's eyes widened as it looked up to where Selen still floated. Realization washed the Seer's features, and its limbs relaxed at its sides. It nodded in some manner of silent understanding.

"If you summon me again, Seer, it will be the last thing you do." There was no mercy in that ancient voice. The shadows swirled as Selen turned to face her.

Deryn didn't want to fear Selen. She knew that the human, however deeply she existed inside Selen's body right now, was not to be feared. But this thing? This was not a harmless human. And it, too, lived within her. Deryn's stomach twisted as she took in those dark, depthless eyes, housed in the body she wanted to cherish.

Selen's head tilted to the side, and she watched Deryn for a moment before speaking. "She favors you." Deryn's brow furrowed. "Do not be foolish."

Deryn recognized it for the threat it was.

The shadows suddenly shot back into Selen's body, and she dropped, crumpling on the ground. Deryn rushed to her side and picked up her limp upper half as Selen's head dangled to the side. She was unconscious.

The Seer slunk into the waters of the pool where it resided.

"Your access to the MistralWood has been blessed. Remove her from my presence." It sounded exhausted as its voice returned to the cold and unyielding force that Deryn had previously known it as.

Varric reached for Selen, helping Deryn to lift her and carry her out. Nys scowled down at Selen, and the look sparked an unfamiliar rage in Deryn that she hadn't expected to feel towards her friend, however unsettling she may be to others.

"Let's get her out of here." There was urgency in Varric's voice as he helped lift her. Deryn felt that urgency in her bones; they needed to get away from the Seer and somewhere where she could check that Selen was okay. Her stomach still twisted as she thought back to the image of Selen's shadowy eyes. The entity that had overtaken her. Why had Selen lied to her? Why wouldn't she just tell her? Deryn had felt her coldness toward her this morning and didn't entirely know what to do with it. She knew she had been harsh after Selen had woken from her nightmare, but Deryn had felt her wanting something that she couldn't give. She could support and comfort her, but she would never enable her to forget her own strength. Maybe she hadn't correctly portrayed that through her words, however.

Or maybe Selen regretted what they had done. Deryn wouldn't be happy about that, but if Selen wanted nothing more than what they'd had last night, she would be okay with it. Deryn had had no idea that it would lead to *that*, anyway—not until two days ago, when they were training. When she had breathed in her scent. When she had seen that desire burning in Selen's eyes. She'd nearly broken right there—had nearly torn Selen's clothes off and enjoyed the sweet taste of her. But she had a mission. One that she couldn't lose focus of. Although that mission was a bit more challenging now that there were some emotional ties... she could get over it. She *had* to get over it.

Deryn and Varric hauled Selen's unconscious body out the tangled branches of an archway that led to the Guardian's lair. They gently laid her down in the grass once they got far enough away from MistralWood that they didn't feel like it would suck them in before they were ready.

"Selen?" Deryn grabbed Selen's face with both hands and tapped her cheek to try and rouse her. She feared that when those onyx eyes opened, they would be filled with shadows. She wasn't sure she'd ever forget that image.

From over her shoulder, she saw Nys's arm move, and before she knew what was happening, water sloshed past her and onto Selen's face. She promptly sputtered awake, breaths fast and eyes panicked—but they were her eyes. Her onyx eyes with gold specks throughout, like fiery stars in the night sky. Deryn sagged back on her heels and sighed in relief. She glared over her shoulder at Nys, who just shrugged and reattached her water canteen to her belt.

"It worked," Nys said without an ounce of remorse, just as Selen turned to the side and vomited.

Deryn reached to make sure that her long, beautiful hair didn't get in her way, tying it into a braid. Deryn untied Selen's canteen from her waist and prepped it for when she was ready to wash the bile out of her mouth. She had no idea what damage the possession might have on Selen. She wanted to throttle her for not preparing her and saying that her magic had a fucking voice. Maybe she hadn't known that was unusual?

The reminder that Varric had known snapped Deryn's attention away from Selen for a brief moment.

"You knew." She wasn't asking, but she needed an explanation.

Varric's eyes went wide and Nys also turned to him with folded arms. Of the years they had worked together, they had rarely kept secrets.

"I did." He put his arms up in the direction of Nys. Deryn couldn't blame him. She was far more likely to physically attack him than Deryn was.

"Why would you keep that from me?" The anger in Nys's voice was laced with her true emotions. Hurt. Hurt that the man she cared for wouldn't tell her something as important as this. Deryn felt the same way, and their relationship wasn't nearly as intimate.

"Varric, you jeopardized our mission by lying to us." Deryn stayed by Selen's side, but kept her attention fixed on her friend.

"Look, it happened when we were training her magic. I saw her tapestry change before my eyes as she let the magic become a part of her. I almost ran back to tell you both in that moment, but..." Varric paused.

"But *what*?" Nys's voice was a near yell.

"But *I* asked him not to." Selen's voice bit through the forming tension. They all turned to look at her. Deryn still had a hand on her back as Selen glared at Nys.

"I asked him not to tell you both in case you wanted to chain me up. Imprison me. I had to find my sister." She leaned away from Deryn's touch. The act was small, but it left an ache in Deryn's chest. "It's not his fault."

"I chose not to tell you guys because we needed her to trust at least one of us." That statement cut more than one person in the group, it seemed. Selen flinched. Deryn could almost feel the cord of trust between them snapping. There was also the implication that Selen didn't trust Deryn, which was evident from how she hadn't told her about this entire other side of herself.

Varric seemed to realize his error, and cringed at his words.

"So that was the game then?" Selen's voice was hollow. So hollow that Deryn couldn't help but watch her. "Find out who could get closest first?" Selen's eyes bore holes in Deryn's.

Oh.

Oh no.

Deryn knew what Selen was thinking. "Selen, that is not why…" Deryn started, but Selen stood and raised a hand, halting Deryn's words. Deryn needed to tell her that she was wrong, that wasn't the reason behind what had happened between them last night, but Deryn could feel their connection severing. She could feel that wall solidifying between them. "Please, Selen, hear me."

Deryn's voice wasn't desperate, but what she felt in her heart might as well have been. How had things gotten so muddled? Deryn ran a hand down her face. The hurt on Selen's face cracked through Deryn as she watched her. Selen just stared at her. Deryn knew that one of those voices in her mind was telling Selen lies, slowly cutting her off from Deryn.

"Selen, I don't know which one is talking right now, but I need you to hear me," Deryn pleaded. "I did not do what you think I did." Even as she begged her to listen, Selen's eyes spoke of vengeance. A look she had never wanted to see from her.

"Don't use my fucked up mind to justify your lies." Selen's words were so cold. The image of fractured boredom slid over her features.

And that was that.

There was no breaking through that wall. Any trust—any emotions that existed between them—closed into whichever room in Selen's mind she stored her pain.

"I'm not." Deryn didn't know what to say to make this better. She didn't know how to get through to her.

Selen stood there for a moment, looking down at Deryn, who was still settled on her knees before her.

"We need to leave. We have to find my sister." Selen spat the last words out before turning and stalking toward the Inn where they'd stayed last night.

Deryn stared at the ground. What could she say? She hadn't done anything out of obligation to the mission. Had she? She hadn't stooped that low.

Varric gripped Deryn's shoulder—an act of comfort that Deryn both appreciated and despised.

Deryn stood and faced her friends.

"Is it real?" he asked. Deryn knew what he was asking.

She nodded in response, and Nys's wide eyes were a sign

that she had thought Deryn had just been trying to get close to Selen in that way. Deryn sent a leveling glare in her direction.

"Then fix it," Varric said.

"She is dangerous," Nys cut in.

It was true. Parts of Selen were dangerous. Especially when that *thing* came through. But Deryn didn't particularly care at that moment.

"Not to me." Was all Deryn said as she turned to follow what could possibly be the most dangerous thing she had ever encountered.

Chapter Thirty-Three

Selen

Selen stalked back to the Inn, head throbbing alongside her aching heart.

Stupid.

She had been so stupid to think that anything other than ulterior motives led Deryn to her bed. Of course they needed her trust to proceed with the mission. Varric with his fake confidence in her secrets. Deryn with her fake intimacy. Had the story about Varric's family even been real? She couldn't imagine anyone making that up, but who knows.

She was a means to an end for them.

She was always a means to an end.

Her heart hardened as she pushed through the doors of the Inn.

"Selen!" Callyn's joyful, booming voice pulled her attention to the bar, and Selen did her best to plaster a smile on her face. It must not have been convincing, however, as the smile lines around Callyn's face slackened.

"We're just heading out." She forced the words out, each one like glass cutting her throat.

Velros's power had been in her organs and leading her body. Their voice had come from her mouth. She'd had no control, and was in darkness for the entire time. Had it been minutes? Hours? She didn't know. Her throat was scratchy. Her mind was scattered. Her heart was forming into the darkness that shaped her mind's wall. Velros had told her while the darkness consumed her that they had no say in what had happened. The Seer had summoned Velros to the surface, pushing Selen into a prison within her own mind. She held no frustration towards Velros, but the panic she had felt in that moment had been unbearable.

Deryn burst through the doors behind her. The look on her face was almost genuine. *Almost* believable. Callyn seemed to spot Deryn's expression and stayed silent, finding something else to do.

"Selen." Deryn's voice was breathless.

Selen just pushed through the door leading up to their room. She didn't want to see it. She had considered leaving all of her stuff if only to avoid the space where she had so blindly given herself to Deryn.

Selen entered their room and made quick work of throwing her things into her pack. She had almost gotten everything when Deryn burst through the door behind her.

She blocked the doorway. Selen tried to push past her but Deryn grabbed her shoulders and pushed her back. Selen gaped at Deryn. Her face was a mix of hurt and anger.

"You don't get to do this," Deryn stated firmly.

"Do what?" Selen threw at her. She wanted to remain calm, but her emotions had other plans.

"You don't get to use this as an excuse to run away." Deryn lowered her brow, eyes digging into Selen's soul.

"You—"

"No." Deryn raised a hand, cutting her off. "No. Fuck that." Deryn pushed forward, startling Selen enough that she backed away further. They kept moving until Selen was pushed against the wall on the opposite side of the room, and Deryn put both hands on either side of Selen's head. Her eyes were dark as she watched Selen.

Selen leveled a glare at her. "You lied to me." Her words shattered. She tried to hold it together, but her eyes stung as tears began to burn.

"I did no such thing." Deryn's voice was low. "You, on the other hand..." Her gaze cut into Selen's flesh.

Selen *had* lied to her. She had exposed so much of herself to Deryn, yet she had lied about a crucial part of herself. But Deryn had also lied. She had used her. Her body. Her emotions.

"I opened up to you." Selen pushed her face closer to Deryn's, not trying to repress the venom that coated her words. "I shared parts of myself I had never—and you used me."

Deryn slammed her hand on the wall behind Selen's

head, but she didn't flinch. She held her stance and bore into Deryn with her glare.

"It is real." Deryn's voice was quiet. "It is fucking real and you know it. You are trying to hide behind this bullshit excuse so you don't have to face that anything between us could be real."

"It's not!" Selen hated her. There was no world where she couldn't hate her. Nothing could be real between them.

"You're a godsdamn coward and a fool if you believe that!" Deryn's voice was raised.

Selen sat with that for a moment, glaring at Deryn. Maybe if she continued to push, she'd finally stay away. She'd finally be rid of this infatuation.

"I am no more than a means to your end." Selen looked Deryn up and down. "A pussy you can fuck your trust into so you can complete your mission."

Selen saw the moment Deryn snapped. Deryn surged forward, and their mouths connected with an intensity that knocked Selen back into the wall.

"You're an idiot," Deryn said breathlessly in between kisses. She lifted both of Selen's feet off the ground until her legs wrapped around Deryn's waist. "You're a fucking idiot, Bird." Her voice cracked.

Selen raked her hands through Deryn's hair and pulled her head back. Deryn growled as she strained against the pressure.

"Don't fucking talk to me like that," Selen hissed. Deryn's eyes flared as she pulled her hand from where she held Selen's hip and wrapped it around her jaw. The utter control in the movement made Selen fall molten to her. She hated this. She hated her touch.

Deryn still gripped her jaw as she slammed their lips together. The kiss was one of desperation and hatred and so many other emotions that Selen had no intention of addressing.

"You have lied to me," Deryn said as she brought her mouth to Selen's neck. "You have pushed me away." She ran her teeth along Selen's ear. "You have fucked with my head." She bit down on her pulse, eliciting an involuntary moan from Selen's throat. "And yet, I can't get enough of you." Deryn punctured Selen's skin with her teeth, and Selen let out a whimper as she felt warmth slip down her neck.

When she pulled back, there was a small bit of Selen's blood on Deryn's lip. Fuck, she *hated* this woman.

"I hate when you touch me." Selen cursed as she lurched for Deryn's lips. She wanted to taste her blood on her lips. "I fucking despise you." She bit her bottom lip, and the groan that worked its way up Deryn's tongue went straight to Selen's core.

A bitter laugh escaped Deryn as she lifted Selen from the wall and carried her over to the bed, throwing her onto it.

"I regret meeting you." Deryn bit out as she ripped open Selen's jacket, along with the shirt below. "And every fucking moment after." She took Selen's breast into her mouth and swirled her tongue, gripping and toying with the other.

Selen glared at the top of Deryn's head as waves of pleasure moved from her sensitive breasts to her molten core.

"Fuck you." There wasn't as much bite in her tone as she'd had hoped for.

Deryn's answering grin sent waves of rage through Selen alongside her pleasure. Deryn slipped Selen's pants off of her until she lay entirely exposed.

"You don't get to be inside of me," Selen ground out.

"Oh, I won't be." Deryn glared down at Selen before grabbing one of her daggers from its sheath, gently running it across Selen's skin. She pressed hard enough to leave lines, but not enough to break skin. Selen didn't break eye contact with Deryn as the blade moved all over her body. The eliciting response was entirely infuriating; a moan was dragged from Selen with every place that the blade dragged, and her responding wetness was proof that her body was betraying her.

Deryn pulled the sheath from her belt and pushed the dagger back into it. She then spat on her hand and rubbed it along the handle of the blade. Selen's eyes widened.

"You want to make a liar of me, Bird?" There was no humor—only resentment—in her words. She ran the cold metal of the dagger's pommel down Selen's center, and Selen let out a raspy moan. Just before she pushed the tip of it past her entrance, Selen could feel the cool metal and the grooves of the handle. Deryn's face was close as she whispered, "Then I'll *fucking* lie to you."

Deryn pushed the dagger the rest of the way into Selen until she could feel the cold steel of the handle's base against her lips.

She pulled it out almost to the tip. "I can't stand you."

Thrust. Retreat. "I hate your fucking smile." Thrust. Retreat. "I hate your laugh." Thrust. Retreat. "And your stupid hair." Thrust. Retreat. "I hate the way your pussy tastes." Thrust. Retreat. "I hate your scent." Thrust. Retreat. "And I feel fucking *nothing* for you." Deryn's voice broke slightly on the last thrust.

Selen felt the sensation of every word along with each thrust. Her breathy moans were the only sound that came from them for a moment before Deryn sank to her knees, keeping a steady pace with the dagger.

"Lie to me, Bird," Deryn whispered against Selen's throbbing clit.

Selen panted as she looked down at Deryn, not daring to break eye contact.

"I hate you." Selen couldn't make her voice meet the words for what they were.

Deryn's mouth closed around Selen, and she let out a helpless wail as pulses of pleasure ran through her with each swipe of Deryn's tongue, accompanied by the thrust of the dagger handle inside of her. Selen crested over that cliff that kept her sanity at bay with the final thrust of Deryn's dagger, and her body pulsed as the climax rocked through her.

She hated her. She hated her for making her feel things. She hated her for the trust she felt for her. She hated her for how quickly her body responded to her touch.

And she was a fucking liar.

Chapter Thirty-Four

Selen worked through a wide range of emotions as she put her clothes back on. Deryn had already gone to meet the others. They had said nothing after they had come down from their releases; Deryn had simply put on her clothes and left the room. Selen attempted to tie her shirt back together from where Deryn had ripped it.

What Varric had admitted still left a stain on Selen's soul. How everything he'd done to help her was just to gain her trust for the mission. She wasn't sure exactly how hurt she should be. The reality was, they were all here for the same goal. Selen had thought that her relationship with them had moved a bit past just using each other for their individual gain, but wasn't that what she had done with Deryn initially? Wasn't that what she had done with all of them?

It was easier to be hurt by them. It was easier to pretend

like her pain kept her from having any form of relationship with any of them. She didn't have space in her head for all her fucking personalities, let alone others. But fucking *Deryn* had forced her way into her emotions.

Selen had wanted it to be a crush—an infatuation she could cure with her tongue—but it had become so much more. After their first encounter, Selen thought she might be able to move past it. She lied to herself and claimed she was cured. But she was far from it. And now? Fuck if she knew. Things were now significantly more complicated because there were actual feelings—feelings Selen hated herself for having developed. All in the span of sixteen godsdamned hours, she had experienced such a wide range of emotions that had brought her to this point.

They were literally moments away from entering the MistralWood, and she was thinking about her complicated emotions for Deryn. She wanted—no, *needed*—to address these feelings, but there was so little time, and Deryn had seemed in no mood to talk when she left. Part of Selen hoped that she had ruined things between them, while another part screamed and tore at her to fight for whatever it was that was forming between them.

Sidra. She was here for Sidra. And to figure out what this weird fucking connection was with this random person who had taken her. Obviously, their magic was connected. Perhaps a Lirium that was related to Velros? She wasn't sure if Lirium had familial ties, but there wasn't anything that said they didn't. Perhaps it was a cousin of sorts. Selen knew she could ask Velros, but anytime it had been brought up, they—or *she,* apparently—had been vague and quickly ended communication.

Selen had kept Velros beyond that wall in her mind since they had taken over her body. While she knew the Seer had summoned them and didn't hold it against Velros, Selen hadn't been entirely prepared to share her functional body with them again. Plus, those moments where Selen had been trapped within her own mind had caused some irreparable damage that Selen needed to address before it drove her to madness.

She took a deep breath, pushing aside all of her feelings surrounding Deryn and Varric and opened the wall just enough for Velros to slip through.

Velros, Selen said quietly.

You know it was not my intention to have taken control of your body, Velros stated it for the fact that it was. No emotions to be found. *Yet, you are troubled by it.*

I'm troubled by the fact that anyone can trap me in my own mind. You taking over my body was not ideal, but it was not my biggest concern. Selen tried to keep her mind's voice level and controlled.

There are not many that can. A Seer is powerful—especially one as old as that one. They have been granted a magic that is both that of the Lirium and of the gods.

Why was it so afraid of you?

To face the very thing you were once sworn to serve can be unsettling to any Being.

Selen sat with that for a moment. She wanted to word the next thing carefully, so as not to have Velros pull back.

Are you still Lirium, even though you gave up your corporeal form?

Velros was silent for a moment. *There is truly no name for those who have bound themselves to a bloodline. So few have done it. I am as much Lirium as I was at the beginning, but I am housed in a realm far from my home.* There was what seemed like... sadness in Velros's voice.

That realm being me.

That realm being this world.

Do you regret it? Binding yourself to my bloodline?

There is no use in regret.

Selen bit her lip as she continued to gather her things from the room. She had gotten better at multitasking while she was communicating with Velros in her mind.

We are entering the Mistral Wood soon...

Ask what you must. Velros's reply was clipped, but did not hold the coldness that was typical when Velros knew what was coming next.

How is my magic connected to the one that took Sidra? What am I in for?

There was a stretch of silence that made Selen think that Velros might not answer.

The one you seek has a shared darkness. A piece of the past that has found its way to the present. I had hoped that they would not find their way here. To you.

Selen stopped in her tracks.

You knew they were coming? You knew she was coming?

I can feel that which shares the darkness. As can you.

Selen wasn't sure what that had meant. Well, she knew

what it was supposed to mean, but she had felt nothing. She had no idea that this person was coming to take Sidra. How could she?

What can I expect from her?

You do not ask the right questions.

What questions should I ask?

That is for you to figure out.

Selen bit at her bottom lip until she felt the coppery taste of blood in her mouth.

Can I defeat her?

Combined, you can do much. Including, perhaps, taking on the one who shares the darkness.

Combined with what?

What combines with darkness to create night?

For a brief moment, an image popped into Selen's mind. It was hazy, but she saw icy blue eyes looking down at her. Sidra's eyes. But they were on a man. He had blonde hair that draped over his mud-covered face. He was looking down at her with tears in his eyes. She saw the tear fall, and the image faded as quickly as it had appeared.

"Starlight," Selen said aloud.

There is much that the night can defeat. Velros's voice faded with their presence as Selen pushed open the door to the stairs that led to the beginning of her journey.

The trio waited for her outside, and Deryn watched her carefully as she exited the building. Varric's gaze was as equally assessing as she approached. Selen didn't want to deal with whatever awkwardness could potentially exist here. They had bigger problems. Selen also had an idea of the solution to their evil, shadow-wielding kidnapper problem.

"Look." Selen turned towards Varric, pointing her entire hand toward him. "I'm pissed at you for pretending to get to know me so you could gain my trust, but I get why."

Varric stepped forward as if to say something, but Selen cut him off by turning her palm toward him. "With that being said, I don't really trust you, but I need to—at least a little bit—in order to be successful in finding and saving my sister."

Varric's brow furrowed, but he nodded and looked down at the ground.

"And you," Selen turned to Deryn, making quick eye contact before moving her gaze down slightly until she was staring blankly at the ground behind her. "I don't have the capacity to discuss anything that's happening here right now."

She briefly looked up to find Deryn's stern eyes watching her, emotions swirling within, but didn't look long enough to identify her emotions. She turned toward the entire group and addressed no one in particular.

"My one and only goal has to be finding my sister, and you all are helping me with that. We don't know what we will find in the MistralWood, even with the Guardian's blessing. So—" Selen took a breath and stood tall. "Any and all other bullshit has to fall to the wayside. I need you all to trust that I am going to do my part in this."

"You have yet to prove that you can be trusted with your magic," Nys quipped from beside Varric. Nys had so far been the only one who hadn't tried to gain Selen's favor on this extravaganza, and while Selen may not like the tiny, angry woman, she respected her.

Selen leveled her gaze at Nys, who returned a challenging glare. "There is nothing I wouldn't do to get my sister back to safety. *Nothing*. If you need trust in something, trust that." Fuck if Selen didn't mean it. Sidra was the thorn in her side that gave her life. Without it, Selen felt as though she would simply fade away. She was, in biology alone, her other half. Losing that... Selen couldn't even *think* about losing Sidra. She had had to accept that she might not be okay, but she was alive. That was what Selen clung to.

Nys didn't respond, which was, in and of itself, a reply. An approval of sorts.

With that, Selen began moving toward the MistralWood with a determination that lit her soul on fire, but stopped as Deryn cleared her throat. She turned to see that none of them had moved.

"The, *uh*..." Deryn started. "The entrance is that way." Deryn pointed a thumb to the right of Selen. Selen glanced between Deryn and the Wood.

"Well, someone else lead, then," Selen huffed. "I don't know where I'm going." Selen's voice fell into a grumble. "You all have been here before. No one else was moving. It's a forest. Why is there a specific entrance?"

A quick grunt that sounded like it was a muffled chuckle slipped from Deryn. And off they went—toward the MistralWood's *special* entrance, with Deryn in the lead.

Chapter Thirty-Five

The hum of the Mistral Wood was intoxicating and nauseating as they approached the *official* entrance. It didn't look any different from any other edge of the Wood.

"How do you know this is the *special* entrance?" Selen asked Deryn.

"It's not-" Deryn glanced over her shoulder and scowled. "It's not a special entrance. It's just the only entrance that is linked to the blessing of the Guardian."

"That sounds pretty *special* to me," Selen said to Nys at her side, who simply growled in response. Selen frowned and looked Nys up and down. Maybe she was a badger internally. Selen had always heard those were far angrier than they should be, considering their size.

"Let the special entrance thing go, Bird." Deryn's voice held a twinge of amusement.

Selen pursed her lips. She was nervous, and everyone was

being too quiet. "Did you know that you can poison someone with cherry pits?" Selen didn't do well in silence, especially when she was anxious.

The three stopped and all looked at Selen with the same bewildered look.

"Not a fun facts group, got it." Selen put her hands up. Deryn was the last to look away as she shook her head.

Selen was pushing all her emotions into tiny boxes in the back of her mind. Those for Deryn were locked in a steel chest with a padlock. All that was left to fill their void was the random trivia she had thanks to Sidra's endless research and a dry humor, courtesy of Aeden.

"There is said to be a river far south that runs the length of the earth. There are also said to be large cats that eat people sometimes." Selen was looking at the ground. The thrumming of the wood reverberated through her skin. She needed a distraction that wasn't going to drive her into a breakdown.

"If you keep speaking, I will personally remove your tongue," Nys hissed.

Selen looked over to her. She didn't doubt that she would do it. But there was little that would keep Selen from spewing random facts until her anxiety eased.

Deryn seemed to have sensed that and fell back slightly until she was next to Selen.

"Cats who eat people?" she asked. Selen knew she was humoring her, but she didn't care. A swirl of emotion ignited in her heart.

Nope. Go back to your home.

"Yes. They are orange and black and have teeth the size of your hand."

"I hope never to meet any of these large cats," Deryn said, looking up at the ceiling of tree branches above them.

"They have a cousin, I think, who's really fast, but a bit smaller. Fastest in the world, if the books are to be believed. Actually, if my *sister* is to be believed." Selen glanced quickly at Deryn, who didn't take her eyes off the path ahead. "She's the one who told me all of this."

"Does your sister often share random facts with you?" Deryn asked.

"She does. She started the research to find out about our magic—or lack thereof. She found a lot of information along the way."

"How did she stumble onto human-eating cats?"

"I suppose learning about human-eating cats may have been more exciting that day than another dead-end about our magic."

"*Hmm.*" It seemed like Deryn was through entertaining Selen's distraction.

The distraction had worked, though. Selen hadn't entirely realized that they had entered the MistralWood until the edge of the wood was a fading light behind them. Selen's heartbeat quickened.

She was ready for this.

She was absolutely not ready for this.

Temple.

Sidra's words slid back into her mind. Gods, she had been so distracted by Sidra becoming that horrifying entity that she had completely forgotten what she had said in the brief moment when she had been herself.

"The fucking temple," Selen whispered.

Deryn looked at her. "What?"

"Sidra is at the fucking temple." Selen wanted to throat punch herself for having forgotten that important detail that would likely guide their entire mission.

"How do you know?" Varric asked from behind her.

Selen looked up at Deryn, who watched her, searching her gaze.

"It was in the dream. In the... fucking nightmare." Selen was stumbling over her words, which typically led to a heightened use of expletive language.

"You didn't think that was pertinent information prior to now?" Nys was clearly speaking through ground teeth.

"Sorry. I was distracted by the fact that my sister turned into a fucking demon nightmare creature, *Nys*."

Nys just growled in response.

Selen's gaze moved back to Deryn, who watched her inquisitively.

After another moment of looking at Selen, Deryn spoke. "Then we go to the temple."

Selen hated that. The temple in the center of the Mistral-Wood was what had created the gods awful place. It had been many things throughout the centuries: a place of worship, a prison, a home to some of the most powerful magic wielders—and many other things. It now sat in ruin. The temple's stones had fallen with time, but the ancient magic that ran through its veins still flowed strong. Like the heart pumped blood to the rest of the body, the temple acted as the heart of the MistralWood, pushing magic from its core and pulling magic back into it to redistribute throughout the veins of the forest. Mostly, the magic that it pulled from the forest came from its own recycled magic; other times, it pulled from those who fell victim to its grip. The more victims, the stronger the magic.

Selen had no intention of becoming one of the victims that fed into the magic of the MistralWood—but it begged her to be. Selen wasn't sure if the others could feel the immense pull, but Selen felt like her magic was being summoned to its core. It called for her. A whisper in the trees. A coaxing breeze, pushing her toward... something.

Her blood seemed to pulse with the magic around them.

The MistralWood was notorious for creating illusions and magical trials that many didn't survive. Selen wasn't sure what it had in store for them, but she had been tense since they entered. No amount of random facts was going to calm Selen's thundering heart.

The tension that came from unease didn't seem to be exclusive to Selen, as the others walked quietly alongside her. Deryn's hand hadn't left the pommel a short sword at her hip, white knuckles gripping it, as if the act itself grounded her. She hadn't had that sword when they arrived at the small town. Had she had weapons stored at Callyn and Devril's place? That was the most likely answer.

The silence left Selen's thoughts far too much space to wander. She felt like she had at least four different thought paths crossing in her mind. It was disorienting. At least conversation—or noise, at the very least—gave her mind something to latch onto, providing one coherent thought. Now there was a mix of jumbled words and sounds, images of past events, and even short parts of songs she had heard. Never a full song. Only a few words or a small part of the tune. Could the magic here be amplifying the intensity of her wandering mind? She didn't often feel this dizzy or over-whelmed by her thoughts.

"Have you been to the temple?" Selen had to break the silence. It felt like shattering a glass in the middle of a test, but there had to be a sound outside of Selen's head or she might pass out.

Deryn's voice seemed equally forced. "I have. We all have." Deryn glanced back at Nys, who shook her head. Selen noted the glance and Nys's reaction. There was obvi-ously a story there, but being that it involved Nys, Selen knew there was no chance they would share.

"Does it feel like this? Like it's pulling at your skin?" Selen wasn't sure if the others felt the pull, but why not find out by asking directly?

"The temple is silent, once you've made it past the outskirts. It's almost as if it allows you a reprieve once you've passed its tests."

"Why were you there?"

There was a beat of silence before anyone made another sound. Nys was the one who broke it with her gravelly voice. "They were there for me."

Selen was surprised at the emotion in her voice and glanced back at her as they continued to move along the path they all seemed to know. Nys stared down at the ground as if deep in thought.

"There are very few reasons to go to the Temple, unless you are trying to perform something that will likely disturb the balance," Nys stated. Selen wasn't used to her speaking to her without that cold bite. "...Something like extracting the rare essence of Thalrion from a person in order to wield it as a weapon."

Selen's eyes widened before she looked at the other two. Their features had darkened, as though they each recalled a horrible memory. There was much to be discerned from those looks; Nys had been brought here by someone who wanted to use her power, to take advantage of her magic. Who would do that? They'd come to save her, though, it seemed. Perhaps that was why they were all so close. Trauma bonded by a shared horrific experience. Selen couldn't imagine coming back here after that. Her gaze lingered on Nys, who continued to stare at the forest floor, before she turned her gaze forward again. The thrum of the forest was no less intense as they ventured deeper into it.

One might consider the wood beautiful if it weren't for the abhorrent energy it emitted. The trees were dense, thickening further the deeper they went. There were no animal sounds, but a breeze called to them. The shrubbery around them grew in tandem with what Selen imagined were the veins of the forest. The setting sun shone through the veil of trees, and there was a slight incline as they approached the foot of the mountains that overlooked the enchanted forest.

'Approached' may be an overstatement. They were a day

out from the mountain's foothills, where the temple sat. Which meant they'd have to stay overnight in the Wood.

That idea made Selen want to sprint back to the small town that sat at the MistralWood's entrance. Shadows already formed from the setting sun, making it seem as though they were being watched. All around, the eyes of the forest peered open as night approached. The shadows moved in the corners of Selen's eyes, but whenever she looked, there was nothing but looming darkness. Where the sunset had granted warm yellows and golds to wash over the tree branches guiding their path, the dusk brought deep blues and grays that seemed to enforce night prematurely. Selen imagined that if they hadn't been within the cover of the trees, they would still be able to see the sun—but the trees brought a new kind of depth to the dark. Selen could not feel the connection she usually did with the night sky. These shadows seemed to mock her.

Before the sun had fully set, they had set up their camp for the evening. They didn't risk a fire. While it wasn't likely that anyone else would be here, forces beyond humans roamed these woods. Even though the constant thrum of the magic around them kept the space a moderate temperature, a shiver ran up Selen's spine. She could feel the presence of shadows around them.

Two would stay up to keep watch, and they would switch halfway through the night. Selen had opted to take the second shift; Varric and Nys were taking the first watch. Selen hadn't objected to taking watch with Deryn, but she genuinely could not get into the emotions of their situationship, so she prayed to whoever was listening that Deryn wouldn't bring it up.

They all stayed close as the night wrapped around them. Without the comfort of a fire, they essentially had to touch in order to ensure that they were all safe in the darkness. Nys and Varric sat at Deryn and Selen's feet, murmuring as they sat shoulder to shoulder, and their gentle conversation was just enough to block out the ringing in her ears.

Deryn and Selen's hands brushed as they both lay on their backs, and the connection sent sparks into her hardening heart. The contact brought clear tension—there was so much unspoken between them. Selen could almost taste the words Deryn wanted to speak, but instead of doing so, she looped her index finger around Selen's pinky. The act was a silent confirmation that her mind had wandered to a similar place, and it was enough of a comfort that Selen soon found herself drifting off. The touch had broken the tension that had built between them.

Chapter Thirty-Six

Selen's eyes shot open. She could feel them. She could *smell* them.

They stunk of copper and rot—no, not just copper; *blood*. Selen gagged as she sat up. The scent was everywhere, and there was a dark, looming presence that Selen could not see, but could perceive. She looked, finding Nys and Varric still sat for their watch, Nys's head leaning onto Varric's shoulder. Could they not smell it? Selen looked over to Deryn, sleeping peacefully beside her.

"Can you guys not smell that?" Selen asked, jumping at the sound of her own voice. It was far away, as though she had spoken from a different room. Her words echoed into the void around her, and she realized everything was dim—not the ordinary dim of the night's darkness, but like a veil had been placed over her surroundings. Selen moved, reaching for Varric, and froze. She looked down at the pinky that wrapped around Deryn's index finger—*Selen's* finger—and her stomach dropped. Slowly, she turned to look down at the body she no longer inhabited. Her face was scrunched as she slept.

Selen looked down at her hands in whatever form she was currently in.

Had she died?

Shadows swarmed her—so much so, she couldn't see any of her pale skin beneath them. She imagined her entire body looked that way. These weren't her shadows though. There was no familiarity in their embrace. It was cold– like the rush of air wrapping around your skin on a windy winter day.

Velros? Selen hoped that this was just a dream she could use Velros to help pull her out of, but the typical swarm of their presence didn't come.

Velros! Selen started to feel that all too familiar panic settle into her. Velros was nowhere to be found. She must still be housed in the body that lay below her.

"You will not find them here." A raspy voice ran its cold fingers along her mind—a voice she knew only from the depths of her mind and her nightmares.

Selen stood and turned to find two hound-shaped shadows, and trepidation blurred her vision. Despite being made up of only shadows, they seemed to bare their teeth at her. They sniffed at her, and Selen froze. She had no idea what to do. There was nowhere to run. She didn't even know if she had control of her body in this form.

She looked around at the people who protected her body —at the person who held a spot so near to her heart. She felt a cold calm wash over her. She had to protect these people.

Even Nys. Selen was the only one who *could* protect them here. Wherever 'here' was.

"What do you want?" She willed strength into her voice, but it still sounded distant.

"You moved quickly." The voice was taunting. The closer the hounds moved towards her, the stronger that horrific scent grew. "We've been expecting you."

Selen didn't know how long she had to try and get answers here. She wasn't sure if she was even going to go back into her body. This was an entirely unprecedented situation.

"Who are you? Why did you take her?" Selen didn't want her fear to seep through, but it tinged her words regardless.

"Your sister is but one part of a two-piece puzzle. You are the other." Her calm voice skittered across Selen's skin in the worst of ways.

"So, you trapped her to get me here?" Selen had thought that it could be a trap, but she hadn't sat down and thought through the reality of what this would mean. She still wasn't entirely sure where the voice was coming from, and couldn't see any figures in the darkness behind the hounds, who still growled at Selen. A moment of silence passed, a seeming answer to her question. "What do you want with us?" Her voice was a near whisper.

Selen could feel the looming power that held the hounds back. It pressed into her skin and called to her shadows. "I want to reunite what was once separated. *Stolen* from me," the voice hissed with an ancient anger that sent a shock through Selen's bones.

"We didn't steal from you." Selen didn't dare move from where she stood. "Why are you taking it out on us?"

"You *were* what was stolen," the voice answered gently, and Selen's blood ran cold. This person knew them. *Knew*, knew them. Had she been from their childhood? Images of the mud covered man with the icy eyes flashed through her mind. Had he taken them? Had Deandra taken them? Was this person she'd never met in real life lying?

"Who are you to us?" Selen was careful with her words, for she feared the answer.

"You know who I am, girl." There was no feeling in those words.

A figure moved in the shadows between the hounds, and Selen's breath caught. She reached for the magic that seemed so far now, but found only a distant ocean she could not access. The form moved from the darkness, shadows opening like a door. Selen dropped to her knees when the vision before her fully formed.

A woman stood before her. A woman with raven hair that hung to her waist. A woman with high cheekbones, and pale skin so deeply in contrast with the darkness around her that she almost shone against it.

Selen felt a sob work through her as she met those eyes— onyx, and flecked with gold. An aged mirror to her own image. Selen didn't need the woman to tell her who she was; the resemblance was uncanny.

Selen breathed heavily. "This is an illusion."

"Do not lie to yourself, girl." The woman tilted her head and looked down at her. "It's not good for the family name to lie." A hissing chuckle escaped her.

Bile rose in Selen's throat. She couldn't meet those eyes. *Her* eyes.

This couldn't be real.

There was no way.

She was dead.

This person who stood before her was supposed to be dead.

"Tell me, girl," she crooned. "Who am I to you?"

"It's a lie. You're lying!" Selen glared up at her.

"Speak the words, Selen." The sound of her name rolling off the woman's tongue had Selen wanting to rip her to shreds.

If it was true.

It couldn't be.

If it was true, then this person had ripped Sidra from Selen. Had caused her pain. Had set a trap for Selen to fall into. Had hunted them with unknown motives.

"There's no way." Selen stared at the ground, her voice a near whisper.

Her head was pounding, blocking out any other sound. Her shadows began absorbing back into her body. Whatever magic had pulled her into this shadow realm was fading.

"Say it!" The woman's voice was raised, piercing through the pounding in Selen's ears.

She couldn't.

It wasn't real.

This wasn't real.

"My night and stars." The voice was a whisper.

Selen's head snapped up. She had heard that before—the faded memory of the icy-eyed man popped into her mind. There was no affection in the eyes that greeted her. Not the kind you'd expect, if she were who she claimed to be.

She got close to Selen's face and hissed, "Say. It."

"It can't be." Selen spat out just before she was shoved back into her body.

The last sound she heard was the sharp laugh of the woman who was supposed to have protected them. The woman who stole Sidra and baited Selen. The person Deandra had protected them from.

Their mother.

Chapter Thirty-Seven

Selen sat up fast enough that it made her head spin, instantly jumping to look behind her at where *she* had been. She unsheathed a dagger. Her breaths were ragged. Nys and Varric were up with her in an instant, their own weapons drawn at whatever danger surrounded them. They looked around frantically, and Deryn joined them in seconds. Selen's heart raced and her mind spun.

There was no way.

There was no *fucking* way.

It couldn't be real.

"What do you see, Bird?" Deryn reached for Selen.

Pain cracked Selen's skull, like her head was tearing in half. She crumpled to the ground, dagger dropping to the forest floor beside her.

"Fuck." Deryn dove for her, wrapping her arms around Selen's shoulders as she wailed from the pain. It ripped her mind apart.

Where were you? Velros's voice stormed through her mind, the magic all-consuming, shredding her mind.

Stop this. Please! Selen begged Velros. She wasn't sure if Velros was behind this, but she had never felt this much pain before. The world was fading around her. The darkness consuming her.

You have to gain control. Release the flow of the magic! Velros was shouting within her mind now. That was what this was: all of the panic Selen felt had built up within her physical body while she was in the shadow form and now pounded against her mind, shredding her from the inside out.

"Get. Back." She pushed the words out like she was pulling a dagger from her flesh. She pushed at Deryn, forcing her to release her hold. "Get back!" she screamed, and a rippling wave of nauseating pain shot through her head.

The ground! The ground will absorb it.

Selen didn't think as she shoved her hands into the dirt in front of her. She envisioned the magic shooting deep below the surface of the ground, and focused her energy directly into her hands, which stung as the shadows released, and she felt them flow from her like a raging river. Relief was almost immediate.

The air seemed to pulse around her. It felt almost *excited*. She knew she was shooting her magic right into the veins of the MistralWood, feeding this never-satiated beast that threatened their lives. But it was either this or explode, likely killing herself and everyone around her.

The excruciating pain in her head eased as the final drop

of power she had unintentionally pulled from the ocean of her magic sunk into the earth. Selen sat back on her heels and put her head in her hands.

"What the *fuck* was that?" Nys's voice was ragged and breathless.

"I know who she is." Selen let her hands drop from her face as she stared at the faded handprints she had left in the ground. "I know who she is." She was breathing hard, unsure if it was from expelling so much magic or from the realization she wasn't entirely sure she was prepared to accept.

"I know who she is," Selen repeated. Her head ached alongside her heart. It's hardened state solidified.

Deryn grabbed Selen's shoulder and kneeled in front of her, face was a blend of caution and concern.

A sob working up Selen's throat. She tilted her head at Deryn as tears stung her eyes. "I know who she is." Her last word ended on a sob. Deryn pulled her into her chest as something within Selen cracked, immediately filling with stone.

The rest of the night was silent. They had used that moment to switch watches, although Selen was sure that none slept after what she told them. Selen explained how she had been pulled from her body to meet the woman, *her mother*, face to face in whatever realm they had been in.

They had all been concerned that *she* had found them, but imagined that Selen and her magic had called to one another, which is why she had found her in that state. The implications of what this meant made Selen's stomach turn.

A numbness had engulfed her over the past few hours, and Deryn watched her warily between looking out into the darkness. Selen simply sat silently, staring aimlessly into the shadows of the night, as images of *her* flashed into her mind.

"I don't imagine there's anything I can do to make you feel any better." Deryn's words were little more than a whisper as she glanced sidelong at Selen.

"I imagine you're right," Selen said dully.

There wasn't anything Deryn could say that would make her feel better. Not only had she found out that her mother was alive, but in the same instant, Selen had learned that she was a heartless monster who had kidnapped Sidra to use her against her. She wanted to use them for whatever nefarious purposes.

That would be her reality. Of course she would have a mother who likely wanted her dead. Why not? Why not tack on a father who sold them off to the highest bidder? Add that onto the fucked up story that was her life. Of course— she had absolutely no evidence that was actually real, but what-fucking-ever.

"Couldn't I have a mom who just abandoned me or died like every other orphan? Why'd she have to be a kidnapping psychopath?" There was no humor in Selen's voice, but she knew that her saying anything cut the tension that radiated from Deryn.

Deryn glanced at her. "How do you know she wasn't lying about who she was to you?"

Selen thought back to the moment that *she* pushed through the shadows to reveal her face. Selen hadn't believed it at first—hadn't wanted to—but there was no denying the resemblance. Any hope that she may have altered her image through magic was squandered as Selen recalled the way her magic had immediately responded to *her*. She had never felt so connected to someone other than Sidra. It was in her blood. In her bones. The draw to *her*—it made her stomach sour.

"I don't know how to describe it. It was beyond recognition. I knew who she was in every part of myself. Our magic wound together as if it were the same." Selen closed her eyes and shook her head.

"Bird, there's not a single part of me that wants to force you to relive that moment, but this raises questions." Deryn placed a hand on Selen's knee, eyes searching Selen's. "Questions that we may need the answer to before we meet her for real."

Selen could tell Deryn was intentionally avoiding the pitying gaze that had caused her previous meltdown. "I know," Selen sighed, "I don't know if I'll have any answers, though."

"Then we brainstorm," Deryn encouraged.

Selen looked over to her. She wasn't used to anyone wanting to tackle problems with her—other than Aeden.

Fucking Aeden. *Gods*, she missed him.

More than anything, Selen wanted to find Sidra. Did she know? Had their mother told her who she was? Or was Sidra just lost and wondering if anyone was coming to save her? Selen's heart ached, and she had to push the image out of her mind or she would crumble. Deryn was right, though. They needed to think about how this impacted what they were doing—the details around everything leading up to this moment.

"Okay." Selen turned towards Deryn. "Brainstorm." She nodded.

A crooked grin grazed Deryn's lips. "Okay." Deryn turned herself towards Selen. "I need you to dissociate from your emotions. This is brainstorming only. No emotions. No panic."

"I'm almost always in some varying stage of dissociation, so bring it on." Selen shifted in her seat, as if getting comfortable. "No emotions. No panic."

"You and your sister were adopted by Deandra. When was that?" Deryn asked.

"We were one."

"Do you remember anything from around that time?"

Selen thought, but the only image that popped into her mind was of the icy-eyed man. "One thing. But it's really just fuzzy images of a man with Sidra's eyes. He was crying."

"That could be your father." Selen looked at Deryn. No emotion. No panic. "Dissociate, Bird." Selen nodded, and Deryn continued, "You grew up at Celestara. You and your sister attended your VeilBinding ceremony at the Mistral-

Wood. That's the first unknown I want to think about; why did Deandra choose the Guardian as the Seer to do your ceremony?"

Selen thought back to that time. Sidra and Selen were a whirlwind of emotions that often led to battles. Had her magic been present? There were parts of her childhood she couldn't remember, but that seemed to be the case with everyone. She hadn't thought it might have something to do with her magic. Could Deandra have suspected that Selen was BloodBound before? Now that she thought about it, she hadn't thought about that horrific experience at all prior to when she'd shattered the veil put over her magic by Deandra. Had she masked herself from that? The memory had never been missing, but she'd never actively *thought* about it before.

"To keep the secret further from the school?" Selen suggested.

"It could be, but why even bring you to a VeilBinding ceremony at all if she suspected you were BloodBound?"

"Maybe she just needed confirmation." It sounded silly, but Selen couldn't come up with another reason.

"Perhaps, but it could go deeper than that. Your amulets." Deryn reached for Selen's neck. "When did you receive these?"

"These were the only things from our parents—that's what Deandra told us, anyway." Selen reached for the twin amulets that swung on her neck after Deryn released them. She'd worn Sidra's ever since Varric had found it.

"*Hm.* We'll come back to that." Deryn scratched her

chin, seemingly deep in thought. "When your magic broke through the veil, did you feel that pull you felt tonight from the person who took Sidra?" She was careful not to acknowledge who they now knew that person to be.

Selen saw herself fall off the cliff and through the air. She had been drawn back to where Sidra was, but that could have just been her desire to protect Sid from Xander. The pull didn't feel any different to whenever they were desperate to get back to the other.

"No. It was as much a pull to Sidra as it had been when I was first guided to her that night." Selen closed her eyes and breathed, pushing out the memory of that feeling. Of the pain that had wrapped around her neck and wrists. Of the fucking *scum* who had put them there.

No emotion. No panic.

Deryn seemed to be schooling her own reactions, as if the thought of that night brought heavy emotions to the surface.

"After that night, you said you started hearing a voice—that it showed you things." Deryn's voice was low. Selen had lied to her about that, or at least hadn't told her. Part of her had wanted to, but she wasn't sure how to address that conversation. "Things you shared with *Varric*," she bit out.

Resentment seemed to linger there. "I only shared that with him because he literally saw my magical, internal—whatever it is—tapestry change when I was woven with Velros."

"*Velros?*"

Selen flinched at Deryn's tone. "I gave them a name."

Selen could feel their presence pushing against her mind as their name was mentioned.

"Of course you did." Deryn almost seemed like she wanted to chuckle. *Almost.*

"It didn't seem right to just keep calling *them* an *it*—or shadow voice." Selen shrugged.

"So," Deryn's brow furrowed. "You just hear this voice, what, all the time? Like in *every* moment?"

The implication of what she was asking was apparent, bringing heat to Selen's cheeks. "No. Not always. They—*she*—taught me how to push them out when I don't want them around. Velros just kind of hangs out outside the walls in my mind."

"What have you seen from it?"

"I sometimes have a hard time determining what is a memory, a nightmare, reality, or a vision of someone else's reality or memories." Selen looked off into the darkness surrounding them. "I've seen both. I've seen through *her* eyes as if they were my own—but it didn't feel like that when I was trapped in my mind when we saw the Seer. I've had nightmares that seem real, and that was a very similar experience. I've also encountered real things that feel like nightmares. Some happen within my mind; some happen in front of me; some apparently happen in a shadow realm that I can randomly enter." Selen threw her arms up in frustration.

No emotion. No Panic.

She breathed in through her nose and out through her mouth.

No emotion. No panic.

"I saw the moment after I went off the cliff from *her* eyes." Selen kept her eyes closed, but she could feel Deryn watching her. "I saw the shadows explode from me. I saw Sidra and... Xander. Then I saw her take Sidra, as if it was my own memory."

Deryn squeezed the hand that was still on Selen's knee. "Did your magic explain how that was possible?"

"Velros said that it was because our magic was connected, but didn't explain that it was because she was my fucking *mother*." Selen's eyes flew open. She put a hand up. "Hold on."

Deryn sat back. "What?"

"Hold on. Just, hang out for a minute," Selen said, settling further into her seat. She glanced at Deryn before closing her eyes. She had yet to address this issue with her magical mental companion.

Hey, Velros? Selen said with as much calm as she could muster.

The wall slid open in her mind and Velros strode through. *Yes?*

Would you care to explain how you failed to mention that this person whose magic I seem to have a connection with happens to be my mother, *whom I thought was dead?*

No.

The audacity.

That's not an option.

Selen could feel Velros roll their eyes. *I could not tell you.*

Could not? Or would *not?*

Could *not.* Velros's voice was stern.

Why?

I am the manifestation of the magic that flows through your blood—but the magic is not singular to you. We are BloodBound, meaning that there was one before who was bound by blood too. I am different depending on the intentions of the magic created. Your intentions, now, but I'll be different depending on whoever's blood I run through.

That's... a lot. *So how does that impact our current situation?*

I am currently split between two people to whom I am bound. Although, the magic that runs through your mother's veins manifests into a different Being that she speaks to.

So, essentially, the magic is split?

Yes.

Does it... Does the magic get stronger if only one exists?

Velros was silent for a moment. *Yes.*

Okie doke. So, she's probably trying to kill me.

Velros again kept silent. Selen wasn't sure if this was another thing that they *physically* couldn't tell her because of their ties to her mother, or if it was by choice. Either way, Selen felt like she'd gotten her answer.

Selen opened her eyes after having closed the door on Velros in her mind, and hesitantly turned toward Deryn, who watched her with uncomfortable intensity.

"So, you can just slip away into the depths of your mind when you want to chat with this little friend of yours?" She sounded almost offended.

Selen lifted a brow. "This *little friend* is an ancient Lirium who bound itself to someone in my familial line and is now in my blood. They also had some interesting things to say, if you care to hear them."

Deryn narrowed her eyes at Selen, then nodded.

"Well I found out that... *she* is likely planning to kill me to absorb the entirety of the magic that runs through both of our blood—and is probably using Sidra to lure me there."

Deryn crossed her arms. "That is information I *did* care to hear."

No emotion. No panic.

"Okay, but Velros said before that mine and Sidra's magic combined can probably defeat her."

"That is also information I care to hear. Preferably before now." Deryn tilted her head at Selen.

Selen huffed. "Okay look. There is a lot going on up here," Selen said, pointing to her head. "I literally do not have enough of a grip on my own reality to be able to tell you what happens in there every moment."

Deryn rolled her eyes. "That is genuinely concerning."

Selen didn't disagree, but she didn't know how to *not* have her mind be a jumbled mess of chaos. "Moving past that," Selen eyed Deryn, "What do we know that can help us tomorrow?"

Deryn sighed but leaned forward, putting her hand on Selen's knee. "We know that... *she* will likely try to harm you. We know that your magic is interconnected. We know that your mind mate claims that Sidra and your magic combined can defeat said *she*. We *don't* know how powerful she is. We also don't know if anything that we've brainstormed is actually true—or whether it's just an assumption." Selen raised her brows and pursed her lips. "Sounds like we're good and fucked, Bird."

"It sure does." Selen nodded.

They made eye contact with each other and Selen couldn't help but let the laugh slip from her lips. Deryn's replying grin moved quickly into laughter as they looked at each other, trying to remain as quiet as possible as they gasped through their giggles. It was the release of emotions they had both pent up throughout the conversation. Nothing was truly funny about their situation except how fucked they likely were.

As their laughter waned, Selen leaned over and set her head on Deryn's lap. She glanced up at Deryn, who smiled down at her and started stroking her hair. It seemed so natural here—even with everything else, this felt like it fit.

"Hey, at least if I die, we don't have to talk about what happened earlier." Fucking neat. In an annoying turn of events, Deryn hadn't brought it up, but Selen had.

Deryn gently tugged her hair as she looked down at her.

"Ow." It hadn't really hurt.

"I wasn't going to bring it up." Deryn flicked Selen's forehead. "But if you're dying tomorrow, why not?"

Selen glared up at Deryn, looking anything but intimidating.

Deryn's face turned serious. "I don't know what this is, Bird. I know I care for you. I know I would prefer it if you didn't meet your demise tomorrow." She gave Selen a solemn grin. "I know that I want to talk about so much more with you when we are out of this."

Selen's smile had vanished. She knew that might not happen. She knew that she might never get to talk about those things with Deryn—she might never get to taste her smile again. So, Selen just stared up at her and memorized the lines of her face. Their emotions had manifested as unhinged during this brainstorming session, and Selen felt the weight of it all wedging itself into her spine.

"When we're out of this," Selen repeated. She didn't move from Deryn's lap, but her gaze flitted to the darkness above them.

The unspoken weight of the world settled onto them, and so they sat in silence until the sun rose, with Deryn's gentle fingers stroking Selen's hair. What a way to watch the sunrise of her last day alive.

Chapter Thirty-Eight

They packed the camp up in silence. From the bags under both Varric's and Nys's eyes, Selen imagined they'd slept as fitfully as she and Deryn.

Selen didn't feel any better about heading into whatever the day held in store after her and Deryn's brainstorming session. They had essentially circled a bunch of questions and come up with loosely developed theories, yet had not figured out anything solid about how to approach the day. If Sidra and Selen's powers could combine, how would they even go about doing so? Just grab a hand and send it? Even then, there was no telling if it would work, let alone defeat *her*.

What was her name?

Selen realized she didn't know her own mother's name. Or her father's.

Had she honestly never asked? Had their names been mentioned, but she hadn't bothered to remember them? She hadn't thought much about them growing up. Occasionally, her heart ached at a loss she couldn't remember, but most of the time, she simply wanted to move on and embrace the love she had now. She had also been so focused on Sidra that she hadn't stopped to think about the people they'd come from.

Her darkness suddenly made far more sense. Sidra's volatile emotions suddenly made more sense. Selen's, too, she supposed. But if they were the spawn of a kidnapping, power-hungry psychopath, was there a chance that Selen had inherited more than just her darkness?

Selen physically shuddered at the idea. She couldn't be a psychopath. If she was concerned about being a psychopath, that would suggest she wasn't one, right? That's how that worked.

Was Sidra?

No.

Maybe?

Selen pushed that thought from her mind. Honestly, it wouldn't truly matter if she were. The only thing that mattered was getting her back—they could deal with everything else later.

Deryn nudged Selen's shoulder with her own as they began their journey. She seemed to be getting better at noticing when Selen was drifting into the depths of her mind. Selen glanced at her. They seemed to have crossed some sort of line last night—and, despite all the other lines they crossed, this one seemed to create a sense of closeness the others hadn't.

Probably trauma bonding.

Selen looked away and took a deep breath. It would be her luck to finally make a connection with someone just to die, probably. Again, the chances that Selen wouldn't be able to combine her magic with Sidra's—and they'd be killed by her mother before doing anything to stop her—were higher. She had several years of experience in honing her magic on Selen. Selen literally had days.

But she didn't care what happened to her, so long as Sidra was okay.

Sidra always had to be okay.

Selen would never forgive herself if she weren't.

"Bird?" Deryn's gentle voice sent shivers up Selen's spine, pulling her mind from its dark hollow.

"Deryn," Selen replied expectantly.

"Can I ask something of you?" Deryn's brow was furrowed, and she looked down at the ground as they walked.

"I don't see why not," Selen shrugged.

Deryn paused for a moment. The tension from whatever she was about to ask radiated from her. "Don't give yourself up."

Selen frowned at Deryn, whose face was still scrunched with some emotion Selen couldn't pinpoint.

"Please, don't give yourself over to her. Even for Sidra." Deryn's voice was low and pleading, and part of Selen broke at that voice. In all the ways they had pretended that this was a joke—in all the ways they had blown off the severity of the situation—Selen hadn't expected Deryn to address the looming idea Selen had developed without directly voicing.

So, yes, part of Selen broke at Deryn's request, not because of the fear in Deryn's voice, which made Selen's heart clench, but because Selen couldn't promise that. She wouldn't lie to her.

Deryn got her answer from Selen's silence, and took a deep breath before closing her eyes. Selen did the same.

No emotions. No panic.

Selen didn't know what the MistralWood had in store for them, but it seemed calm. As if it had taken Selen's expelled magic through the ground as a peace offering. As if it were hungry, and she had satiated its hunger. For now, at least. Hopefully, it would be enough that they wouldn't face any of its trials as they trudged toward the temple that acted as the wood's heart.

Of course that would be where she had taken Sidra. It seemed melodramatic, although the absolute power that emanated from that part of the land had to be where she intended to drain Selen of her magic and her life—just as that mystery terror had tried to do to Nys. She'd had an entire society, Varric, and Deryn to save her. Selen had all three from the group, but she wasn't entirely sure Nys and Varric would be very driven to save her.

Selen, too, was an imbalance in the world. If Selen and Sidra did somehow defeat their mother, that would mean that the entirety of Velros's magic would flow through Selen, making her a bigger threat. Would Deryn even be able to stand up to her, then? Would she try to take Selen down once her powers became too strong?

Not going there. The chances of Selen being the one to make it out of that interaction were slim to none, anyway.

Velros had been silent all morning—no gentle raps against the wall in her mind. Selen wondered if they were repulsed by the magic that flowed here. While the Mistral-Wood's hunger seemed to be held temporarily at bay, Selen couldn't help but feel its presence all around. Watching them—almost in warning of what was to come.

"We need to discuss the plan." Nys's voice cut through the stagnant silence. Selen hadn't been sure she would ever be happy to hear Nys's voice, but turns out she had been wrong.

"Is there already a plan?" Selen asked, glancing briefly throughout the group.

"We wouldn't go into any situation without a plan. That's how you die," Varric stated firmly.

"Why couldn't I be a part of the planning process?" Selen frowned.

"Because, in this situation, you are too rooted in emotion. It's compromising." Nys looked Selen up and down. "And you're a liability with your magic. *And* you've never done this before."

"Is that all?" Selen tilted her head at Nys, who hissed at her in return.

"The plan is relatively simple, Bird." Deryn's smooth voice interjected before Selen stirred the pot further by simply existing in Nys's presence without a mediator.

She was like a small, angry cat.

Selen winked at Nys before turning to Deryn. The scuffling sound behind her indicated that Varric probably held her back from pouncing.

Deryn shook her head, but a small grin grazed her lips. "We don't know where Sidra is located within the temple, but we know that you are our best chance of actually tracking her down. So, you and I will be responsible for finding Sidra while Varric and Nys focus on your... *her*." Deryn paused, as if contemplating whether to tell her the next part. "We have to anticipate that she will have set traps, and will likely be near Sidra. She will surely be waiting for you. Varric will try to get close enough to figure out any weaknesses, I will be looking for holes in her magic, and Nys will be prepared to act on any of those weaknesses. We get Sidra, and we get out. *All* of us."

"And what will I do?"

"*You* will try not to get us all killed," Nys snipped.

Selen sent her a glare.

Deryn also shot a look at Nys. "You will solely focus on finding Sidra through your bond."

Selen thought through their plan. She supposed it was fine, but there was one piece that didn't make a lot of sense.

"Wouldn't it make more sense for Varric to go with me?" Selen asked.

Varric glanced up at Deryn, whose features had shifted slightly. After a moment of uncomfortable silence, Deryn spoke.

"Why?" Deryn still wasn't looking at her.

"Well, your magic allows you to identify weaknesses in magic; Varric's could be helpful against *her*, in understanding her motives and identifying psychological weaknesses, but that won't be of any use if she kills us with her magic before we learn anything about her. It would make more sense if you go with Nys to keep her at bay, while Varric and I work together."

Deryn sighed and squeezed her eyes shut. She glanced back at the other two, who had matching 'I told you so' looks in their eyes. Selen glanced between them a few times. It didn't take a genius to realize that Deryn was the only person who didn't agree with the change in plan.

"I'm going with you, Bird." Deryn's voice was violently low as she spoke.

Selen softened her voice. "Deryn, it doesn't make sense."

Her words pulled Deryn's attention from the ground and back to her. She knew why Deryn wanted to go with her. If it came down to it, Selen would sacrifice herself to save her sister—and Deryn knew it. Varric might let it happen; he might not. But Deryn damn sure wouldn't allow her to do so.

But that wasn't entirely why Selen didn't want Deryn to come with her. Selen needed to save Sidra, and if Deryn's focus was on saving Selen, the whole plan would go to shit. Feelings aside, it didn't make sense for Deryn to *not* go with Nys.

Deryn clenched her jaw as she watched Selen. "I can't let you get hurt." There was an intense desperation in her gaze.

It was hidden behind her harsh exterior, but Selen could see it.

"Varric won't let me get hurt either," Selen said, looking back at Varric expectantly. He held her gaze for a moment. His stare was intense. He knew, better than Deryn, maybe, the depths she would go to further their goal. To get her sister back. He had seen it in the tapestry of her Being. He had seen it when she had willingly welcomed Velros to become woven with that tapestry. He knew her motives. So, he knew that her motive right now was to appease Deryn, so she could remove the risk of Deryn trying to stop her from making the sacrifice she had asked her not to make.

Varric's eyes flicked to Deryn, then back to Selen. Selen barely shifted her head, but Varric seemed to understand that he needed to answer quickly.

Beside Selen, Deryn still brooded, missing the unspoken moment. Nys caught it, though. She watched Selen carefully before exchanging an understanding nod with Varric.

"Yes. I will make sure she doesn't get hurt." He spoke stiffly and without breaking eye contact.

Selen didn't need anyone to protect her, but she couldn't allow Deryn to jeopardize Sidra because of her feelings and own stubbornness. That wasn't an option, even if Deryn's desire to protect her made Selen's heart warm.

No emotions. No panic.

Deryn looked at Selen, then glanced back at Varric. She gave Selen one more pleading look, angling her head as though she were forcing off the urge to fight back and get her way. Selen held her ground on this. She was honestly surprised they were letting her have any say in the plan at all, but based on the looks Nys and Varric had given Deryn, it seemed that they had already proposed her version.

"Fine," Deryn grumbled.

Selen's victory was short-lived as the image of temple ruins formed in the distance. They all stopped. The push from the temple was now muted in comparison to the pull Selen had felt in her chest. Her bond with Sidra went taught, as if she, too, had realized how close she was.

Selen immediately knew where to go, where to find her —and a wave of emotions swept over her at the familiarity of that tug. There was nothing that could stop her from getting to Sidra.

Nothing.

Chapter Thirty-Nine

Surrounding the temple ruins were trees, along with jagged, moss-covered rocks—that seemed part of what may have once been a huge, stone building. The stone still standing was weather-worn, and appeared as though it could topple at any moment. One wall was fully erect, and housed the entrance. The gothic archway reminded Selen of the entrance to Celestara—gaudy and overwhelmingly large. The roof of the temple had long since given way to time, leaving the area entirely exposed to the elements—which was apparent from the greenery that wrapped itself in and around the ruins. The vast foundation of the building held little of its structure, but Selen knew that there were places that could easily act as a hiding spot for whatever lay within.

Tree roots had begun to mingle with the stones of the walkway that led to the temple, and Selen found she had to consistently look down at her feet to ensure she didn't stumble. She couldn't help but feel like the roots were reaching for her, begging her to trip so they could absorb her alongside the rest of the magic it pushed and pulled throughout the MistralWood.

Selen could feel *her*, then. There was no smell like the one that had accompanied the shadows from last night, and she could feel those shadow hounds lurking in the trees. She knew they were being watched from all sides, and from the unease emanating from the trio, they knew it, too. The woods had fallen silent. There had been much sound throughout their journey, but the air was eerily still here. Even the pulse of the magic seemed to pause as they approached.

It had become apparent that Selen might not leave this place. Even though she had known that, she didn't like the stone that settled in her stomach as her reality neared. The reality that her sister was traumatized—potentially beyond repair. The reality that it was their mother that had been the cause of all of this. The reality that it was potentially her father that had gotten them away from her. The reality that she had no idea what had happened to him. The reality that Selen was so deeply interconnected with a monster.

No emotions. No panic.

Deryn's hand brushed Selen's—seemingly as much to reassure herself as it was to reassure Selen. Selen looped her index finger around Deryn's pinky, and a small shudder seemed to run through Deryn. Selen felt the warmth of their small connection. She could savor this. She *would* savor this.

Soon they would separate, and she may never see Deryn again.

Deryn sighed and halted their approach a few hundred feet from the ruins, where the trees blocked them enough that they could step off the path and not be seen—although, the looming presence of shadows reminded Selen that they were still in enemy territory.

Still holding onto Selen, Deryn turned to the group and relayed the plan again.

Selen's mind drifted as Deryn was speaking. She leaned around the nearest tree until the ruins were just barely visible between the branches. She felt like her vision was tunneling in on the entrance of the ruins, the rest of the world fading around her as she stared. A small light flickered in the archway. Beckoning. Calling her to it.

Deryn gripped Selen's chin with her thumb and forefinger, turning her head back to her.

"Did you hear me, Bird?" Deryn's eyes shifted between hers, searching their depths.

"No. Sorry." Selen shook her head. Her vision returned to its normal state.

"We have to stick with the plan." She continued to hold her chin. "No matter what happens." She dropped her chin, and her intense gaze was unavoidable as Selen squirmed. This was the look of the leader of this group, but just as quickly as her gaze had intensified, it softened. Deryn's brow furrowed again, and Selen wanted to reach up and smooth out those lines with her thumb. She almost did.

No emotions. No panic.

Worrying about seeing Deryn again couldn't be Selen's focus; it had to be Sidra. It had to be about saving her. Only her.

No emotions.

No panic.

Deryn's jaw flexed as if Selen had just said those words out loud. She released Selen's chin and turned back toward Varric and Nys.

"You know your orders?" Deryn asked sternly.

They both nodded at her before exchanging a look. They didn't want to be separated either, but they were mission driven. Their gazes held, and Selen saw a softness in Nys's eyes that she hadn't thought her capable of. She then proceeded to shove Varric's shoulder and turn back to face Deryn, face returning to its permanent sneer. Varric grinned slightly and settled back into his stance.

Suddenly, Selen realized that she didn't just want Sidra to get out of this. She wanted all three of these people to get out of this. If her life was as valuable to *her* as she thought it might be, then she could trade herself for them if need be. She already had the idea for Sidra, so she didn't mind doing it for them, if only so that Nys's sneer lines didn't end up permanently ingrained in her face. Varric and Nys deserved a chance.

"She knows we're here," Selen said at a near whisper, turning her eyes back toward the ruins. "She's watching us."

"We know," Varric stated. "What do you feel?"

"A pull." Selen glanced back at him. "I can't tell if it's from Sidra or…" She couldn't bring herself to say her relation to this Being. She also didn't know her name, so she would either have no name or just be referred to as *her*.

"Where is it pulling you?" Deryn asked quietly, staying close to Selen as they moved closer to the temple.

"To the archway." Selen's focus was solely focused there. "There is nothing beyond that right now."

The tugging in her chest grew and grew with each step they took, and Selen tried to take deep breaths to ease the pressure building within her. Her sights were set on that archway, and the deep green of the moss on the surrounding trees and fallen stone began to fade away as her vision again tunneled on the entrance. Varric might have been talking again, but his voice grew as muffled as the pull within Selen deepened.

The world became calm and slow. She blinked and looked to her side, finding Varric looking at the archway before them. Where had Nys and Deryn gone? She had missed that entire interaction. Had Deryn said anything to her?

Varric's head slowly turned towards her, and when he spoke, his voice was low and slow. "You ready?"

His face was fuzzy. Selen blinked, but her lids felt so heavy. She nodded, and it felt like her head had grown too big for her shoulders.

They moved up the steps to the archway in painfully slow movements, the world wobbling and tilting as they did. As they reached the top of the steps, Selen took a moment to steady herself on the stone of the archway. She had to get it together if she was going to be successful, but the entrance called to her. She knew that if she stepped foot in there, it would stop whatever was happening to her. She didn't know why, but she needed the relief that would come from stepping into the ruins. She thought she might have felt hands on her shoulders and muffled yelling, but she pushed off the wall and stepped through the archway.

Immediately, her senses came back to her—as if she had finally answered the call that had been pulling her here. She took a breath, filled with the scent of sage and rosemary. She closed her eyes and inhaled deeply again. As she released, she opened her eyes and found a deep red cushioned rug beneath her feet. The walls around her were of a beautiful, dark stone, and sconces in the shapes of hands holding candles lined them. The vast entryway led to two wide staircases, spiraling to meet at the same level where a statue of one of the goddesses that Selen didn't recognize sat. To her left, she could see a bright room filled with books and tables. To her right there was what seemed like a dining area.

She knew this place. She recognized it.

Selen looked behind her. Had she come here alone? The archway housed a large door that had intricate carvings in the dark wood. It sounded almost like someone was pounding on it, but it was so distant she must have imagined it.

Selen felt that pull in her chest again. She moved forward.

Was this home?

Selen's foot caught on something, and she stumbled

forward, but when she looked down, confusion cascaded over her. There was nothing there but the plush rug.

The pull in her refocused Selen on her mission.

To go home.

It called to her.

That was her mission, right?

To find this place and stay here.

She smiled as the sconces around her seemed to move with her, guiding her between the large staircases and to the back of her home.

Her hip smacked into a table that she hadn't realized was there, and she hissed in pain. For a wooden table, it sure felt like stone. She stood again, ignoring the ache in her now-bruised hip.

Selen pushed through a set of large, wooden doors and out into a covered terrace. She could smell the freshly-brewed tea and greenery that covered the space. There was a small table in the corner, looking out into the vast forest.

Selen's heart softened as she saw who sat there. Her dark hair and strong features matched her own—and, though aged, there was a warmth to her features that Selen loved to see.

"You're home," she whispered with a smile. It brightened her onyx eyes.

"Hi, Mom." Selen grinned and sat at the table with her.

"It's been some time since you've been here." She grinned as she sipped from her glass.

"I had quite a journey getting back here." Selen couldn't

remember much of her journey now; she just gave in to the peace of finally being home.

"Have some tea." Her mother waved her hand, and a cup appeared that already had the perfect portions of tea, sugar, and milk.

Selen picked up the cup and almost brought it to her mouth when her mother's voice distracted her. She set it back down to listen. "I know you've just returned, but it's almost time to go on another journey." As her mother spoke, the smile she had previously worn slowly faded.

"There is no need to concern her with such things when she's only just come back to us," a deep voice said from the doors behind them. Selen's heart skipped just as her stomach dropped.

He stood tall, with blonde hair that flowed down to the nape of his neck, pushed back by his fingers. He had rugged features and icy eyes. Selen knew those eyes. She cherished those eyes. Selen stood and ran over to her father, who embraced her in a warm hug that ignited Selen's soul. She melted into his embrace as if she had never experienced it before.

"Father," she whispered, tightening her hold.

"I trust that you found your way home well?" He lifted her chin with his finger, examining her face for injury. His eyes were the color of the ice caps on the mountains that surrounded their home, but there was no limit of warmth in them.

"It calls to me." She stepped back from him as they sat at the table.

"Tell us, daughter, do you fair well at school?" Her father's deep voice was a symphony.

Selen thought back to school. It was fuzzy. She remembered icy eyes—but on someone else. Selen's brow furrowed.

"Where might my sister be?" Selen asked as she glanced between her parents.

They exchanged amused looks. "You don't have a sister, silly girl," her mother chuckled.

Something twisted in Selen.

Didn't she?

Selen stared down at the tea in front of her as she sat back at the table.

"Has your education been so challenging that it is eating away at your mind?" Her father chuckled alongside her mother.

Something seemed off. Who had those icy eyes belonged to if not her father?

A warm hand wrapped around hers as she stared into her tea. She could almost swear she saw trees above her in the reflection, but when she looked up she saw only the ceiling above them.

"I know it is lonely at school." Her mothers warm voice coated her senses, pulling her focus back to her. "I imagine that your friends do come to feel like your sisters. Like Aleya?"

Selen's gaze shot to her mother's.

Aleya?

Green eyes and chestnut curls popped into her mind.

She hadn't discussed Aleya with her mom. She hadn't discussed her with anyone. "How?" Selen's brow furrowed.

"We know much, my dear girl. Especially when the Headmaster is our close friend."

Selen shook her head.

"Drink your tea, my love. It will sooth the stress that your schooling has put on your mind." Selen smiled up at her mother, but it felt more forced than before.

Deandra. The headmaster. Was that all she was? A family friend?

Selen took a sip of her drink. It was as delicious as it looked and smelled, with hints of vanilla and cream swirling within the perfectly-steeped black tea.

Vanilla. There was something else that smelled like that. Something that she cared for. And leather. Vanilla and leather.

Flashes of the desert passed through her mind.

Selen had never been to the desert. She stared down at her glass.

The cup felt rough against her palm and lips, and she glanced down at the smooth glass. It didn't make sense. Her senses were confusing her.

She shook her head again and set down the cup.

"Something feels off," Selen said, looking at her mother. Something flashed in those onyx eyes that startled Selen. She'd never felt unease from her mother—only love and adoration.

What had changed since she was last here?

When had she last been here?

Home.

Her home.

Selen glanced around her as the room itself seemed to become unfamiliar.

"Mom?" Selen looked to her mother for comfort, as she always had. Selen pushed back in her chair as the image of a blonde woman with age lines and kind eyes dabbed a wound on her knee.

That wasn't her mother.

Those onyx eyes watched her carefully.

"What's going on?" Selen asked.

"You're home." Her mothers grin was anything but comforting. "You're finally home."

Unease crept over Selen as she looked to her father. He was frozen with a grin that seemed to shift from the warm gaze she had first looked upon to a forced, painful look that sent Selen's heart to her stomach.

His eyes glazed and his skin began to droop, and Selen stood, horror racking through her.

She had seen this before.

When?

Selen closed her eyes and shook her head. This wasn't real.

But what was?

When she opened them, her father's skin had drooped further, and shadows spilled from him. His eyes. His nose. His mouth. His ears.

Selen screamed and dropped to the floor. "Mom, what's

happening?" she wailed. She was too terrified to take her gaze off of whatever was happening to her father.

"You're home." She stood and came closer to Selen. "You're finally home."

Selen's gaze shot to her approaching mother as her heartrate pounded in her ears.

Her mother's smile had grown too big for her face, and her eyes were bloodshot. Selen felt her breath quicken.

"What?" She tried to push further back into the wall, but her mother's face was now centimeters from hers. Selen whimpered, turning her face to the side. She needed to get away from whatever was happening.

This couldn't be real.

Something slithered from her mother's gaped mouth and caressed Selen's cheek. It was cold and felt like death, and Selen's lip trembled and she pushed and pushed into the wall, only to be met by an unmoving force behind her.

"You're home." Selen's mother's eyes darkened as the onyx of her irises spread out and into her skin, until it looked like a rot had spread from them. "You're finally home."

The scream that left Selen was that of absolute terror.

Chapter Forty

Selen continued to scream as she faced the creature that had once been her mother as her body contorted and shifted, bones cracking and bending into unnatural positions. With each move, her skin was further consumed by darkness, until she was nothing but a snarling shadow figure.

The walls began to fall into shadowy swirls, and the lights that had previously brightened the room vanished, blanketing the crumbling stone in darkness. Selen watched as the world around her faded into nothing but ruins.

Ruins.

Of a temple.

Of *the* temple.

Selen shook her head. Her mind was racing.

None of it had been real.

A choked sob left her. Her mother, her father—the life

that she didn't have, wouldn't have, was robbed from her. It was all fake?

Why was she here?

Her mission. Her goal.

To find... *something*.

She squeezed her eyes shut.

Icy eyes. Silver hair.

They weren't her father's.

Mischievous smile.

Her eyes shot open.

Sidra.

Her sister.

Her fucking *sister*.

Selen gasped as reality crashed into her like a wave. She looked at the shadow hound in front of her and slowly stood.

Dried tears pulled at her skin as she watched the shadow creature that had once been her mother. She knew who had done this. It didn't seem to be moving toward her, but as she slid against the stone wall, its shadowy gaze watched her every move.

Selen finally looked up at the ruins. The archway that acted as an entrance was nowhere to be found. How far into the ruins had she gone?

Her gaze snapped to where the table had been, and there sat the woman who had caused so much terror and destruction in her life.

Selen sneered at her.

"Is that any way to greet your mother?" Her cold voice radiated through Selen.

Selen forced herself to stand tall. "You're no mother to me." A sense of calm had surged through Selen now that she faced this person, and she briefly glanced around them.

Where was Varric? And the other two? Deryn.

"I gave you life, girl. You should show some respect." She angled her head at Selen, the act predatory.

"Where is she?" Selen stepped forward, and the hound growled low in its chest. Selen stopped but held her ground.

"We can get to that." She flicked her wrist dismissively. "First, I'd like to... *catch up.*" She grinned just before shadowy tendrils wrapped around Selen's waist and pulled her to sit on the broken stone that she was using as a table. Selen pulled at the tendrils, but they didn't budge.

She sat, wrapped and bound by shadows. Her fear had been replaced with rage. She was sure she wouldn't leave here now—there was no humanity in those dark eyes. Her hair seemed to swirl alongside the shadows and her eyes.

Those *eyes.*

They were rotten to the core.

"Where. Is. She." Selen ground the words out.

"She lives." Her gaze roamed over Selen. "Since you cannot think of anything else without that knowledge."

"Where?"

"In time, dear girl." She chuckled, and it sounded like nails scratching on a chalkboard.

Selen looked around her for anything that could help— any sign that the other three were alive.

That *Deryn* was alive.

No emotions. No panic.

Selen squeezed her eyes shut and took a deep breath, opening them to find her mother watching her inquisitively. "What do you know of me, girl?" There was a genuine curiosity in her voice.

Selen settled in her seat and frowned. "I know nothing of you. I don't even know your name." She hoped that cut her.

"That *witch* didn't even give you the name of the one that gave you life and power?" she hissed at Selen.

"I had no need of it." Selen glared.

Her mother sat back against the stone and crossed her arms. "She's bold. Much like her mother," she crooned.

"I'm nothing like you." Selen shoved against the shadows.

"Oh we are so much more alike than you could even imagine, dark one."

Selen broke the wall in her mind.

Velros! She screamed into the void. *Velros, where are you?*

She sprinted into the darkness of her mind.

"Ah, ah, ah." Her mother's cold fingers lifted Selen's chin. "Do not call for your dark friend. She cannot save you."

Selen scowled. How did she know that she was calling for Velros?

"You gave yours a name. How peculiar." She sat back again, staring up at the trees that drooped over the tops of the ruins. "Mine was always cruel." Her tone was almost a sing-song lilt.

"Because you are cruel." Selen steadied her voice.

She laughed. "I suppose that's true." She reached forward and grabbed a few strands of Selen's hair and rubbed it between her fingers. "I always imagined you'd look like me." Her eyes glaze slightly. "When I saw *her*, I knew that she took after your father."

Selen's heart skipped.

"Those *eyes*." She stood and began pacing. "So similar to his that I almost forgot what he'd done to me." She stopped and turned her head slightly back towards Selen. "I imagine that hers will look the same as his did when the life fades from them."

Selen thrashed against the shadows. "You can't hurt her!" Selen screamed. All of the rage she felt manifested in that scream.

"Oh!" She clapped her hands together. "There's so much potential! You almost let her out."

Selen's breath was ragged as she glared, and while her head drooped, her gaze tore into her mother. "What is your name?" Selen growled.

Her mother tilted her head at Selen. "I suppose that if we are to work together, you should know my name."

"I will never work with you."

"Won't you?" She waved her hand, and Sidra appeared on the ground beside her. Selen shoved forward, tears immediately stinging her eyes.

"Sid," she whispered.

Sidra didn't move, though. Her unconscious body continued to lie, unmoving, on the hard, stone floor. Bruises still lined her neck and wrists, but were now accompanied by a cut lip, a bruised cheek, and a black eye —not to mention the countless scrapes that bloodied her pale skin.

Selen angled her head in anguish as she looked at her. "What did you do to her?" Selen screamed.

"She served her purpose." Her mother raised her hand, and Selen wasn't sure what she was going to do, but fear entombed her more intensely than ever before.

"No!" Selen cried. "Gods, please no. Don't hurt her."

"Oh?" Her mother stopped whatever she was planning to do. "And what will you give for her life?"

Selen glared up at her, defeat clenching her heart.

She thought of Aeden and his sarcastic sense of humor. She thought of Deandra and her comforting warmth.

She thought of desert eyes. She thought of vanilla and leather. She thought of soft hands against her skin—hands she'd never feel again.

"Anything," Selen crumbled. "I'll do anything to save her."

"That"—her mother shot at her with a speed she wasn't sure was possible—"that is much to give for a useless life."

"How can you say that? She's your daughter," Selen growled.

"And she played her daughterly part so very well." She stroked her cold finger down the side of Selen's face.

"You're a monster!" Selen couldn't help the sob that came from her.

"And your emotions make you *weak*," she hissed as she got into Selen's face.

"Take my life. Just... just let her and the others go." Selen hung her head.

"Take your life?" She stood back up and a ruthless cackle came from her. "I'm not going to kill you, stupid girl," she scoffed.

"What?" Selen looked up at her. "Why not?"

"Do you seek death so badly you ask why I won't give it to you?" She tilted her head.

"What do you want from me?" Selen shook her head. Her hair clung to her neck and cheeks and crawled along her skin.

"If I were to absorb the magic you have now, I would gain nothing but a drop. What a waste of a life that would be."

"So, what? You're going to train me?" Selen pushed and pulled at the magic around her.

"I'm going to *mold* you. Conform you until you're the perfect. Little. Magician." She tapped Selen's nose in between each word.

"I hate you."

"Good," she sighed, as if it was expected. As if she were bored. "That will fuel you. Hate corrupts your soul and drives you to darkness—right where I want you."

A small shuffling behind her mother startled Selen. Sidra's tear-streaked and swollen eyes looked up at them.

"Selen?" Sidra choked on a sob.

"It's going to be okay, Sid. It's going to be okay. Just stay there. Don't move," Selen pleaded, but Sidra began to slide to her feet.

Her mother's gaze never left Selen, as if Sidra was no threat at all. Maybe she wasn't. Maybe neither of them were.

She didn't even want to try and use Sidra's magic with hers to try and defeat their mother. Their mother had warped Selen's reality so much that she had genuinely thought that was her life—she had no power that could match that. She would crush them in a minute if they tried.

Selen could at least save them for now. She could save Sidra, Deryn, Nys, and Varric. At least they could have a chance. Nys and Varric could give whatever weird relationship they had a chance. Sidra could return to school and learn her magic the way she should have. Deryn could find someone else—she could fall in love, and have someone to sit on a stone wall with and look at lovingly.

Selen let out a gentle sob.

"Please. Let them live," Selen whispered. "I'll give you all of me. Just let them live."

A broken roar came from the side of them, and both Selen and her mother's heads snapped to the side as Deryn beat against the invisible wall that kept her out.

Selen tilted her head, and another sob came out. "*No,*" She whispered as tears slid down her cheeks. Selen briefly leaned into the shadows and pushed everything down to watch her. Deryn's eyes were so filled with pain and panic.

Selen had never wanted to cause her any harm. She had a chance to remove that pain by removing herself.

Deryn beat and beat at the wall of magic until her hands were bloodied. Her look of agony and desperation was all Selen could see on her face, teeth gritted as she clearly used her magic to find any holes in Selen's mother's magic. She punched the wall again when she found none.

"Oh, young love," her mother crooned in Selen's ear as they watched Deryn, and her heart cracked and hardened. "So fragile."

"Bird, please." Her scream broke through the magic, or her mother had let it through. "Don't do this, Selen, please!" she screamed.

Selen watched as tears streamed down her face. It always had to be this way.

"Let me go," Selen whispered. Deryn seemed to hear her, and she dropped to her knees, but kept beating the wall. "Let me go." Selen's voice broke.

A tear dropped down Deryn's cheek, and she stopped hitting the wall. Her eyes met Selen's, and there was so much pain—so much heartbreak. Selen had never wanted to cause her this kind of pain, but there was no other way to save them all. This was the *only* way.

"No!" Sidra's voice reached Selen, and before she realized what she was doing, Sidra sent a wave of light from her hand that sent their mother back a few feet.

Sidra using magic was something Selen wasn't sure she'd been prepared for, and she was right; the sight of Sidra's entire body trembling after releasing the blast had the hairs on Selen's arms standing on end.

"That's inconvenient." Their mother glanced at Sidra as she wiped her dress. With a flick of her wrist, a wave of shadows shot for Sidra, knocking her back so hard that Selen could hear the crack of her skull on the stone behind her.

The world stopped.

Selen let out a blood-curdling scream that she was sure could be heard throughout the forest. The world darkened around her as she watched Sidra's body fall to the ground. Every emotion turned to rage and hatred, pulling at that ocean within her. It raged. The calm waters of her magic began to flow and splash until they were rampant waves, breaking against the wall of her mind.

She felt Velros's presence crash into her like they had just used all their strength to break through a barrier. Her shadows mingled with those binding her and pried them away, and Selen stood slowly as she felt the power form around her like a cocoon.

She wasn't afraid anymore.

She felt only the darkness, mingling with her soul and her blood. It pulsed through her, visibly disturbing the stones around them.

Her mother's gaze moved back to Selen, and she seemed thrilled. Selen's hatred for her spread from her heart to every other part of her. She felt it under her skin, seeping out of every pore. She was darkness. She *was* power.

Selen felt her feet lift off the ground, but it felt so natural.

Her mother's laugh ignited her magic like a log to a flame.

Selen released a primal scream as her hands shot towards her mother. Shadows shot from her palms and wrapped around her mother's body and throat. The laughter didn't stop, though.

Selen hated that laugh. She wanted to rip her vocal chords from her throat. Selen squeezed her shadows, and the gurgling sound that became her mother's laugh showed her efforts were working.

Selen floated closer, and the darkness swarming her vision darkened. Selen felt herself slipping, like she was falling within her own mind. All she knew was that this person was a threat that needed to be eliminated.

"Can you feel it?" Her mother's strained voice pushed through Selen's mind. "The call of the darkness?"

Selen tilted her head, and she squeezed her shadows further. Her mother coughed, and blood dripped from her mouth, but her smile didn't fade.

Selen was drifting further and further into her mind. The darkness pulled her in, welcoming her like an old friend. She fell and fell until the image of this horrible woman was nothing but a swirl of shadows.

Then she was standing on the cliff.

She was looking out at the waters of her magic, far shallower than they typically were.

She felt Velros's presence next to her without having to look.

You're pulling too much. Velros's voice was calm as they addressed Selen.

Selen looked out and watched as the ocean drained.

I don't care, she said, and she meant it. She didn't care if she was left with nothing if it took down the monster that had brought them here.

You should. Velros didn't move as they, too, watched the waters drop. *You can fight back.*

I am fighting back. Selen glanced at Velros, who wore her skin.

Velros's eyes were almost sorrowful as Selen looked at her. She couldn't feel anything, though, as she watched her magic fade with her life. She felt nothing.

I mean against this. Velros waved their arm to the ever-shrinking body of water.

Why should I? If she goes down with me, then it's worth it.

She won't. Selen snapped her head to where Velros stood. They finally turned their eyes to meet hers. *You will have died for nothing.*

Just like Sidra? A gentle pull at Selen's heart reminded her that there were emotions within her. She shoved them back down.

She lives. Velros spoke quietly.

A light sparked in Selen but quickly fizzled out. *But I can't save her.*

Velros looked back at the waters. *The stars shine brighter in the presence of darkness, yet darkness exists without starlight.*

Selen furrowed her brow. That light sparked again. Selen recognized it for hope.

Velros looked sidelong at Selen, and those shadowy eyes tore into her soul. She was looking at a mirror of herself. Velros grinned slightly as what looked like a sunrise crested over the draining sea. Selen watched as it rose and rose, then realized it was shooting towards her.

A star, shooting through the night.

Chapter Forty-One

The star shot towards her and lit up the darkness of her mind. Selen had no idea where this was coming from. It felt foreign, but welcome.

The star hit Selen's chest with an unexpectedly desperate force, pushing her back into the darkness of her mind. It pushed her until she could see the image of her horrifying mother in front of her. It shoved her back into her physical body.

Selen gasped. Her shadows wrapped almost entirely around her mother's face, threatening to drag her under, but something made her pause. A new light in her soul. She looked down and saw Sidra, broken and bleeding, grabbing Selen's wrist. Light flowed from her into Selen. Her starlight. Selen stared down at where their magic connected, and the shadows transformed into something different. It turned into night. A wash of deep blacks and grays intermingled with the bright lights of stars.

Selen's breath caught as she saw the determination in her sister's eyes. Her sister, who had experienced so much hell in these last two weeks, stood by her side, blood coating her silver hair. Selen reached out with a tendril of darkness and stroked her sister's cheek. A small tear slipped from Sidra's eye, and Selen wiped it away.

She lived.

Sidra lived.

Selen felt her control slip. It was just enough weakness that their mother blew them back with a burst of shadows. Selen caught Sidra before they hit the ground.

They stood together, fingers interlocked as they held hands.

"You can't win," she cackled, spitting blood on the stone floor.

"We have to try!" Sidra yelled. The power in her voice almost brought Selen to her knees. It gave her a renewed sense of strength.

Magic exploded from their mother—a tornado of shadows, that encompassed the three of them until Selen and Sidra's hair swirled around them. The air thinned as their magic built, and Selen could feel the mingling of their power. It transformed and turned to night, pushing around them, protecting them from the stones that swirled with the shadows.

Sidra turned toward Selen until they were face to face. Selen moved, too. They grabbed each other's hands, and the world stood still as soon as their eyes met. The mischievous look in Sidra's eyes blazed alongside a stifled rage that lit her like a fire.

She grinned. "We do this together."

Selen shook her head in disbelief and wonder at Sidra's ability to smile, but couldn't help the grin that spread across her own face.

"Together," Selen agreed.

"Do you know what to do?" Sidra asked.

"Not a fucking clue," Selen said as she drew from the small bit of power that still lingered in her.

"Let's fuck up the bitch who birthed us." Sidra's grin was feral.

Selen released her left hand from Sidra's right, and they unleashed their power on their mother.

The wretched smile fell from her face as the force of night collided with her, sending her flying back against the stone of the ruined wall.

The shadows around them stilled and turned into whisps.

The whole forest seemed to stop moving, and they glanced at each other in unease before looking to where their mother lay.

They approached, and she limply sat against the stone wall.

She grinned up at them, blood coating her teeth. "Oh, how you've grown." She spat the blood on the ground before them. "My girls." Her tone was condescending, even in her broken state.

"We aren't your anything, bitch," Sidra hissed at her.

She laughed. It was a raspy, horrible sound. "End it, then," she challenged.

Selen reached out a hand to do just that, but the slight tug from Sidra's hand—still held in hers—stopped her. Selen furrowed her brow and looked at her sister in question.

Sidra took a small breath and nodded her head.

Selen turned back toward their mother, whose gaze had turned dark, and almost released her power when the icy sound of her mother's voice made her pause.

"My name is Selmara." Her voice had become soft. Selen felt the weight of that name settle on her.

Selmara.

She recognized it without having ever known it, as if it pulled at memories so deeply-sewn in her mind that she couldn't access them.

Her mother's sharp cackle broke Selen's thoughts, and a wave of power pushed her and Sidra back again. But this time, when they looked up, she was gone.

Selen released Sidra's hand and rushed the spot her mother had been. The foul odor of her shadows—even her presence—had disappeared.

Selen spun in circles and frantically searched around them. "Where is she?" she whispered. "Where is she?"

Her whispers quickly developed into a scream as she kept repeating the phrase until warm hands gripped her shoulders. Selen's eyes still shot from place to place, panic encasing around her, when they met desert eyes and stopped.

Selen dropped to her knees, and the owner of those eyes dropped with her.

"You're a fucking fool, Bird." Deryn's smooth voice tucked over Selen like a blanket. Selen focused on her face. On the curve of her lips. On the silver of her scars. She couldn't help the well of emotions that spilled from her as she fell into Deryn.

Deryn embraced her, and it felt like home. *True* home. Like everything she had fought for had led to this. With her.

"So, it seems like you've got some shit to explain." Sidra strode up beside them.

Selen shot to her feet and wrapped her arms around her sister. She let her sobs out freely now.

"Fucking gods, Selen. I'm severely concussed," Sidra said, but wrapped her arms around Selen anyway.

"I thought you were dead." Selen moved back and placed her hands on either side of Sidra's face, gently tilting her face so she could examine her injuries. The joy she felt faded as she took them in. "We have to get you to a healer."

"Well, yeah." Sidra shoved Selen's hands down. "But can we get the fuck outa here first?"

Selen grinned, a fresh set of tears lining her eyes. Sidra glanced behind Selen for a moment. "Do you think she'll be back?"

Selen's grin fell. She was sure she would; It seemed as though their mother, Selmara, had bigger plans for her, and couldn't imagine this was a win at all. Selmara wouldn't be gone for long, but hopefully long enough that Selen and Sidra could master whatever magic it was that had given them the strength to fight her. She had to believe that they had that time. Until then, they had to get out of this godsforsaken forest.

Varric moved up the stairs where Deryn had come from, carrying Nys. Her head was pressed into his shoulder. Selen startled.

"Is she—" She couldn't say it.

Varric shook his head and looked down at Nys. "She's unconscious." He looked back at Selen. "Her hounds fought us the entire time." His eyes were dark, and an unspoken concern lingered there. "I couldn't get in." He dropped his gaze.

"It wasn't your fault." Selen approached him, briefly looking down at Nys. Her face was peaceful—far more peaceful than she was used to seeing from her. "She warped my mind."

"And you're better now?" His question was genuine. Selen didn't know the answer though. So much had altered her brain in the last week that she didn't know what was real and what wasn't.

Varric took her silence and nodded.

Many questions that needed to be answered. An evil Being who threatened Selen's very existence was somewhere in the world. But she looked at Deryn, who still sat on her knees. Her gaze held so much hope as she looked up at Selen.

Selen had genuinely thought she would never see her again, and all of the feelings she had pushed aside throughout their journey knocked into her. She didn't move, however, and just looked at the woman who'd welcomed her fall. Who'd caught her, even though she didn't want to.

Selen stared down at her sister. Her silver hair gently blew in the breeze as the wagon bounced along the road. Deryn sat to Selen's right, hand gripping her knee like she might slip away. Nys and Varric shared the driver's seat. As it turns out, they really *could* have acquired a wagon to haul her in an iron box if they had wanted to, and had found this one immediately upon exiting the MistralWood.

Deryn had said her goodbyes to Devril and Callyn, and they left almost as soon as they could. No one bothered to bathe before hitting the road. While they smelled, they cared more about getting back to Celestara.

Sidra would need a lot of healing. Selen, too. Both had gone through different types of psychological torment. Selen just prayed to the gods that Xander had died. She didn't typically care to pray for another's death, but she would not allow Sidra to be cared for in the same infirmary he occupied.

Selen gently ran her hand down Sidra's hair. Somehow, it was still soft despite how she doubted Sidra had been able to bathe since being taken. Any indifference she had felt for her sister no longer pulled at her mind. She cared only that she was safe. Selen would do everything in her power to keep her safe.

"What will you do when you return, Bird?" Deryn's voice sent a shiver up Selen's spine.

She kept her gaze on Sidra. Afraid that if she looked away, she'd disappear.

"Probably kill Xander," Selen said. There was humor in her tone, but she was serious. If she returned and he was there, she wouldn't hesitate to disembowel him.

Deryn chuckled, and the sound was enough to force Selen's attention away from her sister. She looked at Deryn, and found so much light in her eyes. Selen never wanted to see that fade, but knew that her own eyes were now tainted. The darkness that had pulled at her had rooted itself in her soul. That wouldn't go away, and Selen didn't want it to. For the first time in her life, she didn't feel powerless.

She grinned at Deryn, who grabbed the back of Selen's head and brought her forehead to her lips. Selen embraced the warmth of Deryn's lips on her skin.

They had been on the road for days now, and Selen knew that they would soon be approaching Celestara. She didn't know what would become of her and Deryn once she re-entered those walls. Nothing would be the same as it had been. She had feared that initially, but now? She welcomed the change. There was no future before—now there were endless possibilities.

All began with Selen mastering her darkness.

For if she didn't master it, it very well may master her.

Epilogue

Sidra

Make her believe she's won.

That was what their mother had told Sidra before she had blackened her eye and bloodied her lip.

She had been happy to do it—to appease their mother. She had finally found someone who appreciated their magic for what it was, and didn't try to steal it from her. Her mother wanted nothing more than to help them reach their full potential. That was what she had shown Sidra during that week. They knew Selen was coming. They had planned for it.

At first, Sidra had felt fear and confusion when she'd realized her mother had been behind everything, but once she knew the truth, she couldn't help but work with her. She'd showed Sidra everything Deandra and the other professors at that godsforsaken school should have.

The school to which she now returned.

She knew that faking her affection for Deandra would be a challenge—she fucking *hated* that woman for all she'd put her and Selen through. Let alone their mom. Deandra had wronged their family. So had their father. It broke Sidra's heart. She'd wanted their family to be reunited once she'd learned the identity of her captor, but that was quickly thwarted when she learned what he had done. *He* was the reason they had ended up here. She could never love someone who put her through such a thing.

The way her mother had shown her what they were capable of was something Sidra still had a hard time wrapping her head around—there was so much that she wanted to tell Selen, but their mother had told her to wait. So she would. The path she'd shown her was clear to follow, there was no question in her mind if it was the right thing to do. Even when she was hurting Selen, Sidra knew it was for the right reasons.

Just like when *she* was hurting her, Sidra had taken the blows like a champ. Even though they hurt like hell.

Sidra dabbed at the newly ripped open lip as she watched Selen and Deryn talk to the two males outside of the Inn. There was something going on between them, that much was clear from how that woman had fought against her mother's magic. She was so desperate to get to Selen. It must be love for her to have thrown herself into so much danger.

Sidra could almost taste it, that love.

It brought her a small spark of joy that her sister could find happiness—if she could even feel that emotion anymore. Sidra had felt happiness when she saw Selen initially, but then the hatred she saw in Selen's eyes as she'd watched their mother. The person who had given them life. The person who would save them from the chains Deandra had shackled them with. Resentment for her sister had wiggled its way into her heart. Sidra wasn't surprised, she supposed. She and Selen had always had a tumultuous relationship. Sidra wasn't afraid to cause her sister pain if it meant bringing her happiness in the long run.

This infatuation she had developed with this *Deryn* could prove to be troublesome. Deryn was intelligent, Sidra had figured that out in the short time she'd spent with this group.

The tiny blonde seemed to only know how to glare—as she was doing now, glaring at Sidra from the seat of the wagon they had commissioned for their journey back to Celestara. Sidra looked her up and down, then sneered at her. Selen had warned her of the tiny one's wrath, but Sidra wasn't afraid.

The one who concerned her most was the beautiful, brown-haired one. *His* eyes watched her the closest, as if he could see into her. At first, she had thought it was interest that caught his gaze, but she soon recognized it for caution.

He was skeptical of her, and Selen was too busy doting on Deryn to notice the look that he was giving Sidra.

She didn't want to provoke this one. There was something beyond the depths of his eyes that told Sidra that he was her biggest threat amongst this group. She couldn't risk exposure before their plan played out; Selen wouldn't understand right now. Plus, they needed to go through their final year of schooling. Selen's magic needed to grow. Hers did, too.

They had missed an entire year of magic training and had a lot to catch up on. So, the seeds would be planted, the traps would be laid, the loose ends disposed of—much like the one that looked at her now. And the one by Selen's side. Pieces of the puzzle that didn't have a place. But, that would all come with time. Patience was new to her, but it was very much essential for the goal ahead.

Selen and Deryn made their way back to the wagon, and Sidra didn't have to fake the smile that pulled at her split lip. She hadn't seen that light in Selen's eyes for years, and she loved it. She hated that it might have to dull before the true light of their magic had room to shine through, because Sidra knew that the light in her sister's eyes was partially due to the tan-skinned beauty she walked beside. So much better than Aleya, truly.

Sidra hated that she would have to rip that joy away from her sister. But just as Sidra had, Selen would have to see the darkest parts of the world and herself in order to reach her full potential. Sidra had every intention of showing her that.

The brush of an icy hand ran along the walls in her mind, and she recognized it as her mother's. It was different from Selen's. More powerful. There were now two open pathways in her mind. One to her sister. One to her mother. Her heart warmed at that.

Slowly, she was piecing her family back together. Once the final piece was in play, then Sidra could finally know peace.

Acknowledgements

I can't thank you enough for taking the time to experience this world. The process of creating it was something incredibly special to me. For something that started as a convoluted nightmare, it sure became a beautiful reality.

To all of my friends who had to listen to me babble on about the characters and detail pieces of this story, thank you for dealing with me for the year and a half I've been on this journey. You all contribute so much to my life.

To my editor, Cameo. Thank you for truly bringing life to this world. You were the first person to experience Selen and Sidra's story and to have you see the beauty of this world was so heartwarming. I can't tell you how beautiful it was to read the manuscript after the editing process. It flowed like a real book!

To my partner and best friend, Drew. This was not a journey I could have taken if it hadn't been for your support. You helped me overcome every bump in the road. Every time I didn't think I could make it happen. You continue to be my wings when I am down and my rock when I fly too close to the sun.

And to my readers. Thank you for immersing yourself in

this story. I hope you loved reading it as much as I loved writing it. Remember that there is always so much beauty to find in the darkness.

This book is just the beginning.

Sneak Peak: Book Two

"Name your price," Deandra repeated to the horrible creature in front of her. The Seers cackle cut through to her bones.

She had known something had gone awry when Sidra had shot out of the MistralWood in a panic. Deandra had never felt so protective of the girls than she had been in the moments following— when she realized that Selen was not behind her. She had wanted to stay and comfort Sidra. But she couldn't leave Selen in there with the Guardian. She tore herself in half trying to decide what to do. The hurt in Sidra's eyes when she left her curled in a ball outside of the darkness of the MistralWood would not be something she forgot. But Selen was alone. Brave and selfless Selen. The child that gave up everything about herself to make sure her sister had everything she needed.

She loved Selen deeply, but she felt *it* there. The same thing she had felt in *her*. It terrified Deandra to no end that

Selen could have the same writhing darkness that had consumed her friend all those years ago. She had felt its presence since she first held her in her arms on that cliffside. When she had given up everything and caused so much damage to the world just for them. For *him*. She'd do it again. She'd leave it all behind *again*. She didn't want to though. She had become attached to them here. Plus the wards would make their movement even more challenging. She knew that Selmara was waiting for her to make an error so she could find them. She had done everything to limit the possibility of that.

Perhaps it had been denial that had kept her from realizing fully that Selen was BloodBound. Perhaps it had been hope. But she had been a fool. She had let the indications that Selen already had her magic throughout her youth go unchecked. She had pushed them aside and pretended like it was her own past experiences coming to the surface. Because Selen looked so much like *her*. Even down to her mannerisms from when she was young. The hope and determination that had existed in Selmara before she gave into the darkness were so prevalent in her daughter's faces. Although, in all honesty, Sidra resembled her personality more than Selen did. Selen had her fathers softness. His selflessness.

So, she had left Sidra curled in a ball at the forest's edge. Maybe that had been a mistake, but when she approached the scene that was the Seer gripping Selen's small face, Deandra knew she had made the right choice. Selen's eyes were so panicked. How could a child be expected to deal with this alone? Fortunately, the Seer had released her when they saw Deandra. She knew she couldn't have fought off a Seer. Not with the magic of the realms behind them.

"You brought me a Bloodbound?" The Seer hissed at Deandra.

"I didn't know." Deandra breathlessly voiced. After running through the warped walls of an entrance to this place, Deandra didn't hide the fact that her breathlessness was laced with fear.

"Either you are a fool or a liar." The Seer pointed its boney finger towards her. She raised her hands in submission. As much as she hated to admit it, the Seer was right. She was a fool, and potentially a liar if she included lying to herself.

Deandra didn't take her eyes off of the Seer as she spoke to Selen.

"Selen. I need you to get up and wait with your sister." Deandra said calmly. She needed to get as far away from here as she could. Why had she brought them to the Guardian? All of her choices leading up to this moment seemed to slap her across the face as she now looked into the milky eyes of the creature.

"This doesn't have to be a battle, Seer. What do you want?" Deandra forced control into her voice. These beings sought balance but thrived on chaos, which included fear.

"There is quite a price for a BloodBound. There's also quite a price for one who hid her." The Seer spoke calmly.

"I will pay more for your silence. Name your price." So, here she was. Negotiating a payoff with a Seer to hide the fact that she had a BloodBound with her. If she had brought

Sidra without Selen, the Seer would've known something was wrong. If she hadn't brought either of them, Sidra would never get magic. That wasn't acceptable. There was no chance for the girls if they didn't have their magic. Although there had been others that had lived comfortably without it for a time.

Deandra's shoulders dropped in relief as the sounds of Selen's footsteps faded. Then it was just her and the Seer, the Guardian of the MistralWood.

"You cannot pay the price that would save your girl." The Seer's head angled. There seemed to be curiosity lacing its features.

"I will give you...I will give you *anything*." Deandra looked away from the Seer. She would give them anything. She'd give her life if that's what it requested.

"I don't doubt that, Headmistress." It floated closer to her. Deandra tried and failed to set her gaze back on its face. It knew too much. Her mind reeled at how to solve this. She had protected them for eleven years. Gods be damned, she would protect them now.

Deandra stayed silent as the Seer floated around her in a circle. She could feel its knowing gaze cutting into her skin.

"Seer, let us come to an agreement and be done with this."

"But your fear smells like spring flowers." The Seer's voice was so near to her ear that Deandra flinched slightly at the closeness of it.

The Seer floated back to where Deandra could see them

and it set its shoulders. "Answer my questions, traveler, and I will do nothing with this knowledge until it is needed."

Deandra started. Answers? That was all it wanted?

"I will answer your questions. Just please...please don't do anything that will harm them." Deandra took a deep breath and closed her eyes. She may have been foolish to make herself so vulnerable in the presence of the Seer, but it wouldn't matter anyways if they hurt them.

"Why did you bring her here?" Deandra glanced at the Seer. She knew they weren't asking about bringing them to the MistralWood.

"There was no other option. They needed out and I was already here." Deandra's stomach dropped as memories of her past flooded into her mind.

"Why now?"

"I told you, I was already here." Deandra bit. The Seer hissed in response, forcing Deandra to shrink back. "I didn't know where else to take them." Deandra's answer was a near whisper at that point.

"An act of convenience then." The Seer floated back. "Why protect them at all? Why not let her have what she craves?" The directness of the questions startled Deandra.

"How could you know where they come from?" Fear slithered its way into her mind. Had Selmara been here?

"I am granted sight from the beyond. Many answers live there, along with many questions."

Deandra sat with that for a moment. She had no choice but to answer their questions. "It was never a question. I would have saved them sooner if I had the chance. My goal wasn't just to keep her from her goals, but to save *them*."

"Hm." The Seers head tilted towards the sky. "You cannot save them."

Deandra met the Seer's eyes with a ferocity that she hadn't thought she'd have in their presence. "You can't know that."

"I know that they cannot exist here without a balance. That balance will come with time."

"I will protect them. I don't know how, but I will protect them." She wanted to pinch herself at admitting that she had no idea how to protect them, but it was out.

"You can try. But you will fail. Just as you will fail to save them both."

"*What*?" Deandra's head snapped up to the Seer.

"When the world crumbles, which falls first? The darkness or the stars?"